Praise fo

M000202727

"Irresistible. An excellen

—**Jennifer Saint**, *Sunday Times* bestselling author of *Ariadne*

"Exquisitely written, wonderfully lyrical, and richly immersive—this is a story we all know made fresh and chillingly relevant, refracted through a feminist lens."

—**Ellery Lloyd**, *New York Times* bestselling author of *The Club*

"A brilliant, feminist reimagining of Romeo and Juliet, *Fair Rosaline* is a gorgeously written version of Verona from Juliet's cousin, Rosaline's, point of view. What does Romeo truly look like through the eyes of a woman on the periphery of the original story? Natasha Solomons skillfully shows us another version of the star-crossed lovers—and the Romeo —we all think we know. I absolutely devoured this thought-provoking, female-centric take on Shakespeare."

—**Jillian Cantor**, *USA Today* bestselling author of *Beautiful Little Fools*

"Intelligent, imaginative, irreverent. Solomons has created a gripping Romeo and Juliet for the twenty-first century."

—**Annabel Abbs**, author of *Miss Eliza's English Kitchen*

"I have not been able to stop thinking about this book… *Fair Rosaline* is a gripping, spellbinding, and wonderfully immersive book—and one that truly makes you think. I would be very surprised if everyone is not talking about it."

—**Elodie Harper**, *Sunday Times* bestselling author of *The Wolf Den*

Also by Natasha Solomons

The House at Tyneford
House of Gold
I, Mona Lisa

FAIR ROSALINE

NATASHA SOLOMONS

sourcebooks
landmark

Published by Sourcebooks Landmark, an imprint of Sourcebooks
P.O. Box 4410, Naperville, Illinois 60567-4410
(630) 961-3900
sourcebooks.com

Cataloging-in-Publication Data is on file with the Library of Congress.

Printed and bound in the United States of America.
VP 10 9 8 7 6 5 4 3 2 1

For my sister, Jo, and my daughter, Lara—
may you be safe from Romeos

"Rosaline?…I have forgot that name, and that name's woe."

(*Romeo and Juliet*, Act 2, Scene 3)

Where the infectious pestilence did reign

The funeral was held at dawn and little more than an hour after Madonna Emelia Capulet passed out of this world. Rosaline trailed behind the bier, disconsolate with loss. Several times, she had to be chided by her father and brother to stay farther back as the corpse—her beloved mother—was pestilent.

The only porters they'd found who were willing to pull the bier were filthy and reeking fellows, not much better than beggars, and even they had to be bribed prodigiously. Rosaline had been forbidden from washing the body. A priest had come, clutching a nosegay of herbs to his mouth, and tossed holy water upon the dead woman's face before scuttling out again. There had been no time to find a golden or purple gravecloth to wrap her in. No one wailed the lament. No relatives gathered at the house or followed the family to the tomb. The mourning party was pitiful, the other Capulets and their neighbors cowering behind locked doors, sniffing posies and oranges studded with cloves to ward off the plague or offering up frantic prayers and hasty confessions. Instead, there was only Rosaline; her father, who wept openly, leaning heavily on Rosaline's arm; and her brother, Valentio.

"You deserved more," she murmured to her mother.

One of the porters stopped abruptly to scratch at the fleas in his groin, fumbling and dropping the handle of the bier.

"You oaf! You wretch!" roared Masetto Capulet, who would have kicked out at him if he hadn't feared that the man would drop the body entirely.

Rosaline hid a smile. Her mother would have found it funny; she'd delighted in the wicked. Two stray dogs had started to follow their pathetic little troop, perhaps in hope of scraps. She'd count them too. Made the numbers almost respectable, even if the congregants themselves were peculiar. She would not mind the absent neighbors: hypocrites and liars, all. Mama had sent them birthing gifts, and wiped their tears and their arses when they were babes, but she had not loved them. *She loved me. And I am here.* At this thought, Rosaline bit her lip hard to stop from crying and tasted blood.

The service in the family tomb was brief. The friar appeared terrified, eyeing the coffin continually, and rushed through the prayers, stumbling over his words in his haste. Rosaline observed the slick of sweat trapped in the sausages of his neck fat, despite the chill of the tomb. There had been no time to purchase wax candles befitting Madonna Emelia Capulet's status, and the chamber was smothered in shadows. A vault in the wall had been pried open in readiness for the coffin, and a rising stink of death and rot, compostable and foul, joined the decaying smell of other bones long sealed up. In the gloom, the waiting hole yawned black, a stairway leading all the way down to the underworld. Rosaline wanted to scream out, to cling onto her mother, much as she had clutched her skirts as a child—how could Emelia Capulet be lowered into that darkness? She would drown among those poisonous vapors, in that black well she could not see. She would be afraid. She must have a candle, but when it stuttered into darkness, what then? In truth Rosaline knew that fear, pain, and love were all beyond her mother now. She belonged here, among the ghosts of other long-departed Capulets.

Rosaline became conscious of her father weeping and tugging at her arm, and felt a nag of resentment as she stroked his head to comfort him as he rested it on her shoulder. He was neither kind nor tenderhearted, and yet she had to surrender her grief to his. He usually had no use for her at all, but now, when she wished to be left alone to her sorrow, he demanded that she attend him.

Her parents had been as a pair of candlesticks purchased together, twinned on either side of the mantle perfect in their polished symmetry. Now only her father was left, and alone, he looked wrong, skinny and lost. She grasped his hand, feeling the fragility of the bones beneath skin transparent as vellum, and he squeezed her fingers, kissing her knuckles. He tried to speak but only a sob came forth.

"Hush," said Rosaline, soothing him like she would a child, conscious that their roles had been momentarily reversed.

Despite his faults—and for once Rosaline resisted listing them—her father had loved her mother. Their marriage had been blessed with joy, and his pain was real and heart-stricken. For that she pitied him.

The friar fidgeted from foot to foot as though he needed to urinate. The family stared at him, puzzled and adrift in misery. Then, Valentio reached into his purse and pulled out several coins. The friar pocketed them, mumbling a hasty blessing.

"My apologies. I have yet more unfortunate souls to bury."

Not souls, thought Rosaline. *Merely their broken and rotting shells. Their souls have fled this charnel house.*

When the dismal party returned to the house, the officers of the watch were waiting for them at the front gate, the red cross of pestilence already daubed across the door. The chief of them nodded to Masetto but stood well back, his face muffled by a nosegay, and declared: "A member of this household has been infected, so you are all to be shut up for twenty days. Warders are here appointed to prevent you from breaking this decree. May the Lord have mercy upon you."

Rosaline saw her father shrug, defeated. There was no use in argument. They could only wait and hope. As she withdrew into the passage, Rosaline heard the hammering of nails as into a coffin lid.

Each day following she watched from her window as the doors along the street became slashed with red crosses, the plague spreading through the city. In the afternoons a procession of holy relics was trailed through the streets to drive out the infection, the friars chanting prayers and wafting incense, the citizens throwing open their windows and standing out on their balconies to join the song, beseeching heaven.

She watched her father drift through the house in his yellowing nightshirt, a daylight ghost, as he muttered prayers for his dead wife. He stumbled as he walked, and in the darkness, she saw him pacing the halls clutching a nightstick, sleepless. And yet, she could not bring herself to send a word of consolation. If it wasn't for him, Emelia would not be dead. Rosaline's sympathy was jumbled with anger and shot through with her own grief.

Soon she felt her life contract to her small room and the endless ringing of the basilica bells. Seven times each day for twenty days it tolled, instructing her to pray. She did not.

On the twentieth day, the watch returned, bringing searchers with them to inspect all the members of the household for signs of pestilence.

A woman came into Rosaline's chamber and bade her strip naked. "Your skin is blacker than your brother's and your father's," said the woman.

"I am my mother's child," replied Rosaline, who was weary of such remarks.

"And a pretty blossom whatever your complexion, although dark beauty 'tis not the fashion."

Rosaline bristled with irritation. Her mother would not have listened to such talk. "Nay, I will not have it. 'Twas in the old ages that dark was not counted fair. My mother's beauty turned the fashion of the day."

Rosaline had the same golden skin as her mother that in summer tanned to a rich terra-cotta. Her brother was more like her father: two veal calves. Rosaline was glad to take after Emelia—this was a part of her mother that could not be taken away from her.

The woman crouched down and peered up at her most private parts. "I see nothing. Not on your back or groin or underneath the arm or breast. There are no marks upon your neck either. You are free from contagion."

"Is Caterina safe?"

The woman balked. "You ask about the maid before your father!"

Rosaline shrugged.

"All are clean," added the searcher. "The household can be opened."

Rosaline smiled for the first time in twenty days.

"We shall not stay in Verona," said Masetto Capulet. "There is nothing for us here now. We will retreat to the hills above the city until this cursed scourge has gone."

A needle of anger, jewel-bright and sharp, pierced Rosaline's heart. Emelia had pleaded with and cajoled her husband to leave the city for cleaner air, to escape from the enemy that they could neither see nor fight. All the other grand houses lay empty, save for a servant or two, and even they deserted their posts daily as more bodies were carried out and abandoned in the streets. Yet this branch of the Capulets had remained in Verona, for Masetto had not desired to leave his business.

If they had departed earlier, two months before, as her mother had asked, then she would not be in her tomb.

"Yes," agreed Valentio. "You should leave. It is an excellent suggestion."

Valentio's own family had fled to the protection of the hills many weeks ago, cossetted in a villa amid a sea of swaying wheat fields, far from calamity. Yet he had not taken his mother and sister's part against his father, no matter how they'd pleaded. His own precious jewels, his own loves were safe. The rage inside Rosaline was a tinder, and she bowed her gaze, unable to look upon father or brother.

Somehow Masetto mistook her down-turned eye as modesty and a signal of compliance, traits not well-known in his daughter. With a sigh, he petted her shoulder, and she longed to cast him off.

"Yes," said Masetto, warming to his theme. "Emelia would have wished it. We'll go to the country and mourn for her there. Pack only what's essential. We leave at once."

My mother was essential, thought Rosaline bitterly. She understood that many were orphaned younger than she, at not yet sixteen. And she did consider herself an orphan. Her father's shoulders were weighted by this new mantle of sorrow. He looked about him unseeing, his only thoughts were of his wife, and when his gaze eventually fell upon Rosaline, it was with bewilderment and irritation.

Rosaline balled her hands into fists, digging her nails into the pale flesh of her palms. The pain reminded her that she was still present, that she had not faded from view—even if her father now wished she would.

Rosaline sat in a corner of her bedchamber with her knees tucked under her chin. She placed at the bottom of a trunk a copy of Dante, another of Petrarch and Boccaccio, and her most precious book, a tattered volume of Ovid's stories, as well as her lute, and declared her packing complete.

Caterina was less convinced. "Where are your stockings? Gowns? A shawl?"

Rosaline shrugged. "If I have books and music, I'm satisfied."

"Music? You cannot think to play. Not while in mourning. There are limits, my lady, even for you."

Rosaline slipped into the trunk a spare length of catgut, should any of her lute strings snap. "I'll make certain that no one hears me."

"Fie, you pretty wretch." Caterina continued to fret, grumbling to herself as she tossed items into the trunk with haste. Rosaline retrieved the Dante and sat on the floor, rereading his visions of the afterlife. She wondered where her mother was and felt a prickling unease along her skin, as if she'd emerged from a river bath on a summer's day only to find the sun had vanished. She found Dante's descriptions of heaven lacking radiance. An eternity in such company threatened tedium. The alternative was fascinating torment among sinners or the chill and oblivion of purgatory.

"You shouldn't read. It brings on the agues in women. Everyone knows."

Rosaline kissed her maid, pinching her plump, well-loved cheek.

They sat in the wagon as it jolted along the road and onto the track, leaving the city behind. Rosaline watched the swaying velvet haunches of the two horses as they hauled the cart, smelling of sweat and hay dust, their harnesses clattering and clinking. Caterina followed behind, her face glossy from the exertion. Lines of cypresses thumbed a brilliant lapis sky. Yet the plague had written itself upon the land: fields lay untilled, woven by weeds; a vineyard tilted at the sun with tiny nubs of gray suckling grapes. Rosaline noticed two women balefully trying to repair fallen posts and scrape back bindweed from choking the vines. There were no men left to help with the heavy work.

The cart wheels bruised the meadowsweet and larkspur as they passed by, releasing their scent into the air. *Everyone desires*

a poultice against this pestilence, decided Rosaline. *Even nature
herself.*

Valentio steered the wagon, driving a stick across the muscled shoulders of the horses if he felt they dawdled. Her father
sat beside her, his shoulders trembling every now and again as
he broke out in sobs.

Rosaline did not cry. The pebble of rage, hard and dry,
lodged inside her, had burned up all her tears.

Valentio maneuvered the cart around a thin bullock riding
a bored-looking cow in the middle of a ragged field, still chewing the cud. Rosaline surveyed the coupling with interest. After
much pleading and pestering, her mother had promised to talk
to her about the physical act between a man and his wife. Two
days before she'd fallen sick, they'd watched two dogs rutting
in the street: the whimpering and grunting of the bitch, the
frantic shuffling of the dog; and then afterwards the animals
locked together, whining and hobbling in the gutter as passersby
kicked out at them. Rosaline had wanted to know whether men
and women were fixed in such a doleful and degrading state
after consummation. Emelia assured her that no, people were not
locked together like dogs and bitches, and that one day soon she
would tell Rosaline what she needed to know. Soon never came,
for Emelia had sickened and died. Rosaline wondered whether
anyone would furnish her with the details now.

Masetto reached into his jacket and handed her a gold chain,
warmed from his skin. "Your mother wanted you to have this."

Rosaline took it. Her mother had worn the chain and

pendant every day. It had seemed a part of her, like her finger or brown eyes or chipped front tooth. A fat green emerald, like the effervescence of a dragonfly wing, gleamed at the center, sealed in shining gold. She inhaled the pendant, hoping it might still contain the scent of her mother—rose hips, pressed sage—but it smelled only of the fleshy leather of Masetto's jacket and his unwashed, sour skin. She looped it around her neck.

"And she left you a letter." Again, he fumbled in his jerkin and produced this time a folded piece of parchment.

Rosaline looked at it for a moment. Her mother could neither read nor write. The letter must have been dictated to her father. He already knew what it said. He licked his lips, the darting tongue of a serpent.

"What does it say?"

"You should read it."

His tears had dried and he was looking furtive, like a dog caught thieving chickens who would not meet its master's eye.

Snatching the letter, she read with creeping horror. "She tells me that I'm to go to a nunnery. This is a lie! She did not want this! You do. You wish to save my dowry!"

A stinging pain rang out in Rosaline's ear, and it took a moment for her to realize that her father had hit her.

"You forget you are mine to dispose of as I choose. But no. This was truly your mother's wish."

Rosaline stared at Masetto, tasting the tang of blood in her mouth. He stared back at her, taken aback at his own sudden violence.

It was clear to Rosaline that even if this had been her mother's wish, Emelia's choice did not displease him. Dowries were expensive. Placing daughters in nunneries cost money—more if one desired them to live well with plentiful food and pleasantly furnished cells—but it was a pittance compared to the ruinous expense of a dowry.

Rubbing her stinging ear, Rosaline stared at the letter. It was full of protestations of love, but all transcribed in her father's hand. What had it cost him to record such scraps of tenderness, the last leavings from a dying woman's table? Rosaline consumed them hungrily—there would be no more. *He has taken every piece of you*, thought Rosaline. *Even your last message can only be glimpsed through him*. It was like staring at a vision of Emelia through a choke of bonfire. Had he merely transcribed the messages of affection to make it appear that the order to enter the convent had truly come from her mother? Yet there was a bleaker thought lapping at the edge of Rosaline's mind like a cold spring tide.

What if Masetto Capulet told the truth? What if her adored mother wanted her only daughter to be sequestered in a nunnery?

Tears needled her eyes. She was damned, if not to hell, then to purgatory.

When they arrived at the villa in the hills above Verona, Rosaline retreated immediately to her bedroom. She lay on her low wooden cot and studied the silvered ceiling beams. A mouse scuttled along one of the beams and hesitated above her head, watchful. The chamber smelled as it always had, of nestling damp and old fires, and the wind tickled the eaves, the rafters creaking like a ship on the water. Outside in the yard, Caterina pumped water from the well, a hiss and squirt as it hit the bucket. Everything was the same and nothing was the same.

Rosaline considered the convent in Mantua that was to be her fate. The building perched on top of the hill like an ill-fitting hat, aloof from the town. Its walls were hewn from purple-gray sandstone mined from the Alps, three feet thick. It was a fortress for the soul. At night, no citizen ventured near. It was whispered that in distant times the nuns from the order could fly and conjure spirits, not always holy ones.

She remembered being taken as a child to visit her mother's sisters at the convent. Rosaline had to be cajoled into the *parlatorio*; this visiting chamber had grated iron bars that kept the nuns safely insulated from the fleshy perils of the world. Visitors pressed their faces up against the cold metal, poking fingers through the grill, desperate to caress their beloved daughters and sisters surrendered to God. While Rosaline wept in misery and fear, her mother had parcelled her up in a blanket and stuffed her into the barrelled *ruota*, spinning it so that she could be quietly plucked out by the nuns on the other side and secreted into the womb of the convent; her aunts smuggled her inside, soothed her tears with embraces, spoiled her with sweets and treats of every kind. The *ruota* was designed for goods like eggs or cakes or biscuits rather than nieces, but it was often used for illicit cargo, and after that first visit, Rosaline had frequently been sneaked into the convent to be doted upon, her infant cheeks like freshly risen dough, ready to be dimpled with kisses.

When Rosaline thought of those visits, she recalled no prayers or penance—that was all hidden from her. Instead, her mother's sisters saved everything they thought would interest or divert her: newly born kittens, fur still birth-slick and eyes blind shut; a baby sparrow that had fallen from its nest in the cloisters, in a box being fed with worms until it was strong enough to fly. Her mother had seized upon each detail of these visits, needing them repeated again and again until Rosaline wearied of their repetition, although now she realized that the rehearsing of them had set them fast in her mind like the livid colors in Murano glass.

The visits had continued for several years. Rosaline had not known at first that they all risked their very souls and excommunication for smuggling her inside and violating the immaculate sanctity of the nunnery; although she was certain that, if asked, her aunts would have answered without hesitation that any price, soul and all, would have been worth it for those chubby, pitted elbows and round, mucky knees.

On her final visit, she had grown too big. She'd become wedged in the *ruota* and stuck fast on the way back for a full half hour until they pried her loose. She'd never touched or embraced her aunts again.

She understood why her father wanted a convent life for her. He was a man without warmth. At gatherings, people delighted in telling her how astonished they had been when he married her mother, a woman of unfashionable looks with a small dowry, for love. The surprise of their union had not lessened even after twenty years.

Unfortunately for Rosaline, Masetto's store of affection had run dry with his wife. He was gratified by his son, but he had no use for her. The beauty that in Emelia enchanted him irked him in Rosaline—he admonished her not to sit too long in the sun, lest her cheeks darken further still, although Rosaline did not heed him.

Rosaline knew that he believed the adage: *A woman should have a husband or a convent wall.* But until now, she did not know that her mother had believed it too. Why had she not spoken to her? Was it cowardice or lack of time? Had she intended to confide her intentions to Rosaline but been cheated by the quickness of death? They had been resolute in refusing Rosaline entry to the sickroom out of fear of fetid vapors.

With a sigh, Rosaline realized that it did not matter that she was ignorant of the details of the marital bed, its terrors or its joy. She was never going to experience it herself.

Sitting up in bed, she saw that the sun was sinking, slung low in the yard, swollen and red like a boil ready to be lanced. Her throat was snuff dry, aching. She picked up a stalk of lavender, gathered last year, from a jar on the dresser. It held the scent of happier times. Bitterly, she rubbed it to dust between her fingers.

Fury with the dead was a hopeless, desiccated thing. Rosaline picked up the jar and hurled it into the grate, where it smashed among the hoary feathers of ash. For the first time in weeks, she gave in to grief and howled. Her face was hot and her ribs ached as though she had been kicked. But there was no release to be found in crying, no comfort to be had.

Growing calmer, she listened as the mice scratched in the rafters and, outside, a barn owl whooped at the moon. She walked across to the open window. All the farmhouses were bathed in darkness now, and she surveyed the spangled canopy of stars, the breeze a balm on her cheek. She closed her eyes.

When she opened them again, she noticed that a lamp burned in the Montague place on the hill. If it had belonged to any other household, the lick of yellow light may have offered some solace, the companionable thought that another unhappy soul was awake at this irreverent, ghoulish hour. As she stared, the lamp blinked into blackness.

For a moment it seemed to Rosaline that no light could ever come again. She felt an invisible chain coil tight around her chest and supposed it to feel much like the rope the Inquisition used upon heretics, and she wondered if she might die. She did not want to be hidden behind a wall. She wanted the world, all its glories and its sorrows and rottenness. How dare they take it from her?

She would not let them. Until the moment came and she was sealed away, she'd delight in every pleasure possible. She spat upon the floor, sealing an oath to herself.

At dawn the sun rose again and Rosaline with it. The dew was fresh upon the grass, laundering it clean and bright and luridly indifferent to her misfortune. Bees diligently pursued dangling lobes of jasmine for pollen, and a woodpecker rapped for breakfast. Caterina carried a tray to Rosaline's room and persuaded her to eat a little bread and drink some milk. She said nothing about her swollen face and purpled lids and, after she was dressed, tied black ribbons around her wrists, a dark mourning cloak about her shoulders.

Putting her hands over her ears to muffle Caterina's protestations at her leaving the house, Rosaline hurried across the fields to call upon Livia, her brother's wife, who was anticipating her seventh lying-in.

When she arrived, Livia was in bed in an upstairs chamber, already jostling with a nurse and her three surviving children. Her face shone with delight on seeing Rosaline, but then, remembering the tragedy, it contorted with sorrow.

Struggling to sit upright, Livia reached for her hand. "O, my dearest Rosaline. May Emelia's soul rest in heaven with the Virgin and all the saints and a thousand prayers. She was too good for this earth. And," she continued, "she made the best almond tarts."

Rosaline nodded dumbly, unwilling to speak in case she should cry again.

Livia squeezed her hand. Her skin was papered thinly across her bones, but her grip was surprisingly strong. "I have lost my mother, all my sisters, and three children. The pain will not lessen, but you will grow used to the burden."

Rosaline draped her arms around her neck and kissed the

pallid cheek, inhaling a sickly smell of unwashed sheets and oil of roses. The swell of the next child sat bulbous and snug beneath Livia's shirt. Her inflated bosom already looked painfully round, the blue veins a confluence of rivers. There were scooped hollows beneath her eyes.

"Do you eat enough?" asked Rosaline, relieved to be thinking of someone else's suffering.

Livia smiled. "Your brother presses endless delicacies upon me."

"Yes, but do you eat them?"

"I try, I try."

Rosaline glanced at the nurse feeding Livia's youngest, a plump infant of nearly one, a wizened nipple in his mouth. "She seems useful and good."

Livia nodded. "Yes, she looks after them all with little ado." She lowered her voice conspiratorially. "She used to be a searcher."

Overhearing, the nurse turned and looked at them both. "This is better. Life over death."

The door opened and Madonna Lauretta Capulet entered, surveying the busy chamber proprietorially, as though all the occupants were bolts of silk she was considering for a gown. There was no sound except the wet suckling from the fat baby on the nurse's nipple. Rosaline stiffened and saw Livia fuss with the blanket. Both of them were as wary of Lauretta as they would be of an asp. She was married to Masetto's older brother, the old Lord Capulet, head of the household.

"Where is Juliet?" demanded Madonna Capulet. "I thought she was here, playing with the babies."

"No longer, Aunt," said Livia. "She was for an hour or more with her nurse. Playing very prettily. But they left."

Madonna Capulet continued to gaze about the room nonetheless, as though Juliet could be hiding beneath the bedclothes or behind the screen.

"I'm sorry to have missed my cousin Juliet," said Rosaline. "I should have liked to have seen her."

Her aunt frowned. "She should be here. Tiresome girl." Then, remembering herself, added, "I am sorry for your mother. Emelia was a women of *virtu*. May she rest with the Virgin in eternal peace. You will honor her memory when you enter the convent."

Rosaline felt pain coil in her belly and found herself unable to speak.

Madonna Lauretta Capulet considered her for a moment before calling for a servant to bring wine. "My niece is unwell. The effect of grief, not pestilence?" she asked, turning to Rosaline, suddenly afraid.

"You knew I was to be sent away?" said Rosaline.

Madonna Capulet perched uncomfortably on the edge of the bed, her expression puzzled. "What else would she want for you, dearest niece? Your brother can't stop producing heirs. Your parents don't need more. You can't carry on your father's name. He doesn't need to whelp you. What use do you have?"

Rosaline slid a dry tongue along paper lips. "But you will marry Juliet."

"God has lent us but one child. All our hopes are now with her. Baggage that she may be."

Rosaline said nothing. She was too young to remember Juliet's sister, carried off by fever, or the brothers, stillborn. She turned to gaze upon her sister-in-law in the bed, the distended stomach. The babies came each year, handed off to the nurse so Valentio could mount her again and she could fall pregnant more quickly.

Children, though, must be useful; Rosaline served no purpose.

"What did you want, Rosaline? You are but fifteen. Did you hope for a husband?" said Madonna Capulet, leaning forward with real interest.

Rosaline did not think herself obliged to answer. Instead she thought about her parents. She did not know if her mother had actually loved Masetto or even if she considered love necessary. He had loved enough for both of them. Sometimes, when there had been much wine drunk with dinner, Emelia had teased him when no one else dared. Rosaline was certain that her mother had moments of happiness with him, like beads of dew strung along a spider's web. They were no less precious because they were fragile and fleeting. Rosaline determined to know something of love before she was locked away, husband or not.

II

His name is Romeo

The plague receded like the waters of a flood, leaving ditches overflowing with hastily buried dead. Crops moldered in the fields, and bridges lay unrepaired as there were no men to hew the trees into timber, no carters to haul the uncut planks to the rivers, and no carpenters to mend the rotten beams.

Rosaline watched in bewilderment as her father went onto his knees to give the Almighty thanks for his deliverance. She would not give thanks. God had seen fit to take from her what mattered most and left a world broken and pitiful.

Yet several times a week, a grudging Rosaline was urged into the small church crammed with penitents and grateful supplicants, all expressing thanks to every saint they could remember that they too had been spared. She noticed that it was those of her father's age who prayed with the most ardor. The younger congregants stifled yawns and were distracted, ignoring even the friar spraying spittle in his fervor as he preached. Rosaline watched enthralled, waiting to see who would be hit by clots of prayer and zeal, lobbed straight from God's messenger. The choral singing used to be joyous, until harmony in church was banned by Rome for inspiring profane and lustful thoughts. Rosaline found plainsong exactly that: plain and tedious. She thought again of her fate at the nunnery. To face a lifetime of prayer and single notes. How was she to bear it?

After church she sought her father in his office, studying his accounts.

Only, he wasn't looking at his ledger. He stared instead at a painted miniature of Emelia, caressing her varnished profile with a forefinger.

Rosaline seized her moment. "If you grant me a year's reprieve, at the end of it, I will enter the convent if not willingly, then without objection."

He frowned. "Why should I bargain with you?"

Rosaline gestured toward the painting of her mother. "She did not want me to be unhappy."

He glanced down again at the tiny painting clasped in his fingers. "Nor do I, Daughter. Even if you do not believe it."

"I do," she said, trying to sound as if she did and reaching for his hand, but the intimacy was too much and she let his fingers fall.

"A year's board and lodging is not inexpensive." Her father was a man of means though, and he cared little for the expense. He just wanted her gone. "Your mother desired you to go. Even if you don't want to hear it."

"And I shall. But give me a year more of the world. Let me fatten myself upon it before I lose it forever."

"Better to cut yourself off quickly. Seal the wound with fire. It will be easier thus."

She knelt down and blanketed his hand with kisses. "I beg you."

He was silent for a moment, considering. He looked unhappy, wavering. "I should like us to know each other a little better, Daughter."

She nodded, eager.

"And when you are admitted to the convent, you will allow me to visit?" he said, a note of sadness in his voice. "I have lost a wife; I shall not lose a daughter too?"

"You shall not," she answered.

"You may have twelve nights."

She looked up, aghast. "So little! That's not enough."

"That or you can leave at once. Do not forget, that for my all kindness, you are my own property to dispose of as I choose."

She agreed, blinking through a film of tears.

"Twelve nights from today you will enter the convent without appeals to the family or dramatic scenes, but quietly accepting your fate?"

She could not speak. There was a stopper of flesh and tears and panic closing her throat. "Yes," she croaked.

"Swear it, Rosaline."

"I swear."

She wanted to hear the sudden dirge of all the bells in

Lombardy or a cacophony of rooks heralding the calamity of her misfortune, but there was nothing, only the distant iron clatter of hoof on stone as the horses were led around the yard and the cheerful *pit-pit* of a chaffinch.

Her father no longer looked at her but now turned to his abacus and his ledger. She was already dismissed. She ran from the room. Only twelve days to be part of the world. Twelve days of color and light and music. She would seize them all. She raced to the kitchen in search of Caterina, as she had since she was a child whenever trouble had found her and her mother was not to be had. But this was no skinned knee, and no sweet posset or candied apple could mend it.

Caterina was baking an eel pie. She did not see her come in but hummed to herself, kneading the crust. Rosaline stood on the threshold wordless, adrift. Watching Caterina, arms snowy with flour as they'd been a thousand times, she felt neither here nor there, as if this could be any moment during her fifteen years. But as soon as she told her that they were to part and heard Caterina cry out, the hourglass would turn and time must run again. She was not ready, not yet.

Rosaline waited a second more. She looked at the tapering slubs of eels on the wooden bench, their slime-slick bodies, inhaled their river stink. The razor glint of the paring knife, globed with blood. The drift of flour, falling in whorls to the floor. She would eat this pie and perhaps the next, but for the one after, she would not be here. Rosaline cleared her throat.

Caterina stopped, pie forgotten, on seeing Rosaline's colorless cheeks, eyes brimful with tears. "What's happened? What is it, ladybird?"

As Rosaline spoke, Caterina cried out and wiped river mud and eel guts across her forehead. The two women clutched one another. Then Caterina pushed her away, pressing a rag into her hands to dab at her eyes. "Here, sit. Livia is safely delivered of her baby. A messenger arrived for your father. A boy."

"I am twice glad. For it is better to be a boy in this world."

"Already he eats and eats. Between him and his brother, they may have to hire a second wet nurse. Perhaps you can call on Livia tomorrow." Caterina opened the larder, rummaging for sweet treats. With a cluck of satisfaction, she pulled out a parcel of candied cherries and plums.

"You can have these. Don't spoil your appetite," she chided.

Rosaline took the sweets, grateful, swallowing down the lump in her throat along with the spittle and sugar. Caterina prattled on about the new babe to distract her.

Rosaline shoved more sugared plums in her mouth. When the children were big enough—but not too big—perhaps Livia would bring them to visit her at the convent one by one and pop them in the *ruota* barrel, and she would stow them in the nunnery for an hour or two. She could not hope for more.

Caterina was still chattering away like a sparrow. "There can't be a proper baptismal celebration because of your poor mother. But the neighbors have been sending gifts and your brother's been holding court like the Prince of Verona himself! But then the birth of a boy must be celebrated. Everyone has sent something. Well, almost everyone. The Montagues haven't, of course."

The Montagues. The name itself was like a foreign isle, distant and separate. Powerful and burdened with sin. The epitome of wickedness and awfulness. If ever Rosaline misbehaved, she would be threatened that the Montagues would get her. How was not made clear. Would she be sent to them packaged up as butcher's meat? Would they appear in her chamber, like devils conjured from a magic circle? She made the sign of the cross.

But like Lucifer himself, the Montagues had not always been wicked, and the Capulets had not always abhorred them. There was a time when the two great houses of Verona had been, if not friends, then they had agreed upon the wisdom in forming an alliance. There had been marriages between the families. However, many years before, during her grandfather's youth, a marriage had been promised and agreed, and then the Capulet bride cast aside. It seemed the groom had chosen the Church and love of God over his bride, rapidly rising to the rank of cardinal.

The insult had not been forgiven but had warped and grown and calcified into hate, hardening with each year that passed. Or so it was said. Rosaline felt certain there was more to the feud than this slight, but could find none who would tell her.

Caterina cast a blizzard of flour upon the bench. "The Montagues are holding a masque. If you can believe it! Everyone else goes to church to give blessings and thanks, and they hold a ball! And the plague dead barely tucked into their pits. But that's the wont of the Montagues. At least we won't need to go nor send our excuses. God can just smite them as he fancies."

Rosaline was only half listening. The Montagues' parties were renowned throughout Verona and the Venetian Republic: fire-eaters, tricksters, jugglers, the best musicians that money could hire (and the Montagues had a good deal), feasts of pigeon pie, bloody venison haunches, oysters heaped in alpine mounds, dissolving orange and lemon ices, and dancing until dawn. But all of that was as nothing. The festivities were held in the Montagues' gardens, a labyrinthine grotto of monsters and marvels that she and no Capulet had glimpsed in the flesh.

The gardens were said to have been built a hundred years ago by a Montague man driven mad with grief after his wife died. Terrified that she was lost in the ravages of hell, he had created the seven circles on the wooded hillside surrounding his villa so he could visit her in his dreams. On carnival nights, men and women caroused among a waking nightmare of visions conjured by a tormented soul and given form in stone and moss amid looming forests of cedar, sycamore, and pine.

All of this Rosaline had gleaned from descriptions passed on by neighbors and acquaintances. Before she had married Valentio, Livia had attended a party there with her family, and Rosaline had made her repeat the details of the gardens again and again. Of course when she became a Capulet, Livia was cast out, unable to experience those wicked pleasures again. No Capulet would consider attending.

The reluctant vow her father had pried from her echoed in

Rosaline's heart: *a dozen days and nights*. If she must surrender the sinful world, then first she'd gorge herself on its pleasure. The thought of the Montagues was frightening, but she had so little time left. She must be brave. If the devil himself was playing host, she would attend with ribbons in her hair.

Rosaline paced her chamber. A mask was useful: it would hide her face from God. But for those on earth who knew her from Verona and who still might recognize her, she preferred a more fulsome disguise. She must not be discovered. Her father might have granted her a twelve-night reprieve, but she knew with cold certainty that this was not how he intended her to spend it. If even a whisper reached his ears, she would be dispatched to the convent immediately. Not only for attending a ball unchaperoned, but at the house of the Montagues, against whom his grudge had petrified into cankered hate. Yet what possible concealment could she procure at this late hour? None of her own clothes would do.

She glanced at a chest at the foot of her wooden cot. This room had once been Valentio's in the years before his marriage, when he did not have a country house of his own. An idea came to Rosaline, and her heart was a bird with frantic wings, hurling against the bars of her ribs. She pried open the trunk. It smelled stale, and a fine larval dust from woodworm was sprinkled across the linen at the top.

It contained little. The torn wings of a long dead moth. A

sheet, yellowed with age. Some old clothes belonging to Valentio from his youth. They had not been passed on to a servant in the usual way but tucked away in this trunk, presumably in hope of being worn by more living sons that had never come. The jacket had slashed black-velvet sleeves, eaten here and there by the moths. The hose were gray, edged with silver brocade, the fabric smooth beneath her fingertips. Yes, she would go to the ball as Valentio. Or as he had been in youth.

In a mask and wearing breeches, none would know her.

With eager fingers she unbuttoned her gown, discarding it on the floor. Keeping on her undershirt, she peered down at her bosom. There was nothing worth the trouble of binding. What little she had would lie snugly concealed beneath the jacket. She tugged this on, along with the hose, fastened the polished mother-of-pearl buttons, and was regretting the lack of hat to hide the long rope of black, treacherous girl's hair, coiled in knots at the nape of her neck, when Caterina walked in and yelped as if she had stubbed her toe.

"Did you think me Valentio?" asked Rosaline, pleased.

"No. You are far too pretty. Your face is too brown and you lack a beard."

Rosaline sagged. It seemed hopeless.

"And why would you wish to ape your brother?"

Rosaline shook her head and would not speak.

"Tell me, Rosaline. I am your friend and I have been since before you were weaned."

Rosaline hesitated. She did not like to reveal her intentions, less in fear of betrayal than the consequences for Caterina should she be discovered. And yet, as she glanced down at the dove-gray breeches, she caught sight of her feet in their fancy rosebud slippers and, reaching up to touch her hair, realized she'd neglected to remove her maiden's veil, which still perched squatly upon her head.

Caterina gave a cry, understanding dawning. "Please, ladybird, you cannot think to go to that place alone! It's full of danger for any woman, but for a girl like you, a Capulet…unchaperoned and who knows less than nothing!" Her hands fluttered to her throat, frantic with dismay. "You're a child."

"I am not a child," said Rosaline. "I do not know what I am. I am never to be a woman. I am to be locked away to slowly wither, a peach unplucked, to rot upon the tree."

"The nuns in the convent are still women."

"Are they? They are married to God. Surrendering all will and desire and thought. I do not have the temperament to be His servant. I am neither meek nor obedient. I want too much."

Rosaline saw that Caterina could not deny this charge, merely repeating: "Don't go. It isn't safe."

"I shall go. The question is, will you help me or shall you tell my father?"

Later, as the two of them walked the unlit path through the fields to the Montague gardens, Signior Rosaline tried not to jump with fear at each rustle in the sycamore leaves or bark of a fox. The evening was as thick and warm as heated milk, cicadas chirruped and bullfrogs belched in the rank dikes at the fields' edges. Stumbling in her borrowed boots, Rosaline swatted at the mosquitos whining around her ears. Though sick with fright, excitement hummed through her. Her father may lock her away, but first she would live. And perhaps there was even the possibility of escape? Might she not yet worm out of fate's horrid grasp?

This hope was faint—a firefly mistaken for a navigational star on a cloudy night—and she squashed it down.

"This trick shan't work," Caterina muttered. "You'll be spanked and sent away at once, and I'll…" She did not finish, too frightened to speak aloud what would happen to her if Rosaline's ruse was found out.

Rosaline stopped, placing her hands upon the other woman's shoulders. "They will not know you helped me. That I swear. Still, you must return to the house. I shall be quite safe from here."

Caterina shook her head. "I will walk with you as far as the gates, imp that you are. You were the sweetest babe I ever tended, and the naughtiest."

"You mean, the sauciest boy."

"If you were a boy, you wouldn't be tripping over your own sword." Caterina smiled. "Come, let me adjust your belt. It dangles too low. And stand like this. With your hips and legs apart, just so."

Rosaline tried, one foot astride the soft pudding of a molehill, another balanced on the edge of a ditch.

"Better. But one would think you'd never actually seen a man. Did you never fight your brother with a wooden sword?"

"Valentio clouted me once on the head, declared himself the winner, and that was it."

Caterina adjusted the angle of her hat and studied her. Rosaline wriggled, uneasy beneath her scrutiny. "Stand still. Men don't squirm. Better. But even in the dark you're too rosy-cheeked for a boy."

Caterina reached down and, dipping her fingers in the crumbed earth of the molehill, smeared a little on Rosaline's cheek. "That will have to do for the shadow of a beard. I should have thought to use charcoal. And you must drink wine or it will seem strange. But not too much. And do not wince if the men swear before you."

"Zounds, I shall not."

"And don't say that word! You'll damn yourself to hell!" Caterina sighed, defeated. "Why you would want to go to that dreadful Montague place, I cannot fathom."

Rosaline smiled. "It whispers of dark delights."

They had nearly reached the far end of the track, where the Montague house and the path leading to the gardens were lit up with a parade of torches dissolving the night. Music and voices sang out into the shadows. Rosaline's breath caught in her throat, and she clutched Caterina's hand, squeezing it with her own inside its too-large, borrowed glove.

"If you are afraid, we can yet go home," said Caterina hopefully. "No one will know we were ever here."

"No," said Rosaline. "Hark at the music. There is nothing terrifying in that!" Releasing Caterina's hand, she followed the sound, led on like a ravenous man sniffing the scent of a joint on a spit.

"Wait! Let me tie your mask." Caterina held up the mask. It was not the comely white one Rosaline had worn to previous carnivals or masquerades but curved and black, a proper gentleman's disguise. She waited impatiently as Caterina pressed it against her skin, prodding at the earth with her boot. The toe was stuffed with paper, the boots being several sizes too large.

The mask fit snugly around her eyes, leaving her cheeks, nose, and mouth exposed.

"It itches."

"Fie."

Rosaline allowed Caterina to fasten the ribbons and then, bidding her anxious companion farewell, hastened toward the music once more.

She paused on the edge of the pool of light, listening. The rest of the garden lay hidden, the cypress trees lining the driveway tall quills dipped in the thick ink of night. She was later than most of the guests and she traveled the path alone. A vast grotesque shape materialized out of the shadows and blocked the path. Her breath caught in her throat. A towering ogre, its cavernous mouth agape, its open jaws the height of a man, a pair of blazing torches pinched in its claws. It leered at her with hollow, cadaverous eyes and she tamped down the urge to turn and run. After a moment she realized that the music was drifting out through the black hole of its throat. By the flicker of the torches, she could just read the words inscribed on the ogre's forehead: *Ogni Pensiero Vola*—abandon all reason.

If she wanted to enter the *feste*, she must do so through the mouth of Hell. Rosaline took a breath and stepped into the ogre's mouth.

She emerged into a glade where frenzied gods cavorted and battled. Hercules tossed Cacus to the ground upon his head, while a sphinx turned her gaze upon the Furies. Great dragons grappled with howling lions and tried to beat back the jaws of frantic hounds. A giant turtle with a nymph balanced upon its back rested by a waterfall where a river goddess bathed. Yet all were caught and turned to stone, as if by Medusa in a single long-ago glance. Their faces were brushed with black moss and silver lichen, and ivy groped long fingers along the hems of granite robes.

Rosaline paced the glade, surveying the statues in wonder. The gardens thronged with masked revelers. No one looked at her. More open-mouthed ogres sneered at her from the shadows at the edges of the wood; some had stone tables for tongues, set with food and drink. She was neither hungry nor thirsty, for also in the glade was the source of the music.

She glanced around for Pan himself or Puck, for who else could it be who played in such a world? The musicians, however, were mortal—stout and perspiring fellows. From their flutes, viols, and a pair of lutes, they played a honeyed motet, accompanying a singer, a woman with a rasping, sugarplum voice.

Rosaline was breathless with joy. As she listened the night became filled with color; she watched the notes rise up and perforate the sky with glowing pinholes. O, to have real music, at last! This was nothing like the drab devotionals in church. How could God not prefer this gilded altarpiece of sound? These were the notes of heaven yet whirling around a wild revelation of hell. She drew closer and closer, elbowing her way to the front of the gathered audience, like a dog nosing to the warmest spot on the hearth on a winter's night.

The singer, seeing Signior Rosaline so enraptured, was amused and pretended to serenade her. A cup of wine was thrust into Rosaline's hands. She sipped and nearly spat it out again. The wine was sour, like tart mulberries not yet ripe, and made her wince. In an instant her cup was filled again. Shuddering, she drained it. The torches blazed and whirled. The music played on and on, and masked dancers wove in and out among the trees and statues, caterwauling with pleasure.

The wine dulled her nerves. Curious, Rosaline glanced around for faces that she knew, but most wore masks—black, white, crimson, harlequin, and here and there horned devils. A few sported hook-beaked masks and dark capes, like those the physicians wore during the outbreaks of the plagues. She did not like to see them; they haunted the party like ghosts of the dead, reminding Rosaline of the fleetingness of this delight.

As the night wore on, and the festivities grew wilder and more drunken, masks became loose or were discarded among the trees; she noticed among the crowd the faces of Signior Martino and Lucio from across the hill. She wondered who among them were the infamous Montagues. Were they the hooded figures of Death and his companions, Despair and Pestilence, who lurked among the guests? She could not tell. There was a tall fellow sporting a diablo mask. Was he a Montague? Or him? She watched a man as he kissed along the line of a woman's neck, lapping at the ridge of her collarbone as she thrashed and gasped, his hand burrowing beneath her skirts. Rosaline had never seen such a carnal display before, and she stared, appalled and fascinated. They stood brazenly beside Poseidon's pool, while the god observed unabashed, trident in hand.

The torches spurted wax and gathered moths, and finally the musicians paused their playing to carouse. The evening waxed late. Rosaline spied a lute left upon a bench. It seemed to call out to her. She tugged off her gloves, picked it up, and plucked upon the strings. At once a steady calm suffused her, and her head, which whirled from the wine, steadied. The instrument was excellent, its throat deep and sweet. She knew that she must not sing or they would discover her secret, so she simply played, her fingers deft and certain. A small crowd gathered to hear her while the music fell from her fingers like rain, cool and restorative in the heat and closeness of the night.

A man drew close. He did not wear a mask. He was neither too tall nor too short, but the ideal height and leanly muscled. He tipped his head to listen better. As he did so, Rosaline noticed that his eyes had an intense expression, as if moved by her song. Beneath his hat, his hair was almost as dark as her own. As she finished each piece, his cheers were the loudest, his applause the most heartfelt and rigorous.

After playing for a full half hour, Rosaline began to feel warm and sick, her mask too tight and slick with sweat around her eyes; she longed to take it off but knew she must not. Glancing up, to her dismay, she noticed a friend of Valentio's who would know her and could betray her, and panic rose in her stomach, hot and acid. She put down the lute and wondered where she could hide. But before she could turn and leave, the stranger's arm was draped around her shoulders, firm but not unfriendly. She smelled pine and leather.

"Come, good sir. Why don't we withdraw awhile? I know a spot," he said, seemingly sensing her discomfort, steering her away from the crowd and toward a quieter part of the garden. He led her along a path beside a stream and lesser Roman gods, to where Pan lolled naked beneath the sycamores' canopy. The stranger was unhurried and walked with a studied ease. Even in her agitation, Rosaline found herself watching him, observing that he was slender and wearing a fetching cloak. His skin was paler than her own.

He noticed her glance and grinned with white, straight teeth. "There was more perfection in your playing tonight, more truth, such as might melt a heart of flint."

Rosaline laughed, unused to hearing such compliments. Unused to being noticed at all.

"Who are you, good sir?" he asked.

"A gentleman of Verona," she stuttered, unable to meet his eye, embarrassed and pleased by his study of her.

The stranger bowed. "Well met, then, gentleman of Verona. We are two gentlemen of Verona, and yet I do not know your face."

He was staring at her intently, and Rosaline felt her cheeks grow hot beneath his scrutiny. She was glad of the shroud of darkness. "How could you know me? My face is hidden."

"Your name, then?"

Rosaline laughed. "What is the use of a mask if I am to simply surrender my name?"

The man bowed his head and smiled.

She had not spoken with many men before, and none like this man. He reminded her of a painting of Saint Sebastian she'd seen in the cathedral in Padua, a perfectly symmetrical and red-lipped Sebastian stripped naked and pierced with arrows that bloodied his breast. She'd been mesmerized by the icon, gazing upon him all through mass, quite unable to concentrate on the sermon or the priest. Now, she forced herself to look away from this stranger as if fearful of burning her eyes from gazing too long upon the sun. It was his civility, the sweetness of his tongue, and, O, his fine looks. Venus herself could not have rendered him more fair.

Rosaline felt conscious of the moth holes in her hose and the dirt smeared upon her cheek. Her own tongue was not lyrical but fat and slow, wedged behind her teeth.

He reached into his jacket and produced a flask. "Have something to drink, friend."

Rosaline shook her head. "Thank you, gentle sir, but alas, I think I've had too much already."

He laughed. "A little more will help." He pressed the flask into her hands. He was so kind, so insistent, that despite the heaviness in her stomach, she drank. The wine was strong and sweet.

He seemed pleased. "Just one more sip."

"I don't think I can. Not without mishap."

"Then you must eat."

She was aware that she was swaying side to side, as if she were on a ship. If she ate, she feared she would vomit. She did not want to do that before this gentleman. This particularly attentive gentleman with a direct, bright eye. And perhaps when men were sick, they did it differently from women, and that would give her away.

He reached out and steadied her, grasping her arm and seating her carefully at Ceres's feet, upon grass already damp from dew. A table was set with food beneath the trees, and he gathered a few choice morsels and brought them to her upon a plate. A little bread. A cup of mead. Dizzy, she lay back and shut her eyes.

"Eat," he pressed, settling beside her. "And the ale is not strong. It will help."

She took them and, as she nibbled, did in truth feel better. She was aware of the closeness of his body, the warmth of him. They were almost touching.

He lay back and stretched, perfectly at ease.

Rosaline wondered what age the stranger was. Older than herself, certainly. Five and twenty. Thirty? It did not matter. Time itself was suspended here. The sand had ceased to run.

She gestured to the statues, half-concealed among the dell of pines. She inhaled their dry scent. "I feel as if I am caught in a waking dream or have been stolen away by Queen Mab. It's at once awful, and yet I do not wish for dawn," she said.

"You've never seen this place before, and yet you're from Verona?" said the man in surprise.

Rosaline feared she'd given away that she was a Capulet. "Yes! I mean, of course. But it seems different each visit. One is not the same each time one enters."

"No, indeed. And it's not just reason that must be abandoned as one enters. See what's written here?" He pointed to another inscription near the fertility goddess. *Solo per sfogar il core.*

"'*The heart must be unburdened,*'" read Rosaline slowly.

"And what makes your heart heavy, friend?" he asked, his voice mild and pliant with sympathy.

"Why do you think me unhappy?"

"No one plays music as you did unless his soul is lined with lead."

Rosaline stared at him in surprise. This was the first kindness a man had ever shown toward her, even if at this particular moment he did not know her to be a woman. She had believed herself long inured to the apathy of her father. She was of no consequence at all to her brother. He thought about his hounds more often. Taken off guard by this stranger's attentions, Rosaline longed to confess her unhappiness. Her throat itched with tears. It was her own fault for drinking too much wine, but he was looking at her with such gentleness, his expression open and frank. She longed to tell him too about her mother's death, about being sent away to the convent. That sometimes it seemed as if no one loved her but Caterina, who was paid to do so, and Juliet, who being so young knew no better. Yet she could not, or she would reveal she was a woman, and women did not sit out in the dark unchaperoned with men they did not know. She must leave. The thought of dawn was tickling the tops of the trees. She scrambled to her feet.

"I did not mean to cause offense," said the stranger, rising. "Do not go."

"It's late. Or rather it is early and soon the house will rise and I must be abed."

"Please. Stay. Just one minute more."

She hesitated.

"What harm is a single minute spent with a friend?"

"Can strangers be friends?"

"Strangers such as we, I think. We have broken bread together. We have listened to rare music. We have lain together side by side on a summer's night beneath the pale-faced moon. I hope that makes us friends."

Rosaline flushed to hear him speak of them lying together, but knew he meant it innocently enough, for how could he not?

"Tell me then, my lord, where you learned to play the lute?" he asked.

Speaking of the lute made Rosaline think about her mother, and she could not bear to do that. "Fie! You ask a lot of questions," she said.

"Very well. You ask me one. Only stay."

Rosaline considered. There was only one thing she really wanted to know. "Will you show me a Montague?"

He did not laugh, only looked puzzled. "I could, but why?"

"I want to see one."

"'*One*'? You make it sound like they are beasts, not men."

"If they are men, then they are all wicked. Monstrous. Like this garden they built."

"It is wild perhaps. Astonishing. But wicked? No."

Rosaline said nothing for a moment, uncertain. "I have heard it said that they are wanton and wicked to a man."

"How so?"

Rosaline frowned. "I cannot say, having never met one."

At this the stranger was provoked. He turned from her, his fingers toying with the hilt of his sword. "You cannot say? You know of no reason?"

Rosaline shook her head, reluctant to recite the origin of the feud and betray herself as a Capulet, and the man faced her again, edging toward her until she was compelled to back away.

"You are full of insinuations and hints, and suggest to me, a stranger, the tired, vile, and vicious rumors that are hissed all around Verona by our enemies, the Capulets. And yet still you come here—to the Montague place—to eat their food and drink their wine and make merry among their guests, and to repeat these dishonors."

Rosaline stared at him confused, uncertain if he was playing a game. If it was a game, she did not understand the rules.

He stopped, his head bent low. "You leave me no choice. You have dishonored me and my family name."

As he spoke this, his voice low and heavy with regret, he stalked again toward her, and she found herself forced backwards along the path.

Rosaline could not believe that she had really caused offense; he must be in jest. She could not fight. The very thought was absurd. She almost laughed. "How have I dishonored you, my lord?"

His gaze met hers. "I am Romeo Montague." His hand rested easily upon the hilt of his sword. "Do you refuse to fight? Will you bring dishonor upon your house, young man of Verona?"

She shook her head, quite unable to speak. She touched her sword; she no longer felt like laughing. Her fingers were sticky on the hilt. She must have lost her gloves. Her heart roared in her ears. Romeo now appeared taller, broader than she'd realized, and he was dancing toward her on the balls of his feet. His smile gleamed in the early dawn light.

She glanced behind her and saw that they'd reached a small tower that appeared to lean precipitously to one side, like a chess piece about to surrender and fall. At first Rosaline thought the angle of the tower to be an effect of all the wine she had drunk, but as Romeo pressed her farther back toward the darkened entrance, she saw that it really leaned, half-toppled.

"Shall we?" asked Romeo, gesturing to the doorway. "In here is as good a place as any to fight a duel."

Rosaline felt truly sick now. She was not certain as to the

rules of a duel but was almost sure she had the right to a second. But who could she call upon? Who would answer her? Not Valentio. Caterina?

Rosaline would not confess her sex to shun the fight, even if that meant death among these grotesques and apparitions.

"After you, my lord," said Romeo.

Rosaline stumbled into the leaning tower and at once found herself disordered. Through the window the horizon was atilt and misangled, the floor bent, and she staggered and almost fell. The world was topsy-turvy, mad and broken, and she wondered if she had indeed fallen helter-skelter into the underworld.

She looked back at Romeo and saw with horror that his sword was ready.

"You must draw," he said in a gentle voice lacking anger.

Doing as she was bid, Rosaline took a breath, wondering if it was to be her last. Within a second, she felt the sword wrenched from her grasp and clatter to the ground. She closed her eyes and waited for the blow that must come. She hoped it would not hurt, or not for long.

Instead she felt only the tug of the ribbons of the mask around the nape of her neck, the warmth of his fingers, his breath. She reached up to stay his hand.

"No, signorina, you lost."

Deftly he removed her mask and, taking her by the hand, drew her to the window where the dawn light was starting to break. He looked down at her and took her face in his hands. He stroked her cheeks gently with the pad of his thumbs, then caressed her eyebrows, then down the ridge of her nose to her top lip. He gave a small sigh. "Indeed, I do not know you, for I would remember such a face," he said. "Ah, the goddess Venus orbits us in heaven above."

He pointed upwards, where the last of the stars had been extinguished, only Venus still blinked in the brightening sky. "See? She witnesses the moment of our meeting." He kissed her hand.

Rosaline had never been spoken to in such a way before and stared at him, confused and aroused. "You knew I was not a man?"

He laughed. "Your lips…two rosebuds…are not those of a man. Your cheek…" Here, he paused with a frown. "My lady, there seems to be some grime smeared upon the perfection of your cheek."

Rosaline swallowed, aware that she was trapped in this peculiar tower with this stranger, and yet she trusted Romeo—or wanted to so very much. The fight had been a mere game. Her heart was still thumping in her chest.

Smiling, Romeo took a step away from her and leaned back against the wall. "Now, you say we Montagues are fiendish, depraved, and take great delight in sin. You are sure of this?"

"If I say yes, you promise not to fight me?"

Romeo laughed. "I swear it. You have disarmed me too, my lady."

"I can only say what I have heard. I will not lie. You are the first Montague I have met. So you must show me the truth as it really is, my lord."

"Very well. Here we are alone, madam, but you are safe." He stepped closer and brushed her cheek with his thumb again. "I want nothing to keep your secret. I do not want a kiss. I do not even want your name." He reached out and pressed her mask back into place, retying it with nimble fingers.

"I shall trust you, then," said Rosaline, looking up at him and meeting his eye. "I don't believe you would betray me for all that you are a Montague."

Rosaline paced her small bedroom, wriggling out of the hose and struggling with the buttons on her jacket. For the first time since Emelia's sickness and death, she was experiencing a fluttering in her chest of something like happiness. It was fragile, like butterfly wings, and might easily be tossed away by the merest wind.

She sat on the edge of her mattress in her linen under-blouse and tried not to think of Romeo. He had escorted her back through the monster garden as dawn probed rosy fingers through the ragged tops of the trees. The gods and gargoyles had peered imperiously upon the slumbering drunks laid out beneath them. Romeo insisted that she did not walk alone, for only the dregs of the guests remained and he did not trust them. Rosaline and Romeo had passed through the ogre's mouth together, but there she told him they must part—she would not have him see the path she took through the fields, or else he would know where she lived.

She did not want him to know she was a Capulet. She liked that he thought well of her, and she did not want the spell confounded. Since she would not see him again, she let the illusion remain.

Now, after slipping back unnoticed into the house full of sleepers, Rosaline could not settle. She paced to and fro as if trying to see how many *bracchia* wide her room was. She was aglow. No one had cared for her before. Or only as they might a fine china cup that if chipped would be spoiled and have no worth. Her reputation and honor was only valued because, if besmirched, it brought shame upon the Capulet name. It was the name that mattered, not Rosaline herself. But Romeo seemed to care about her. Her fingers. Her cheek. Her lips. Even if he was a Montague. And she would not see him again.

But what if she did? What if Romeo could pry her away from the set path laid out for her? He was the finest man she'd ever seen, and he was kind to her, but most of all, he offered hope.

She climbed into bed but did not close her eyes. Caterina would be along shortly to check she was safely returned. It did not matter; she could not sleep.

Outside, the wind tapped the shutters, softly at first, then with more persistence. It took Rosaline a moment to realize it was not the wind but someone knocking.

A voice called out, "Rosaline!"

She slipped out of bed and raced to the window. It could not be; it was not possible! Her bedroom window and the small balcony that it opened onto was beneath the eaves at the very top of the house. Whoever it was must have climbed up the apple trees outside and then edged along the narrow wall. Her heart was a drum beneath her breast. Her skin prickled, stung with fear and anticipation. She eased open the shutters.

"Rosaline!" came the voice again, urgent and soft.

"Who goes there?" she called, her voice low.

"Why? Do you not know me? Has it really been so long?" he asked.

Rosaline opened the windows and stepped out onto the narrow balcony. At first she couldn't see anyone in the easeful light, the shadows congealed and mingled with the trunks of wisteria and ivy. Then she saw a hand gripping a thick wrist of ivy and nearly cried out in alarm.

"Help me in, Cousin. It would be a waste of youth and beauty if I fell and broke my neck upon the cobbles below."

"Tybalt!"

She grasped his hand and pulled, tugging him down onto the balcony. He landed agilely on his feet and grinned. Rosaline hurled herself into his arms, knocking him back against the rail and then, suddenly shy, stepped back. She stared at him—taller, though his flesh didn't quite fill out the bones of his frame, a beard prickling his chin—taken aback at the realization of how much time had passed.

Tybalt stared back at her. "You are no longer a child," he said, sounding half in awe and half afraid of her.

"Neither are you."

The two of them gaped at one another, full of sudden

reserve, as they realized that their old intimacy must be reforged. Strangers had often mistaken them for brother and sister, they were so alike in coloring and mischief, and now they searched one another's faces for themselves. This Tybalt's smile was an echo of both her own and Tybalt the boy. The figure before her was tall with a man's shoulders. He was at once familiar and strange, with the same quick, restless movements.

Rosaline was horribly aware of how long they had been apart, of the years taken that could not be returned. She wondered if he still had a scar upon his knee from when they'd gone fishing for carp together and he'd slipped on the slick rocks, slicing it deeply. He'd cried bitter tears to see himself bleed so and made her promise never, ever to tell Valentio, for fear the older boy would tease and laugh at him. Now Tybalt stood outside her bedroom covered in mud and leaves, hat drooping over one eye, unable to meet her gaze. Yet the color of those eyes was the same rich brown as ever. Like a river after rain.

Why couldn't *he* have been her brother, and not Valentio? If Tybalt had been her brother, he would never let her father send her away. But there was nothing he could do.

Finally, he cleared his throat and looked at her. "I am sorry about your mother. A thousand blessings upon her soul. Emelia was my favorite aunt. I came as soon as I heard. But the letter took weeks to reach me in Padua, and by then you were nailed in."

"I am glad that you are come now," she said, finding as she said it that it was true. "Will you stay awhile?"

Tybalt nodded. "Yes. My studies are finished. I'm returned to Verona. I'm to stay with Valentio."

"You'll find Valentio just the same, only fatter. He was always greedy. Only now it shows."

Tybalt had been orphaned as a boy, and afterwards he'd been shared like a cold between the surviving Capulets, never belonging to any one of them, and handed off quickly and with enthusiasm.

Only Rosaline had wanted him. They were close in age, disposition, and looks, separated only by sex.

Rosaline sighed. She wished that Tybalt could live with them, but her father disliked guests, even if they were family. After all, he was even trying to rid himself of her.

"O, I've missed you, Cousin. But now we have time," said Tybalt.

We don't, thought Rosaline. But since it seemed he did not know about the nunnery, she would not tell him and spoil the joy of his return. Instead she said, "Yes, coz, it's almost like old times. But for now you must go. See, it's nearly fully light. Caterina will be here any moment. She can't find you with me. We're not children anymore. Come again in the morning? In the more usual manner? Through a door."

Grumbling but with good humor, Tybalt allowed himself to be led back to the edge of the balcony. Nimbly, he heaved himself back over the rail and clambered down the wall into the apple trees below.

Rosaline returned to bed. She lay back down, considering

this new Tybalt. Not quite a stranger, nor the companion from her girlhood. They could no longer spend the night tucked up together in the same bunk, reading aloud pages from Ovid or Homer to terrify one another in delight. She shivered and felt even lonelier. Curling up, she tried to remember snatches of how Tybalt used to whisper Ovid's *Metamorphosis* to her in the dark, but it was too long ago, and when she tried to picture one of the tales, she could only see "Venus and Adonis." And Adonis had Romeo Montague's face.

She awoke to see Caterina clattering the shutters. Caterina gave a shrill cry, and Rosaline buried her face in the bolster: her companion had likely found a mouse again.

"I came to no harm at all. I told you all would be well," said Rosaline, hoping she would leave her to sleep, but Caterina continued to mutter in bewilderment.

"What madness is this?"

Reluctant and bleary with sleep, Rosaline slid from her bed to the window and stared out onto the balcony. A carpet of roses had been lain out and scattered across the wooden floor while she was sleeping. A forest of dark green stems. A hundred, two hundred flowered crowns in pink and white and bloody red. Their petals lay unfurling in the sunlight, releasing a sweet, earthy fragrance. The air was thick with bees.

"Who climbed up and did this?" demanded Caterina.

"Tybalt," said Rosaline. "He's home from Padua."

"O, dearest Tybalt! Now, he was the sauciest boy I knew, and the sweetest. And this disarray I suppose is typical of him. A sweet-smelling muddle from your old playmate."

"Aye. And now, sweet Caterina, go. Let me pick up these fallen roses."

"You'll need twenty jars to put them in—that's if they're not all crushed and spoiled."

Rosaline shooed her away to her chores, assuring her that she'd find plenty of jars.

Once Caterina had finally departed, Rosaline stepped out onto the narrow balcony in her undershirt. Tybalt had not done this, of that she was certain. For there, in the middle of the bed of roses, nestled among the green leaves, thorny stems, and fallen petals browning in the sun, lay the gloves she had worn last night to the Montague place and then lost somewhere among the monsters.

She tiptoed barefoot across the thick layers of green, trying not to pierce her feet upon the thorns, and reached out for a glove. It felt stiff as she picked it up. Inside one of the fingers was rolled a note.

> Roses for fair Rosaline. I return your gloves,
> not to declare a duel, but to withdraw from
> one, as you withdraw this note. I would that I
> could have been a glove upon those fingers, as
> I would that I could be this letter, secreted
> inside your palm.

Rosaline glanced up, blinking against the glare of day. The sky was a vestal cobalt blue and the sun gilded and gleamed. Had it ever been so bright before? Her cheeks were hot. She turned and retreated into her bedroom but did not look where she trod and in her distraction stepped upon a bee. The pain was instant and acute. She felt light-headed and inhaled slowly and deeply, the sweet and heady scent of roses swirling all around her. But the pain did not matter. For Romeo Montague knew that she was a Capulet. And he prized her still.

III

I conjure thee by Rosaline's bright eyes

As she came down the stairs carrying armfuls of snapped rose stems, through the open doorway leading out through the hall, Rosaline spied the grooms readying the horses and preparing the wagon in the yard. Setting down the compost, she hurried out, wincing at the pain in her foot.

Her father stood among servants, upbraiding them for idleness—the bridles weren't gleaming, the wagon was sprayed with mud, the horses' manes improperly groomed. She waited for a pause in his diatribe.

"Where are you going, Papa?"

"Verona. And I'm to be back by sunset, if these buffoons would ever finish!"

"Will you take me with you? Please, Papa. I want to say prayers in the tomb for Mama's soul."

Masetto hesitated, and Rosaline guessed that he was torn between his desire to be alone with his grief and his desire for the safe passage through purgatory of Emelia's soul. He had paid monks and nuns to recite the essential masses, but so many in Verona had died that there were still hundreds of masses waiting to be said. Rosaline knew he fretted about the lost souls trapped in purgatory, circling like black clouds of starlings stuck in between worlds.

"I promise not to talk the entire way to Verona," she pressed.

"Very well, Daughter. You miss her too," he said, not unkindly, and gestured for the groom to hand her up.

Rosaline passed the trip in dutiful silence, looking out at the groves of olives, their leaves silver curls in the midday heat. She slipped down to pick a nosegay of wildflowers to leave upon the grave, limping beside the sweating horses. Every now and again, she glimpsed a rider on a black mount a little way behind them. Whoever this rider was, he kept a careful distance, as whenever he seemed certain to catch up to them, his horse would slow.

After a while, Rosaline saw the towers of the city's churches straining heavenwards and stood up in the wagon to see them better. Soon, they were crossing the stone bridge into the town itself, the green waters surging and foaming beneath. As they entered the city gates, Rosaline observed the emptiness of the streets—whether people had sought to escape the midday sun or it was an aftereffect of plague, she did not know.

When they reached the churchyard containing the family tomb, the wagon halted, and Rosaline jumped down.

"I'll return in an hour or two. Do not stray from the crypt," warned her father.

Rosaline nodded, taking these crumbs of concern as the only tenderness she was likely to receive from him.

As she walked along the twisting path, the heat thickened and congealed like soup. The family tomb stood in a large cemetery, crammed with graves alongside the mounds of new burial pits. The old bones sieved from the earth to make way for the newly rotten dead, and each of these had been tossed in more shallowly than the last. In the July heat, the smell was fetid and sour, and she could taste it on the back of her tongue, briny and foul. Her skin was slick with sweat and death. Everywhere the earth had been wrenched and cracked open, and more forced inside its skin. It was squirming, brimful, and, just beneath the surface, liquid and oozing. Crows perched on the headstones or circled above with their glottal laughter.

Rosaline shuddered despite the press of heat and picked up her pace through the churchyard, desperate to escape. She retreated with relief into the cool tomb. At least in there, the smell was better. Here the dead were locked away inside the stone vault.

It was dark, as she lacked either candle or lamp. She hadn't liked to take the time to fetch one in case Masetto changed his mind about her coming.

She knelt to say her prayers, muttering incantations for Emelia's safe passage into the next life.

Once she was finished, she sat back on her heels and stared

at the stone that hid her mother's remains. The stone mason had not yet chiseled her name, and the carved effigy of Emelia that Masetto had ordered would not be finished for another twelve months at least. There was just a blank. Emelia had been erased. No name, no likeness. Anger rose up in Rosaline's chest like bile as she laid down the few flowers she had picked—rue, rosemary, fennel, stalks of long-stemmed purple-speckled orchids, and daisies. The posy was wilting and wrung damp from her hands, but she did not care. "Here you are. Tybalt always called these long purple ones 'dead men's fingers.' Such a wretched name for a pretty flower." She pulled out the orchids and set them on the cool slab. "I always thought that one day you'd strew my bridal chamber. Now I'm strewing your grave and there will be no bridal bed for me. I am to be entombed in a living death. And I cannot even ask you why!"

Rosaline's voice rose and echoed around the tomb. Then— from somewhere—another joined it. For a second she thought the sound was some phantasm of grief—perhaps even her mother come to answer her. She looked around, startled.

"Do not weep, sweet Rosaline," it called.

Rosaline saw Romeo standing in the half-light of the entranceway.

"How are you here?" she asked, bewildered, and yet out of the dull fog of grief, she experienced a thrill like a lightning flash skim her heart. She stared at him, almost forgetting to breathe. He smiled at her, then stepped into the tomb.

"Please, forgive me. I came to your house this morning

hoping to speak to you, and when I saw that you were coming along the road to Verona, I thought that perhaps I might find a chance to talk to you more freely here."

Rosaline turned his words over in her mind. He had ridden into the city just for her.

"Please, dearest Rosaline, speak. I did not mean to frighten you."

"I'm not frightened."

She was quiet for a moment, and he stepped closer. "Do not be sad. Your mother is in paradise, not in this dark and fetid tomb."

He spoke so sincerely and gazed at her with such concern that Rosaline was moved. "Why did you come to my house? If my kinsmen found you there, they'd kill you."

Romeo shrugged. "I hid, hoping for a glimpse of you. I could not wait, fair Rosaline. I'm more afraid of your indifference than of their swords."

Rosaline shook her head and rubbed her eyes. She had slept little, and the heat and rancid stink made her nose prickle and eyes itch. For a moment she was not entirely sure if he was real or some mirage. In the darkling light, he was so still and the angle of his chin and throat so finely turned, that she could almost believe him one of the statues, carved to flatter the deceased and lie in stone for all time.

And yet, he was not marble but flesh. He blinked. His tongue, moist and soft, licked out across curved lips.

"Why did you have to be a Montague?" she whispered.

"I shall not be from this minute if you dislike it."

He came and sat beside her. He was close enough for her to smell pine and leather, although this time it was mingled with the warm, earthy aroma of his horse. It was a relief to have anything overpower the stink of rot and death.

"How did you find me? How did you find out my name?" demanded Rosaline.

"By love."

Rosaline laughed. "That is not an answer."

"It is the answer I shall give."

Rosaline was bewildered that anyone, least of all this remarkable man, would go to such lengths to seek her out. Only the stirrings of real affection could have driven him to do so. Her pulse was a bead in her throat, as tight beneath her skin as the fluttering wings of a moth. She wanted to reach out and touch his hand, feel the rough fingertips worn from the leather of his horse's bridle and the solid muscle of his thigh. Was this impulse, this need to touch, love?

In the hours they'd been apart, Rosaline had tried to conjure his cheek, his chin, his lip, the turn of his leg, but for all that she knew they were excellent, she could not quite bring them to mind. Now that he was before her, she saw that she had remembered him imperfectly. He was broader, his eyes blacker. In death, the Capulets surrounding them had been perfected as statues, but Romeo Montague would need no improvements or flattery. Such beauty in a man was unsettling, and beside him she felt clumsy and childish. Even in the wavering light, she could see that he was at least of an age as Valentio, or older. Compared to Romeo, her playmate Tybalt was merely a boy.

Impatient, she wanted him to move out of the gloom and into the daylight so she could see him better. As he smiled, she caught the bright gleam of his teeth.

"When I'm with you, I think myself already in paradise," he murmured. "It is not dark in here, for you are more luminous than the moon."

Rosaline stared at him for a moment, listening to the hurried beat of her heart. No one spoke to her like this—often they didn't speak to her at all. Mostly she felt invisible, as if she had no body at all, and here was this man of the mighty house of Montague telling her of her loveliness. It was as if she'd never had form until this moment, and with his words he conjured her into a being of solid flesh and beauty. She shed her girlish skin and felt herself metamorphose into the woman he described.

Romeo smiled, edging closer still. Her breath caught in her throat. He gestured to the effigy of an angel, poised upon one of the Capulet tombs above. All the departed Capulets carved or cast in plaster seemed to be gazing down upon them, an audience of the benevolent dead.

"The alabaster of your cheek is purer than that of this angel who looks down at us and weeps."

At this Rosaline put up her hand to stay him. She longed to believe every delicious word, but for that he must speak the truth. "Sweet Romeo, your honeyed tongue is over-sweetened by courtly tropes. What you say is true of…my cousin… Juliet's skin is alabaster perhaps, but not mine. I'm darker than is modish. Some have even wondered if I have Moorish blood."

"And you are perfect for it."

"Then speak how I really am, not how I am supposed to be. Love is blind, not lovers."

"So we are lovers, then?" he asked, smiling and placing his hand upon her cheek.

Rosaline frowned a little. "I cannot think of love or life, surrounded and mocked by death on every side. It makes me see the end before we've yet begun."

At this, to her wonder, Romeo stood abruptly and took her by the hand. The touch of his hand on hers made her fingers tingle, the dull throb of a nettle sting.

"Come then. Let us leave this stale and noisome air," he said, tugging her on.

Rosaline allowed him to lead her, murmuring, "The stench is worse outside."

"Ah, yes, that way indeed it is. But not this."

He led her out of the tomb, but instead of proceeding into the churchyard, he showed her into a passageway that opened immediately into the street leading down toward the river. As if by some blessed miracle, the air was clean and fresh there, laundered by the waters. He paused in order to tug her veil low to hide her face and then drew her arm through his and stroked her fingers, kissing them one by one.

Rosaline basked in his adoration. Her fingers tingled from his touch, thawed by his attentions. In the daylight he was fine-looking, with black hair like a raven's wing, his arms lean and strong, his hands restless at his sides, long fingers drumming against the muscles of his thigh. His lips were curved and full, and as he squinted against the sunlight, fine creases appeared in the corners of his eyes.

"None who know us will come to this part of the river," he said.

He hurried her down some steps near the bank, where the air was fresher still, and the streets teemed with people once again. She forgot the ache in her foot. The shade was stuffed with hawkers selling wheels of cheese swaddled in damp cloths, round globes of oranges dimpled and fat, gray coils of whiskered shrimp, and glittering trout in bloody heaps, eyes blurred, bellies slit.

Rosaline inhaled in gulps the pleasure of it all. Here the world was sharp and awake, and she felt the last of her low and lumpish mood dissipate.

"What would you like?" asked Romeo.

"An orange."

Romeo handed over a coin, and then, as they ambled farther from the stalls and found a spot looking down upon the waters, he began to peel it for her with his knife. Rosaline lifted her veil and ate the segments one by one. The juice was sharp and, O, so sweet, and trickled down her chin and then her throat.

Romeo watched her, then caught the spill of juice with his fingertip. He hesitated before leaning forward again and kissing the bare skin of her throat. His mouth was warm, his breath soft, ticklish as a feather. For a moment she forgot to breathe.

He pressed closer, and that morning's unshaved beard scraped against her skin.

She inhaled again and tasted the sharp perfume of oranges.

Romeo leaned back, his eyes half-closed. "It's sticky. I wouldn't want to attract flies."

"No," agreed Rosaline, shocked that he had licked away the juice so shamelessly, more shocked that she had let him.

She ate another piece, allowing the juice to dribble and ooze again, hoping he would kiss it away. He did, making a low noise in his throat that surprised and intrigued Rosaline.

She watched him as he sat up. He remained almost the perfect statue in the daylight, only he looked older than twenty-five. Could he be more than thirty? She could not tell. Perhaps it was the effect of the light, but there appeared to be flecks of gray in his black hair around his ears, like fallen snow. She did not dislike it. He moved, and the snow seemed to melt away. Perhaps it was the glint of the light after all.

She remembered, too late, that she was not supposed to leave the tomb or churchyard. "I must go," she said, rising.

"No. You cannot," he said, catching her hand and trying to pull her back.

"My father will return and be furious when he cannot find me."

"Rosaline! You can't leave me here. Not so unsatisfied."

"Unsatisfied?"

"I must know when I shall see you again."

Rosaline shook her head and closed her eyes tightly against the luminous glare of the sun. Beneath the tang of the orange, she could smell the ripe reek of the trout, and then as she took another breath, there was the stench of the grave again. She would be a fool to allow Romeo to court her. He was a Montague. And even if he was not, her father had already decided her fate. Before the summer faded, she would be locked away. Rosaline already had sufficient griefs to bear. She could while away hours in her cell counting out her sorrows on her rosary beads and the parts of the hurly world that she missed; she did not need to add to her impending unhappiness by encouraging a courtship that she knew was star-crossed.

She stood and pulled down her veil. "Do not look for me again." She started to walk away and then paused, turning to call: "You cannot save me, Romeo Montague."

Masetto was outraged when he could not find Rosaline in either the churchyard or at the tomb. When she returned, he was torn between fury that she had risked her honor by taking a walk alone without a chaperone and the horror of his being made to wait a full quarter hour. They sat in the wagon as he railed at her, journeying back out of the city; and while the air was more pleasant, with a light wind blowing, none of zephyr's charms were enough to soothe Masetto's choler.

"I paced to and fro! I was hot! And what if the convent heard of this disgrace and refused you admission? What then?"

What then indeed? thought Rosaline. This was a boon she had not considered.

"You've broken our agreement after a single day, Daughter.

You're a baggage that I cannot manage. Twelve days! Indeed, you must leave at once."

"No, Father, please! I beg you. I was hot. The smell. I could not stomach it."

But Masetto shook off her pleas as though she were a cur and would not speak or heed her. "Hush! I'll consult with your brother. Do not whimper; it annoys me."

When they arrived home, Masetto led the evening prayers, the entire household gathered together in the hall. Masetto knelt upon an embroidered cushion depicting pomegranates and pine cones that had been worked by Emelia. There was an empty space on his right side where Emelia herself used to sit, the miniature portrait of her propped upon a cushion. Rosaline knelt to his left on a silken pad, while Caterina and the kitchen maids and the few men servants groveled behind them without cushions to soften the waxed stone floor.

"O, divine and Holy Father, we beg your mercy and forgiveness! We must have sinned for you to have sent such a scourge of pestilence among us," called Masetto, scraping low. "Please deliver us from further divine disfavor and grant us your heavenly light and mercy."

When he was finished, Rosaline and the household recited their catechism without thought or choice. Afterwards they stood, surreptitiously rubbing life into tingling limbs as Masetto addressed them all.

"We must be vigilant. I've heard news that there is sickness in the monastery at Santa Maria. We pray with renewed vigor that it is merely fever and not plague. This shattered world must be restored to order."

Rosaline glanced around and saw fear painted across the faces of the servants. She sighed. Did her father believe that through acts of Christian goodness, he could protect himself and his house from a pestilence carried by the miasmas? Was prayer another posy against death, just less herbal and sweet-smelling? She was not sure if she believed in its power any more than she did the packets of cloves, mace, and sorrel.

She came back to herself. Her father was staring at her with outrage and dismay, as if he could read her thoughts upon her face. She rearranged her features in what she imagined was a display of maidenly timidity. She would not incite him further.

"Rosaline, are you ill?"

"No, Father."

"What acts of Christian charity will you carry out tonight?" demanded Masetto.

"I shall read the Bible with our tenants."

"Read?" He exhaled the word as if it were a flame that burnt his tongue as he spoke it.

"Recite prayers with them, then," soothed Rosaline.

"Your mother could not read. And it did her no harm."

Nor good neither, since she is dead, thought Rosaline. Then, she noticed Tybalt waiting just beyond the open doorway, lingering half out of sight. As a boy he had been afraid of her father, who'd always been quick with the strap. Even now it seemed the aversion held. She curtseyed low to Masetto and, before he could speak again, hurried out, leading Tybalt farther into the yard.

"You cannot hide here. You must go and speak with my father and tell him of your sadness at my mother's death."

"I do not hide! I am no coward! I came this morning early. I've come to take you to Livia. But if you wish to quarrel, I shall go."

Rosaline caught hold of his elbow as he turned. Tybalt's temper was like yeast in the sun: fast to rise but easily subsiding when pricked. "No! I don't wish to quarrel. See, here are my hands. I do not bite my thumb at you." She smiled.

Tybalt gave a tight smile in return. She nudged him again in his ribs and he yielded. She'd always known how to appease him and was satisfied that time had not lessened her skill.

"How is Livia today?" she asked.

"Well."

"Then let us go at once," said Rosaline, slipping her arm though his.

"Don't you need a cloak? Better shoes?" he asked, looking askance at her lambskin slippers.

"No. Let us make haste," said Rosaline with a hurried glance over her shoulder. She did not wish to either read or recite prayers to tenants any more than they wished to hear them.

The sun was a polished gold coin suspended high above the strips of barley, wheat, and vines. Every fourth or fifth strip lay fallow, gripped by weeds. A hot wind swirled around them, carrying motes of dust from distant shores so her skin was covered in fine grit. A kite circled in loops as Rosaline limped on, the beesting on her foot sore now and swollen. She paused and removed her slippers and hobbled on barefoot, as Tybalt stared at her in bemusement.

"Don't stare," she snapped. "I stung my foot."

"If you wore shoes more often, then perhaps it would not have happened."

Rosaline glared at him and Tybalt wisely fell silent. She stumbled on, seething, though it was not Tybalt at fault.

"The world is broken," Rosaline said after a moment. "My father wishes it to be mended. But nothing can make it whole again. She is gone." Her voice faltered, her temper dissipating. "This earth was disordered by death and disease, and I cannot believe it will be whole through either wishes or prayers."

"All will heal in time."

"And also die."

Tybalt gave a wry smile. "You were always cleverer than me, Ros."

"You know that the plague's come again to the monks' house at Santa Maria?" she asked.

"It might just be summer fever."

Rosaline shrugged. "But when priests and friars and nuns sicken and die, what hope is there for us sinners? What use is there in prayer? For what else do nuns and monks do other than pray?"

Tybalt looked worried. "Hush, fie! You speak like a heretic."

"Do I? Do I speak like one or am I one? I do not feel like one, Tybalt. I feel like myself."

"Speak however you like for my sake, Ros. It's only if others should hear you. 'Tis them I fear."

"What others?" said Rosaline with a laugh, gesturing to the bare and open fields. "If I am a heretic, will you still be my friend?"

"Always. And you will be so reasoned in your arguments that I shall think myself one too. But, Ros, for pity's sake, hush," pleaded Tybalt, reaching for her.

"There are none here but birds and ghosts," she cried, dodging away from him.

"Ghosts can speak, and the fields have eyes."

They reached a wide strip of land, fallow and filled with white dandelions, the seed clocks a summer snowdrift, catching in the balmy breeze and in their eyelashes, turning their hair hoary and white.

Rosaline plucked dandelion fur from her eyebrows, declaring, "See, if you leave again, when you next come back, this is how changed I shall be!"

"I did not want to go, Ros," said Tybalt softly. "I had no choice in it. Forgive me."

Rosaline was silent. She had not known till now she was angry that he had left her. He had been her truest friend, the sharer in her woes. Then he had gone to Padua to learn as boys must.

She touched his arm. "There's nothing to be forgiven," she said.

Turning, she caught the feathered seeds between her fingertips and between her bare toes, where the fluff had drifted into tufts upon the bare earth. She picked up a handful soft as duckling down, rolling it into a ball upon her palm, and blew it at Tybalt, who caught it and then tried to keep it aloft with his breath like a shuttlecock. Rosaline clapped her hands in glee, almost forgetting the beesting, and for a few minutes the pair were playing as children, the last unease and awkwardness between them puffed away with the tufts of dandelion snow.

When they finished their game, they sat on a tree stump, clammy and out of breath. Rosaline rested her head on Tybalt's shoulder, and he tugged her plaits as though they were ten years old again, tired after a day's dawdling in the woods.

He rose to pick a ragged bunch of cornflowers, dusty from the heat, then sat back beside her on the stump. "These were my mother's favorite, or so I've been told. I do not know for certain, any more than can I know if she loved me."

"By the stars above, you can be certain that she loved you," said Rosaline, turning to look at him.

"Why? For all mothers must love their babes? She loved me only for an instant, amid pain in the midst of death. All three at once. But you, Ros, you were loved by Emelia. She is carried with you; for so long as you live, she does not die. But how can I carry my mother with me when I cannot remember her? She's but a stranger."

He crushed the bedraggled cornflowers between his fingers,

tucking them into his belt, saying, "I gather flowers to wilt on her tomb. They molder with her."

Rosaline turned to him, her eyes bright with concern, but he grinned. "My wound is old and long scabbed over. I only say this to remind you that you were loved and known by Emelia."

Rosaline's anger began to kindle again, hot and fierce. "If my mother loved me so, then why send me away? Curtail my life?" She plucked a piece of dandelion fluff from her eyelash. "I'm not my father's to sacrifice to God. I won't pray for him. Even at the convent. My father is to dispatch me—"

She stopped, seeing Tybalt's face. He said nothing, only looked wretched and forlorn.

"You already know my fate?" said Rosaline.

Tybalt would not look at her. "Your brother told me this morning." He paused. "I can't imagine you as a nun."

"Neither can I."

"And I can't believe your mother wanted it."

"I'll never know for certain, since the dead can't speak." She sighed. "I have eleven days left till I must have a living death of my own. Or perhaps even fewer. I disobeyed my father, and he threatened to change his mind and send me at once."

"O, Rosaline…"

"Fie! I can bear anything but your pity. Even when I cracked my nose falling from the turkey oak and we thought it was broken, you did not pity me but laughed."

"I laughed because I was frightened, Rosaline. You spat blood all the way home."

"I liked your laughing better. Laugh now."

"I cannot."

"Then speak of other things." She slid off the stump and began to walk slowly now. "Tell me of Padua. Nay, tell me a story. Something fantastical. Like you used to."

It was Tybalt who had taught Rosaline to read, not with the dreary primers like the boys, but with a copy of Ovid stolen from Valentio for the purpose. The young Rosaline's mind had been fattened on myth and monster. She loved Tybalt for teaching her and enduring the beating that it had earned him; girls' minds ought not to be risked with the exploits of the Greeks.

Rosaline owed Tybalt a debt of love for this gift. She liked to repay him by reading to him and retelling him her versions of the stories that she'd found, but this afternoon her spirits were too leaden. She only wanted to listen.

Tybalt pondered for a moment and then obeyed. "Today you visited your mother's tomb, but, Ros, it does not always follow that a tomb is the end. A tomb is a door. Orpheus follows Eurydice down, down into the underworld to bring her back. As I would you," he added with a grin.

Rosaline raised an eyebrow. "A poor choice, Cousin," she chided. "Orpheus fails. He falls over his own feet."

"He is tricked! By a god! What chance do mortals have?"

"In any case, Eurydice is lost. The tomb is the end for them."

Tybalt considered for a minute. "You were always better at games." Then he clapped his hands in triumph. "Pyramus and

Thisbe! They meet at Ninus's tomb. For them, the tomb spells not death but a beginning…"

Tybalt spoke on of love; Rosaline did not listen. She thought instead of Romeo in the Capulet tomb. She wished that if their love was to begin, it had not started there, that the scent of rue, rosemary, and fennel had not been laced with decay. And when at last she did listen, she was not certain that Tybalt had remembered the story quite right, but the sound of his voice was pleasing and familiar, and she did not like to interrupt. Around them the luminous rays of sunlight broke through the spinning sycamore leaves lining the path.

Rosaline sat with Livia's newest babe perched stiffly upon her knee, its layers of swaddling making it rigid. The child glanced about it with furious eyes, a bruised blue, as if still angry to have been born and placed upon this wretched earth. Livia sat back among a nest of pillows, her face paler and thinner than before, while Tybalt leaned against the wall, silent and still as his cousins squabbled. Rosaline was once again relieved to have her old ally returned while she pleaded with her brother.

"Father promised," she insisted. "He cannot go back on his word. I have twelve days. Nay, eleven."

"Our poor father is unmanned by grief," complained Valentio. "He does not know what to do with a daughter. And certainly not at such a time as this! And then you flouted his command."

"For a moment. It was hot and noxious in the churchyard. And I begged his forgiveness," said Rosaline.

"You should not have used his good nature so."

"Good nature! Toward you, perhaps. Not to me. The animals that heap his dunghills he views with as much interest as me. At least their muck he can use upon his fields."

"Rosaline," said Valentio, chiding her gently. "Your words bite worse than horseflies."

Rosaline was too upset to take them back.

"As you are to go in any case, then delay is futile," added Valentio.

"Only to you, who has all the time to squander as you choose. For me every hour, every minute in the world before I am sequestered and walled up is as a jewel. When I am in the convent and victim to monastic law, I cannot hold your children or touch or kiss them unless it's through bars. I cannot clasp the hand of another person. I am not allowed to play upon my lute or see a field of sunflowers unfurl and turn toward the sun. And yet, brother of mine, you wish to hurry me through these last days."

"You speak as if it's an execution."

"To me it is. Of my very self."

Her brother rubbed his forehead. "Then let us think, Sister, of what is to be done."

Valentio set down his cup in annoyance, spilling the contents. Livia reached for his hand. Rosaline glanced at Tybalt. He was staring at her in dismay.

"Speak, Tybalt, in my defense, but do not offer piteous looks. They are no good to me," she said.

"I will speak when it's useful," he replied.

Livia interjected, turning to Valentio. "She is helpful to me here, Husband. She is good with the children," she said, her tone pleading.

Valentio snorted. "Nonsense. She holds the infant as though he were a jug of ale. You must think of something else, Livia, if you wish to delay her leaving."

Rosaline bounced the baby, but it began to fuss and whimper. The nurse appeared, removing him from her lap, and stowed him away in his crib.

Now, Tybalt stepped forward, saying, "The difficulty, as I understand it, is that Masetto wishes to dedicate himself to his grief and supplications to Madonna Emelia's beloved memory."

Rosaline began to object. Surely the best way for her father to dedicate himself to his wife's memory was to take care of her daughter.

"For once, Ros, I beg you, hush," said Tybalt, not without affection.

Grumbling, she bit her tongue.

"Earlier, I called upon Madonna Lauretta Capulet. I saw little Juliet too. What if Rosaline were to spend these last days of freedom with her?"

"No!" cried Rosaline. "Juliet is dear to me, but she's a child. She's barely thirteen."

"She's fourteen on Lammastide," said Livia quietly.

"She still has a nurse," said Rosaline.

"She does," agreed Tybalt. "A peculiar creature getting on in years. I remember her well from my own boyhood. She's kind enough and dotes upon Juliet, but prattles all sorts of nonsense. She can't be much of a companion for Juliet."

"I believe Father would agree to it," said Valentio after a moment's thought.

"So this is my choice, then?" cried Rosaline. "The nunnery or the nursery?" She gazed at the array of faces and hurried from the chamber, stuffing her sleeve into her mouth to muffle her sobs. She would not have any of them see her cry. She heard Tybalt's foot upon the stair as he tried to follow and comfort her, but Livia called him back. For that small kindness, she was grateful.

That night Rosaline could not sleep. She lay in her bed listening to the click and rustle of the mice in the attic above. Where was Romeo? Was he in the city, or had he ridden back to the countryside? Even to wonder about a Montague was a kind of treachery, and yet she longed for another, deeper treachery. If only he could slide into her chamber like a shadow and steal her away. She buried her hot cheek into the sheet and tried to forget his face, forget hope.

Rosaline and Juliet sat in the orchard on a bench beneath the nascent bulbs of apples. Juliet was swinging her legs. Nurse had not stopped talking for a full half hour.

Her nest of chins wobbled in happiness as she chattered. "Two angels instead of one! What heaven! Will you not stay the night, Rosaline, and fill up my nursery, my little coop with chicks? It's been years since it was nicely stuffed."

Rosaline shook her head. "My father agreed I can go home to sleep. I want my last nights in my own bed."

Nurse squeezed her hand in understanding, but a shadow of disappointment crossed Juliet's face.

Rosaline experienced a nudge of guilt. She had known Juliet as long as she could remember. At times she appeared but a child, milk-fed and pleading with Rosaline to play hopscotch with her in the scrubby patch of shade, and yet she was also fast-tongued and nimble-witted from having spent too long in the company of adults. Rosaline liked it better with her than she'd thought. Juliet might be young, but she was fun.

In the fierce July light, Juliet's hair was gold, like the ripening ears of corn. It fell in drifting curls around her face, as fair as Rosaline was dark. She was slight and small, one of Titania's fairy maidens, and she looked even younger than thirteen.

The sickness in the monastery was not plague but summer fever, and so Masetto and Juliet's father had decreed that they might return to Verona. All the other Capulets had followed suit, and Rosaline was glad to spend her last days of freedom in the city, among the stink and hum of life.

She blinked up at the sun. Another quarter hour at least had passed and Nurse was still talking. "O, I have watched her run and waddle about all these years! Even when she tipped backward upon her little bum, she did not cry. Eleven years it's been since she was weaned. She didn't want the milk sup to end.

No! Not Jule. I had to rub wormwood upon my dug before she would stop."

At this Juliet had had enough and abruptly stood. "Rosaline, we have racquets. Shall we play?"

Rosaline trailed her to a patch of grass, parched in the heat and marked out for tennis. Juliet smiled sideways at her as she tossed her a leather ball. "Unless you prefer to hear more of how I was swaddled from left to right and left again, and angels descended from the firmament above to sing me to sleep?"

"O, that I remember. The sound was heavenly indeed."

They played despite the heat, eager for a refuge from the prattle. Poor Nurse was unsure who to cheer on, and so contented herself by trumpeting for them both, commiserating with every lost ball or missed shot with agony, as though she were lamenting a man fallen in battle. Rosaline saw that Juliet bore it all with practiced fortitude and was so distracted by observing them both that she continually lost until Juliet grew cross.

"Come, coz," she complained when Rosaline missed the third easy pass in a row. "You are older than me, but not yet an old maid. A little sport, please! Unless you wish to choose a different game?"

"You are as quick on your feet as you are with your tongue," said Rosaline, pausing to catch her breath.

After a while they saw that Nurse had surrendered to the warmth and dozed off. Juliet nudged Rosaline and threw down her racquet. "Come here. Under the trees. She won't find us even if she wakes."

Juliet clambered into a cupped hollow beneath the spread of apple trees, and Rosaline followed. It was cooler there, and the shade dappled and green. They lay back and looked up at the spangled canopy of leaves.

"I always envied you and your kind, sensible mother," said Juliet.

"Your nurse is kind."

"But she is not sensible. And my mother is not kind."

Rosaline did not think it either sensible or kind to agree, even if both observations were true.

"I'm glad you are here, coz," said Juliet, turning to look at her. Her face was flushed from sunshine and exercise, her eyes blue and clear. "You don't want to be a nun, I know. But what do you want, dear Rosaline? If you were free to choose your fortune, do you think you could love a man in earnest?"

"In earnest?"

"Well, I could not love one in earnest. Only in jest or sport. Men are odd creatures. Not like us at all."

Rosaline thought for a moment before answering. "I do not know if I could love. I only know that I cannot. Must not." While she spoke, Romeo's image conjured itself before her eyes. She pushed it away. She remembered the warmth of his lips against her throat. The sharp scent of oranges. She must not think of him. She must not. "Since I cannot choose my fortune, Juliet, I can only surrender to my fate."

Juliet smiled. "None of us can really choose our fate. We only pretend we can. You are wiser than most, Rosaline, for men or women who think they can control fortune as if she's a housewife are the fools. She'll spin and spin whatever we do."

"Fortune is blind, and she is supposed to bestow her gifts evenly, but I do not believe she does—she does not give her bounty equally to women," said Rosaline quietly, picking a bulb of apple and squashing it between her fingers.

Juliet considered her. "I don't agree with what the family says."

"What *do* they say?"

"That'll you'll make a wonderful nun. I think you'll make a rotten one."

"Thank you," said Rosaline, grateful.

They lay beneath the trees in silence, staring at the sky filtered through the wavering green. They watched the polished plume of a lapwing, like a centurion's helmet, as he hopped up and down in the unscythed grass at the edge of the orchard, scouring for bugs for his chicks. Slowly, the heat of the afternoon lost its ferocity and faded into the drowsy warmth of early evening. Nurse awoke and began to cluck and call for them.

"Juliet! Rosaline! Come."

Juliet winced and took a breath and called, "By and by, I come!"

"At once, madam!"

Rosaline led Juliet out from their hiding place. To her surprise she saw that Tybalt stood beside Nurse. He winked at Rosaline and she smiled, glad that he'd come. Juliet clapped her hands in delight, and he held open his arms for the younger girl as she hurled herself into them. A moment later he was twirling her around and around on the grass, as she shrieked with exuberance, finally collapsing, dizzy, in a heap.

Grinning, Tybalt turned to Rosaline. "Rosaline, your turn?"

"No, thank you very much."

"Nurse?" he inquired with a bow.

"Not with these aching bones. I'd fall in twenty pieces."

Tybalt chuckled and looked at Rosaline. "I've come to return my cousin to her father's house."

Juliet chewed the end of her plait and looked so forlorn at the prospect of her leaving that Rosaline crouched down on the grass beside her, placing her hands upon the girl's thin shoulders. "Dear Juliet, I will be back in the morning. And I'll take you with me in my heart tonight."

"Just take me with you. I'm little. I could sleep beside you in your bed, and you'd hardly notice."

Rosaline tried not to laugh. She was unused to professions of affection. She hugged her close, whispering, "I'll see you tomorrow, sweet Juliet."

Leaving the others in the garden, Rosaline retreated into the house to change her dress and retrieve her outdoor shoes from Juliet's chamber. Inside it was cool and still, and there was the smell of sweet pastry cooling, straight from the oven. She hurried up the stairs. Her overdress lay waiting for her upon Juliet's truckle bed. She stooped to pick it up and, bending low, spied a family of dolls stashed beneath the cot in a small pine box, stacked neatly side by side as if they were sharing a coffin, all hastily buried. Rosaline pulled them out. They'd been tenderly tucked in to their resting place, well-worn rag faces and cross-stitch eyes gazing at her blankly. There was no dust. They'd not been long stored but were shoved well back beneath the bed. If she had to guess, she'd hazard that this was that morning's work—Juliet had put her childhood away neatly out of sight before her older cousin had arrived, so she would not think her ways too babyish. Rosaline was pricked with tenderness. She returned the box to its tomb beneath the bed as if it had never been disturbed.

Juliet had asked her if she could love a man. In truth she did not know. All she knew was that she loved Juliet already.

"This is not the way home," said Rosaline, glancing about the unfamiliar street. It led not to her father's house but out of Verona, toward the vast amphitheater at the edge of the city, and then to the countryside and fields beyond.

"O? Is it not?" said Tybalt, pleased with his surprise. He smiled. "The prince has decreed the theaters may open again now the pestilence has waned."

Rosaline squeezed Tybalt's hand in delight. "O! Which play are we to see? A comedy?" She saw his face fall. "So, 'tis a tragedy then, no matter!"

Tybalt looked discouraged. "A wrestling match. I persuaded your father to permit me to take you to the prince's wrestling match. He has a new fighter. Reputed to be the best in all Verona, and he is eager for a goodly crowd at this first bout."

He examined her face eagerly, and Rosaline managed to smile. She had little interest in wrestling, but any diversion pleased her.

"We must fill every moment till you go to the nunnery with debauched delights," said Tybalt. "It shall take you a lifetime to repent of your sins."

Rosaline laughed. "Indeed, I'll be the worst of nuns."

"The very worst," he agreed.

She looked at Tybalt. She was moved that he understood how she wished to spend her last days. The years apart had separated them in body but not in mind.

As they approached the amphitheater, she could hear the crowd like the rumble of an approaching storm. There was the smell of roasting pig and honeyed nuts. In the lane, jugglers dressed in Roman garb tossed batons into the air, while admirers threw coins and cheered, and fools hit each other with sticks. Tybalt stopped to watch and laugh.

"See? Are you not glad we came?" he asked.

"Indeed I am," she said, taking pleasure in his merriment.

A fire-eater with livid, bloodshot eyes saw Rosaline and swallowed down his flame and then, leaning close, leered at her, breathing it out so near to her that she flinched and yelped.

Tybalt chuckled again. "Come, let's away inside."

Their seats were near the front, among the prosperous and noble citizens of the city, affording them an excellent view of both the amusement in the ring and the crowd. The prince himself was seated on a dais a little way apart, the royal standard in blue and gold snapping in the breeze. The rows in the common stands were rigid with spectators. Most of the onlookers were men, but here and there women stood out among the crowd in their livid dress, some ladies, like Rosaline, distinguished by their gowns of damask and silk brocade, dyed blue and emerald and saffron, and stitched with tiny seed pearls, subtly denoting their high rank. Yet more intriguing to Rosaline were the whores and courtesans, who ignored the sumptuary laws and, in flagrant disregard of Rome's decree, mimicked their betters, wearing overdresses of crimson velvet, frilled collars, and frothing lace sleeves, with gleaming jewels upon their breasts. These women laughed the loudest and gathered together unchaperoned by husbands, brothers, fathers, or cousins. They drank wine or ale without a care. However, Rosaline wondered whether each sip, each giggle as they threw back their heads and exposed smooth and supple white throats, was an act of theater as studied as that of the wrestlers now strutting in their leather hose and beating upon their chests as they roamed the ring. Every now and then, a man would approach the women, and their fans would all flutter at once, like dozens of spangled butterfly wings, as he made his choice.

"What are you looking upon with such intent?" asked Tybalt. "The wrestlers? They are splendid fellows."

"No," replied Rosaline slowly. "The ladies there."

Tybalt followed her gaze. "They are not ladies, and a lady such as you ought not to look upon them." He licked dry lips. "And yet, they belong to a world you must surrender to, so look, look with stealth. I shall not be your judge."

Next came a massive shaggy bear missing an eye, straining on its chain, and prowling around the pit with its keeper, its fur bedraggled and matted. It stood up on its haunches beside the school of courtesans and gave a fearsome snarl. One of the women leaned over the rail and growled back at it to a chorus of cheers from the crowd.

"The bear is on next week. We can come again, if you like?" said Tybalt.

"I think I can manage without the bear. He looks sad."

"He has but one eye—he can barely look at all."

She couldn't help but observe that the sawdust covering the ring was already well doused with blood and gore—from what or whom, she preferred not to dwell on. There was a disturbance along their row as a young man elbowed his way toward them, stepping on feet in leather slippers and nudging the rotund bellies of Verona's most prominent citizens.

Tybalt spied him eagerly. "Petruchio! My friend! Come, sit with us. Ros, you do not mind?"

Petruchio did not wait for her reply, and Rosaline found herself shoved to the side to make way. The young man wore a red mantle in the German fashion, a velvet collar with four long slashes, and gold buttons at the throat and upon his chest. He kissed her hand with a flourish and then, turning his back upon her, spoke only to Tybalt, who gave Rosaline a helpless and apologetic smile.

"I'm so glad you're returned from Padua," declared Petruchio. "I've had more fun these last few days than I've had in three years. Come, let us drink and toast to your return!"

They drank and surveyed the arena with fervor. Soon, Rosaline grew hot and bored. Tybalt tried again and again to include her in the conversation, but Petruchio had no wit when it came to women and limited himself to covering her hand with damp kisses that she quietly wiped on her mantle. Tybalt looked at her and mouthed another apology for his neglect, but she could see he was already in his cups: his cheeks were flushed damson-pink, like a maiden's. The bench before them was set with empty jugs of ale, and the two youths were soon toasting the courtesans across the ring.

"A toast to Beetle Brows! May she blush for me tonight," cried Petruchio.

"And if love is rough with you, be rough with love!"

Rosaline wondered to herself what either of them knew of love, but suspected that the whores sizing them for easy money would be content to teach them for a price.

As Petruchio raised his tankard high above his head, he spilled ale upon the bald pate of the lord in the stand in front, who turned around and scolded him. Petruchio bowed an apology, dropping his hat.

"O, they are no fun at all, these old men of rank," he muttered.

"No, and the smell is terrible," replied Tybalt, and both young men chuckled.

Rosaline wearied of their boasts and verbal jousting, and longed for more sensible company. She neither wished to be jostled nor doused in beer. Tybalt she loved well; he was a fellow of both tact and charm, but his friend was boorish.

She edged away from them both and, as she did so, spied at the far side of the theater Romeo Montague. Her heart began to pound; she was speared with delight that he had come. Surely in a moment he would notice her? She strained to see him better, but he was too far away and was speaking intently with another man and did not observe her.

How could he be here? She scolded herself. Why should Romeo Montague not be here? This was Verona, and all were welcome to this display of the prince's. The Montagues were among his friends. She simply had not known them before as they were not among hers. She watched Romeo for another minute, the gentle seriousness of his expression and then how, like the sun bursting forth from behind a cloud, he would laugh.

Seeming to feel her eyes upon him, he at last looked up and met her gaze. He did not wave or smile. Rosaline stared back and felt her cheeks grow warm.

Then, Romeo bent to speak to his companion and disappeared.

Where had he gone? She glanced about the theater but could not see him. To her surprise, Rosaline discovered that she was bereft. She had no interest in the wrestlers who had now entered the ring, ready to fight, oiled and baring their teeth at one another, as the crowd roared and the arena itself seemed to tremble and quake. The prince himself was out of his seat and shouting with the rest of them, his face red and inflamed with choler.

The yells echoed in Rosaline's chest, their collective

excitement passing through her, but she did not share in it. She did not care who triumphed or who was cast down, bloody, onto the filth and sawdust. If she could not talk to Romeo, then she wanted to be gone. She was restless and wished she had not come.

A hand slid into hers. Warm lips pressed against her ear. Her heart pounded and her breath caught in her throat.

"Come with me," murmured Romeo.

Without a thought she followed him.

No one saw them leave. All eyes were fixed upon the battle being fought in the dust in the ring as Romeo led her away from the rows of people, behind the arches of the amphitheater. The noise was brutish, and Rosaline glimpsed the two men grappling, barefoot and stripped to the waist, slippery with sweat as they tried to strangle one another. The crowd was chanting now, eager for blood and death. There had been so much of that wreaked upon the city, but this time it was at their choosing.

"Will one of them die?" asked Rosaline.

"Perhaps."

Romeo appeared neither stirred by the closeness of death nor saddened. He drew her farther back and out of sight. "The prince might intervene and order the loser spared, if it is not too late and his neck isn't already snapped."

"Will your friend come looking for you?" she asked, her heart thumping even faster against her chest.

"Mercutio? No."

The crackle of violence in the air was like the spark before a lightning storm. Rosaline could feel it prickling the down upon her skin.

Then Romeo leaned in and kissed her.

She kissed him back, and as she did, through half-closed lids, she glimpsed their shadow selves on the wall opposite. Romeo's shadow was long and lean, with talon fingers that combed through Rosaline's hair and clawed down her neck. She closed her eyes tight shut, giddy and disordered, suffused with warmth. She gripped him fiercely, her fingertips turning white.

Romeo whispered into her ear. "To your shadow I make love."

She watched as the shadows drew close again upon the wall, joining together.

"In shadow then, until I can have your perfect self," said Romeo.

"No," said Rosaline. "Kiss me alone. Know me. Do not worship shadows."

"Very well," said Romeo, turning her away and kissing her again.

He drew back to look at her once more, and she wished he would not. She did not want his words but his mouth. "My lady Rosaline, by the moon above, I vow—"

"What moon?" Rosaline frowned. "There is no moon tonight." She gestured up at the swirling clouds above.

Romeo laughed. "Very well. Then by what shall I swear my love?"

Rosaline stared at him. "Your love? You love me?"

Romeo kissed her again. "By my troth, I do, fair Rosaline."

Rosaline looked at him in amazement. Was it possible that he loved her? In the hours since they had met, she had dreamt of little else but him. All possibilities had been closed to her, and then love and light had appeared. And here they stood, their fingers knotted together. His breath hot upon her cheek. His leg pressed firm against hers. It was marvelous to be loved. To be seen.

"How shall I swear my love?" he asked again.

Rosaline shook her head. "Do not swear at all."

Romeo stepped away from her and paced, wounded, full of sudden heat. "For you do not love me? If you do not, O, then under love's heavy burden, I will sink and die."

Rosaline stared at him, confused by this sudden irritability, unsure whether his words had become untethered from their meaning. He could not mean to die for love of her—the very thought was absurd. She, who was nothing to anyone. And she did not want him to die for her or even to wish for death on her account. And yet, she did want to be loved. Even though it was a useless, unhappy longing. She hurried to him. "I say do not swear it for it is hopeless. I'm to be walled up in a nunnery. I'm to belong to no man. Even if you were not a Montague, it would not matter."

He stopped walking and turned back to her staring at her so intently that she blinked and had to look away. "Rosaline Capulet, I will not let them take you from me." He grasped her hands, turning them over and placing a kiss upon the tender flesh on the inside of her wrist.

She shivered as a spectral glimmer of hope slid through her. No. It was no good. Romeo did not know her father or her brother. They were resolute, and if they knew that she was even speaking to a Montague, she would be sent away before the cock crowed the next morning. She knew it was doomed, even if Romeo did not. "O, Romeo, you cannot tilt at fate. You'll lose."

"A man in love understands no constraints, my sweet Rosaline. Only tell me that you love me too."

Rosaline looked up at him. He smiled down at her with eyes round and black with love. The most beautiful man she'd ever seen, and he wanted *her*, the other Capulet girl who no one wanted. The girl whose name most people forgot. She wanted to be the woman Romeo saw, one exquisite and rare.

Beside them, the noise of the crowd had altered. Ten thousand feet stamping at once on wooden boards and the rumble of raised voices. The fight had been won and lost. *A man is dead*, she realized, *and another is champion*. Yet here they stood, just the two of them, apart from it all.

Romeo studied her, only her, with quiet resolve, waiting. Out of the cacophony of noise, she heard Tybalt calling for her, his voice increasingly frantic. She must hurry. She felt herself poised at the edge of the world, ready to fall. Until this moment, she always believed that love was something that happened without one's choosing; it was unconscious and inevitable, like the turning of the seasons or the tide. Laura and Beatrice were beloved ladies, adored by Petrarch and Dante, but no one ever talked about how they felt or if they loved in turn. Romeo was asking her not just to be beloved, but to love. He demanded it from her. She understood now that she must decide whether to step across the threshold into this other world and agree to love Romeo back.

She looked at him, the dark curl of his hair, tousled from her own fingers. She could still feel his skin, the warmth of him. A muscle ticked in his jaw—she longed to reach out and touch it.

He gazed at her from beneath thick lashes with smiling eyes.

"Yes to love," she answered, and turned and ran as the crowd emptied out of the stands and swallowed her.

IV

Thou chid'st me oft for loving Rosaline

The days were honeycombed with heat, white and parched, leaving Rosaline and Juliet listless in the spinning shade beneath the willows. The grass had lost its polished June green and was now the color of wheat-straw, burnished with a Midas touch. They felt to Rosaline like the end of days. There were now only ten remaining to her in Verona.

Whether she escaped with Romeo or was dispatched to the convent, her home would be lost to her.

Juliet worked at the brown scabs on her knees until tiny garnets of blood appeared. Thoughts of Romeo constantly intruding, Rosaline read again and again the same three lines of Ovid until, unable to bear the heat any longer, the two girls retreated inside to the relative cool of Juliet's bedchamber to play rounds of knucklebone and dice. There Juliet lay sprawled upon her belly, her grubby toes wiggling in the air, winning each throw, partly from luck and partly from Rosaline's inattention.

"I've cheated thrice and you've not said a word."

"But you rob me so prettily."

"Play properly or don't play at all."

Rosaline knew she neglected Juliet, but she could think of little else except the curve of Romeo's brow. How his expression was invariably grave and then transformed into playfulness and mirth when he smiled at her. His eyes were—with dismay, she realized that she could not recall the precise color of his eyes. They were dark, but were they pumice-gray or a stormy shade of blue like the sea at night? Was it possible to be a lover and not know the color of one's beloved's eyes?

"You've lost again. You must pay a forfeit. I'm taking this necklace from you."

Rosaline clutched the gold chain around her throat protectively, caressing the fat smooth stone. "No. Not this. I'm sorry. I'll pay more attention, Jule. The necklace was my mother's."

Juliet crept closer and scrutinized the emerald, bright as a cat's eye, and let the gold chain run through her fingers, fluid as water.

"Very well. You keep it. But play properly. You're as addled as Nurse today."

"O, you wound me!" Rosaline fell back upon the wooden floor, clutching at a feigned stab wound to her chest.

Juliet laughed and tickled her as Rosaline shrieked.

The door to the chamber opened. "You're both too loud," declared Madonna Lauretta Capulet, leaning against the lintel. "My head aches. This infernal heat. I'm sure that July is never usually so close."

"I'm sorry, Aunt," said Rosaline, as Juliet snapped upright, her laughter withering.

Lauretta was the draft that sucked all warmth from a room. Her eyes moved around the bedchamber with disapproval. "Where is Nurse? She has not tidied today," she complained.

"She has," said Juliet. "We just unraveled things. I wanted to play."

"And everything at once, so it seems, by the mess."

"Aunt, tell me," interrupted Rosaline, sensing a row in the making. "How came you to meet Juliet's father? I never heard the tale."

Lauretta surveyed Rosaline with casual interest. "I was young. I was dutiful to my parents. Francesco Capulet was introduced to me as a man of good name and decent rank, and I, a daughter who was amenable, understanding that she must bring honor to her family, did as my father bid me."

She said all this while staring at Juliet, who continued to toss the counters from knucklebone between her palm and the back of her hand and pretended not to hear.

"And did you love him, Aunt?"

Lauretta snorted. "O, you girls! What is love? You listen to too many stories. He gave me a house and clothes and children, and God in his mercy spared us Juliet. Not all couplings are like that of your parents, Rosaline. It's why your father grieves so piteously for Emelia. With love comes loss at its passing."

Rosaline studied her aunt. She was not sure whether Lauretta was envious or relieved that she would be spared such pain.

"Put away these childish things, Juliet," Lauretta snapped. "One day, not so long hence, your father will come here to inform you he has a match for you. This place is stuffed with games and toys. What will your husband think?"

Juliet sat up on her heels. "I do not mind, madam, so long as he can play dice and knucklebone and shovelboard."

Lauretta left the room, knocking over the stack of games with her skirts as she passed. "Do as you will," she called, "for I have done with you, Juliet."

Rosaline started to gather the games and their counters, sweeping them into piles. Juliet sat with her knees drawn up to her chin, chewing her nail. Rosaline put her arm around her shoulder, but too angry to be comforted, Juliet pushed her away.

After dinner, Masetto lingered on the loggia sipping wine and gazing out at the spray of stars fired out across the night's sky. From a canopy of vines above, a peewit called and the evening bustled with the hurry of wings. The pump in the yard dripped like a clock, and the cicadas began their evensong.

"Stay and sit awhile with me, Rosaline," said her father. "Let us try and be friends."

So rather than fleeing the moment as was her wont, Rosaline remained at the table with him.

Her father seemed lost; he did not know how to begin.

"Do I remind you of my mother?" asked Rosaline.

Masetto poured himself another goblet of wine from the jug.

"A little. When you laugh. Although I don't hear it very often, Rosaline, for I don't amuse you."

"But, Father, you aren't funny."

Masetto shook his head sadly. "No, the only person I made laugh was Emelia. You see? That is love. I am not funny, but she found me so. I was a better man with her. Or I believed I was. Perhaps I was still the same rose after all, with the same sour scent; only to her, I smelled sweet. And I only minded how I was to her, not to anyone else. O, Rosaline, the surprise of her love when she gave it to me, the ferocity of it." He sighed. "The light has gone out of the world."

An owl stirred the darkness. Rosaline studied her father's face. He had withered in the time since her mother had been gone, as if each meal he'd eaten was mixed with grave dirt. His skin was taut across his skull, and his hair thin stalks across his mottled scalp.

"Did she love me too?" she asked softly.

She'd always believed she had, but such was the bond of affection between her parents that now she wondered whether there had been room for her; the seal between them had been so tight, could any light have stolen beneath it?

"Yes, she did. Better than your brother. For all that mothers are supposed to love their boys more."

Rosaline felt a pressure give in her chest like a puncture in a ball. "But, Father, then why did she want me to go? Why lock me away in the convent?"

"Not all marriages are happy, Rosaline. Is Livia happy, for all her brood? Your mother thought not. Not all men and women are as we were. Most are discontent. She wanted you free."

"Free! A convent is not freedom!"

"There you are free to have your own thoughts and not run a household, and the money I shall provide will ensure your comfort and ease. You are bound to God, but not to a man. Yes, your mother believed it was a freedom. The best she could provide."

"Then let me choose."

"You are too young to know what's best. It's a father's burden to make the choice for his daughter. You believe me a tyrant, but I do not want you to be unhappy. I still hope you will let me visit you. I hope you are not so full of hate."

She paused and thought for a minute. "I do not hate you," she said. "I could have loved you too."

Masetto looked at her with tired eyes that were red-rimmed. "Couldn't you try now a little?"

"There isn't enough time left."

"No, I suppose there isn't," he agreed sadly.

The lamp on the table flickered, and a moth fanned it with paper wings. They lingered in the darkness, each lost to their own thoughts, considering a love between them that might once have taken root. At last the hours waxed long, and Rosaline withdrew inside.

Rosaline could not sleep. It was still too warm in her chamber beneath the eaves, and her shirt stuck to her skin. The air was honeyed and thick. She lay awake, listening to the toll of the bell from the basilica of St. Peter dispensing the hours to the living and dead.

When at last she slept, her dreams were fretful and wild. She roamed barefoot through the Montagues' garden, searching for Romeo among the ogres and fallen gods, but he hid from her.

She woke suddenly, full of terror, moving from one nightmare into the next. She was drowning; she gulped for air but there was only fire. A hand pressed against her mouth.

"Hush! Do not cry out! Fair Rosaline, 'tis I, your Romeo!" His voice spoke in her ear, and his face hovered just above her own. He took his hand from her mouth. Her heart hammered in her ears. He pressed her hand to his lips. His eyes were dark and beautiful.

"I did not mean to frighten you. I curse my own name. Hateful, wretched man." He studied Rosaline, his features contorted with worry. "O, how is it with you now?"

She sat up, shaking off sleep and fear, and took his face in her hands and kissed him. The window was open and the shutters knocked, and she saw how he'd stolen into her room.

He'd risked injury and death for a few moments in her company. What else could this be but love?

"How come you are here?" she said, still half-unsure if he was a dream.

"I had to see you, my lady. I count the hours, nay the minutes, until I take you from this place."

Rosaline found a tinderbox and lit a candle, then studied him in wonderment, amazed that he was hers and that he loved her.

This man, this Montague, with such fine looks that he could choose any woman—one whose name did not spell death but wealth and prosperity—had still chosen her, loved her.

Romeo reached into his jerkin and pulled out a box, slightly crushed, and passed it to her.

She took it from him, grateful and bewildered, unused as she was to receiving gifts. She unfastened the ribbon and opened the lid to find inside a marzipan rose, painted a rich ruby red and so real that at first she thought it a living flower.

"Another rose for my Rosaline. And yet, however sweet it tastes, there are no kisses as sweet as those of my fair Rosaline."

"Thank you."

"Every rose in nature is unique. Just like you. I had it made especially for you, and the confectioner promised me he'd never make another."

Rosaline gazed down at the rose. She swore to herself that she would never eat it but would put it aside, preserve it forever as a crystalline symbol of their love and the maidenhood that she now longed to shed.

He stood and prowled the room, looking at her things, and she felt as if he looked at her, into her. Upon her table lay her *trousse de toilette,* with a comb her mother had given her for her twelfth birthday. Once a week before bed, Emelia had dismissed Caterina and, unpinning Rosaline's hair, had combed it out herself. It was always tangled, thicker and darker than Juliet's or the other girls', and she'd tug through, teasing knots while Rosaline closed her eyes, half-mesmerized. The process took a long time, and all the while Emelia sang as she plaited, combed, and refastened her hair. Now Romeo picked up the comb, his thick forefinger upon its fragile teeth. For a moment Rosaline wanted to cry out and order him to put it down. It was sacred. None must touch it but her mother. But her voice caught in her throat. She did not want him to touch or comb her hair.

He stalked toward her, the carved ivory comb clasped in his fingers, and leaned over her, pinning her to the cot. She held her breath, half afraid of him.

"It's a pretty thing for a pretty thing," he whispered. "What is carved upon it? I see the siege of the Castle of Love. Will I win this siege?"

Then, to her relief, setting down the comb, he drew back with a low laugh and reached up with gentle fingers to stroke her cheek, tucking her plaits behind her ear. With absolute tenderness he brushed his fingertip across her neck with warm hands, skimming kisses along the tip of her ear so she shuddered with pleasure.

He reached into his jerkin and produced a flask of wine, unstoppered it, and passed it to her. "Here, sweet girl, drink."

She took it from him and sipped. It was strong and tasted of honey and summers gone. She tried to give it back, but Romeo pressed it upon her again. "No, wine will give you strength after a fright."

Dutifully, she drank, although she did not feel frightened anymore. Under his watchful gaze, she drank deeper this time, the wine burning and warming her throat. He smiled to see her swallow, and to make him smile more, she drank again.

"Let us make a toast," he said, raising up the flask. "To our love, sweeter than this wine, and our passion, stronger than its fumes, and to my lady, more beautiful than its amber hue."

They took turns sipping again, lifting the bottle with each tribute and taking another swallow until, by the final one, Rosaline realized the flask was empty.

Romeo leaned forward and kissed her again, his lips doused with honey. She laughed and fell back, the wine making the room spin. She was warm and steeped with love.

Perhaps this was all he had come into her chamber for, to ply her with wine and kisses? Rosaline's disappointment was edged with relief. But then, Romeo set aside the empty flask and shuffled down beside her on the low wooden bed. Slowly he ran his fingers along the bare skin of her arm. She shivered with longing, and he smiled and began toying with the silk fastening of her linen undershirt, tugging it low, revealing the slope of her shoulder, and then again, lower. He pulled at the long rope of her hair, winding it around his wrist.

"You see? I'm love's captive. And I shall not let you go into the nunnery. We'll leave Verona together. And live free. Not as Montague or Capulet, but as man and woman."

"Husband and wife?"

He did not answer but stopped her mouth with another kiss. He lifted her nightshirt over her head so she lay naked upon the sheet. Exposed and uncertain, she reached to cover herself but Romeo stayed her hand.

"No, blushes are for babies. O, sweet mistress, your beauty is like the sun. No, not the sun. The brightness of your eyes would shame the stars."

Rosaline laughed, amazed to hear herself described so wondrously. She did not cover herself again, for she did not want him to think her a baby but a woman of wit and beauty, deserving of a man such as he. She wished she weren't so thin or her breasts so small—she was aware of the rigging of her ribs. If only she had the ripe plumpness of one of her older Capulet cousins. Before she'd started breeding like one of Catrina's kitchen cats, Livia had had enviable curves, like an autumn poplin pear.

Despite Rosaline's love and new rush of desire for him, she had to clench her fists to stop herself from tugging at the sheet to cover herself once more. Now the moment was so near, she was not sure if she was as eager as she had thought. A ball of tears caught in her throat, like a crust of bread, but she did not know why. She swallowed it down before he could see. He must not think her childish or sullen. She wanted his love. She must be like a sunflower that turns to face the sun.

"You think this is your foot," he whispered, holding it. "But you are mistaken, for it is mine." As he spoke, his covered her instep with tiny kisses, light as coils of ash. "And this is not your leg, for it is mine." His mouth, the warmth of his breath, the scrape of his beard as he moved upwards to her thigh, then higher still. Desire kindled in her again. He was practiced and well-schooled not only in words, but in matters of the flesh.

"This is not your breast, nor this your heart, for they are mine now. Each and every part of you belongs to me."

She did not want him to stop, but his lips no longer touched her skin. He stared down at her.

"Promise me that you're mine."

"I am yours."

"Swear it."

She did not know how to swear so that he would be satisfied, but she longed for him to touch her again, for him to love her. She would say almost anything for that. "I swear by the moon above."

To her relief, he bent and kissed her. She watched as Romeo shed his clothes like a snake discards its skin, easing out of them until he too was naked, lying beside her. The ridge of his hip, the crock of hair at his pelvis.

She tried to sit up, but he pressed her shoulders down again, gently but with intent. "All is well, my love," he whispered.

"We are to be married?" asked Rosaline. Her voice sounded thin and not her own.

"I swear to you that I will not let them shut you away in a nunnery. They will not take you from me," he said and kissed her again.

He pulled her arms above her head and she found she could not move if she had wanted to. He pushed against her. It hurt, and she cried out at the surprise and indignity of the invasion. Even though she whimpered, he did not slow and wait a moment. His breath was ragged and his eyes screwed shut as he shoved at her. And then at last he lay still. He did not move from her but lay upon her sticky and wet, heavy as death.

She slept and dreamed of nothing. He woke her gently, whispering to her of her beauty. "You are everything. I had no need for eyes before you. Your voice is music."

She smiled, preening in the array of his love. His fingers raked through her hair as she continued to doze, listening to the swell of rain.

"In time you will learn to take pleasure in the act of love," he said.

She exhaled, relieved that he had recognized her unhappiness.

"I will teach you little by little."

His knuckles rubbed the soft moraine at the base of her spine, but this time he touched her slowly, whispering only of love, until she felt as if another world was opening up. It was someplace that she had never seen before, except perhaps in that space between half waking and dreaming. The basilica on the hill began to toll once more, in time with her own breath, and Rosaline understood that she wanted this new world to open up to her, that she liked how it felt there, and she wished to return to it again and again.

Afterward, as Romeo began to dress, Rosaline lay on her belly and watched him. The light was changing, spilling blood across the sky. She did not want him to put his clothes on; she preferred him naked, for then he belonged only to her and this room, to this hour and this world that had shrunk to the two of them. As he pulled on his shirt and then his hose, his jerkin, his stockings, and finally his leather boots, she felt her spirits sink.

Romeo sat beside her and ran a fingertip along the bony protrusion of her ribs, the tiny cupped shell of her navel, the ridge of her collarbone. "You are perfect. In beauty and character. You are gentle and shy. You may be afraid, but I shall protect you from all things."

Rosaline listened to his description of her in growing confusion. She was not gentle nor shy, and was always scolded by her father and brother and even Caterina for speaking when she ought to hold her tongue. She was only afraid tonight because Romeo had appeared like a spirit in her bedroom, conjured out of the shadows. "I am not shy. Nor perfect or gentle."

"Hush. You are indeed perfect. That you do not see it only adds to your perfection, my fair Rosaline."

Rosaline frowned. *Fair*. She preferred his other endearments. My sweet Rosaline. Dearest Rosaline. He called her fair for her beauty, yet her beauty was not fair and pale, but rich and deep. She wanted Romeo to love her and adore her as she was, not as some vision of a woman she was supposed to fit.

He sat beside her, smoothing her hair to one side and toying with her earlobe. Leaning closer, he breathed into her ear. "And, my Rosaline, you understand that you cannot tell anyone about our love? It would mean death to me. And banishment for you."

The knot of tears rose again in her throat, and it seemed for a moment that they would choke her. Even though she knew it must be done, and neither she nor Romeo had any choice, she did not like to keep secrets from Juliet nor Tybalt or even Caterina. For the first time since she'd met Romeo, instead of feeling brushed with new joy, she felt alone.

He seemed to sense her unease and pulled her close, whispering, "The world is against us, my love. It is you and me, dear sweet lady. The two of us are together in this cruel and ill-tempered sea."

Rosaline knew what he said was true. If her father or brother discovered their love, she would immediately be dispatched to the convent before she and Romeo could escape. Romeo might well be killed. As long as they remained lovers, her family and friends were their enemies. After what she had done tonight, she was already a cuckoo in the Capulet nest.

Fingers clawed at her insides. She could cast aside Romeo, and choose duty and loyalty to her father and the memory of her mother; to elope would betray Emelia too. No one ever need know what she had done tonight or that she had lain with Romeo; she could carry her love for him into the convent and let it shrivel there.

Even as she considered this, she knew it was impossible. Her choice was already made.

He covered her in yet more kisses and then rising, retreated to the balcony. There, he stood against the window with the morning light catching in his hair, his own love for her reflecting back at her, dazzling her like the midday sun in a reflecting pool. She felt herself soften and unclenched her jaw. She understood that she could not take her vows, not now, not ever. She wanted him, her Romeo. She wanted this new world he had given her.

The swell of heat was rising already so each breath inhaled was dust filled. The rows of houses emitted steady warmth like the blackened range in the kitchen. Biting flies pestered the strays in the sweltering shade. Masetto and his brother, old Lord Capulet, declared the fetid city unendurable and hurried to St. Peter's together to pray and make confession. The onslaught of the heat wave after the woe of the plague could only mean that the Almighty was still angry, and they must plead forgiveness and undertake great penance.

But while the older generation plied the heavens with devotions, the younger Capulets sought more earthly and rapid escape from the heat. At Tybalt's suggestion, they planned a day's escapade to the woods to enjoy their meals in its sylvan shade, intending to remain there until the cool of nightfall. If they were to be damned by plague or heat or some other pestilence, then they would enjoy a carnival first.

Rosaline, however, did not wish to go with the others into the forest. She wanted to remain in her room, to lie upon her sheets and think only of Romeo. She was awash with love. She ached with it. Her tongue clacked in her mouth, sticky with salt. She still tasted him. Her head ached from all the wine she had drunk with Romeo, and as the morning wore on, the pain behind her temples grew. At first, she tried pleading with Caterina that she would not go, that her head hurt, she was ill. Caterina brought her mint tea to soothe her stomach. Next, Rosaline tried cajoling and at last a fit of pique and temper. None did any good. No one listened. Not to her. They never did. She was loaded onto the wagon alongside the slab of cured ham, the melons, figs, flagons of beer and wine, jar of honey, and stack of napkins.

Juliet was handed up last and squeezed in beside her. "Isn't it thrilling to leave the city, coz?" she said, nudging Rosaline.

Juliet's face was rosy with happiness, and Rosaline could not help but smile and take pleasure in the younger girl's joy.

Rosaline tried to listen to her own thoughts as the wagon rolled along the lanes among spatters of scarlet poppies and swarms of flies, but Juliet was a sparrow of chattering excitement. She could hardly attend to Juliet, thinking only of Romeo. When would he come for her, and when would she see him next?

Perplexed, the younger girl turned to lobbing grapes from the basket lodged between her feet at Tybalt, who rode beside them and tried to catch them in his mouth. Usually such antics would have diverted Rosaline, and she would have cannoned grapes at Tybalt with glee, but this morning she was too distracted.

"Rosaline!" Tybalt called. "I've addressed you three times and you've not answered. Are you ill or out of temper?"

"Why must you think there is something wrong with a woman merely if she does not prattle away or wish to join childish games?"

To her relief, Tybalt addressed her no further but watched

her in silence, his brow furrowed with worry. The fresh air was starting to soothe her roiling stomach and aching head.

When they reached the woods, the girls jumped down, while the servants unhitched the horses and began to unload the vittles from the wagons, hauling them the rest of the way. The horses led the way along the snaking path into the forest, throwing up leaf litter and muck with their hooves, swatting flies with their tails. The air was moist and smelled of the bright ferns that fanned out on either side of the track, forming a canopy for the creatures that scuttled beneath.

As they proceeded into this other world, Rosaline felt that she had entered a cloistered chapel where the light that filtered through the stained glass of the leaves was every hue of green. The stillness was sepulchral, charged only with the breeze. She walked deeper and deeper among the trees, longing to lose herself among the swaying green. Even the birdsong seemed muted and distant.

After a while, the horses were brought to a halt in a clearing, and Rosaline observed that the servants were setting down their baskets of bread, flagons, and haunches of ham, ready to prepare the first meal. Juliet lingered to help Caterina and the other servants unwrap the parcels of food, but Rosaline was not hungry. She wanted only to be alone, so instead of lingering in the dell with the others, she continued to weave her way through the forest. Tiny white flowers bloomed, spangling the ground like mislaid stars. Serpents of ivy swung from birches and oaks, their colossal necks muscular as they writhed up the trees, hunting for the light. Brambles scratched and bit at her ankles, and a flotilla of vermillion butterflies no larger than her fingernail wove in and out of a holly tree like living berries magicked into life by Oberon. She hurried on, stepping over falling branches that concealed the route, deeper and deeper into the wood, until at last the path was hidden, and she could not tell which way she had come. Breathless and hot, she sat down to rest on a toppled trunk padded with moss.

Then, a man's voice was calling for her, and for a moment the blood swished in her ears, ringing with joy—it was Romeo! She stood, happy and eager, flushed with delight, but it was Tybalt who pushed his way through the knot of branches. Red-faced, he came to sit beside her, smearing the sweat from his brow.

Stifling her disappointment, Rosaline sat back down. She tried to be happy to see her friend, but if she could not have Romeo, then she only wanted to be alone.

Tybalt unfastened a flask from his jacket and drank deeply, then offered it to her. She sipped, grateful. Tybalt grinned at her, and her irritation at the intrusion began to dissipate like the tiny gnats Tybalt flicked away with his hand.

"I'm puffed from chasing you. You do not walk upon trodden paths, Rosaline. There are burs clinging to your petticoats."

"Those I can shake off. What about the burs in my heart?"

"O, I would try and pluck them out, for I see that you are unhappy."

"I believe you, Cousin," said Rosaline, taking his hand.

Tybalt did not release it but gripped it tightly, and Rosaline rested her head on his shoulder for a moment. She wondered if he could tell that she was different. That she loved a man and was loved in return, her maidenhood now discarded. She thrummed with excitement.

"You are so very quiet. Your silence tells me how unhappy and frightened you must be," he said.

Rosaline did not answer.

"I would save you from the nunnery, Rosaline. What if you were to marry me?"

"You, Cousin?" She sat up, startled, and released his hand. She thought at first that he was teasing her, but as she turned to look at the boyish face beside her, flushed from hunting for her through the wood, a rind of sweat and soft fur coating his upper lip, she saw the sweetness of his expression. He frowned, heavy with concern for her, his eyes cast down. A fierce pang of tenderness toward her friend stirred deep in her belly.

Long ago, she had sent a bird she'd made of gold paper soaring high into a thick hedge and sobbed when she'd realized it was lost. Tybalt had combed through that hedge for hours to find it for her, lacerating his arms and legs and face with holly and thorns. He had not found it but stayed out until it was full dark, searching for her paper bird. Now, she was the gold bird and he was still trying to yank her out of the dark.

She nudged his knee with her own. "O, Tybalt. It's impossible. They'd never let us. You're poor. You must marry a rich girl with a handsome dowry. And my father wishes to save mine, such as it is."

Tybalt dismissed her concerns with a wave. "Fie. I've lived on less. And you seem happy in a wood. We could run away— walk through these trees and keep on walking and then come out together on the other side. We'll elope."

Tybalt had been her most cherished companion in child- hood, the hoarder of all her secrets. They'd fought bitterly, and she'd hit him, bitten him, stolen his toys, tried to drown him once or twice, but whatever treasures she possessed, she'd shared with him and he with her. Worms. Sweet treats. Books. Joys and punishments. Now he watched her steadily, blinking away sweat from his eyes. She understood that time and distance had not diminished his friendship and affection for her. He sought to share this too. "This calamity is mine alone. You cannot take it from me, Tybalt."

Even as she spoke the words, Rosaline understood that, for the first time in their friendship, she was lying to Tybalt. The lie twisted in her stomach, squirming deep within her, as if she'd eaten something rotten. She could not tell him that she was going to marry Romeo to escape the misery of the convent. Neither could she confess to him her love for Romeo. For Romeo was not like the nest of robin's eggs in the long patch of thistles or the thrashing Valentio had given them both when he suspected them of stealing his books. Romeo was a Montague, and if she told Tybalt that she loved him, he would kill Romeo. Or die himself in the attempt.

He turned his face from hers and would not look at her. He stared up at the vaulted green above. "If they lock you away, you'll wither. What about your lute and songs? You need music and saucy humor to fatten you. I know you. You're not godly, Ros. You are fire and mischief."

Rosaline almost smiled at this assessment of her character. All of it was true, if not quite flattering.

"How can I live, knowing that you suffer and are miserable," he continued, his voice heavy with feeling. "We've shared in all things always. The two disregarded Capulets."

"We've always been the best of friends."

"Indeed. And why would the others mind what we do? We're little to them. Come, Ros, let us marry." He paused, his face shiny with confusion and growing hurt. "Why would you choose the convent life rather than a life with me?"

He took her hand in his, and gently, she pried it away again. "I don't love you, Tybalt, and you don't love me. It would not be fair. You are my brother. Better than my brother. The brother of my heart. But I am grateful," she said, resting her head upon his shoulder again. "You are the very best of men."

She placed a fond kiss upon his cheek. At this he stood abruptly and, when she reached for him, shook her off. To her bewilderment, he did not appear as relieved as she expected. He had done his duty by offering, and she had released him from any obligation, and yet he did not seem like a man gratefully relieved of a burden.

He turned his back to her and did not speak for some time before saying briskly, "Let's away to the others."

Rosaline studied him in confusion. "Do you know the path?"

Tybalt did not reply but turned and walked quickly back the way he had come, hacking at the briars with a stick.

Rosaline hurried after him. She attempted to talk of many things, but upon every avenue of conversation, she stumbled and faltered, for Tybalt appeared not to hear her, and they walked the rest of the way in uneasy silence, save for the flutelike song of a wood thrush.

Rosaline lay down on a rug in the glade, drowsy, slapping at the mosquitos that emerged as the light filtering through the leaves faded from green to gold. Juliet passed her another glass of mead, and Rosaline drank it quickly, hoping Caterina would not notice. She surveyed the discarded heaps of rocky oyster shells and yellowing ham rinds now speckled with ants. The wind shivered in the larch and spruce like absent rain, and a cuckoo echoed from across the wood.

Juliet crouched beside her. The servants lit lamps, bright yolks in the gloom.

"Kiss me, Juliet," said Rosaline. "Tell me you love me, for I love you, my sweet cousin."

Juliet took her face in her hands and kissed her quickly. "O, Rosaline, you and I are one. I am thankful every day that fortune sent you to me."

"Ah, here you are mistaken, it was not fortune but Tybalt who bid me come to you."

"Then I thank the bountiful blind woman called fortune

and Tybalt, who is neither blind nor a woman, but is still bountiful."

Hearing his name, Tybalt glanced toward the two girls across the glade, catching Rosaline's eye and then immediately looking away, his face taut with unhappiness.

Rosaline sighed, disconcerted and annoyed. She had so little time left for joy she would not allow Tybalt to tarnish what remained, and yet she found she could not be happy when he was not. The hours were spinning through the glass, faster and faster. Why would he not join in the holiday foolery?

There was a lute lying on a rug, and retrieving it, she plucked at the strings and began to sing as the other girls stood up to dance. As always, the lute's melancholy tone soothed her, lulling her into another space, between day and dusk, made entirely of music. There was a wildness in the air; she felt it snap in the darkness all around her.

> *Under the greenwood tree*
> *Who loves to lie with me,*
> *And turn his merry note*
> *Unto the sweet bird's throat,*
> *Come hither, come hither, come hither:*
> *Here shall he see*
> *No enemy*
> *But winter and rough weather.*

Her voice, usually as clear as a lark in spring, wavered and cracked. These people were her family, and yet she and Tybalt had never quite fit so easily among them; they were second-rank Capulets, less precious except to one another. What would happen if all these Capulets knew she loved a Montague?

As she played, Juliet danced among the black yew trees, her eyes closed, her dress half-unbuttoned and hitched up to her knees. She'd lost her slippers and was skipping barefoot among the fallen leaves and celandine, dark lobes of violets and ghostly spears of enchanter's nightshade crushed beneath her soles. Setting down her lute, Rosaline rose to join her, discarding her own shoes and clasping Juliet's hand. Another player picked up the instrument and took her place. Rosaline and Juliet swayed and danced. Other girls joined them, as the youths clapped and cheered, spongy with wine.

As Rosaline spun around and around, the trees became a blur of green and black and gold. She felt her hair come loose from its fastening and tickle her hot cheeks. All was music and shouting and noise and the ribald chatter of the birds.

Whispers hissed through the dark that the Prince of Verona himself was there among them, watching the dancing. He too had ridden out into the forest and found them making merry in the lamplight. He had brought a friend with him, a rich one. A handsome one. The girls around them whirled faster still, laughed harder.

Rosaline saw the prince. His cape was lined with ermine despite the heat, but he sported a jaunty straw hat apparently in testament to the rustic expedition into the forest. Two servants in his livery stood sentry on either side. They did not belong here in this green place. They'd brought the city and its rules and hierarchies with them, and they did not understand that in the wood at dusk, all was music and dancing and wine. And they would not stop looking at them. They spelled discord, and their very presence unsettled her.

The prince's friend was a tall well-built man of middle years whose jerkin could not quite contain his stomach. The evening was warm and sweat glistened on his forehead. Servants hurried to and fro, providing the pair oysters and flasks of mead that had been cooling in the river.

The man could not stop watching Juliet, like a sheepdog eyeing its flock unblinkingly. No, he looked as if he wanted to eat her. Rosaline shuddered, despite the heat.

He spoke to the prince in a too-loud voice, a man who enjoyed being overheard. "Who is that girl?" he said. "The little one?"

"Who do you mean, Paris? That child over there?" asked the prince, gesturing to Juliet.

The men's voices were not welcome. Not now, in this place. Rosaline danced Juliet away before they could speak about her further. She heard the bark of a fox and saw the slick red tail slide between the trunks of the trees, and then somewhere more distant, the howl of a wolf, the answer of another. Some part of her, feral and once prey, shivered. But she was not afraid of the wolf; she was more afraid of the prince and Paris.

Paris still eyed Juliet, drink forgotten, licking already wet lips.

Rosaline saw Tybalt sitting some way off, watching her,

miserable, and tried not to notice. They edged yet farther away, away from them all. From the prince, from his friend, from Tybalt, from all the eyes, away from the light and into the companionable darkness of the wood.

V

My heart is here

Time slowed and shuffled to a stop. It was no longer grains of sand flowing through the hourglass but thickened treacle; the gap between each toll of the duomo bell not a quarter hour but an entire year. Rosaline could not bear it. It was not possible that he had forsaken her now there were only nine nights left. Eight nights. Seven. She could not believe it. She would not.

Why did he not come? Did he now harbor doubts about their love? She cursed that she was born a Capulet and her breath was full of sighs. *Wherefore was he?* He did not send word.

Each evening she left the window open, but he did not come for her. No rose was left upon her balcony. She ached with silence. She had been so sure of his love.

There was nothing that could console her. Only Romeo himself. His absence made her pine for her mother. Grief was a stomachache that rolled over her in waves, sometimes crippling her. Her mother's ghost was the only one to whom she could confide her secret love, but it was an empty confidence, for Emelia did not reply, not even to admonish or berate her. Her fury would be better than this deathly indifference.

In desperation, Rosaline sought her mother's pendant to hold for some little comfort. It was all she had left of her. Yet to her dismay and confusion, the jewel was not inside her cedar box; in the space where it ought to lie, there was only the assorted treasure of her girlhood: an array of tinted pebbles and shells, a yellow feather from a goldfinch, the speckled turquoise of a blown robin's egg, a copy of Ovid's stories, stolen from Valentio by Tybalt and given to Rosaline. Out of habit, she thumbed through the well-loved illustrations: Thisbe waiting for Pyramus at the tomb; Daphne mid-transformation, half-nymph and half-free, metamorphosing to escape Apollo's pursuit. Lovely as these riches were, there was no chain and no emerald pendant. She checked the carved cassone chest and the tray beside her bed, but there was no gleam of green, no flash of gold. Her room was sparsely furnished and there were few places to scour. Frantic now, Rosaline groveled on the floor and peered beneath her bed to see if it had slipped beneath the gaps of the boards.

This was how Caterina discovered her: crawling on all fours with grime beneath her nails. The pair of them scoured the room, checking in every crevice, but it was not to be found.

Caterina moved from sympathy to annoyance. "You ought to have been more careful! That pendant was a good portion of your mother's dowry. Now go, be off to Juliet's. Stop your weeping before your father asks why and discovers what you have lost."

Rosaline crept off to her cousin's, damp with disgrace. How could she have been so careless? Yet in her heart, she knew she was more miserable at Romeo's silence than she was over the missing necklace. The shame of this made her more wretched still.

All through the morning, Juliet chided Rosaline for her lack of attention in their games, but she barely heeded her sighs or rebukes.

"Come, coz, shall I sing to distract you?" asked Juliet.

"You can't sing," said Rosaline. "You have many gifts, my love, but not music."

"Indeed, my voice is ragged, but that may amuse you and make you laugh," said Juliet. Her eyes grew round with concern. "And if I cannot make you laugh, then let me bear your sorrows. Do not suffer your griefs alone, sweet Rosaline."

Juliet stared up at her, her face open and guileless, a golden stray curl tickling her cheek. For a moment, Rosaline longed to confess her love for Romeo the Montague. Her hands were restless in her lap, a fresh pain burned in her chest. She longed to see him, to hold him, hear him whisper his love. He was both the infection and the cure to her sickness.

"I will visit you in the convent, coz," said Juliet, taking her hand. "As often as I can."

Rosaline nodded and blinked, turning her face so that Juliet would not see her eyes fill with tears. Juliet mistook the source of her unhappiness. Her body colluded in her betrayal as each sigh, each tear became a signal to be misunderstood. And yet, she could not confess the truth and be forsworn to Romeo.

Rosaline declined to go down for the midday meal, saying she was tired and had not slept well. Juliet offered to stay with her, but Rosaline, wanting only to be alone, pressed her to go.

While she lay upon the bed, lost in thought and misery, there was a knock on the door, and a messenger asked for admittance. Rosaline called for him to come in without looking up.

"I have a letter."

"Mistress Juliet is not here. Put whatever you have for her upon the table."

"It is for Mistress Rosaline. The maidservant said I would find her here. I must give it to her and no one else."

She sat up. "I am Rosaline." Quickly, she took the letter and dismissed him, her blood running hot in her veins. The missive was penned in Romeo's hand.

Seek permission to come to confession. Meet me at St. Peter's. 6 o'clock.

When Juliet returned, bringing bread, salted fish, and plump, furred peaches with her, she found Rosaline transformed, with color returned to her cheeks and ready to smile once more.

They played a little longer, the hours dawdling and dragging, until at last, at half past five, Rosaline sought permission from her aunt to attend confession on her way home. It was duly given.

Rosaline longed to run to the church, as if the spirit moved her and she had sins to cast upon the water. Yet what did she have to confess but love? The heat of the day was only just beginning to slacken, and blackflies gathered in the gutters and around the tawny puddings of dung in the middle of the street. The stalls and shops had been closed and barricaded against the sun; now their shutters were opening again like bleary eyes, but Rosaline hastened by, eager only to reach St. Peter's.

The streets thinned as she reached the basilica, the church walls stippled in afternoon light, turning the stone a rich yellow ocher. The air was perfumed with the scents of both heaven and earth: incense and the lingering effluence of the city—shit, river mud, and fish. It grazed the back of Rosaline's throat, but she did not care for she was about to see Romeo.

She raced up the steps, past the pair of squat stone lions keeping guard and into the stillness of the nave. She ignored the pillared heights, the striped marble arches, and the ceiling of stars, scouring the darkened crevices for Romeo. A monk nodded to her and gestured to the stairs leading down into the crypt. Gathering her cloak around her, she walked quickly to them and descended into the cavern beneath the church, Persephone plunging into Hades.

Despite the heat, it was chilled in the tomb. The air was dank, and mildew made slick tidemarks upon the walls. Torches spat and hissed in their sconces. This crypt was where the Montagues guarded their dead and other treasures. Rosaline had heard that the Montagues' power could be glimpsed through their cache of holy objects, but she'd not had the chance to pore over them before. She'd never ventured into this crypt. St. Peter's belonged to the city, but the crypt belonged to the Montagues.

As she peered into the cabinets, she was compelled and revolted, and a little afraid. A pair of golden angels clasped a glass reliquary box containing the gray and jawless skull of a holy saint—its teeth and mandible the benediction of another blessed family. In a minute crystal coffin, she glimpsed a desiccated hand manacled in rosary beads, the wrist bones yellowed and shrunken in death to the size of a child's, the edge of the hand-shaped coffin set with rubies and emeralds. She hunted for the relic in a golden shell adorned with pearls, until she realized that the pearls were teeth, lumpy and cracked with age. And a crystal vial of powdered earth that, as she leaned closer, it dawned upon her, was, in fact, blood, now dried and desiccated. She frowned. To kneel before the vials of blood and scavenged scraps of the saints, and pray for blessings upon her life did not feel like a holy ritual bringing her closer to God but grisly.

She knew her father and the priests would not agree and that her very thoughts were close to heresy. Each one of these relics were objects of real power. The first power was mystical and one of faith. Her father believed that objects like this had the ability to alleviate sickness or bestow good fortune upon the devotee, but the other power each item possessed was tangible and absolute, and even Rosaline dared not question it: the relics were treasures coveted by popes and princes, and to own such precious things marked the Montagues as a family of wealth and influence.

Yet the thought of becoming a Montague filled Rosaline with scant joy. She loved Romeo and looked forward to being his wife but wished she could cleave to her own name. The name of Montague seemed to belong in this crypt, with its marvelous dead that hissed of power and saints and decay.

Beside the jeweled teeth, she saw the effigy of a snow-white Montague maid, lying as if asleep on a carved stone bed, her head appearing to softly indent the marble pillow. She looked to be somewhere between her own and Juliet's age.

Montague or Capulet no longer mattered in death.

Rosaline heard the soft pad of footsteps behind her and, turning, saw Romeo. With a murmur of happiness, she ran to him, pressing herself into his arms, seeking his embrace. He stood absolutely still and turned his face from her. She recoiled immediately, hurt and bewildered, and then reached out for him a second time, willing him to look at her, into her. He would not meet her eye. He was pale, hands restless at his sides.

"Please, Romeo." She reached up and kissed him. He hesitated and then, after a moment, kissed her back. His tongue prodded her teeth for entry. The reliquary skulls in their glass boxes watched them with empty eye holes.

"My anger gutters out when it sees you," he said with a sigh.

"Anger, my lord?" asked Rosaline, bewildered.

"I spoke with our Prince of Verona. Our good and noble prince. He saw you dancing with other men in the forest."

Rosaline shook her head. "I danced, and I cannot help it if they were watching. I did not ask them to. Nor did I wish it." She took his hand. "I love only you."

Romeo eyed her in silence, his face lined with shadows. He stroked the tops of her arms. She could see that she had hurt or injured him in some way, but she did not understand how. Was this why he had not visited her chamber for two long, lonely nights?

"You have an inviting eye," he said, testing her.

"An inviting eye?" asked Rosaline, confused.

"And you are an exquisite lady with an inviting eye, and thus you invite men to look."

"I did not invite them." The skin under her arms grew damp. His jealousy was new and strange. She must please and placate him, persuade him of his mistake.

He examined her minutely, turning her chin to one side. Rosaline squirmed beneath his scrutiny.

"But you danced?"

"Aye. But with my cousin."

"Tybalt?"

"Juliet."

"Juliet. Then, I'm sorry, fair Rosaline."

He pulled her close and kissed the top of her head. She breathed in the scent of his skin and leaned into him. She was unused to love, and jealousy and doubt were as novel to her as its passions. All she knew of courting was from books and poems and music, and she understood from those that love was full of torment and she must expect it. Still, she wanted love's roses, not its thorns.

"And yet you went into the woods with that prick, Tybalt. For hours, so I heard," complained Romeo, kissing her wrist.

Rosaline squirmed for she did not like to hear him abuse Tybalt. And yet, she also experienced relief. If this was truly what had riled him, then it was easily remedied. "My cousin Tybalt? We have been friends since we were children. I love him like a brother."

"And he?" asked Romeo with a shrewd glance. "How does he love you?"

Rosaline blinked and fidgeted and knew enough that here she must dissemble. "I cannot say how he loves me, as I cannot see with his eyes or speak with his tongue. I can only say how I love him. With a sister's love."

At this Romeo laughed. "That's altogether too much love. I want it all for me, fair Rosaline. I'm greedy for it with a hunger that cannot be sated. None will love you as I do." His expression became more serious. "You're not to talk to him again. Will you swear to it?"

She stared back at him, trying to see if he was teasing her. "I cannot."

"So you would choose him over me?"

He stood so close that she could feel his breath upon her

cheek. His pupils were a pair of flickering tinderboxes, reflecting the torch flames in the gloom. It was a game after all. It must be. He did not really want her to swear such a silly thing. She was relieved. "You. Always you. But he's my cousin and my oldest friend. He would be a friend to you too, if you would let him."

Romeo gave a low laugh. "As if I could lose you to Tybalt the Prick."

Rosaline drew away from him. "He's dear to me as my own self. He is the brother of my heart."

At once Romeo saw that he had offended her and was chastised, bowing his head. "Forgive me. Tybalt is indeed your friend and cousin, and when we are married, he shall be my cousin too."

Rosaline watched carefully as Romeo continued. "I'm jealous of the moon for she gets to shine upon you and look upon your face when I'm not there." He withdrew her lambskin glove from her mantle and shook it out so it flapped limply. "I'm jealous of this little glove for it can caress these fingers when I'm gone." He slid his hand beneath the folds of her dress and found the smooth flesh of her thigh. "I'm envious of the worm who made the silk for this skirt, for he was cocooned day and night in the fibers that now stroke the place where I long to be."

He withdrew his hand, dropping the fabric of her skirts, and placed his palms on her shoulders. "Can you forgive me yet?"

Rosaline shrugged, starting to enjoy the game. "Perhaps. Perhaps not."

He bowed and moved away, prowling among the tombs and the gleaming reliquary boxes, the riches of the dead. Rosaline inhaled frankincense and the scent of the grave. At last he turned again to look at her and, as he reached her, stooped on one knee, lowering his head. "Please, I beg you, my love, forgive me my jealousy. My love runs too hot. How can all men not adore you when I worship you so?" Holding both her hands, he turned them over and over, kissing them.

Rosaline smiled down at him. "I forgive you then, my lord." She knelt down beside him on the floor of the chapel, and he took her face gently and kissed her, softly at first and then with resolve. The stone where they crouched was chilled and dank, and she shuddered both with her longing for him and from cold. She wished they could be in some other place: beside the willows at the river bend perhaps, where the kingfisher dabbled and the air was blue and clean. Yet so long as she was with Romeo, she was content.

He placed his head upon her lap, and as she drew her fingers through the coarse curls of his hair, she tried to picture the riverbank and imagine that the dripping they could hear was the music of a stream, and not the water running down the mossy walls.

"I sent a letter to the friar some days past, and he at last replied," said Romeo. "The friar is saying mass for the plague dead in Mantua, but he'll return to Verona within three days, and he'll marry us here in St. Peter's."

"In this crypt?" murmured Rosaline, wishing it could be in some other, more auspicious place.

"It is my family chapel. Ten generations of Montagues have been married and christened and laid to rest upon this very spot."

Rosaline closed her eyes against those long-dead Montagues. She felt their ghostly breath as freezing fog upon her neck.

"I will send for you when he arrives, and you'll meet me here. Then, we'll away to Mantua," said Romeo.

Perturbed by the prospect of marrying him in the crypt, Rosaline was too slow in expressing her happiness, and Romeo sat up, disappointed by her quietness. "I fear your heart is not full of joy at this. Is it Tybalt? Or some other man?" He paused, his voice heavy with dismay. "For you deceive your father and may me."

"I deceive him in loving you. How could you speak such words? My very soul is cut in two."

"And I unlaced my soul and gave it to you."

Rosaline could not understand how Romeo could still doubt her devotion to him.

"How else can I prove my love, sweet Romeo? I have given you myself, my honor."

"I believe thee, sweet lady," said Romeo, brushing her cheek with his fingers.

The basilica's bell began to toll the hour, and Rosaline realized she needed to hurry. Caterina would be waiting for her, and she'd be scolded severely if she was late.

"A moment more! This kiss"—he placed a tender kiss upon her lips—"there can be no betrothal ceremony for us but this, my love," whispered Romeo. "We can have no feasting and dancing amid guests brimming with tears of joy. So we must celebrate, we two." He reached into his jerkin and plucked out a single pomegranate. "Since you have no pomegranates embroidered on your gown to bring us both good fortune, I brought us this for our betrothal feast."

Rosaline was raw with love once more. Romeo sliced the fruit in half with his knife, the seeds bloody and wet, and fed several to Rosaline with his fingers. They were sweet and bitter at once, bursting upon her tongue, the juice staining their teeth red and purple.

The only witness to this betrothal ceremony was the marble statue of the dead Montague girl. She would not betray them. As Rosaline reluctantly turned away, lowering her maiden's veil, she glanced back at the marble effigy, and for a moment she did not like to leave her there alone among the relics and mildew or the shadows from the torches that tongued the walls.

Rosaline's fingers were stained crimson from the pomegranate, and as she looked at the sleeping girl frozen on her stone pillow, the immaculate white of the girl's lips appeared to be bloodied with pomegranate juice, as if the statue was metamorphosing into Persephone herself. Persephone, who by eating seeds of the pomegranate, was forced into becoming Hades's bride. All at once Rosaline had the frantic desire to flee this dank place, lest she too be trapped in the dark with the Montague dead.

That night Rosaline waited for her love to come to her. She listened for him and waited, breathless with hope. He'd never come to her this late before, but perhaps tonight? That was not the cockerel; it was but the screech of an owl. There was still time. But what if he'd been caught? What if he lay dead or bleeding and she had not known to rush to his side? Or else, perhaps she had displeased him and that was why he had not come? Her eyes were hot with tears that would not fall. She felt feverish with longing and could not sleep. No one had *seen* her before him. She was nothing to any of them but an inconvenient child. An expense and a burden to the family name, to be locked away before she could bring shame upon them.

And yet, even to herself she could not pretend this was quite true. Tybalt was her most constant friend. He'd even offered her himself to free her from the confines of her future. It was a different kind of love from Romeo's and yet it was still love: older, softer, and one grown from friendship, not passion. Uneasy, she tucked thoughts of Tybalt away. She did not want to think of him and how quiet he had become when she'd said no to his offer of marriage.

And then the window snapped and swung open, there was a foot upon the floorboards, and Romeo was there! *O, the stars fire brighter in the sky tonight!* She was dizzy with gratitude that he had come. She covered him with kisses, half ashamed of her hunger for him.

"Has the friar returned? It's been so long."

Romeo smiled. "I said three days, little one. Love is making you impatient, but there are so many dead. The moment he's here, I shall send for you."

Rosaline longed to be gone from this place. The convent loomed bleakly in her thoughts. There were but seven nights of freedom left to her. Yet Romeo distracted her with his lips as he peeled off each layer from her. As she trembled for him, he made her swear her devotion to him, and she obeyed. He liked to hear her say how she loved him in a hundred different ways. "My passion for you is hotter than the sun and as undimmable. You are fairer than the first July morning." She enjoyed this game. Even if she could not find the words as easily or quickly as him, he would always love her and not waver. Of course he would.

Afterwards, she lay naked on the bed, her knees tucked beneath her chin, feeling the slick ooze from him between her thighs, thick and lumpy as frog spawn. Abelard in his passion for Heloise or Dante in his fervor for Beatrice never mentioned the frog spawn, or that afterwards as they lay together naked, rather than experiencing rapturous and perfect union, she felt alone, marooned in her own thoughts, thinking more of death than of love. Romeo liked to speak rapturously again of his feelings for her, and to hear her describe her passion and devotion to him, but sometimes it seemed to Rosaline that he did not always listen to how she felt about anything beyond their love. Their world was only the two of them. Anything that stood apart from this did not matter to him. She basked in his devotion and if, for a fleeting moment, she desired anything more, she blamed the poets for not preparing her properly. Also, she supposed, Dante's love for Beatrice remained perfect in its lack of consummation. He walked behind Beatrice in the street, breathing her air and admiring the way the sunlight dappled her skin, but it was not clear whether the poet had ever even spoken to her, let alone caressed her thigh.

Rosaline and Romeo lay side by side, sharing sips from Romeo's flask. The liquor was honeyed and strong, and made her head whirl with light. When she drank, she did not feel like a child-woman any longer. The candle sputtered, and she traced the shadows on his stomach with her finger, and he shuddered, hairs rising across his arms and chest like miniature legionnaires. Rosaline giggled, marveling at her own power and his beauty. His skin was as smooth and unblemished as the kernel of a nut, pale beside her own. He made a guttural noise of desire in his throat, and Rosaline laughed again.

There was a sound outside the room, and to her dismay, Rosaline realized that under the effect of the liquor in their pleasure they'd forgotten to be quiet.

"Who's there?" whispered Romeo, sitting up at once, his cock shriveling.

Rosaline shook her head and clutched at him. He fumbled beneath the bed for his sword but could not find it.

The door opened. "What is this?" called a voice, and Caterina's face appeared in the gloom, lit by her nightstick, large-eyed with fear and worry.

Rosaline leaped from the bed and quickly closed the door behind them both, sealing Caterina inside the chamber. The maid stared at the lovers in dismay and then turned her back while they dressed themselves with fumbling, wretched fingers.

Rosaline tried to plead for mercy. "Good Caterina, do not

wake my father. I love Romeo. We are to be married within days. Please, Caterina. Do not betray me. I beg you. He's a Montague and you know his name is death in this house."

Caterina eyed them both with horror, her hand fluttering to cover her mouth, and looked ready to weep. "O, Rosaline, what have you done?"

Romeo stepped forward, having now shaken all fear from him like droplets of water. He spoke softly but with resolve: "Please, madam. Let them kill me, but do not let them send away my Rosaline. She does not deserve to be locked away. I only want to set her free with my love."

"And marriage?" Caterina asked, her voice sharp.

"The instant my good friend the friar returns to St. Peter's. I hope tomorrow."

"No, you shall not persuade me of this. She is too young for marriage. She is not yet sixteen." Caterina turned away as if unwilling to look directly at him, as though the unreal beauty of his face might weaken her resolve. Her voice was unsteady. "Sir, you are of an age to know better, and if you truly loved her, you should have waited twelve months at least."

Romeo bowed his head, contrite. "Madam, you speak the truth. I would not hurt her. Love blinded to me everything but her beauty and my own impatience. She is an angel that loves me, and I am truly blessed. If I must die now, then I die happy and rich in the jewels of her love."

"O, you practiced seducer!" Caterina's expression contorted in disgust, turning from him in revulsion. "You speak prettily!

And look prettily too. I can see how this thing was done."
Caterina leaned against the wall, her face in her hands, wretched.
"I should have prevented you from going to the masquerade,
Rosaline. Your mother would not forgive me. She did not want
this for you. What have I done?"

Rosaline ran to the maid and threw her arms about her.
"Truly, Caterina, my love for Romeo was freely given. And I
cannot, I shall not, live without him!"

"Fie. Peace! You are a child and do not know what you say."

"I am not a child and I know that Cupid shoots his arrow
blind. Love will not be bound by a lover's age nor by a name nor
time. I saw Romeo and at once we loved."

"It is true, good lady. I saw this bright angel, this winged
messenger, and I loved her."

Caterina gave a snort. "Perhaps it's love after all if you believe
this willful girl, this pretty baggage, to be an angel."

Rosaline continued to study her in trepidation. Caterina's
eyes flicked between them.

Romeo shook his head. "I am bewitched. I can have no peace
until she is mine and we are married. I swear to you, lady, that I
will make her a good and faithful husband."

Caterina moved to sit on a low wooden stool. She glanced at
the rumpled sheets upon the bed and turned away unhappily. She
looked older than Rosaline had ever seen her, her face lined with
concern, and Rosaline's heart was pricked with both tenderness and
fear. She took Romeo's flask and gave it to her, and Caterina drank.

"It shall be the duty and honor of my life to make her happy,"

Romeo continued. "My only task will be to deserve the daughter of your departed friend."

Caterina blinked but did not speak. She seemed to waver, but if it was enough, Rosaline could not tell. She could bear it no longer, demanding, "Will you tell my father? For then Romeo will die and you will have killed him."

"Hush, Rosaline, my love," soothed Romeo. He turned the beacon of his attention back upon Caterina. "You shall come and live with us, gentle Caterina. Not as our servant. I see how high my Rosaline holds you in her affection, and I know what she has lost. So be as a mother to her, then, and I shall tend to you both." He knelt before her and kissed her hand, looking up at her with the steady gaze of his black eyes.

Caterina said nothing, and then, at last, she nodded, and Rosaline saw to her relief that she too was lost to his charms.

Caterina left the lovers to their parting. Rosaline brimmed with happiness now at the prospect that she had a friend with whom she could share her joy. It made their relationship more substantial, less of an imagined delight.

On seeing her expression, Romeo laughed. "Till tomorrow, sweet Rosaline."

He leaned over and captured her chin in his hand. As he did so, a glint of green, bright as spring grass, swinging from his sleeve caught her eye. A fat emerald pendant, oval in shape and encased in gold. Rosaline knew it at once to be hers.

Her guts twisted, full of snakes. "That's mine. It was my mother's."

Romeo smiled at her in confusion. "Yes, my love. You gave it to me, as a token of your affection." He laughed. "I see we're playing a game!"

Rosaline shook her head. "I did not give it you."

"Of course you did. I asked you for a token of your regard, and you presented me this. It's wondrous fair and I do love you for it."

Rosaline continued to gaze at him in puzzlement, her heart beating wildly. She had not given it to him. Had she? She remembered now, him asking her for some lover's gift, but not her giving it to him. Was he right? Had she forgotten? But she would not have given him this and then forgotten the gifting of it, would she? She was wormy with doubt.

Romeo was staring at her, his features rigid with disappointment. He fumbled with his sleeve and wrenched the pendant from its fastening and thrust it at her. He no longer smiled. His expression was grave, heavy with regret. "Here. Take it. The only jewel I need is your regard."

Rosaline longed to snatch it from him. Her fingers itched to curl around it. She could already feel the weight of it in her palm. His brows furrowed. She knew she could not take it. To take the jewel would be to lose her Romeo.

She swallowed and tossed her head. Smiled. Her teeth ached. "Keep it. A token of my love. Until we are married."

His face was transformed, his features radiant as high

summer; the storm had blown out to sea. "Pin it back upon my sleeve."

She did, with fingers that trembled and longed to pry it away. She loved him. She must have been mistaken.

VI

I do love a woman

Rosaline discovered Juliet in an ill temper, eyes red from angry tears. She had quarrelled with her mother. She would say nothing of the dispute, but she bore a red welt across her cheek, a five-fingered crimson star only now fading. Nurse had a headache and had not been there to defuse the argument and even now remained in her quarters with a poultice strapped to her forehead. Rosaline tried to distract and soothe Juliet, but she sat crouched beside her bed with her knees tucked beneath her chin and would not stir.

"Come, let's outside. Let's sit inside the apple trees awhile. I'll read to you."

"I care not for books."

"I'll sing or play the lute."

"I care not for music."

Guilt probed Rosaline with jagged fingers; she ought to have been there earlier. Then perhaps the fight would not have

happened. Yet even now she was distracted with longing for
Romeo. The warmth of his arms. The sunshine of his gaze. How
his voice lit up with joy when she pleased him. When she was
removed from his presence, she felt like a crocus that closes its
petals in the cold glare of the moon. Sometimes she wondered if,
had he not seen her, she would have simply faded from the world
like Echo's disregarded nymph.

Then, she saw before her the hard nub of the emerald, its lush
glare, pinned upon his sleeve.

From beneath the layers of her skirts, she produced Romeo's
flask. He had neglected to take it with him, leaving it behind in
her chamber. She nudged Juliet, who folded her arms and sucked
her bottom lip. This would distract and cheer her cousin.

"Let's sit in the apple tree and drink a little of this," said
Rosaline, showing her the flask. "We'll forget our cares. Nothing
will seem so bad that it cannot be mended. It's like sipping
sunlight."

Juliet smirked and took it from her, turning it over. "Is it
Valentio's?"

"No."

"Tybalt's?"

"No. Don't ask questions; just come."

Rosaline tugged her by the arm, and the two girls ventured
down the stairs, already clutching one another, giggling and
hoping that they would not be caught as they hastened out into
the dazzle of the afternoon. They settled in the cradle of the
apple tree, passing the flagon between them. Juliet sipped and

spluttered. A slow smile spread across her features. She thrust the flask back at Rosaline, who drank and laughed. The liquid was cool and sweet and tasted of Romeo's kisses.

"Do you think you shall love one day, Juliet?"

"Definitely not any man my mother finds for me," answered Juliet, a note of stubborn fury in her voice.

Rosaline did not press her further. It was delightful in the drowsy shade. The leaves spun and danced. Juliet tried to catch one and, in grabbing it, fell from her perch and landed in the dust beneath; Rosaline laughed so hard, the stitches in her bodice creaked.

The flask was soon empty. Juliet climbed back into her spot beside Rosaline and stretched out. "Tell me the truth, coz… Have you ever kissed a man?" asked Juliet.

Rosaline shook her head and smiled. "I cannot answer. You forget, I'm to be a nun."

"O, you tease; you're not yet sworn to holy orders."

"Fie, I shall not answer. Give me a forfeit."

"Then, the answer is yes. But if you will not tell me who, there is no fun in it. I'm guessing it must be Tybalt. He has a fine face. Though his beard is not good."

"What's wrong with his beard?"

"It is too thin and the shape is poor, but that you like it shows that you are partial. Yes, indeed I think you have kissed Tybalt."

Rosaline, despite the spinning of the apple leaves above her head and the tossing of the grass below, would not be tricked by Juliet. By denying Tybalt, she would be admitting the possibility of another. Juliet leaned forward in eagerness for her confession. Rosaline shook her head; she could not tell. Her cousin pouted in annoyance and Rosaline sighed—Tybalt had asked her to marry him, and Juliet would have been delighted if Rosaline had agreed. It would have been a happy secret, a shared treasure between friends. Her illicit betrothal to Romeo brimmed with as much sadness as it did joy.

Juliet nudged her, impatient.

"A forfeit, coz," said Rosaline.

Juliet sighed. She became quiet, deliberating. "Strip naked and run three times around the orchard."

Rosaline shrieked. "I might be seen and, if seen, punished!"

Juliet shrugged and yawned, displaying the inside of her mouth, soft and pink as a snake's. "That is why 'tis called a forfeit."

Muttering with displeasure, Rosaline unfastened her dress, stepped out of her underskirt, and, discarding her slippers, raced through the orchard. For a moment she was mortified, fearful of who might spy her—servants, her aunt, or, worse, her uncle Capulet—and she wove among the trees, frantic and ashamed. Then, she noticed how the leaves made shifting patterns upon her bare skin, and the grass in the shade was mossy and springy underfoot. Breathless and hot she slowed, the sensation of the sun warm upon her back and even more pleasant upon other parts that it had not touched before. She was dizzy from mead and running, and the heat was too much. She stood and dragged a toe through the dust, watching the polished carapace of a beetle the color of waxed mahogany as it navigated an alp of dung.

Making a decision, she discarded her shame as if it were a cloak; it was agreeable to be naked in the orchard among the burgeoning stubs of apples and the whir of the bees.

"Cousin?"

Rosaline glanced behind her to find Tybalt standing at the edge of the trees, a look of bewilderment displayed across his features. Rosaline laughed at him. He was a muddle of embarrassment and keen curiosity, both knowing he ought to look away and unable to do so. Her head full of the hum of mead, she turned her back to watch the beetle and pretended to ignore him. She felt him watch her still, but she would not hide. She'd learned from Romeo that there was power in her nakedness.

Tybalt waited for her to cover herself and, then when she did not, ran to her, throwing his cape across her shoulders. She wriggled free and began to dance, naked. She was unsteady on her feet, and she bowed to him, giggling, performing a sarabande with mock solemnity, to unheard music.

"Will you not join me, Cousin?" she asked. "'Tis our uncle's ball on Sunday, and I only think to practice a few steps."

"Cousin, what madness is this? Are you afflicted by the sun?" He shook his head as he came closer.

"It shall be my last Capulet ball. I should like to enjoy it and dance my very best."

"Cousin. Rosaline. I beg you, stop."

Rosaline took no notice and continued to dance around him out of reach until Tybalt surrendered and began to laugh too at

her absurdity, joining in, their fingertips touching. Juliet cheered
and clapped.

As she laughed, Rosaline thought hazily through the mead
that she laughed a good deal with Tybalt.

She tried to remember when she had laughed with Romeo.
She could not.

"What a pretty pair!" called Juliet.

"Why, thank you," replied Rosaline. "You, sir, are over-
dressed," she said.

"No, Rosaline. You have led me into many capers, but I'm no
capon, for I'm keeping my cape on."

Staggering with wine, Rosaline decided this was the funni-
est joke she'd ever heard and tripped over her own feet. Tybalt,
apparently concerned that the jape had gone on long enough,
seized the opportunity to throw his cape around Rosaline's
shoulders. "You reek of drink. Come, before the servants or our
aunt sees you."

Juliet ambled toward them, following a meandering line
across the orchard and steadying herself against a tree.

Tybalt clicked his tongue in annoyance. "You too, little one?"
He glanced about for Rosaline's discarded clothes and, spying
them in the crook of the apple tree, strode over and gathered
them up, then tossed the bundle to her. "Stand here, both of you.
Give me the flask. And you, coz, need to dress, and quickly—
there are others not far off." He turned his back to her and continued to reproach her. "Rosaline, this is your doing. You'll both
be whipped if they catch you."

At that prospect Rosaline began to pull on her clothes again with some assistance from Juliet, who, after several attempts, managed to help fasten her buttons, half of them in the wrong holes.

"Where did you get the mead?" demanded Tybalt.

"Rosaline," answered Juliet.

"The flask," replied Rosaline, arch.

"Why?" asked Tybalt, irritated and realizing he was not going to get a proper answer from the two sozzled girls.

"I was unhappy. And the little cheer she has, she gave to me," said Juliet.

"Good cheer is not found in a flask," said Tybalt. He shook his head. "Let us linger here awhile in the open air until you both feel well enough to return to the house."

The three of them settled back down in the crook beneath the conspiracy of apple trees, where they were hidden from view. Juliet disappeared to surreptitiously vomit into the long grass and then joined them again.

"I'm sorry," said Rosaline, contrite. "Tybalt is right. I shouldn't have let you do this. How are you now? This is all my fault."

Juliet smiled and closed her eyes. "Indeed it is, coz, and I am glad. I'm tired of being cosseted."

Rosaline was grateful for her forgiveness but not entirely sure if she deserved it. She stood and nearly fell. Tybalt seized her arm and steadied her. She glared at him.

"Do not mock me," she said.

"I would not dare," he said with a smile.

Juliet crawled beside Rosaline, placing her head in Rosaline's lap. She stroked her hair, smoothing her golden curls. The three were silent for a few minutes, listening to the wind comb the grass and the servants call to one another in the house. Juliet's eyes slowly closed, and she appeared so peaceful as to be not quite of this world. Something about the paleness of her skin and her perfect stillness made Rosaline recall the Montague maid in the crypt. Despite the heat of the afternoon, she shivered.

She turned to Tybalt and spoke in a whisper: "I want to know about the Montague feud."

Tybalt frowned. "Why?"

"It interests me on a hot afternoon. I heard that a Capulet maid and a Montague man were to be married. And then, he abandoned her to take holy orders. He chose God over love?"

Tybalt gave a low laugh. "Your view of it is too soft, too full of poetry."

"How so?"

He propped himself upon his elbow. "They were betrothed. But then, the Montague groom had the chance to become a cardinal. It was not love of God but love of power that made him abandon her."

"And that began the feud?"

"The Capulets were outraged. And then less than a month after his ordination, the new Montague cardinal died. The rumors were that he'd been poisoned. At the hands of the Capulets."

"Did we poison him? He would've deserved it."

Tybalt chuckled and shook his head. "Truthfully, I don't know. It's so long ago. I'm not sure that anyone still alive knows the truth."

Rosaline stared at him. "And what happened to the Capulet bride?"

Tybalt yawned. "She's not important."

"How can you say that?"

Hearing Rosaline's outrage, Tybalt held up his hands. "In some versions she married someone else. Or died of a broken heart. Or became a nun."

"That is every single possibility," said Rosaline, annoyed. "To not choose an ending for her is to say she doesn't matter."

Juliet opened her eyes. "I think she's the one who poisoned him," she said softly. "She sought her own revenge."

Tybalt walked with Rosaline back to her father's house. Without Juliet, they were awkward with one another, their former easiness tarnished and rubbed. Tybalt glowered and marched at such a pace that Rosaline was breathless from trying to keep up, but she would not ask him to slow. Her head ached badly now, and her mouth was dry and tasted foul.

As they reached the enclave of the house, he finally turned to her and said, his voice thick with hurt, "You are so unhappy, you stole drink and made yourself and your cousin sick, but you will not think to run away with me to escape your fate? Am I so repulsive to you, Rosaline?"

His face was tight with hurt. Pierced with shame, Rosaline reached for his arm, but he had already gone, vanished among the hurry of the passersby.

Rosaline let out a roar, banging the passage door so that it rattled like loose teeth.

Lying to her friends was a misery she could hardly bear. And yet, she understood that once they knew she loved a Montague, the truth would be worse than the lie. Her marriage would be like her death to them. She would be forbidden from seeing Juliet or Livia and the children. No Capulet would utter her name except as a warning, a hiss to other wayward girls. Tybalt would hate her as his enemy.

But wasn't she already his enemy, full of lies and dissemblance? He just did not know it yet.

Rosaline leaned against the cool of the wall, feeling the roughness of the stone beneath her fingertips, and for a moment could not breathe. What had she done?

For a time Rosaline wished Romeo would not come to her that night. How could she give up Tybalt? The thought of him grieving for her, despising her, made her stomach cramp. And Juliet? She loved her too. But there was no color in the world without Romeo. Everything was ash when he was not there. She could not be without him. So when she heard his step upon the floorboard, she was out of bed and in his arms, covering him in kisses as he laughed and caressed her. All doubts, all others forgotten. There was no one else. Only Rosaline and Romeo.

They lay together upon her bed. He stroked the indent of her back, the freckle on her cheek. "Once we are married, we must elope at once. The hatred between our two families demands nothing else."

Rosaline swallowed. The tears that she'd forgotten rose again like a spring tide. She imagined Tybalt and Juliet watching her, silent with reproach and her betrayal. *I love you both*, she thought. *I love you too.*

"And yet you lie with a Montague," said Tybalt.

"And you leave us for him," said Juliet.

Rosaline blinked, her eyes liquid with tears, as the vision of her friends gradually dissipated. Romeo lay beside her talking, and it took her moment to heed him.

"I cannot ask my father Montague for the usual bridal *contra-donora*,"—gifts from the groom—he was saying. "And you will receive no dowry. We shall both be cast out of our houses."

He saw the expression on her face and, smiling, traced her collarbone with his fingertips. "Do not be unhappy, little one. We shall be free. The two of us drunk on joy and hope. What else do we need of the hurly-burly world?"

"Nothing," said Rosaline, trying to smile, wanting it to be true.

"And yet," said Romeo, kissing a line from her earlobe to the puckering skin of her nipple, "if you could get from your father the ducats he was giving to the convent as settlement for you, our lives in Mantua would be easier with some coin."

Rosaline stared at him in horror. "You want me to steal from my father?"

Romeo laughed, as if astounded she could consider such a notion as theft. "No. It is your money, little one. He was going to give it to the convent as payment for your keep. But since you won't be there, they shall not need it. It's for our life together, sweet Rosaline. The nuns won't be in want of it. And it isn't their money. It's yours."

"It's my father's," she said in a soft voice that was barely a whisper, as she did not like to contradict him.

"It's your dowry. Or it should be. Beauty such as yours ought not be hidden away in a convent. It's a cruelty to the world."

Rosaline frowned and twisted her hair around her finger.

Romeo kissed her nose. "It's a matter of trifling importance. Think on it," he said. "A small act of love to ease our way in Mantua. And if you do decide to…borrow…the ducats, send them to me and I'll keep them safe. Send them to me with good Caterina."

Rosaline did not reply. She would not do it. She absolutely would not. Anger hummed beneath her skin like bees. How could he even ask her? And yet he did not consider it theft. His words were so reasoned. So why then did the very thought repel her? She would *not* do it…but then she envisioned his look of gratitude and love. And it was intended for her nun's dowry at the convent. Could Rosaline really steal what was already hers?

She knew that if she did as he asked, she would never send the coins with Caterina. The consequences for her if caught stealing from her master would be death. Did Romeo not know this? He could not, or good, sweet Romeo would not suggest it.

The following morning, when Caterina came to wake her, Romeo had gone.

Rosaline was bereft. She allowed herself to be helped into her clothes and made her way down the stairs, lagging at each step as Caterina gestured to various household items.

"The rug with moth damage. Or this wall hanging with the deer hunt. Your mother never liked it, and so your father has decided he dislikes it too, even though it's valuable. Or this Moorish design?" asked Caterina. "You must choose. Your father orders it. They are to be sent ahead to the convent, your cell prepared for your arrival."

"I do not care," answered Rosaline. "It is not for my comfort. It's for his reputation. It must appear that Masetto Capulet has provided decently for his daughter. And you know as well as I that I shall not go. I'll be in Mantua with my love."

Caterina considered for a moment. "Very well. But we must make a show of choosing." She paused and then smiled. "Perhaps, if Romeo can find a way, these things can furnish your new home."

Rosaline shook her head vigorously. "I do not want them."

"As you wish. But you must choose one or two things, or your father will be displeased."

Rosaline knew she would do well to heed her warning.

Leaving her, Caterina returned to the kitchen and her myriad chores while Rosaline dallied through the house. If she had a choice, would she take anything with her into her new life? That painting of the petulant Madonna? The carved daybed where her mother used to doze through the afternoons upon heaped pillows? No, not even those. Instead she wanted be a like a newborn chick and discard everything she'd come from and emerge naked into this new existence. And yet, Romeo's words nagged at her. They would have no money in Mantua. Or not at first. She already felt like a thief sliding through her father's house. Her father could not love her—there was a shriveled walnut where his heart was supposed to be—and yet, for all her revulsion and bright anger, she did not want to rob him of either goods or gold. She was still his daughter, and once she could have loved him.

Looking down, she saw that her hands were shaking. While Romeo's delight was radiant, his displeasure and disappointed looks were the cold of winter. She dreaded telling him that she could not do it. Perhaps if she borrowed just a little—her father was rich and would not notice. Then, once they were settled in Mantua and Romeo was established in his endeavors, they could return the ducats. Then it would not be a theft at all but a loan, if an unwitting one.

All the same, Rosaline was not sure whether she deceived her father or herself.

She was excused from spending the day with Juliet in order to pack and retreated to her chamber. Yet she did not order her belongings but paced the room, chewing on her fingernails. She did not want to do this thing, though her father would never discover it.

She lay upon the bed, a queasiness lying heavily inside her guts like curdled milk. She did not come down to eat nor touch the tray Caterina left outside her door.

Later in the afternoon, Rosaline heard her father leave and venture out into the city to visit traders, as was his habit. He would be gone for several hours. Caterina would be occupied in the kitchen, and the two maids in the outhouses busy with the slops and other rough work. As if in a dream, Rosaline rose from the bed and crept downstairs. She was a phantom in her own house. It was hot and still. Nothing stirred—there was only the click and tick of the deathwatch beetle in the beams.

Every moment expecting that she would be caught, Rosaline slunk along the stone passage and into her father's room. The door was ajar. She hesitated, her hand reaching out to touch the handle. She could turn around and run back upstairs and tell Romeo that no, she couldn't do it, she wouldn't.

She pushed open the door.

The room was tidy and newly dusted. The maids had rubbed the floor with beeswax, but even that couldn't rid the room of the stale smell. No matter how many fires were lit, this room was always damp and cold. She saw a patch of mildew bloom in one corner, lettuce green.

Masetto had left the portrait of Emelia upon his desk.

She reproached Rosaline from the blotter. Reaching out with trembling fingers, she turned her facedown so that she would not witness her daughter's crime and her horrible descent into wickedness.

"I will atone for this," whispered Rosaline.

She crouched and retrieved the key to her father's chest from where he always kept it behind one of the metalwork firedogs. The key was heavy and fashioned from wrought iron and would not turn in the lock of the chest. With relief, she decided that she could return to Romeo and tell him quite honestly that she had tried but the lock was stuck fast. He would soothe and forgive her. They'd find another way. She breathed again. Yanking it hard, she tried to withdraw the key. It clicked open.

She'd only ever glimpsed inside the chest once or twice before, many years ago, and it had gleamed with gold—piles of it, daffodil-yellow light reflecting back upon her father's sallow face. Now, Rosaline lifted the lid of the chest, dread pooling. But there was no glorious glow of daffodil yellow. Or not enough to fill a flower bed, merely a few meager pots. Where had it gone? Masetto must instead be keeping his gold in one of the banks in the city.

She could not take much or he would discover the theft at once. Taking the small bag she'd secreted about her for this purpose, she counted out thirty ducats, hoping that enough coins remained that he would not notice those she had borrowed.

Closing the lid again, she locked it and hastened upstairs to her chamber. She lay upon her bed, a sheen of sweat upon her lip. Closing her eyes, she longed for a sleep that would not come. She knew Romeo would be pleased with what she had done and furnished herself with his joy. She felt none of her own.

Rosaline sent a message with Caterina to her love that she must see him, but when the maid returned, it was to tell her that Romeo had been ordered by his father to their villa in the hills above the city. He could not return to Verona this night. Instead, he asked if Rosaline would meet him in the place where they had first encountered one another.

"The Montague garden. But how shall I get there?" asked Rosaline, full of apprehension.

Caterina paused, considering. "My brother is a groom in another household. He shall take you and wait for you there," she said. "We shall not ask any of the servants here. It is too dangerous."

Rosaline agreed to Caterina's plan, her dread and guilt at what she had done giving way to eagerness at the prospect of seeing Romeo. She did not confess her offense to Caterina. It was better that she did not know.

As the hours waxed late and the rest of the house was long in bed, Rosaline lay in a small cart beneath a loose covering of sacks that reeked of mildew and grain. Her eyes itched. She kept her fist tightly wrapped around the small bag of coins.

"You can come out; we're nearly there," called Caterina's brother. "There's no one around."

With relief, Rosaline threw off the sacking and gulped a breath of cool night air. Thousands of stars had been tossed up against the black backing curtain of the sky and shone so bright and clear that they seemed to quiver. The only other light was that of the Montague place, coming closer and closer with each pull of the horses. There were no blazing torches this time, only the faint glow of a few candles in the windows.

"Here, this is as close as I should get," said her escort, drawing up the cart. "I'll wait by these trees. We must be back in the city before dawn."

Rosaline nodded and jumped down, teasing stray kernels of stale grain from her hair and ears.

She ran along the track leading to the garden at the far side of the grand villa. It was draped in darkness, only sparse light coming from the skinny, white moon that peeked down at her, half-hidden behind trees. Her feet across the gravel path seemed to echo, piercing the stillness. Any moment she anticipated a band of servants rushing out and seizing her. Then she heard raised voices and, falling to her knees, cowered beside the low hedge, blood swirling in her ears.

Two men appeared, in the midst of an argument with one another, not prowling for her.

"You're a coxcomb and a fool," yelled a man, his voice deep and resonant with anger.

"I am none, my lord," replied a second familiar voice.

Rosaline peered through the film of darkness at the two figures pacing on the loggia before the villa. Romeo she recognized at once. He appeared slight beside the corpulent figure of the other man, whom she took to be his father. The moonlight caught in his silver hair, making it shine and spool out behind him like spilled mercury.

"You are what I say you are. And I say you are a fool, a rascal, and a pretty knave. Aye, prettier than your sister, poor wretch," said Signior Montague, his voice treacled with scorn.

"I say again, I am none."

"You are none?" He scoffed. "You are indeed nothing. And, boy, nothing can be made of nothing."

With this, he shoved Romeo with both hands. To her surprise, Romeo did not resist, only staggered backwards. Rosaline wished she could move or retreat farther into the garden, but could not stir out of fear of being seen. Her feet would make noise upon the gravel. Yet staying there and watching this argument was an intrusion.

Signior Montague hissed at Romeo, poking his chest with his forefinger. "Alas, you are too big for whipping. If you were my dog or my daughter, I'd kennel you or starve you. But fate has seen fit to make you my son."

"I try to please you—"

"You do not! You please yourself. Do not contradict me, else you take *me* for a fool. Do you call me a fool?"

"No, my lord."

Signior Montague muttered something that Rosaline could

not hear and turned away in contempt. He paced upon the loggia before saying loudly, "I don't like that Franciscan, Laurence. He fattens himself upon you. Rid yourself of his company."

At this Romeo replied in a stronger voice, "You do not choose my friends, Father."

"No, but I tug your purse strings."

With this he pulled on Romeo's ears before dragging him along the terrace as though he were a schoolboy, while Romeo thumped his arm to release him, trying not hurt the old man until, finally losing patience and humiliated, he shoved him away, hard, so that Signior Montague staggered into the stone balustrade of the loggia.

He fell to the ground, roaring with laughter, wiping what appeared to be blood from his mouth. "So you do have some heat! You can fight and not just whine or wine."

Rosaline longed to flee. Romeo's father was a tyrant, not unlike her own. Yet, while it was something that they shared, she sensed he would not like her to see him thus.

A few moments later, the old man rose and a door slammed as he vanished inside the house. Romeo swore and muttered bitterly to himself and then, as she watched, walked quickly across the terrace toward the path. She dared not call out to him, and then he disappeared through the ogre gate.

Sliding from her hiding place, she followed him. She hesitated at the ogre gate before stepping through the mouth of hell and into the glade of fallen gods. The stillness there was absolute. She wondered where he'd gone. A dragon roared in darkness as a hound tore at its flank and the tall pines blotted out the stars. Proteus, wearing the mask of madness, gawped and screamed in endless despair, while a little farther on Venus stared out blankly.

Rosaline glanced around the glade looking for Romeo. Then, hands slid around her waist and a voice murmured in her ear, "Do not be afraid, my love."

She kissed him.

"Come," said Romeo, taking her hands and drawing her on. "Let us to another part. More cheerful, perhaps."

Rosaline allowed herself to be pulled deeper in.

"I saw your father."

Romeo stiffened.

"I do not think he's gentle or good," said Rosaline. "My father is unkind too. He was good to my mother but no one else."

"My father is a cock. To my poor mother most of all," snapped Romeo. "And he's a rich cock too, used to people groveling before him. I will not grovel."

Rosaline decided not to mention Signior Montague again; the wound was too bloody and not yet scabbed.

He guided her to a clearing, to a kind of theater of raked grass banks where sculpted heads peered down at them disdainfully from mighty plinths. They looked to Rosaline horribly like the decapitated heads of kings and queens.

"The players come on summer nights to entertain us here," said Romeo. "But tonight we are the only actors upon this grassy stage."

The audience of severed stone heads eyed them imperiously.

Romeo had prepared a blanket and a basket of treats, but Rosaline found that she was not hungry. This place that had delighted and intrigued her, now unsettled her. The scent of the cedars and the far-off waterfall made her recall the incense and steady drip of the crypt. And yet, when Romeo leaned in and kissed her, his warm fingers in her hair, she was lost to him again. With him she became lighter than a dandelion seed. There was nothing but him. His breath that tasted of honeyed wine. She only wanted to lie here under the trees and kiss him and talk, but Romeo had insistent fingers.

"Let us speak awhile. Or tell me a story."

He grinned. "I shall tell you a story of Romeo and his Rosaline."

Romeo pressed against her and she tried to wriggle away but found she could not. Her body did not move as she asked it to. She found that she lay perfectly still and watched herself along with the statues that gazed down at them, unblinking. She allowed him to unfasten her dress and lie her naked upon the blanket. He lay heavily upon her, and it pained her, but she could not confess her dislike to him, for he might laugh and think her fears childish. Instead, she found herself pretending a joy she did not feel.

Afterwards, as they sat wrapped in blankets, sipping glasses of Vin Santo, Rosaline took the bag of coins and presented them to him, flushed with pride, eager to see how pleased he would be.

"My lady? You did it?" he said, lacing her fingers in his and kissing her knuckles.

She nodded, pleased.

He embraced her so that she fell back upon the blanket, spilling the wine. "How I love you," he declared.

She laughed, pushing him back. Sitting up, he opened the bag and scrutinized the contents, his smile and good cheer fading like the light at dusk.

"'Tis all here? These thirty ducats are everything?"

Rosaline frowned. "The chest had little in it, my love. If I had taken more, my father would have known the theft at once."

"It's no matter. You must simply try again."

"No!" Her voice came out shrill and loud in the still night air.

Romeo stared at her, taken aback by her vehemence. "Hush. If you won't, I shan't make you. I only wish you would try again. It is a terrible shame and we will suffer in Mantua with so little. But if you say this is your best, I must believe you."

Rosaline's veins were full of beetles scurrying through her. She was not angry—that would not be fair. Romeo simply did not understand what the theft had cost her of herself.

A breeze started and shivered the larches like coming rain. The statues stared down at her piteously. She wished they'd look away and turned her back upon them. If this was how it was to be a player upon the stage, she did not like it, even if the audience was silent and lacked all applause.

"I can't."

"Here," said Romeo, filling her glass again. "It is true my father summoned me to the country villa, but I also wanted us to be here, in this garden where I first saw your face. I have news. My old friend the friar will return to Verona and marry us tomorrow night."

She looked back at him in joy and rapture, all doubt and fears blown to the wind.

"In a day's time we'll be in Mantua. We two," he said.

"And Caterina," said Rosaline, although she knew he would not have forgotten.

"As you wish. All as you wish," he said, capturing her fingers.

At once all was well again. The statues were benevolent, not nightmares but strange dreams. These gods and goddesses would bestow their blessing and favor upon their outlawed love.

Rosaline lay hidden beneath the sacks once more for the journey back into the city. The groom was displeased. It was later than she'd intended when she returned to the spot, and the first hint of dawn was already in the sky. He offered no rebuke, but she could see that he was frightened. She felt too happy for fear. She was a leaf borne upon the air, ready to slide into the woods and join Titania's company. All thoughts were crowded from her brain unless they were of Romeo. She was restless, all pins. Exhaustion suffused her limbs, but despite the steady jolt of the wagon, she could not sleep. Why would she dream when she could consider the perfection of him?

They would meet in the crypt tomorrow night at eleven. And then, they would away to Mantua. He had friends there.

She must not think of her own friends. Of Juliet and Tybalt

or Livia. She must not think of what would be lost, only what was to be gained. And yet, seeping through her delight, she found that she wept a little as she considered those faces. She loved Romeo but she loved them too. She was so tired, she ached. Above her, greylag geese honked as they flew, the light igniting their wings, turning them for a moment into a flock of Icaruses.

There could not be a beginning without an end. She hoped her friends would not hate her.

"We're at the city gates," called the groom. "You must hide yourself now, mistress."

She pulled up the sacking, listening to the rapid beat of her heart. Soon the cart stopped and she lay still, waiting. Even through the gaps in the hessian weave she could see that it was nearly light.

"Come, quickly now. Through the side gate. Caterina is waiting."

Rosaline climbed down, the groom taking her hand, glancing over his shoulder anxiously. The streets were still empty save for a rat, who eyed her from the gutter. She thrust some coins into the groom's pocket, thanking him hurriedly, and raced down the cobbled passage at the side of the building.

The watchman wasn't at his post; instead, in the half-light she could see that a woman waited for her there. Caterina. At once her nerves eased and she let out a breath she didn't know she'd been holding. Yet, as she drew closer, she saw the woman was smaller than Caterina, slighter too. Almost a child except for the noticeable swell of her stomach.

Rosaline stopped quickly, drew back again.

"Please, mistress," called the girl. "I've waited here for you so long. I beg you, do not turn and go!"

Rosaline hesitated. The child's voice held a note of desperation. Even in the shadow, she didn't look more than eleven or twelve, although it was possible she was older. Her face was thin and pinched. The massive swell of her stomach looked painful and unnatural on a girl so young. Rosaline approached her, reluctant and unsure.

"It isn't me who you want," she said. "I can take you to the kitchen. Someone there will find you a proper meal."

The girl looked steadily at Rosaline. She had the same wide blue eyes as Juliet. "You are Rosaline Capulet?"

Rosaline nodded.

"Then, madam, it is you who I came to see. You are to be Romeo Montague's wife. Or so he promised you?"

Rosaline stared at her in astonishment. How was it possible that this child knew her secret?

"I was a maid in the Montague house. But do not worry. I know when to talk and when to say nothing."

"But what do you want with me? Money to keep my secret?" asked Rosaline, her tone rough with panic.

"No," said the girl, with a vehement shake of her head. "Please don't be afraid. Not of me. I come to beg your help. Him and me"—she stroked the enormous protrusion of her belly— "well, this is Romeo Montague's child."

Rosaline shrunk back against the stone of the passage. "I

don't believe you," she said. Her blood roared in her ears. She tried to push past the girl, but she stood squarely in her path and continued to talk.

"He told me he loved me. O, mistress. He said so many words that were nothing but breath. That he never saw true beauty till he saw me. That the moment we met was marked out by fate. Or was it Venus? I forget." She gave a tiny, sad laugh. "It no longer seems important. He swore that we would marry and that we'd away to Mantua. He had a friar, you see, an old friend who would marry us and who would not balk at either my youth or my lowly station. But then, he kept delaying. The friar was away. We could not marry in the midst of the summer fever. And then the plague came. But you see, good mistress, in truth I feared his interest waned. He did not like that I was with child. He liked me better when I was thin and small."

Rosaline stared at the girl in shock and revulsion. She closed her eyes and blinked them, hoping that when she opened them again, the maid would have dissipated in the wind like some foul odor or fairy, but no, there she was still speaking, disgorging her filth about Romeo.

"He brought all sorts of remedies to get rid of the child, but I wouldn't take them and he grew angry with me." She shook her head. "I didn't want to be rid of it. This"—she stroked her bulge again—"is a baby. I have no family but him. And then Romeo met you. Loved you. I was nothing to him anymore. Discarded. Broken crockery upon the kitchen shit heap."

At last Rosaline could bear it no longer. "Stop! It isn't true!

Nothing you say is true!" Rosaline stamped her foot and put her hands over her ears. She would not listen to another word. It was spite and nonsense. The girl was out for money, that was all. Some act of petty cruelty, fueled by bitterness—why, she did not know. Perhaps Romeo's beauty fueled such madness. She would not listen, she would not.

The girl stood there, still and pale, and did not move aside, only waited and stared at her with those too-blue eyes. "I am sorry. I see that you love him. As I did once." Her voice was full of pity.

How dare this unfortunate, wretched thing, pity her? Rosaline stared back at her, willing herself not to cry. "What do you want from me?"

"I wanted to look at you. To see who it was he loved now. And to warn you, even though truly I always knew you would not listen. I wouldn't have listened either. When he loves you, the world is full of goodness. I was alone, without a friend, and then I had him. He wanted me, grub that I am. He's too delightful. Like mead on a summer's night or them marzipan flowers he brings."

Rosaline swallowed. The girl had researched her lie well. She felt hot and cold, like a fever was breaking. A sheen of sweat was upon her brow like dew.

Still the girl did not move aside.

"Why do you not go?" said Rosaline with a cry of exasperation.

For the first time, the girl looked awkward, glanced down at the ground. "I need coin. Each time I see him, he whispers to me that I should die for shame at my situation. But I don't want to die, Mistress Rosaline. I am not ashamed. If I die when bringing this child into the world, then that's God's will and so be it, but I shall not perish by my own hand." She reached out to Rosaline. "Will you help me?"

Rosaline looked down at the small hand gripping hers, the coarse skin rubbed and raw from rough work. She unpeeled the fingers from her own. "It's not true. None of it is true. I won't believe it."

The girl nodded. "I wasn't the first, you know," she said after a moment.

"You know?" demanded Rosaline scornfully. "Or you heard a rumor?"

The girl hesitated, swallowed, and Rosaline experienced a tiny flutter of triumph.

"Whispers," she conceded at last. "Rustling in the rafters like the *scratch-scratch* of mice when you're trying to sleep."

Rosaline folded her arms and shook her head. She would not believe a single word.

"Mantua. That's where he took one of them. Or so I heard. Far from Verona so the whispers stayed away from the prince and his friends." The girl swallowed. "She vanished. Ashes into the wind."

"Enough! Fie! Get away from me!"

At this the girl stepped aside so that at last Rosaline could pass her, but not without knocking against her hard, distended belly.

Rosaline rushed along the passageway feeling the girl stare, afraid to turn around. She clattered the door to the courtyard in her haste to get away. *I must seal her on the other side. Lock the girl and her lies in the passageway.* She half expected the handle to turn and for the child with her massive belly to push her way inside.

But all was still in the courtyard. Only Caterina was waiting for her on the far side, pacing in silent fury. "You're late! And now you make a noise? Your father will rise soon. You risk us all. Quickly now."

Shaken and dismayed, Rosaline said nothing as Caterina led her swiftly up the backstairs and into the peace of her chamber. When she was sitting on her bed, the maid began to ply her with questions. "What happened? You look pale. Did you quarrel?"

"No. We're to be married tomorrow. Nay, this very night."

Caterina frowned and turned her face toward her, examining her closely. "Then why aren't you painted with delight?"

Rosaline hesitated. She said nothing of the child. It was all falsehoods. There was no need to repeat the slander. The girl had admitted she wanted money. It was a trick, that's all. She wondered again how old the girl was.

With almost physical effort, she shoved the thought of the child from her mind. "I am happy. I have been up all night and I'm tired."

"Well, sleep a little. I shall be along soon to wake you again." Caterina stroked her cheek and tucked her into bed.

After she'd gone, Rosaline lay awake, whispering to herself again and again like a shibboleth: *Lies, 'tis all a lie.*

Too late, she realized she'd not even asked the girl her name.

Rosaline chewed her finger and did not sleep. *Mantua.* The word had become a prayer to her. The place where she and Romeo would be together and happy. She did not like that the servant girl had spoken its name and violated its sanctity. It was as if she had uttered a secret of Rosaline's own heart and transformed it into something darker. Everything the girl had said was a lie, and yet Rosaline needed confirmation.

If the truth lay hidden in Mantua, then Rosaline must find it.

She dressed herself and, as soon as she heard the noise of her father rising and descending the stair, hurried down to speak with him.

He was busy with his morning devotions and looked up in surprise.

"I want to go Mantua. To visit the convent at Sant'Orsola. If I'm to be sent there, I wish to see the place that is to be my home before I go there to live."

He surveyed her for a moment and then nodded, gratified. "Very well. We shall go tomorrow morning."

"No!" Rosaline forced herself to smile. "I should very much like to go today, if it might please you, Father. May I join your morning prayers?"

Her father stared at her for a long moment, uncertain if she was teasing him, and then seeing that her expression was sincere, gestured for her to join him, pleased. "You may. While we pray, we'll see to it that your belongings are loaded into the cart." He rang a bell. "Have the servants bring Rosaline's things"—he turned to his daughter—"we may as well have them ready your cell for arrival in a few days." He called out to the servants. "We leave for Mantua after the morning meal. We return tonight."

Fear began to spike inside Rosaline—what if her father decided he must take some of the ducats for her nun's dowry with him too and discovered he'd been robbed? Dread swelled into a drumming pain behind her left eye. Yet no servant came to whisper in her father's ear, and no sudden shouts or accusations from him disturbed the sunshine of the morning. Still, the guilt at what she had done would not go. This was not a sin that she could rid herself from in confession.

She wanted to return the coins to the chest, but she'd given them to Romeo.

When the packing was complete, Rosaline was handed up into the wagon beside her father. She sat beside him, her hands clenched in her lap, nails white, her veil drawn low over her face, hiding the dark shadows rubbed beneath her eyes. For once she did not need to be told to stop chattering.

In four days, if I take the convent wall or I elope to Mantua, I shall not see Verona again.

Every glimpse of the city became precious. The stink of the fish market. The stone bridges spanning the broad river with the boats dawdling beneath, the wash of mudflats.

Rosaline hoped that at the convent she would find out that there was no truth at all to the servant girl's story. The convent might be outside the city, but words were breath and, like drafts, still found the gaps between stones and permeated walls. If a girl came to Mantua from Verona and disappeared, surely even the nuns would hear of it. They were not so far removed from the world. The servant girl had spoken of "whispers," but what did that really mean? They were nothing more than rumors, which made no more sense than the rustling of leaves and were as unstoppable. The maid's sad story had nothing to do with her Romeo; it was another man who'd disgraced and abandoned her. And yet, if Rosaline believed that with such certainty, why was she journeying to the convent to chase down gossip on one of her last days of freedom?

Rosaline began to feel dizzy and sick. She closed her eyes, and the rattle and squeal of the wheels became grinding finger-nails scraping inside her skull.

After nearly two hours, they came to the convent. Masetto shook his daughter awake. The pain in her head was pulsing with light, and her tongue felt thick and strange. The horse pulled them through the gates, hooves echoing on the cobbles. Here at least it was cool, the walled convent a rocky fortress perched at the top of the hill. Rosaline had not visited it since her aunts had died many years before. When she'd been a child, the place had seemed vast, and even now it brooded above the town, snooping on the wayward souls below.

Father and daughter crossed the cobbles to the door of
the convent, where a female servant let them into the *parlatorio*. Masetto explained to the servant that Rosaline wished to
see the abbey that was to be her home and asked her to bring
Rosaline to the abbess. The visiting room was whitewashed,
with a single wooden crucifix on the wall and a bowl of oranges
laid upon a table. The oranges were too bright. A bowl of suns
in a bleached room. Rosaline's head throbbed. The servant disappeared through a low side door.

A low bench was set before the grated window into the convent, above the barrel of the *ruota*, which Rosaline recalled being
stuffed into as a child. After a few minutes, the servant returned.

"Please wait here," said the servant to Masetto with a little
bow. "Rosaline is to come with me."

"I've business in Mantua." Masetto kissed Rosaline's cheek.
"I'll return for you later in the afternoon."

For the first time, Rosaline watched him leave with reluctance and then followed the servant through the door and into
the secret heart of the convent. No one was usually allowed
inside, but she supposed since she was soon to join the order—or
so they believed—it was permitted.

The ache in her head was affecting her vision. The place
was all light and shadows and pools of color, red and black and
green. She lurched from side to side as if aboard a ship, and the
servant reached out to steady her, but then it wasn't the servant
but the abbess herself. She felt so sick now that she hoped she
didn't vomit on the good mother's robes.

"Come, child, sit. No, here, out in the air."

Rosaline found herself led out into the cloisters. A fresh breeze blew, scented with rosemary and pine. She had not expected so much light, only cold stone and darkness.

"You are in pain," said the abbess. "Which side of your head? The temple?"

Rosaline nodded but found that sent showering sparks firing from her eye. She rubbed it but the pain wouldn't dissipate. The abbess murmured something to another nun. Time blurred and stuttered. There was only the hurting and the light and the white sails of the clouds against the tossing blue sky. A vial was pressed into her hands.

"Drink," said the abbess gently. "A draft to make it better."

"What is it?" asked Rosaline, half afraid.

"Herbs. We are herbalists. You must drink it all at once and then sleep a little. We'll talk after. It doesn't taste pleasant."

Rosaline sipped. She shuddered. It was bitter and yet the smell was aromatic. She swallowed the rest in a gulp, too tired to disobey. There were questions she needed to ask, but exhaustion and a desperate need to sleep overwhelmed her. Tender hands drew her onto the green lawn, where a rug had been laid out for her beneath a yew tree. Softly, the abbess herself tucked her in. She had hands like Emelia. Someone loosened the tight knot of her hair and fanned it out and smoothed another blanket around her. She slept.

Rosaline did not know for how long she lay beneath the yew in a dreamless sleep, but when she opened her eyes, the pain and

sickness had gone. The light had altered from the fierce brightness of morning to the buttered glow of afternoon.

She sat up and found that she was alone on the lawn in the
cloisters. Beyond, where the grass sloped away, lay the town and
countryside far below. She was sailing above the world. The tiny
strips of field below were dappled with sunflowers that from here
appeared as a burnished mass of gold leaf, stitched together with
rows of vineyards. The orange roofs of the town caught in the
sun, glowing like embers. An *aquilone*, eagle, surfed on the air's
high currents, wings taut, intent upon murder.

The abbess walked across the cloisters, shading her eyes,
coming to sit beside Rosaline on the rug. "You are better now,
Rosaline?"

"Yes."

Rosaline felt a lightness to her. The pain had gone and left air
in its place. A novice brought out fruit, bread, and cheese, and laid
it on a cloth. No meat. Rosaline realized that along with the sound
of the wind, she could hear music. Women's voices. She guessed
from the hour they must be singing Sext or even None. And it was
not merely singing she could hear but a lute, a viol, and perhaps
even a flute, and the deep notes of a *contra basso* viola? And while
she could not distinguish the words, there was a melody—and
harmony. With a thrill, Rosaline understood this was not plainsong but real music. She was not entirely convinced it was holy.

"But Rome has banned all music in our churches!"

"But we are not in a church; we're in a garden. And Rome is
so very far away." The abbess gave a tiny smile.

As she looked about her, Rosaline decided that the convent was not what she'd expected. It was like a cobnut: its dark hard shell belied the sweetness of its white interior. "What do you do here?"

The abbess laughed. "We're nuns, Rosaline. We're dedicated to the service of God. But God can be served in many ways. And as your father will pay handsomely for your keep, that will free you from many duties. You shan't need to rise in the night to observe Matins."

Rosaline studied the abbess of Sant'Orsola. She was clearly a holy woman of wisdom but also, it appeared, of mischief. In appearance she reminded her tenderly of her mother and aunts: her countenance had the same dark golden hue and brown eyes.

Next the abbess gestured to the orchards of plum and medlar trees, and to the low walls leading into a series of connected garden rooms. In the first, several nuns were tending the earth with hoes and harvesting seeds. "As well as our devotions, we're excellent gardeners. We grow the herbs ourselves in the physic garden that we grind for our remedies. Women from all over Mantua and as far as Venice come to us to seek advice for their ailments."

"Remarkable as your skills are, Abbess, and truly I am grateful, I don't want to grind pastes from snail shells and mustard seed for the sick in the name of the Lord."

Rosaline looked up at the abbess, who suppressed a smile. The starkness of her nun's habit made her appear almost ageless. "I teach the novices to write myself. Every abbess for a thousand years has kept a chronicle of our history and our order."

"A history of women and nuns? But who would read such a work?"

The abbess laughed. "We do. We prefer our own history to that of men's."

Rosaline was certain that if her father had known the unusual character of the abbess, he would have insisted upon her being sent to one of the strict Franciscan orders in Mantua, or even to Venice.

The convent might not have been what she was expecting but, she reminded herself, this was not why she had come. She licked dry lips and glanced sidelong at the abbess. "I heard whispers that a girl came to Mantua from Verona and disappeared," she said.

The abbess frowned and stiffened. "I do not listen to whispers or gossip. There is more wisdom in the burbling of a brook."

"So no girl came?" pressed Rosaline.

"No, I said I do not listen to gossip. Girls come to Mantua every week from Verona and from all over the Venetian Republic, hoping to find something better. Perhaps some do find it. But most do not. They don't disappear, Rosaline—they're swallowed whole. Gobbled down. They don't *want* to be found."

At this, the abbess rose with a sigh, ending the conversation.

Relief washed over Rosaline. The rumors the servant girl had heard were likely nothing but devil's talk. Unfortunate girls chose to run away. Their vanishing did not have anything to do with Romeo.

As she considered her journey there, she felt prickly with resentment at the servant girl's accusation and innuendo.

The abbess proffered her hand to Rosaline, which she took

with surprise. She knew that nuns were forbidden from any physical contact even with one another. Their cells were single for a
reason.

They walked on a little while and entered a stone building
that housed the dormitory with its individual cells, some cramped
and tiny, and others richly frescoed. The Abbess paused outside
the door to a cell, then pushed it open to reveal the brightly pat-
terned Ottoman rug from Rosaline's father's house laid upon the
floor, a tapestry of a hunting scene with a mauled stag pinned
upon the wall. A few of Rosaline's books—she'd only packed
her least precious but had needed to pack a few so as not to rouse
suspicion—had now been laid out upon the single table beside a
candleholder. A feathered plume of lavender was set in a small
jug to try and disguise the cold smell of damp and stone. There
was a square window with the view out across the landscape,
high above the world. On the wall, a fresco of a wounded Christ
wept bloody tears, showing his butchered wrists.

Rosaline appreciated the nuns' kindness and understood
they wished for her to be happy. Yet for all its comfort, this was
still a small, solitary room that would be cold in winter.

Rosaline emerged from the dormitory like a swimmer
coming up for air and inhaled deeply the scent of fennel and
scythed grass in the physic garden. High walls sheltered the more
delicate plants from wind and frost, and chickens pecked at grit
around her feet.

Rosaline was relieved that she had found nothing there.
Soon she would be in the arms of her Romeo.

As the abbess continued on the obligatory convent tour past the chicken house, orchards, the bright, high-windowed refectory, the attics full of silkworm hutches, the library, the physic garden, Rosaline said little, offering only a few words of admiration. Each nun they passed eyed her with benign curiosity before hurrying about her business.

The abbess showed her into the rather dank chapel. As Rosaline glanced about, she noted vaguely that all the saints worshipped there were women. There were no Peters nor Pauls nor Josephs in this place. There were unusual carvings and frescos before each altar of the saints. Rosaline examined a fresco dedicated to the Virgin. Then, she moved on to another: a carmine and gold fresco of Saint Anne. There were scraps of parchment on the altar, and Rosaline picked several up and read them, realizing they were scribbled prayers from expectant mothers and their friends imploring Anne to keep them safe in childbed. A constellation of candles flickered in the gloom around Saint Anne's altarpiece, while rags of ribbon and offerings of nosegays were tied to the wooden altar rail.

At the next side chapel, she saw that here was Saint Katherine, patron saint of single women and, Rosaline supposed, of nuns.

"I shall leave you here," said the abbess. "One of the sisters will bring you tea and cakes, and then you can return to your father."

Rosaline thanked her and made her farewells. She left the chapel and sat on a bench in the garden beside the low hedges of fennel and lavender, listening to thrum of the bees. At the far end of the garden, among tangles of red campion and cornflowers, stood a trio of beehives, like bishop's miters. Rosaline watched, intrigued, as a nervous and unhappy nun wielded a smoking plate that, from its foul stench, she guessed to be smoldering cow dung. The young nun was coughing, her eyes streaming as she edged closer to the hives at the urging of another nun. The nuns wore over their habits mesh visors, leather aprons, and long leather gloves. Rosaline watched with fascination, craning forward to see better. The novice held the smoke as close as she dared, while the other opened the top of one of the hives and slowly eased out a sticky rack that dripped with golden wax and honey. Bees coated her leather gloves, but she didn't flinch and simply placed the rack on a waiting tray, allowing yellow honey to ooze out. Yet a bee must have stung the novice, or else slid inside her habit, and as she began to panic, she screamed and flapped and waved her arms. The other nun shouted to her to calm herself, but it was too late. The dung was no longer enough to soothe the bees, and they filed out of the hive in a black cloud so that in a minute they filled the sky like smoke, obscuring the sun. A growl of thunder rolled around the garden, and Rosaline realized it was the reverberation of the now-furious swarm.

She turned and ran inside the convent, retreating farther and farther for safety, the panicked cries of the two nuns fading behind her. After a few minutes, she found herself alone in the corridor leading to the dormitories. Here it was deserted and still. She walked past the cell that was to be hers, but feeling no desire to enter it again, continued to walk. As she moved along the dormitory, the cells became more cramped and dark, and a dank smell began to grow.

Rosaline slowed and peered into a narrow room. The bed was neatly made up, a palm cross on one wall, a spare habit hanging on a nail like a ghost. Turning away with a slight shudder, she noticed that the door of the cell opposite was ajar, revealing a stripped cot in a cell so narrow that when Rosaline ventured inside and held out her arms, her fingers brushed the damp stone walls on either side.

Curious, she looked around. A few books were placed upon a pine table: a book of hours, a Bible with an embossed blue leather cover. They'd all been neatly dusted. She traced the coat of arms on the Bible with her finger as she picked it up. Idly, she flicked it open.

"This cell belonged to one of the lost girls," said the abbess in a low voice, appearing behind her.

Rosaline jumped and closed the bible. "Where is she now?" she asked. "Did she leave?"

"She died." The abbess hesitated for a moment before continuing. "That's why the cell is empty. No one came to claim her things. We'll move them when the cell is needed, but no one wants to sleep here. It's too sad."

"What happened?" asked Rosaline.

"We found her huddled outside the gates one morning. Some friend must have helped her up here. She was very sick. She couldn't speak. We only ever discovered her Christian name written in her Bible. She wasted away and died."

Rosaline glanced down at the small blue Bible still in her hands and opened its front cover. *For Cecilia* was inked on the frontispiece. She looked up and sighed, studying the sad little cell, trying to imagine what suffering and struggle had forced Cecilia to come here. The walls seemed to press inward. This girl did not have a father to bestow a gift upon the convent. Yet the narrow window still displayed the same magnificent view, and a shaft of light fell into the small chamber, brightening it. She hoped it had offered her some little respite.

"I believe Cecilia was from Verona, like you. Her clothes were in the city style," said the abbess.

"What did she die from?"

"She'd suffered a kind of palsy that weakened her faculties and made her lose the power of speech. It was very sad. It did not kill her…or not at once… She withered before she died. I fear we weren't the first to try to cure her. She reacted with terror to any draft we gave her."

Rosaline frowned a little. "Who do you think might have tried to help her?"

The abbess shrugged. "I cannot be sure. The brother friars perhaps. They also believe they know the meaning and uses of plants, but in the wrong hands, they can make the body sicker. We dedicate ourselves to plants and how they affect the humors. We are experts here—she is known as 'Mother' Nature after all—and such things are the business of women."

Rosaline noticed a set of wooden rosary beads, polished by the dead girl's dead fingers, on the table beside the book of hours.

This was the sum of a life. She turned to leave. Then, she saw a small paper box upon the nightstand. She reached out and took it, unfolding the paper flaps.

Inside was a crimson marzipan rose. The petals were faded and the sugar had crystallized like frost. No, it wasn't possible. How could Cecilia have the same rose as Rosaline, only withered in age? Rosaline felt the pain above her eye pulse and quiver once more.

Cecilia had treasured this rose, had never been tempted to eat it, opening the box to admire it and then closing the lid again, secreting it among her meager possessions.

She knew that Cecilia had done this, for Rosaline had done the same each night, picturing Romeo's face as she did so.

Rosaline's breath became ragged and strange. Her skin felt cold and her palms clammy. She possessed a rose that was almost the same, hidden in a matching paper box beside her bed, bearing the identical crimson stamp of the Verona confectioner. She closed her eyes and heard Romeo's words: *I had it made especially for you... The confectioner promised me he'd never make another.* What else was it he'd said? *Every rose in nature is unique. Just like you.* Only it seemed it wasn't unique. Here was another in a dead girl's room.

Was it possible that Romeo had given it to her? This other girl from Verona? Rosaline shuddered and felt queasy, as though she'd gorged herself on too many sweets. But it wasn't sugar that was making her feel ill; it was the possibility that Romeo had lied. It was such a small thing, a flower of almond paste and sugar, rolled and shaped, and the lie equally tiny, hardly bigger than the rose. She could crush it to dust between her fingers.

Rosaline feared that Romeo *had* lied, one way or another. Either the sweet was not unique at all and they were being purchased by suitors all over Verona, or there was the darker possibility that only Romeo Montague commissioned them, and it was his practice to present a sugar flower to his lovers, every rose in a different shade of red.

And that he had been Cecilia's lover before she had come here, faded, and died.

If Cecilia had been Romeo's lover, then *had* the servant girl too? Was the child in her belly really his? The heavy, sick feeling inside Rosaline grew. She had wondered if she was the first girl he'd loved, but he'd sworn that she was the one he loved the best. She was his bright angel, his heart's dear love. No woman mattered before her. Their love was peerless and extraordinary, inscribed upon the heavens and witnessed by Venus. Now she began to fret again that his words came too easily, well-practiced and shaped by his lips into sounds that aped love, as the confectioner molded paste into a bloom that mimicked life.

She held the flower aloft on her palm, but now it looked fragile and grubby. The dye had spoiled and run. Two of the petals had snapped.

"Are you feeling well?" asked the abbess. "You're pale again. It's this room and its sad history." She opened the door. "Come, let's go out of here. We must not dwell on melancholy things."

The pulse above her eye ticked. Romeo loved her. She

yearned for his love as for air to breathe. Without him, she must become invisible once more. He was a good man for all that he was a Montague. He would never have abandoned a young girl with a child in her belly. Cecilia had been broken by some other man, perhaps one she'd met here in Mantua. Rosaline was mistaken. She had to be. She'd chosen to love and to be loved. These doubts were merely the effect of shadows playing upon an unquiet mind made uneasy by lies a servant girl had told her.

She breathed in deeply and tried to calm herself as they walked back through the physic gardens. Music drifted out from the chapel, catching on the wind and floating out above the town below. The hives now sat quiet and peaceful among the wildflowers, while the same two nuns as earlier, apparently unharmed, labeled jars of honey.

Rosaline glanced down and saw that she grasped Cecilia's Bible in her trembling hands. She felt reluctant to relinquish it. "May I keep it? I'll pray for her."

The abbess gave a sad smile. "Yes. I would like that. And so would Cecilia."

They walked on for a moment in silence.

"We are content here," said the abbess softly, pausing. "I think you could be too. If gardening, beekeeping, or healing isn't your choice, then I think perhaps music? Or you might assist me in writing our history."

Rosaline sighed. The convent was brighter than she'd expected and the abbess intrigued her, yet still she could not see herself living here. "I can see you're happy and I'm glad. But a prison, however prettily furnished, is still cage." She shook her head. "I don't want to be kept behind a wall. I want to be seen. I want love."

"There's the love of God. The love of your sisters."

"I don't have any sisters."

The abbess examined her face for a moment but said nothing further.

VII

The sweetest honey is loathsome in its own deliciousness

Masetto tried to question his daughter on the journey back to Verona. How did Rosaline find the convent? Was her cell prettily furnished? She answered him with grunts and monosyllables, and to her relief he soon gave up. Her wedding to Romeo was to take place that night, and yet she was not filled with bridal joy and blissful anticipation. She was tormented with thoughts of Cecilia, a girl she'd never met, and the young servant with the swollen belly. Had Cecilia been with child too? Had a friar tried not to heal her but to make her sicker out of some malevolency? Rosaline's mind churned with unhappy possibilities as the horses pulled eagerly, refreshed. It was late afternoon and there were mere hours until the wedding. Soon she must meet Romeo.

He would soothe her disquiet. She longed for him to persuade her that she was mistaken. There was another truth. There had to be.

Rosaline informed her father that she wished to go to confession at St. Peter's, that the abbess had suggested she seek to cleanse her soul before admission to the convent. The lie flowed easily as water from a jug. Masetto rapidly consented, pleased and gratified by his daughter's seeming newfound piety.

Rosaline left the house shortly before dusk. As she hurried through the streets, she drew her veil tightly across her face.

The white stone tuff of the basilica of St. Peter's appeared to glow in the evening light like bones. Rosaline glanced up at the rose window in the upper façade above the door. It was split into segments with a pithy, gleaming sun at its heart and small figures of men pinioned at quarter hours along the vast turning wheel of fate.

She had walked beneath this image of the wheel a thousand times and paid it no heed, but now, as she stared up at it, Rosaline wondered where upon fortune's wheel she was fixed. Was she the happy soul, hoisted just before the midnight hour, about to marry and enjoy fate's happy gifts? Or was the wheel turning and she already spinning, poised to fall?

Despite the warmth of the evening, the cathedral was cold, smelling of age and damp. It took her eyes a moment to adjust to the gloom. She walked quickly through the nave where mass was being uttered, and the air was thick with prayer, descending the steps into the chapel crypt. Here, it was darker still, the only light coming from the torches strapped in their sconces and spitting wax. The walls were slime-slick, spinach green. At the front of the chapel, beside the altar, lingered Romeo. She'd entered softly in her lambskin slippers, and he did not notice her.

Although she'd arrived with a ball of tears clogged in her throat and brimful of questions and fears, on seeing him her breath caught. This kind of beauty in a man was rare indeed. At once she ached for him to talk away her doubts. Surely such a handsome visage outside could not belie a rotten core within? His eyes were as fair as they were honest, his lips as red and perfectly arched as his kisses were sweet; the words those lips spoke must be true. God would not be so cruel to make it otherwise.

As Romeo saw her, his entire countenance brightened with delight. Her stomach twisted. Her body was not her own. She was a marionette on strings ordered by forces of love and desire. Hardly knowing what she did, she hurled herself into his embrace. He gripped her fast within the cage of his arms until she heard her joints crack. As he leaned down toward her, she kissed him back, shoving down all thoughts except those of him.

After a few minutes he pulled away, resting his chin on the top of her head. She inhaled the scent of him. Leather and sweat and cedarwood. Rosaline swallowed and felt the world rush in upon her once more.

Let it be, Ros.

She did not have to give voice to this tiny niggle of doubt. She could drink in his adoration and marry him and all would be well.

Licking dry lips, Rosaline toyed with the fabric of her sleeve, tugged at a stray thread. Above them, the goddess Fortuna spun her wheel. She glanced up at him. Met his black eyes.

Say nothing. Say nothing.

"A girl came to see me," she said. "A servant. Not much more than a child. And fat with child herself."

Romeo frowned, impatient. "What's this to do with us?"

"She said the baby was yours."

He pulled back and looked at her. "And you believed her?" he asked, incredulous and hurt.

Rosaline hesitated and then shook her head, her cheeks hot. She chewed her lip in confusion. "No, I thought she lied. She wanted money."

"Then there's your answer," said Romeo. "Why then bring this to me on what is supposed to be our wedding night?" His voice rose with indignation.

Why indeed? His face was grave, and yet despite the roiling inside her, Rosaline could not stop. She studied the ancient floor of foot-worn gravestones, the names rubbed bare. "The girl says she worked in the Montague household here in Verona."

"And what is her name?" His voice was a hiss of steam.

Rosaline studied the floor. "I didn't ask."

All color drained from Romeo's face as he recoiled from her. He looked as white as the marble effigies in the crypt. "A girl whose name you don't know told you lies about me, the man you profess to love, and it appears to me—despite your protestations—that you believed her!"

"I did not. I pitied her and her situation, but I thought she lied."

At first she had indeed thought the girl had lied. Now, she

was not sure. Yet whether it was true or not, as she looked upon his face—the imperious tilt of his chin, the perfect turn of his throat—Rosaline wanted to plead his forgiveness, to rub her cheek against his, to suck his thumb. Yet somehow, still she could not stop. Something made her hesitate and keep asking questions even as his lips tightened with dismay and he stared at her through thick lashes, bewildered and wounded.

Glancing down, she noticed that her hands were shaking. She placed them behind her back so he would not see. "At the abbey, I saw the cell of a dead girl who'd died for love. She pined away." Rosaline swallowed. "She had a marzipan flower. Like the one you gave me." Her words tumbled out in a muddled torrent.

Romeo shook his head, puzzled. "So? Another girl at a convent was given a sweetmeat?"

She could see how much her words hurt him. They were arrow tips.

"It was made in Verona. The box bore the city mark, and you told me the confectioner never made them for anyone else." Even as she spoke, the charge sounded thin and absurd. A girlish accusation.

"He doesn't, Ros, but who's to say that another won't? I haven't spoken to every confectioner in the city."

His words were tempting and plausible. She yearned to accept to them. The friar would be there soon. But she could not push away the thought of the child's swollen stomach. Nor the stillness of the dead girl's abbey cell. Rosaline believed that Romeo loved her, and she adored him—the very thought of him was honey—and yet a voice needled her: *How many others has he loved before me? One? Two? Ten?* And then, the voice hissed louder: *How long until he discards me like them?*

Reaching out, she took his hand, traced her fingers along his knuckles, the skin worn and calloused, chaffed and rubbed from the leather of his horse's reins. Each piece of him was precious to her. She could trace his habits upon his skin and their shared history upon her own body.

"My love, will you swear to me that you never gave another girl a marzipan rose? And that the servant girl's child is not yours?"

Romeo stared at her, his eyes round with hurt. "Do you not love me and trust in our love?" He took her chin in his hands. "I want to marry you. Rosaline, you are to me as moon is to night."

He gazed at her with frank sincerity. She felt as if she had kicked him, and mingling with her guilt, she felt a flutter of relief. Of course he was a good man. He had wooed her gently, not demanding so much as a kiss until she was ready to offer it. They were two souls who had put the enmity of their families aside to unite in love. She was about to plead his forgiveness when, turning to look at her, he spoke again, his voice brimming with regret.

"I would wed you this very minute, but the friar has been delayed."

"What reason did he give?"

"The dead, the dead. This foul plague."

Rosaline knew she ought to be full of understanding, but

once again fears began to tug at her. Romeo seemed to sense them. "He will be here tomorrow to marry us," he said, "and then we will away to Mantua and our new lives, little mouse. Delay only makes appetites more keen, my love."

"Will this delay be forever? After all, you've had your satisfaction," said Rosaline, her doubts blooming once again. Had Romeo ever intended to marry her, or had it all been part of his practiced maneuvering? He was full of promises but had never given her anything more than a candied sweet or a sip of wine— which had made her head swim and his words easier to swallow down. "Your vows are nothing but breath and air," she said.

Romeo stared at her aghast. "How could you utter such a thing? Or even think it?" He reached into his pocket and pulled out a box and held it out to her. "Here, I was going to wait until our wedding, but take it now."

He thrust at her the small wooden box. She opened it and saw inside a gold ring, set with a fat, bright emerald.

Her mother's jewel.

There was a knot of joy tangled in her throat. She gave the box back to him. "No, you keep it safely and give it to me when you slide it on my finger."

He kissed her again. "You're mine," he whispered. "Our love is inscribed in the heavens above. We swore our oaths to one another; I'll see to it that they are not broken in this life nor the next."

He smiled at her with tenderness and love, leaning back against one of the cabinets of reliquaries, stuffed with its fragments of dead men. The air was heavy with the scent of incense and death.

Rosaline was cold. She glanced across at the statue of the eternally sleeping Montague maiden. For once, she did not seem to resemble Juliet but her.

"We do not have to wait for this tardy friar," Romeo said, his voice low in her ear.

"We don't?"

"If you prefer, we can die together on this night," he said softly. "That is a right and fitting end for a love such as ours. Then, we will lie together in eternity and none can part us. Not your father nor mine. Neither God nor fate."

Rosaline stared at him aghast and then laughed. "This is dark humor indeed, especially in such a place as this."

His words had an odd familiarity to them. For wasn't that what the servant girl had said to her? *I don't want to die.* But he was smiling at her now; it was a joke, black-edged. He reached out to caress her cheek. Of course, it was only a game, a tease. He had not intended to commit tender violence upon her.

"Tomorrow then, my love. Your uncle holds a ball at his house?"

"He does."

"I will meet you there and afterwards, we shall be married and away to Mantua."

Rosaline stared at him in amazement and trepidation. "The ball is for the Capulets and their kin. Your presence there risks death for you."

"I do not fear death. Only being apart from you."

"I shall look for you then," she said, still afraid for him.

He smiled. "With one more kiss, we part." He tilted her chin up and kissed her fondly and gently. Rosaline heard the blood swirl once more in her ears.

"Swear to me you are my own, forever," he said.

Rosaline stared up at him and blinked. His countenance was more beautiful than it had ever been. The light from the tapers played upon his skin.

"I am your own forever," she said, and with a final kiss, she hurried out into the night air.

As soon as Rosaline was released from Romeo's presence, the unease returned. As she walked through the basilica, she observed it was filled with friars and monks. They were not all so busy with the dead as Romeo's friend. And why did Romeo want to marry her? Was it simply love? She had no dowry to offer him. The thirty ducats from her father's chest would soon be gone. And, she reminded herself, Romeo had possession of those already. Perhaps a wife was easier to order and rule. In Mantua, she would be far from her friends and family—the family who did not want her. She sighed and chided herself. Of course he loved her and wanted to marry her. Tomorrow was almost here and the delay was not his doing.

She'd walked at such a pace that she'd already reached the doorway leading to her father's house. Rosaline took several breaths and smoothed her hair, adjusted her veil. Daylight faded into dusk. She opened the door to the passage and hurried through. The courtyard at the end was empty. The water pump dripped, cicadas creaked, and a nightjar called from an olive tree.

To her relief the hall was similarly deserted, and no one saw her climb the stairs to her chamber.

As she readied herself for bed, the door to her room opened and she started with a cry.

"It's only I. Is your husband here?" asked Caterina in a low voice, glancing about the room.

Rosaline forced a smile. "No. The friar was delayed."

Caterina quickly concealed a look of concern and embraced her. "All will be well."

As Caterina left her, Rosaline closed her eyes. She would not tell Caterina of her worries. There was someone who would help her without wavering or question.

Early the following day, Tybalt walked Rosaline to Juliet's. She asked him to carry out a favor on her behalf. He was puzzled by the request for it was peculiar, but he agreed at once as she knew he would. He looked as if he had slept little, and she knew he had not quite forgiven her—but his hurt had faded.

They fell into step as they walked, not quite at ease but wanting to mend things with one another. Rosaline vowed to herself to tend their friendship most carefully, whatever fate decided for her.

When they arrived, the entire Capulet household was in chaos making preparations for that evening's ball. Servants hurtled from room to room, eager to appear occupied, more in fear of their mistress Lauretta than to be useful. Lauretta's fury had built into a hurricane—it seemed that many of the guests had not received their invitations. Her ire and dismay rattled the villa. The widow of Vitruvio and Signior Placentio and his lovely nieces were smarting from the insult. A serving man was dispatched with a letter and hurried apologies. Somewhere a maid sobbed.

"Don't tell her that neither your brother, Livia, nor I have had ours either," said Tybalt with a grin.

"I'll see that you are added to the list. Whoever drew up the cards neglected Father and me too."

"Our aunt inspires terror but not efficiency," said Tybalt. "Fetch me the cards and I'll deliver them while carrying out your errand."

She thanked him with real gratitude.

For the remainder of the morning, Rosaline played tennis with Juliet. Already it was too hot for games and the leaves coiled on the trees, desiccated. The ground was dry and cracked, and a blackbird pecked desolately for worms and grubs in the dust.

Rosaline needed a distraction. Sweat trickled into her eyes, stinging them, so she missed a shot.

Juliet remained on the edge of the grass, racquet limp at her side. She blew out a puff of hair. "It's too hot, coz. Let's away inside. We can sit in the cool and discuss who will come to the ball and who will not."

"Anon, anon." Rosaline tossed up her ball, but the fierce midday sun dazzled her and the shot was lousy, thudding into the mulberry tree. Muttering in annoyance, she sauntered to find it among the scuff of leaves.

Flies nipped at her arms and she swatted at them. Then, with a prickle along her neck, Rosaline felt someone watching her. She stiffened. The leaves stirred despite the lack of wind. A prickle of goose bumps rose all along her arm. Had Romeo followed her? For the first time she wasn't filled with joyful anticipation but apprehension. Glancing up, she saw the dark eyes of a blackbird surveying her, a plump mulberry in its beak. For a moment she felt haunted by Romeo. This courtship didn't feel like a joyous dance any longer; it was a pursuit, and she the prey.

And yet she loved him still.

VIII

Is Rosaline, that thou did love so dear, so soon forsaken?

The long gallery was so humid that Rosaline felt as if she were one of the violets wilting in its crystal bowl, petals curling and dropping along the tabletop. The jugs of meadowsweet and Saint Anne's lace drooped too and silted a layer of pollen-like dandruff along the polished sideboard. Everyone's face looked greased and buttered, ready for the oven. Even though all the windows had been thrown wide, the walls were slick with moisture and the ceiling dripped as if with drizzle. In the cavernous inglenook fireplace, a boar orbited on a spit, its ribs stripped bare, flesh guzzled by hungry revelers, the fat and juices sliding onto the coals and making them hiss. The house was suffused with the scent of roasting pig, pastries, and spices—cinnamon, cloves, and nutmeg—but their fragrance mingled with that of the lobsters and oysters, which had begun to stink as the ice they'd sat in had melted. The shellfish floated in meltwater in their capsized shells. Rosaline hoped no one would eat them.

She scoured the gallery for Romeo as dread warred with joy. Would he really venture here into Capulet territory to see her? Suppose the guards recognized him to be a Montague and killed him? The thought was agony. Even now she pined for him, her lips parched for his kisses. Without him, chatter was tedious, music only noise.

In much of the room, the ceiling was low and the sound echoed. No one could hear one another's jokes so the punch lines had to be shouted again and again until they were no longer funny. The music was frantic, and in the feverish heat, the strings on the lutes and viols kept snagging out of tune. Yet the dancers did not seem to mind and they thrust up and down the gallery with shouts of glee. Even Livia and Valentio trotted to and fro with eager pleasure.

Rosaline leaned back against the wall beside her father, who surveyed her with approval.

"Good. Such ribald entertainment isn't fit for a novice nun."

"I'm not a nun yet."

At the far end of the gallery, she observed Juliet partnered with a perspiring man for a lively galliard. He kept reaching into his sleeve for a silken handkerchief to dab his forehead and lip. Her cousin did not smile and her feet scuffed against the floor as she shuffled along the line. Even so, decided Rosaline, she was the most charming of all the young girls there, and in a few years she would be among the loveliest of women. Her nurse had curled and dressed her hair, and she looked older, except that she'd discarded her shoes and kept fiddling with the lacework on her gown, sporting a most unladylike scowl.

For the first time that evening, Rosaline smiled, amused. A moment later, her expression faded as she recognized the man with whom Juliet danced. He was the friend of the Prince of Verona who'd ridden with him into the forest. She tried to remember his name. He must be thirty at least, well into his middle years, and presumably prowling for a wife. Well, let him hunt elsewhere. *Paris*. Yes, that was his name. *Perspiring Paris*. He dabbed his chin again. It was too hot. Even Juliet wilted.

Seeing her discomfort, Paris, with careful attentions, led her from the dancing to find a cooler place and a drink. He was solicitous and kind but still Rosaline longed to pry Juliet from his hands and take her far from this feverish cacophony.

The music grew louder and more discordant. Angry voices rose among the guests at some disturbance and Rosaline looked up. It must be Romeo. Heart thrumming with pleasure and anxiety, she stepped forward and then saw Tybalt strutting, bawdy with ale, shoving his way through the crowd.

Quickly, she moved toward him, weaving amid the dancers. Waving to him, she drew him away from the other guests and toward an open doorway where there was the wisp of a breeze. Above his eye there was a swelling bruise, and his lip was seeping blood. "What happened? You've been brawling," she chastised.

He glanced around, unfocused, his eyes glassy as a fish's. "I met them on my way back from carrying out your errand. But it began with the Montagues. I could not walk away. I am no coward, Ros. No one bites their thumb at me. I won't have it said that I lack courage!"

"Peace! You do not lack courage but sense. Speak quietly now, for our uncle Capulet looks this way."

Tybalt stared about him wildly. Even above the din, revelers had turned to look at them. Rosaline reached inside her sleeve for a napkin and pressed it on his lip as he winced. Aunt Lauretta and their uncle Lord Capulet began to mutter together in displeasure.

Rosaline tugged Tybalt's arm, leading him out onto the loggia. They stood outside in the cool, away from prying eyes. "And tell me now, did you find me an answer on your errand?" she asked.

"I did," said Tybalt, frowning. "Though I understand it not. I visited every confectioner in Verona. Just one man makes the marzipan roses such as you described, and he only makes them for one man—Romeo Montague."

Rosaline covered her face with her hands. She felt lightheaded, and the leaves from the vines above seemed to swirl about her. Taking a gulp of the evening air, she forced herself to ask, "How many has he made? One? Two?"

"I have no idea! A dozen of them for all I know. All shapes and sizes. Red, pink, peach, dark and light, curved and plump. I do know that Montague's his very best customer."

A tiny cry escaped Rosaline's lips and Tybalt gaped at her, puzzled that she could be so distressed by a sweetmeat.

He bowed and offered her his arm. "Come, Ros, you look ill. Let us cool our feet in the fountain as when we were children."

Woodsmoke and the smell of roasting pig floated outside

and into the night sky. Rosaline looked up at the stars, shattered at the realization of Romeo's betrayal. It seemed that she was nothing to him, his love was quickly given and withdrawn, his favors hollow. She was but one in a chain of a girls. *He loved us all, then let us fall from his fingers, desiccated as the rose petals on the flowers he had made.*

She was porous and exposed, full of holes. She wanted to scream, but she stood mute and dumbstruck at the agony of his treachery. He was not the man she'd thought. She loved a ghost.

Tybalt took her arm, pulling her away through the far reaches of the garden toward the rill and fountain. It was smothered in darkness, and the merriment of the revelers grew distant. Discarding her shoes, Rosaline paddled in the shallow water, her dress tucked up, the stones slippery beneath her toes. Tybalt lounged on the edge, skimming stones along the surface of the long pool. They bounded, weightless for a moment, before sinking again. He laughed with boyish glee.

Perhaps if she closed her eyes, they could stay here hidden beneath the swaying skirts of willow and not be found. This world was dark and safe. The only scourge was the mosquitos whining in her ears.

"Ros. Why do you look so ill? What do you care about some marzipan roses?"

Fiercely, Rosaline shook her head and plucked up a stone to skim it herself, but her fear was in her wrist and it sank at once. "No." She would not tell. She could not bear to see his look of disgust when he knew what she had done.

"Ros, come." He crouched beside her, and as she turned away from him, unable to look at him, with a quick smile, he brought his nose close to hers so that she could not help but stare right into his eyes. Still, she shook her head.

"Why, Ros?"

"If I tell you, you will fight," she said. "And I love you as a brother; nay, you are far more dear to me than Valentio. And I do not want you hurt."

At this Tybalt laughed. Deftly, he jumped to his feet and plucked out his sword from its scabbard. Shaking a branch of the willow so the leaves swam down to the earth like tiny blackfish, he swiped at them with his blade. He danced against the phantom enemy, crying out, "Do not be frightened for me! In Padua they called me 'the King of Cats.' I might be young, but I'm as swift as Mercury himself." He sat down on the ground, grinning and sheathing his sword. "And if it's my time, then nothing can be done. Destiny is unshunnable, like death itself."

Rosaline chewed her lip and was silent. She did not know whether to laugh or weep at the boy fighting leaves. He spoke with resolve and solemnity, but still she would not have him injured for her sake. She brimmed with affection and fear.

"Please, coz. I've known and loved you all my life," he said, coming to sit beside her on the edge of the rill. "If you are unhappy, abused, then so am I. If one of us is cursed, then so are we both."

She considered the truth of this. They had been whipped together as children for mutual crimes: chasing and harassing the unfortunate chickens so that the eggs they laid had no shells, racing the goats among the haystacks. Many of these trivial sins had been Rosaline's notion, but Tybalt had been her eager accomplice, seeking to elaborate upon the wickedness, knowing that punishment was inevitable.

When she had thought Romeo honest and their passion pure, lying to Tybalt had been the poison in the well of their affection. To feel joy and not to share it with Tybalt had tarnished it. Now, to be in such agony and not to share her burden with him only increased her pain. Still, she could not confess. He had fought with the Montagues already that day. He had been ill-met by them while carrying out the errand at her behest.

Coming and sitting close beside her, he put his arm around her and then, dropping it, gave her an affectionate nudge in the ribs with his elbow. "Don't make me beg you, Ros. 'Tis unmanly."

He stared at her with his brown eyes, and the sweetness of their expression made her look away. Perhaps she had lied enough already.

"I will tell you, then, if you promise not to seek vengeance." He grunted in assent.

"I, I love—" She could not say the words—not to Tybalt, while he watched her with his guileless expression, full of tenderness and concern. She recalled how he had offered to marry her to save her from the convent. He'd offered her his life, his love. She'd rejected him easily, running over his feelings like water over a rock. Her hands shook. He waited.

"I love, *loved*...Romeo Montague." She paused after

correcting herself, willing this new truth to be true. "And I thought he loved me too, but he does not, and I am a fool and am disgraced, my honor lost."

She watched him, waiting for Tybalt to look away from her, repulsed, but he did not. He flinched and his left eye began to tick, but still he did not speak. Unable to meet his gaze any longer, she confessed how she came to love Romeo. She sat beside Tybalt, her knees tucked beneath her chin, and she told him of her love and shame.

He listened without interrupting, toying with the hilt of his sword, his brow creased in unhappiness.

"I thought he was honest," she said softly when she was finished. "Men should be what they seem and he was not. His looks were false and I am deceived." At last, she looked up at her friend, through lashes jeweled with tears. "Now you've heard the very worst of it, do you think my virtue entirely blackened?"

His eyes were downcast, his shoulders sagging, utterly dejected. When he finally looked at her, she was almost frightened to see his absolute misery. He looked older in a few minutes; something in him was broken, and she had done it to him. She had shown him what it was to have a friend, someone you loved, lie. Shame trickled through her like cold. She had not known that it was possible to be more unhappy. Yet she wanted no more secrets, so with humiliation and regret, she told him how she'd been persuaded by Romeo to steal ducats from her own father.

"Is my soul turned to pitch?" she asked again.

He reached for her hand and pressed it to his lips. "No. Never, sweet Rosaline. I know your goodness. That villain Montague is pestilence. A plague upon him!"

With this he dropped her hand, his anger warming.

Rosaline tried to hush him. It grieved her to hear Romeo spoken of in such terms, however deserved. What a fool she'd been for listening to a nightingale's song and taking it as truth. Her self-loathing was rancorous and deep. Her very flesh smelled sour and hot, and every part of her that Romeo had touched now felt polluted. The water of the fountain was cool, and she longed to wade into it until it flowed over her head, cleansing her, but there was no water deep nor cold enough to purify her of this.

As Tybalt looked at her, she feared that he could no longer see the girl she'd been but the whore she'd become. Yet to her bewilderment, all his anger and his mettle he hurled upon Romeo and not upon her. "I shall find him this very minute and kill him dead! That vile worm. Dishonorable rogue! That hound of hell!" He stood and drew his sword once more. He cursed the gods above and fiends below.

It took all Rosaline's strength to hold him back from seeking out Romeo that very moment to declare a duel. "You swore to me you would not do this very thing. Do not burn so hot! Be reasonable! For what will come of it?" She grabbed his wrists and made him look at her.

At this Tybalt swore again, and Rosaline soothed him. "You tell me that my soul is not blackened. You must show it to be so by not seeking revenge."

Like a mad dog restrained, slowly Tybalt became more

temperate. He breathed deeply of the night air. Then he spat upon the ground, anger growing once more. "As I hate hell, I hate all Montagues."

"Do not be so full of hate. Peace, I say." Rosaline took his hands in hers. "Unfasten your sword, wash your face, and calm yourself, for you cannot go back inside until your temper is cooled and your humors restored." She looked back toward the house. "I must go—we've been out here too long."

She kissed him and then, turning, walked back through the gardens, glancing back to look at his desolate figure. She ought not have told him. No good would come of this. Tybalt had too much choler and blood in him. And yet everything that made him intemperate and impetuous also made him loyal. Even Valentio, who had little heart to spare for anyone except himself, was fond of young Tybalt.

Rosaline felt arrow-struck with grief at Romeo's betrayal. She knew that in the months and years to come, in lonely hours in the convent, she would regret that she had squandered hours with Romeo both in his company and thinking on him when she could have spent them more richly with her true friend. There was to be no escape to Mantua, no marriage spangled with love. Only a life inured as a nun. And now there was little time left to spend with Tybalt, the best of friends and the best of men. Her heart was broken afresh.

She slid back inside the long gallery, and a wave of heat sloshed over her. Glancing up and down the chamber, she tried to see Juliet but could not. The music grew louder. A dog howled.

"Fair lady, will you dance?" said a voice.

Rosaline jumped as if pierced by a dagger blade. The voice was Romeo's.

"You came," she said.

"If I cannot, then perchance I am a ghost." He reached out and stroked her arm, planting tiny kisses along the bare skin of her shoulder, conjuring gooseflesh. Rosaline scrubbed at her skin, despising her body for its betrayal. "See," he said, smiling. "I'm real enough."

She jerked away from him, turning her head from his beauty. "I am not for you, Romeo. No longer."

He surveyed her, perplexed. "Toss those cruel words aside."

Rosaline glanced about her, but everyone was dancing or eating, and no one noticed her or Romeo the Montague.

Frowning, Romeo stepped forward and covered her hand with kisses, only releasing it with great reluctance. "Why? Why would you say such a cruel thing, my love?"

"You lied to me. I know there were others."

Romeo dismissed her concerns with a wave. "Shadows. I did not know love till I knew you. They were such dreams of love as a schoolboy has."

Rosaline stared at him, wanting it to be true. He smiled at her. Something deep inside her snagged and caught. She was knotted with confusion. He leaned closer; she could smell the honey of his breath.

"The friar is come. He is here in Verona. Come, let's from this place to St. Peter's this very moment, and then to Mantua."

She felt her feet move. Let him take her hand.

"Leave all these people. They are nothing," he said.

At this, Rosaline faltered. Tybalt was not nothing. Neither was Juliet nor Caterina nor Livia. The word *Mantua* was a bell tolling her back to herself. She remembered the dead girl's room in the convent. The crumbled rose.

She yearned to trust him, and yet she must not.

She shook him off. "No," she whispered. "I want to, but you tell such pretty lies, more tempting than sweet treats."

"Stay with me, my darling, and I will love and protect and treasure you always. We will forget this as a bad dream, pressed upon us by Queen Mab." He took her wrist, but his fingers as they wrapped around her skin were too tight.

"No," said Rosaline, trying to pry herself free.

He released her, leaving red marks upon her skin.

"You must leave this place before my kinsmen see you here," she said.

"O, let them kill us both, sweet angel Rosaline," he said, raising his voice loudly enough that other revelers began to turn and glance toward them.

"You're a madman to talk thus," she whispered.

"Mad with love! You bewitched me when I first saw you. Do not forswear to love me now, else I already live in death."

Until this night Rosaline had marveled at his exquisite speech and worried that unpracticed as she was in courtly arts, her own tongue could not match his. Now as he spoke, she heard his words, but like arrows fired false, they did not hit their mark.

He had spoken thus to a dozen other girls before her. Her love was real and had been sincerely given along with her virginity, but she doubted his affection. It was too easily lent. He would love again and quickly. His talk of love came on like a sudden fever and then moved all too rapidly to that of death and violence.

She swallowed a sob. "I will not marry you, Romeo. Not tonight or any night. Your siege is lost."

"Love is not tender," said Romeo bitterly, shaking his head. "It pricks like a thorn. I only came here to woo you. But instead of wooing, I am full of woe."

She turned to go, but he blocked her way. She bit her cheek so as not to cry out and draw attention to his presence. But then, to her surprise, he was wrenched away from her.

Tybalt, his face inflamed with outrage, shoved Romeo to the ground, prodding his throat with the heel of his boot. Romeo knocked the foot aside with his fist and tried to scramble to his feet, but Tybalt kept him pinned, his boot on his neck again, pressing it.

"This must be Romeo Montague. Fetch me my rapier!" shouted Tybalt, nudging him harder. "Now, by the honor of my kin, to kill you, strike you dead, I do not think a sin!"

Each time Romeo tried to rise, Tybalt thrust him down again. Rosaline tried to wrench Tybalt from him, but he shooed her away, lost to anger and, turning, hissed at her to leave.

Seizing the opportunity of his enemy's distraction, Romeo rolled to the side and leaped to his feet and out of reach, rubbing at the flesh of his neck.

The guests had begun to gather around them, muttering in

interest and confusion. Masetto and Old Capulet strode across the room, displeased at the ruckus in the midst of the party.

"Now, young kinsman, wherefore do you storm so?" objected Old Capulet.

"Uncle, this is a Montague. A villain that is come hither in spite."

Rosaline felt panic rise in her throat in fear that Tybalt, far gone in drink, would tell their uncle and her father too much and reveal her shame—that she had lain with Romeo.

"Young Romeo, is it?" asked old Lord Capulet.

"'Tis he, that villain Romeo," said Tybalt, chancing another kick.

Romeo darted away again.

"Content thee, gentle coz, let him alone," said Tybalt's uncle in a voice that demanded obedience. "To say the truth, the Prince of Verona brags of him as virtuous man. I would not, for all the wealth of this town, here in my house, disparage him. Therefore, be patient and take no notice of him."

Tybalt began to object but his uncle raised his hand. "It is my will. Put off your frowns. They are ill-fitting for such a feast."

"It fits when such a villain is a guest. I'll not endure him!"

"He shall be endured, boy! I say he shall. Go!"

Still Tybalt did not move.

"Am I the master here or you? Go to!" cried his uncle.

To Rosaline's dismay, Tybalt made as if to speak again. Her uncle stared at him, agape in fury. "Be quiet and go, for shame, or I'll make you quiet," said the old man, raising his fist.

Rosaline looked at her uncle in fear. No one defied the host at his own party. Tybalt's disobedience strayed close to outright insult. If he lacked all restraint, then she must think for them both.

Slipping her arm through Tybalt's, she led him away from the melee.

"This intrusion makes my flesh tremble," he muttered.

"Hush, coz, not here," she said. "They watch us still."

She glanced over her shoulder and saw to her relief that Romeo did not move to follow them.

Noticing her gaze, like a horse resisting the bridle, Tybalt yanked to turn back to Romeo and fight again, but she squeezed his hand, hard. "If you cannot be peaceful, then you must leave," she said. "Our uncle cannot see you again this night. You know what he is like. Easy enough, but once riled and fixed upon something, he is dangerous. Do not let him fix on you."

"I will withdraw," muttered Tybalt, the skin of his neck mottled with fury. "Even though it fills me with bitt'rest gall. But I don't want to leave you here while that villain Romeo prowls the night."

The very thought of speaking to Romeo filled Rosaline with dread. She glanced around the packed chamber. Dancers were beginning to take to the floor again, moving prettily in a motet. Juliet stood in a corner whispering with her nurse. Up in the minstrels' gallery, the musicians played on, a viol player leaning out over the balcony to gaze down, clearly having relished the quarrel as the best entertainment of the evening.

"I'll slide away up there," said Rosaline, gesturing to the balcony. "None shall see me. I'll be well hidden. Now, you must go too. See, Uncle Capulet watches still, and his expression is severe."

With great reluctance, Tybalt kissed her hand and, after seeing her run up the stairs to the gallery, disappeared out into the night.

On the landing among the musicians, it was even warmer, the breath and sweat of a hundred bodies creating a summer inferno. The plaster roses on the ceiling moldings were beginning to slough and turn leprous. Rosaline wondered that the minstrels could play at all—their fingers must slip from the strings.

She perched on a ledge at the far side, where she was happily concealed behind a wooden strut, and peered down over the revelers. There were two boys playing chase with a ball among the dancers—someone was about to slip and fall, and yes, there tumbled the good widow Vitruvio, while the two miscreants were led out into the yard for a hiding. In one corner, two newlyweds gazed at one another—their fingers linked, noses touching, the night and stars created only for them, while in another, a greyhound relieved itself beneath the table on which rested the trays of cheese and figs and a bowl of punch, leaving a yellow puddle on the floor.

Scouring the crowd, she could not now see Romeo. Perhaps he had fled. There was a restlessness within her that was nothing to do with the heat. She searched again for Juliet but could not find her either with Nurse, who lingered gossiping with the servants, nor cavorting with the dancers. There was Paris, alone, picking forlornly at a bunch of grapes and scouring the crowd. If she had to guess, she'd hazard that he was seeking Juliet. *Good. Let him seek and not find.* Still, she could see neither Juliet nor Romeo among the dozens of revelers.

The windows and doors stood open, and Rosaline looked out to the loggia beyond, which was lit with a dozen torches. Then, to her bewilderment, she spied them both: Juliet and Romeo, two figures, conspiring together beneath the canopy of vines. Rosaline caught her breath. She leaned far out over the balcony to make them out better. Juliet appeared so slight beside him, not yet a woman at all. Why was Romeo with Juliet? Were they speaking of her? She could make no sense of it all.

As she saw him, her heart snagged in her chest, and her pulse raced. A treacherous part of her still wanted to run to him, feel the warmth of his arms around her. Then, to her dismay, Juliet appeared to giggle, leaning in a little closer to him. Romeo twined her fingers with his, touched the shining gold of her hair.

There was a pain low in Rosaline's belly. Jealousy, cool and clear, slid into her. For a brief moment, she wanted only to be adored again by Romeo, radiant in his affection, bathed in his love. Together, Romeo and Juliet were both so beautiful. Only he was a fiend angelical.

Had he loved her at all? Rosaline's heart congealed against him. He was neither honest nor good. She felt grim sorrow at his betrayal, and a kindling of rage and hurt. She tasted it in her mouth, metallic as blood.

Every part of Rosaline yearned to howl for Juliet to run, run as fast as she could, far away from this man. That he was beautiful malice.

But even if she did and she yelled so her lungs and throat were raw, her cousin would not hear her above the din.

And would she want to listen?

Rosaline understood the honeyed delight of Romeo's words.

O, could no one else see them? Why was she their only audience? Where was her uncle Capulet now?

As she watched in revulsion, Romeo reached for Juliet's hand. He bent to kiss her.

Rosaline cried out. No one heard.

Her heart skittered with horror. She could bear it no longer. It was no use hiding up here in the gods while he wreaked havoc down below. Skidding on the stairs in her leather slippers, she hurtled down from the gallery. She could not let Romeo near Juliet. She would not. She knew who and what he was. No one had saved her, and now she was filled with mud and dirt, and no one would want her. She did not want herself. She was fouled, and she would not let him break Juliet too. Only she could keep her cousin safe.

There was a dismal drumming in her ears, her heart thundering a warning knell, as she tried to thrust her way among the carousers who grumbled at her, sniping in irritation at her poor manners and sharp elbows. Someone stamped on her toe, deliberate and hard.

Wincing, she rushed to the open door and ran out onto

the loggia. It was cooler and smelled oversweet of jasmine and honeysuckle. Moths ringed the torch flames. For a moment she thought that no one was there, that she was already too late. They had gone.

And then, she saw him. He stood alone beneath a lilac tree, black in the dark.

She willed herself to be resolute. "Do not play with her to spite and torment me," she said, trying to keep her voice steady. "Juliet is a child."

"Juliet! The loveliest name I ever heard. I'm unworthy to even speak it with these profane lips," answered Romeo with breathless delight.

"On this we can agree."

Rosaline stared at him. His eyes glinted with rapture—whether entirely overwhelmed by Juliet's beauty or also taking foul pleasure in wounding Rosaline, she could not tell.

"She is a saint," he said.

"No. She is a girl. Not yet fourteen. Younger even than me. Let her be."

"Alas, I cannot. As I kissed her, all my sins were purged."

Rosaline stared at him in disgust. "Your love does not lie in your heart but in your eyes. It is soon forsaken."

Romeo laughed bitterly. "You told me to bury my love for you."

"In a grave. Not in my cousin, who is still a child."

Romeo appeared unperturbed by her rebuke. "Did my heart love till now? I forswear it. For I never saw true beauty till this night."

Rosaline made herself smile at him, in order to remind him that earlier it had been her he'd wanted, to her he'd sworn his love, for her he'd been eager to die. Yet his words cut into her, and she wondered that they did not leave a mark upon her skin.

She took a step toward him, reached out and took his thumb, biting it gently between her teeth. Then, letting his hand fall, she spoke quietly. "I will marry you this very night if you will let Juliet be."

Romeo surveyed her with contempt. "Marry you? I have already forgotten your name. I love only Juliet. My sighs are all for Juliet. You are nothing to me."

Even though she knew what he was, his words still hurt, twisting inside her. He'd withdrawn his love, and to her dismay, she found she craved it still now that it belonged to Juliet—or appeared to.

He looked her up and down. "Juliet is the sun and you are the envious moon, sick and green. And do not tell lies to Juliet. No one likes bawdy whispers and tattle. Get you to your convent and cease to buzz us."

Her breath caught in her throat, a knot of tears choking her. "I will tell all Verona the rogue you are."

He stood perfectly still, unsmiling—handsome, perfect, monstrous. "Remember, no other man will take you," he said softly. "Your family will cast you out as a common harlot because you've lain with me. They will not pay your dowry to the convent. I'm a Montague after all. The stain of lying with me is darker than that of being with any other man."

Rosaline stared at him, unnerved by his cruelty. "You would not tell them—?"

How had his love so quickly turned to vengeance? Perhaps it had always been there beneath the surface, like mud and filth beneath the hardened crust on a marsh.

He studied her for a moment and then spoke slowly. "Out of old affection toward you, I do not think I could. To see you shunned, no. I do not think I could bear it. But remember—hush, little bird."

His voice was gentle and he moved toward her. Rosaline refused to flinch. For a moment she thought that he was about to try and kiss her, and then he walked past her and was gone.

Rosaline stood alone under the canopy of jasmine and vines, watching bats skim beneath the curd of the moon. She'd glimpsed the tyrannical soul behind the angelic visage. Had he ever intended to marry her, or had it all been a cruel ruse? She was relieved that he had released her from the prison of his affection, and yet he'd been everything to her. He appalled her, and yet he'd taught her what it was to desire, and as he discarded her, he took a piece of her with him.

She felt, as she began to walk back to the house, that she did so on uneven ground, that nothing was as it was supposed to be. Her body was not her own. What or how had she been before Romeo, before he'd taken her apart, sliced her up, rearranged her? Now that he'd forgotten her, despised her, would she simply fade from view?

It did not matter. She must consider only how to save Juliet from the villain Romeo.

IX

Beautiful tyrant!
Fiend angelical!

Unable to sleep, Rosaline rose early the next morning and paced her chamber, toying with the ropes of her hair. She mourned for the man she loved as bitterly as if he moldered in his grave. Yet Romeo had pretended to be a man he was not, and she had loved a lie. Real or imagined, though, she'd adored him and now he was gone. The thought of him that had once been joy to her was now only torment. O, that deceit had such a gorgeous face.

She hoped her reputation was safe. But he couldn't expose that she had lain with him without revealing their unhappy history and his true nature to Juliet.

Still, a cool dread like a winter's chill trickled into her and she shivered. She did not believe that Romeo would try to visit her, and yet every creak of wood, each noise of wind, filled her with disquiet. She felt helpless and afraid, like when she was a child and noisy spirits seemingly prowled the attics above. Now, it was the living who frightened her.

If, in his malevolence, Romeo revealed Rosaline to be guilty of the theft of Masetto's gold, she would declare to all Verona how and why she came to take her father's coin and who had bid her steal it. Perhaps on hearing the horrid tale, Juliet would be revolted and thus be safe from Romeo's seduction. An unpleasant thought squirmed its way into Rosaline's mind—was this then what she ought to do? She considered for a moment. Maybe she need not tell it to all Verona. *Just to confide the truth to Juliet is enough.* Yes, she would confess her crime to Juliet this very morning and persuade her of Romeo's wickedness.

Early, Rosaline hurried to see her cousin. The household was quiet. Even the servants seemed reluctant to rise, late to bed after the previous evening's ribald festivities. The bleary watchman opened the gate to Rosaline, who hastened through the courtyard and ran straight up the stairs to Juliet's chamber. The air was still tinged with woodsmoke and the smell of roasted pig.

Her cousin was not asleep but sat wide-awake on her bed, cheeks pink, eyes fever-lit. She greeted Rosaline with a happy shout and patted the space beside her. "Come, kiss me, coz! Isn't the day bright? Indeed, 'tis the fairest day ever I saw!"

"It is already too hot and it's hardly yet nine o'clock."

"No. It is perfection. I'll not hear anything else."

Juliet was restless and kept on fidgeting, quite unable to sit still, as though her sheets were full of biting fleas. Rosaline surveyed her with growing apprehension. She seemed already like a girl besotted, poisoned with a dream of love.

"I know you will not betray me," said Juliet, wriggling off the bed and glancing over her shoulder as if the very walls had sprung holes. "For if they knew I loved him, they would murder him."

"Wherefore, what it is his name?" asked Rosaline, although she already knew.

"Romeo Montague." Juliet smiled sweetly up at her, blue eyes love-drunk.

"O, Juliet, a thousand times, no. It is too soon to speak of love."

Her cousin's expression darkened, and for a moment she looked anxious. "Our meeting was like lightning, so bright and sudden that the whole world was lit. But then lightning also in an instant vanishes. I have joy in him, but not in our contract."

Rosaline inhaled in shock. "What contract, Juliet?"

"O, my soul already calls his name and soon I shall have his!"

Rosaline stared at her, appalled. "You cannot be married, Juliet. Not so soon. Not to someone you've only known a few brief hours. It is not love but madness. You are thirteen."

"Fourteen on Lammastide, in two weeks' time," said Juliet stubbornly, her pride wounded.

She looked at the floor and poked at a ball of dust with a grubby toe. Rosaline wasn't sure if she wanted to hug her or shake her.

"O, little one," said Rosaline. "This is not love; you just believe it is."

Juliet looked at her. "When you see him, you cannot but love him too. I tell you, Ros. 'Tis only his name that is Montague."

"No," said Rosaline, "it's not his name that I abhor but himself. His looks are charmed but his soul is wicked."

Juliet stared at her in puzzlement and growing consternation. Rosaline swallowed and drew a deep breath. She took Juliet's hand and then dropped it again. Her mouth was dry. "I loved Romeo once," said Rosaline softly. "Was taken in by his quick tongue and handsome face."

Juliet looked puzzled and then laughed. "He is indeed beautiful. The best man I have ever seen."

Rosaline tried again. "We too were to marry. I was his bright angel."

Juliet stared at Rosaline in confusion and doubt, as though her cousin's mind was addled. "I am his bright angel, his dear saint."

"So too was I, the very same. I adored and worshiped him. His love was sun and rain to me. I bloomed or withered according to his affections. We were to marry and elope together to Mantua. Against all my better nature, and to my deepest shame, he persuaded me to take gold from my father's chest, money that would have been gifted to the nunnery for my upkeep. He told me to take it as my dowry and give it to him. To my shame, I did as he bid me."

It had been awful to confess the sin to Tybalt and yet a relief to receive his forgiveness—better than any priest's absolution. She watched Juliet, not knowing what she would say yet bright with hope.

Juliet gaped at her for a moment and then laughed. "Dearest Rosaline. You love me too well. You make up stories to frighten me so I will not go with my Romeo. But, sweet Ros, you do not need to be afraid for me. He gave me love's faithful vow, and my love for him is wide and deep."

A short cry of exasperation escaped Rosaline's lips. "O, Jule! You have scarce known him twelve hours! You do not know what he is! How cruel and fickle. What does your nurse say?"

Juliet grinned and curled up beside her, smug as a cat. "She has just gone to speak with him for me."

Rosaline cursed Nurse under her breath. She should have known better than to have expected anything sensible from her. In all her years of tending for Juliet she had scarce told the girl no, eager to please her charge, trying to placate and recompense for Lauretta's callous indifference and petty cruelty.

Rosaline sat for a moment listening to the stirrings of the household, the scrape of benches far below, the slamming of heavy wooden doors, the clucking of the chickens in the yard. An unpleasant thought struck her. "Did you speak to him after the ball?"

Juliet pinked with pleasure. "He clambered up the vines to my chamber. He was not frightened of our kin, but rather had to see me, speak to me. He says there lies more peril in my eyes than twenty of their swords."

"O, Juliet, he's a practiced prattler. He said the very same to me."

"No, coz, I won't believe it. You wish to frighten me for you love me, but it isn't kind. I wish now that I had not told you."

The two cousins sat in angry silence for a minute. Rosaline tried to remember that when the servant girl had come to speak with her, she too had not wanted to listen, and she was nearly two years older than Juliet. Of course Juliet was besotted; she was at the mercy of a clever and accomplished flatterer.

With great effort, Rosaline forced herself to speak calmly. "Only tell me, Cousin, did you lie with him last night?"

Juliet shot her look of scornful derision. "We are not yet married."

Rosaline was grateful for the younger girl's staunch morality. It had kept her body safe from Romeo for at least one more night. But not her heart.

Juliet gave a tiny sigh. "I am eager to be married. I count the hours, minutes, until the blessed night."

Rosaline winced. Juliet was deceived by the serpent's heart that lay behind Romeo's sweet face. Silently, she vowed to save her despite the girl's own desires. This wedding must be prevented.

It was already hot as Rosaline paced along the river in the tinder scorch of the morning sun. In frustration she picked up a stone and hurled it into the water, watching it vanish. She longed to confide in Tybalt. They were better as a pair than alone. He had accepted her account of Romeo without hesitation or doubt. Tybalt. Apart from the quickness of his temper, she could trust him as her own better self. Tybalt would hasten to her side and aid her without hesitation. His sword, his humor, and his loyalty—all were hers. But it was her deep affection for him that prevented her from running to him now. He had already run into one brawl with the Montagues, while Juliet would not have met Romeo if it had not been for her; he had come to the Capulet ball hunting her and instead snared Juliet. This calamity was her fault. So now if Tybalt, on hearing how matters stood, ran hot-tempered into another dispute and was hurt or banished, then all blame must lie with her.

No, she must attempt to save Juliet from Romeo without Tybalt's help, alone.

She had little choice left to her but to plead with Nurse to prevent the union. Juliet had confessed that she'd dispatched Nurse to talk to Romeo, who would likely still be at the Montague house at this hour, so that's where Rosaline would seek her. At least Nurse's heart was honest and good. Her only offense was loving Juliet too well and refusing to say no to her out of fear of disappointing her. But when Juliet was a babe, Nurse would not have let her caress an adder merely because she'd longed to stroke its neck so smooth and warm with her fingertips. Now, she must persuade Nurse that Romeo was the adder, his bite venomous, and it was Nurse's duty to keep her safe against Juliet's own pleas.

The sun was rising higher in the sky, a polished brass plate, buffed to a gleam. The river hurtled across the stones in the channel below, and in its sound Rosaline imagined she could hear minutes pouring through time's hourglass. She quickened her pace.

She had never seen the Montague house in Verona so closely

before. After the prince's palace, it was the grandest residence in all of the city, larger even than her Uncle Capulet's place. A baker came out of his shop, setting out his sign, and after he left she loitered in the entrance, hiding from the sun and from casual passersby, hoping to spy the familiar figure of Nurse puffing on her way home. The smell of yeast and almond *cantuccini* surrounded her, making her stomach gurgle. She'd been out since very early and missed the morning meal.

Looking down, she realized her clothes were snowed in flour dust from sitting in the baker's doorway. Her father would be furious if he caught her, filthy and without a chaperone.

She lingered in the shade for another quarter hour, waiting.

At last she saw the plump figure of Nurse bustle along the alley. Rosaline rushed to her, seizing her hand.

Nurse startled and cried out in alarm. "Rosaline! Why are you here?"

"Why are you, Nurse?"

Nurse shook her head. "I cannot say. I'm sworn to secrecy. Do not press me, for I shall surely tell."

Nurse scurried quickly on, as fast as her legs would allow, perspiring in the heat.

Rosaline easily kept step with her. "Nurse, tell me honestly, whom did you speak to?"

"Truly, I can't tell, dearest girl. I'm sworn to Juliet. Though I shall say, your cousin knows how to choose a man. He's handsome. And courteous. And his body—though it is not to be talked of, Rosaline—is past compare. And so handsome, or did

I say already? And I warrant virtuous. And, O, his face is better than any other man's. And he speaks like an honest gentleman."

Rosaline tugged on Nurse's cloak, forcing her to stop and face her. "Please, Nurse, believe me when I say, he only speaks like an honest gentleman, but he is none. I know who you met. It was Romeo."

"Truly, you know of him?" asked Nurse in surprise.

Rosaline swallowed, her mouth dry. "I do. So please, trust me when I beg you—you must not let Romeo marry Juliet."

Puffed from her exertions, Nurse paused for a moment and gaped at Rosaline. "Ah, poor child. You are about to go to a nunnery and she's to be married. But even so, she will come and see you there. She loves you."

Rosaline bit her lip in frustration. "It is not envy that makes me speak but concern. She is too young, and he is wicked. Can't you see? It is too quick. She's young and his behavior is gross. He was the same with me. He loved me only yesterday."

Nurse gave a tut of sympathy. "Romeo loved you? He is mad with love for Juliet." She stroked a strand of Rosaline's hair behind her ear and, producing her handkerchief, tried to wipe some flour from Rosaline's cheek. "I fear it's awful trying for you girls who are destined to be wed only to Jesus and to God. It does strange things to your minds. I've heard it said, but never seen it till now."

Pushing aside her frustration, Rosaline blinked away the sweat that trickled, smarting, into her eyes. She considered another tack. She could not bear for Romeo to touch Juliet. The thought of them together was poison. Nor would she have Juliet filled with this roiling self-disgust.

Licking dry, furred teeth, she forced a smile. "Perhaps what you say is true. Good Nurse, tell me where they will marry. Let me come that I may wish the happy couple well."

Nurse frowned and looked perturbed. She said nothing for a moment, as if hesitating over Rosaline's request. She glanced from side to side and started to walk on. Then, seeming to change her mind, she turned on her heel and came back.

Rosaline thought her behavior odd.

With the same expression on her face, Nurse said quietly, "The crypt at St. Peter's this very afternoon."

She kissed Rosaline, who stood fixed to the spot, appalled that it was so soon. She'd hoped for at least a few more hours or a day's reprieve. Romeo had delayed and delayed their wedding. She opened her mouth to object again, but Nurse stopped her, saying, "Hush. My head throbs as it is; I cannot listen to any more of your chattering." She rubbed her temples. "Enough, you should away home."

Dejected and stinging with her failure, Rosaline stood in the street and watched as Nurse scurried on her way, back to Juliet.

She would not go home. She would not yield to fate and Romeo. "You will not have her, fiend," she muttered.

Yet every path seemed blocked to her. She dawdled along the alley, trying to keep in the shade and out of sight in case any of the Capulet household were abroad. Was there no one who would help her other than Tybalt? She longed for him, and yet she would not court more danger. She was steeped in enough guilt; it sickened her. There must be someone else. To speak with Romeo was a forlorn task—he wanted nothing but to torment her. Yet with sudden hope, she grasped that there was someone connected to him: Romeo's friar. He was the man who had the power to prevent the wedding, if it was truly to take place. Perhaps the holy man would be more ready to listen to reason and logic than Nurse?

Quickening her pace, Rosaline turned and hurried to the chapter house near St. Peter's where the holy friars lodged, determined to persuade the friar against the match.

Rosaline glanced upwards as she passed through the arched entrance of a low stone building. She found herself in the first of a series of rectangular physic gardens. A patch of lawn was covered with drifts of white clover that was vibrating and humming, the blooms spread with bees. In a flower bed, two monks raked out weeds, and another knelt, watering seedlings with paternal care.

She walked over to them and asked if they knew where she could find Friar Laurence. The monk kneeling with his can pointed in silence through an arch of laurel into another garden. Rosaline thanked him and hurried on.

The next garden was wilder and unkempt, filled with swaying grasses and fragrant with rosemary, lavender, and sage. She observed an elderly man, stooped as the bent willow whips he tended, twisting tendrils of bindweed around them, a walking stick propped beside him. He continued with his task but, sensing Rosaline's presence even with his back turned, said quietly, "I trail the bindweed here so that it does not strangle the rue. It's easier than plucking it out. It grows happily and harmlessly up the willow canes, fooled into benevolence."

Taking a pair of scissors from a pouch around his waist, he snipped some of the rue and then a little of another plant with tiny, white, starlike flowers, placing them both in the osier basket at his feet. Then he turned to look at her, rolling one of the tiny flowers in his fingers. "I must fill this basket with precious-juiced flowers. Much power and grace lies in plants, herbs, stones, and they harbor true qualities. Used right, they give medicine. But without due care, abuse."

Rosaline examined his face. "You are learned in such matters, ghostly father?"

He gave a chuckle. "We are all children in the face of nature. Even me," he said, giving a tug on his beard, hoary and white as dandelion fluff. "Come." Standing, he ambled over to a felled tree at the edge of the garden. He sat, setting his basket at his feet. Propping his stick beside him, he surveyed her. He indicated the space beside him. "Sit awhile."

Rosaline hesitated for a moment and then sat. He seemed cordial and pleasant, but still she was wary. He had known Romeo for many years, and she wondered if he was mindful of his true nature. The friar cultivated his friendship like the fennel and sage that flourished all about them.

She paused before asking, "Do you know of me, holy father? I am Rosaline."

He frowned, then peered at her as if remembering. His expression altered. "Yes, alas, my poor child." He sighed, his shoulders slumping as if in dejected sympathy for her plight. He cleared his throat and shook his head, muttering unhappily, "Holy Saint Francis, what a change. Rosaline whom Romeo did love so dear and so soon forsaken." His voice was low and sticky with regret. "O, my dear. All himself and his woe was for you, for his Rosaline. And now he is changed, and you are not. Is this why you are here?" He caressed his beard, a look of great commiseration upon his face.

"Holy father, no. I love him not."

"Jesu Maria!" he declared, looking relieved. "He has made me agree to marry him with another."

Rosaline inhaled sharply and grasped the edge of his cassock. "My cousin Juliet. Friar, I beg you, no. She's a child. Thirteen. This match is too hasty. It shall prove rancorous and rotten."

The friar looked worried, his mouth tight.

"I can see the alliance also troubles you. It is too rash. Too sudden," she continued.

"As was your own with Romeo," reminded the friar, his voice sharp, the benevolent grandfather forgotten. Then he smiled once more and continued, with an indulgent expression: "He wrote me letters twice each day hurrying me back to Verona to marry you, so hasty and hot were you for Romeo then."

"Until I knew what he was. Romeo is too inconstant. Too uncertain. As you say, until yesterday his love was all for me."

The friar looked troubled again and then stood, smoothing his robes and his countenance. He smiled broadly. "I gave him my word, daughter. And this alliance between Capulet and Montague, if happy, may unite your households and please the Prince of Verona himself."

So it was true then: Romeo really did mean to marry Juliet.

The friar continued to gaze at her with smiling anxiety, full of apparent concern. Rosaline felt her temper rise but suppressed it. "Please, holy father, you are a man of God. If you listen to her wedding vows at thirteen, you will be saying prayers over her tomb before too long."

The friar shifted uncomfortably. His long, pale fingers rested on his cassock. He would not look at her.

Rosaline rose and stood over him. "If this bud of love is meant to grow, then by all means marry them, ghostly father, but in two or three years hence. Then that love will flower into a mighty and beauteous rose that will please all Verona, even our proud prince. The union will not be hasty but strong, with roots enough to weather the storms our warring families bring." Rosaline paused. "And Juliet will be a woman grown and a proper match for your Romeo."

The friar shook his head, startled at the power of her speech. "This very morning—barely dawn—Romeo found me here and begged me to consent to marry him today to Juliet." He gave a groan. "When only yesterday Romeo was thine. He swore his heart was all for Rosaline. Young men's love, I fear, lies not truly in their hearts but in their eyes."

He looked down sadly.

"Do not mock me," said Rosaline, uncertain.

He held up his hands. "By my troth, I do not, my lady. I am persuaded. Despite your youth and sex, you speak with sense as well as passion."

"You shall prevent the match, then?" said Rosaline, scarcely daring to hope.

"I shall do what is in my power."

Rosaline stared at him in amazement and disbelief. He smiled back at her passively, like a reflection in a looking glass.

"You swear to me?" she said. She must know that it was true and Juliet was safe.

The friar chuckled with wry amusement. "You cannot ask a holy man to swear." Seeing that she was somewhat unsatisfied, he took out his bible and said gently, "Let us pray together for sweet Juliet's safety and happiness."

"And for her marriage to Romeo being delayed."

The friar smiled.

Mollified, Rosaline knelt beside him on the grass. Red ants teemed from the fallen log in a cardinal procession across her shoe. She flicked them away before they could bite.

The friar draped his rosary beads around the Bible's leather cover and clasped his hands in prayer. "God, pardon sin—"

The friar continued to pray, but Rosaline wasn't listening; she'd noticed the small blue leather-bound Bible in his grasp. It was the twin of the one she'd discovered in Cecilia's cell, the same soft cobalt lambskin cover with an embossed stamp. Now, as she studied it, she realized the stamp was the symbol of the Franciscan order: a shield with a cross, a raven, and a flower. Why did Cecilia have a Franciscan bible in her cell when she died?

Something pricked Rosaline's skin, and despite the heat, the downy hairs along her arms rose sentinel. Friar Laurence had boasted only a few minutes ago of his knowledge of plants, of how they could be medicinal or malevolent. Rosaline tried to remember what the abbess had said: that when Cecilia had been ill, that it was possible she'd been treated at first by "*the brother friars perhaps. They also believe they know the meaning and uses of plants, but in the wrong hands, they can make the body sicker.*"

Rosaline was suddenly aware that they were now alone in the garden. The other monks had withdrawn to another part of the friary. She did not know exactly how, but Friar Laurence or the Franciscans seemed to have some unnatural connection to Cecilia She had no faith in this friar; he did not seem quite holy. Nor did she trust that he would prevent the wedding. He only whispered what she wanted to hear; she wondered if he lied as easily as he prayed. She wanted to flee from this garden, its beauty no longer serene.

Friar Laurence rocked to and fro as he murmured implorations to heaven, the rosary beads sliding between his fingers, but he showed no sign of stopping.

To her relief, half a minute later, a party of monks entered the garden, and at last, the friar finished his prayers. Standing up and picking up his basket, he walked slowly to a tangle of a roses. He turned to her for a moment saying, "I must return to my roses, sweet Rosaline." Then, taking his scissors from a pocket hung about his waist, he began to deadhead them.

Rising, she watched him for a moment. He snipped her one and held it out to her. She took it. At first glance it was a perfect bloom, pure white, but then as she looked, tucked inside the innermost petals was a fat black beetle.

She bade the friar farewell. Crushing the flower and discarding it, she walked away, the buzzing of the bees reverberating in her ears.

There was no other choice left for Rosaline. She must find Tybalt. She bit her lip, willing herself not to cry. He would help her as soon as she asked, but she worried that Tybalt, loathing all Montagues, would be too eager to find another reason to hate them. She must hope that fortune would smile on them, for, alone and unaided, it was becoming apparent that she could not save Juliet. As a woman, few heeded her, and as a girl about to enter a convent, her voice was little more than the chatter of starlings. But with Tybalt's joining hers, maybe she could make them listen. She did not want his sword but his voice. Perhaps together, they could prevent the calamity of this ill-fated wedding.

Rosaline tried to think where Tybalt would be at this hour. *Valentio's house.* He dined each day with her brother.

She half ran through the streets to her brother's place; most residents of the city had retreated inside to escape the fiercest heat of the day. She tried not to dwell on what Valentio would say if he glimpsed her present disheveled appearance.

But as she reached the great wooden door studded with brass nailheads marking the entrance to Valentio's house, she hesitated before lifting the lion's head knocker. She did not want to venture inside; if she did, Valentio would scold her for her slovenly looks and dispatch her back to her father's place at once. Her brother would not listen to anything she had to say and, even if he did, would have no sympathy for her disgrace. At best she would be sent to the convent immediately, and she still feared for Juliet's safety. No, she could not trust Valentio.

She glanced around, noticing a ragged boy curled up and snoozing in the shade beneath a stone pine. She shook him awake, tucking a coin into his fist. He opened his eyes. "Take this coin, good fellow, and knock upon that gate. Say that Petruchio has sent most urgently for Tybalt, who must come at once. Say that faithfully, and I shall give you another coin and be most thankful."

The boy looked up at her and blinked, secreting the coin into his jerkin in an instant. "Yes, my lady."

He was on his feet in a moment, and while Rosaline concealed herself behind the trunk of the pine tree, he rapped loudly on the door and repeated the message as he was bid.

Rosaline could scarcely breathe. Would it work and Tybalt come? What if out of worry and concern for Petruchio, Valentio followed him? What then?

Minutes passed and dragged in the dirt. The boy returned and resumed his place in the dust beneath the tree. She paid him his second coin, and he settled and fell back to sleep in his bed of discarded pine needles.

Tybalt was not coming. She did not know what else to do. The cause was hopeless and Juliet lost. And Rosaline needed to pass water. She would have to squat in the street and urinate like one of the beggars and strays. Retreating behind the tree, she lifted her skirts and crouched. The relief was instant.

At once the gate opened and slammed. *Tybalt!* Quickly, she gathered her petticoats and ran after him, trailing him into a small and deserted square opening off the narrow street. The square was parched with heat, the shutters barred on every side, like closed eyes.

"Tybalt, stay!"

Tybalt frowned, and Rosaline was self-conscious as he took in her sunburned cheeks, unkempt gown, and frantic, wild air.

"You are out alone again without permission, Rosaline," said Tybalt, resigned.

Rosaline began to respond but Tybalt interrupted. "Petruchio has summoned me. I am in haste. Verily, I do not know what has happened."

"Nothing. Not with Petruchio. Or rather, I am Petruchio."

Tybalt surveyed her in confusion.

"I sent the message," explained Rosaline. "I needed you to come and meet me here without my brother's knowledge."

Tybalt looked again at her disheveled appearance.

"Has Romeo hurt you?" he asked softly. "You do not look like yourself." His forehead creased with concern.

"Romeo has forgotten me—"

"This is good news indeed!" Tybalt's face brightened but Rosaline's expression remained grave. "Why still so moody, then?" he continued.

"He now loves Juliet. Desires to marry Juliet."

"Our Juliet?" he asked, staggered in disbelief. "Our little Juliet?"

Rosaline bowed her head. She was filled with remorse that she had not done more to protect her cousin from such a monster. She'd been so love-drunk that she'd not seen her dove was really a raven. All her selfish fears had been that they might be discovered.

Screwing her hands into fists, she prayed with uncharacteristic fervor that they were not too late. She glanced at Tybalt through reddened, dust-rimmed lids. "He saw her at the ball, called her his bright angel, and says he loves her now."

Tybalt stood very still, seemingly unwilling to believe this news. "And she loves him too?" he asked.

"She does. With excess. Or believes she does."

At this, Tybalt began to curse. Rosaline flinched, fearing that he must blame her excessively for her part in this—it was only due to her that Romeo had even ventured forth to the Capulet ball and chanced upon his new prey. She had acted wretchedly and as blindly as Cupid in this unlucky romance.

Yet to her relief, all Tybalt's wrath was preserved for Romeo. "O, this coxcomb! This scurvy waverer! This whoreson prick!"

He spat the words, running his hands through his hair, shaking with rage. "Let me at him before he leads her into a fool's paradise! She is too young for this!"

Rosaline's relief gave way to irritation. The quick anger of these men was not useful. "Be more temperate," she scolded. "It clouds your judgment and cannot help us. I did not tell you to listen to you spout choler and steam like a teakettle." She reached out and caught his chin, trying to make him look at her. "Yes, coz, we must prevent the match but by reason and clever thinking. I sought out and spoke to the friar who is to marry them. He promised me he would not do it. But something in my soul warns me that he false."

"Then I know it to be so," said Tybalt with certainty.

"And I've tried to talk with Juliet and Nurse but they will not listen, or not to me." The shame of this caused tears to graze her throat.

Tybalt placed his palms firmly upon her shoulders. The weight of them was comforting. "So, together then, we shall prevent this unholy match. Where is it taking place?" he said.

"St. Peter's. This very afternoon."

"So quick, alas! Come then, we must go there now. But if reason and prattle fails, then I must fight him and restore honor to you both."

"No!" insisted Rosaline. "I do not want your sword! Honor is useless to me without you! I want you to make them listen. If they hear that you believe me, then perhaps Juliet also will be persuaded. If you cannot keep from violence, then do not come."

Rosaline wished that she could unbuckle his sword and hurl it into the river. His eagerness to decide each dispute by fighting infuriated and terrified her. Did life mean so little to these men that they were all so eager to cast it aside?

"Swear it or go!" she said, patience worn to a nub.

Tybalt grumbled reluctant assent.

Anxious and irritable with one another, they walked for several minutes in silence. Gradually Rosaline's annoyance with her cousin dissipated and was gone. Holding on to a grievance toward Tybalt was like trying to hold on to smoke.

Next to the river, beside the wide span of the bridge, there was more shade where the stallholders gathered hawking fish and a painter's palette of vegetables and fruit—puckered lemons, split melons with pips like children's teeth, shriveled dates. Gazing hungrily at the array, Rosaline stumbled and Tybalt caught her arm, steadying her.

He surveyed her with concern. "When did you last eat, Ros? Drink?"

She shook him off. "I don't remember. It's not important. We must make haste."

Ignoring her objections, he bought her a cup of ale and half a melon, overripe and smelling rotten-sweet, and tripe sausage, strong and hot. The melon they passed in silence between them as they walked on apace, again falling in easy, rapid step together.

Rosaline's fingers were soon sticky, and she smeared sausage grease and melon sap upon her skirts. She recalled the last time she'd eaten at the marketplace—with Romeo. The thought of him kissing away the juice of the orange made her shudder.

She glanced sidelong at Tybalt. "You believed me at once when I told you of Romeo's crimes?"

He shrugged and spat a piece of gristle into the gutter. "Of course, gentle Rosaline. I trust you in all things; you are all the world to me."

He spoke with open frankness, unabashed yet tender.

"But," she pressed, "you hate all Montagues and always seek for a reason to quarrel with them and fight. Did you me believe me out of hate?"

He sighed and stopped walking so he could look at her. "No, Ros, I believed you out of love. I've always loved you. Since we were children sucking on lemons for a bet. And you told me that you'd loved Romeo and he'd wronged you, so I believed you. Not out of hate for him but love for you."

He threw the rind of the melon in the gutter and wiped his mouth upon his sleeve. He looked so young standing before her, hopeful and guileless.

He slid closer to her and then stopped, suddenly unsure of himself. "You say I am a brother to you. And so I shall be until you say otherwise."

Rosaline stared at him.

"You may love me as a brother, Ros. And I love you, but not as a sister."

He continued to gaze at her. She squirmed, sticky beneath her arms and aware of the rime of dirt stuck under her nails and the spatters of grease upon her skirts. There was something tangled and itchy in her hair. Yet still he stared at her as if he noticed nothing else but her.

"Rosaline, I love you; by my life, I do."

She found she could not speak. He continued.

"You thought me selfless when I asked for your hand before and tried to save you from the convent. But it was selfish for I love you more than mine own self."

He placed a tender kiss upon her palm and closed her fingers over it as though it were a jewel. Rosaline sighed—if only his word and easy affection could restore her very self as the food had satisfied her belly. He had known her all his life, the good and ill, and yet loved her all the same. She had never pretended to be other than who she was with Tybalt. A muscle in her jaw ticked, and she flinched, knowing that she was undeserving of such affection or acceptance. If he could see into her, he'd understand that she was tainted, soiled with blood and obscenity. The girl she'd been, the one he'd known, was gone.

Tybalt did not understand. He edged closer. His eyes were so wide and brimful of love that she could not bear it; she had to blink and look away. The girl she'd once been could have loved him as he wanted and deserved, that other Rosaline who Romeo had done and left undone. She loved Tybalt. She always had. Whether she could love him as a husband, she was less certain; there were too many layers of blood and hurt and filth. She wanted to. And perhaps wanting could make it so.

Given time enough, could his love wash away the dirt and pain?

"Your silence gives me hope. My life, my soul, my Rosaline."

She spoke at last. "I am amazed and don't know what to say."

Tybalt grinned. "Say that you will marry me. We can stay here in Verona and live out our days until we are old, or else run away with me. After this thing is done, let's elope. Escape together through the green wood and live in Venice. Rome. Athens! Truly, I care not if I'm with you."

Something about his expression made Rosaline laugh. It felt like the first time she had laughed in months. Tybalt was her playmate. They were two berries sprouting on the same branch.

Tybalt smiled. He pressed his nose against hers and kissed her tentatively, uncertainly. She let him and found she did not dislike it. He was not as practiced as Romeo. He had time to learn. His beard was soft upon his chin. Was it possible? She did not know if she could be whole again. Tybalt would help her. He knew how she used to be.

"How are you now?" he asked, stepping back, uncertain.

"Full of joy and sorrow."

She looked at the familiar face, known and unknown. Playfellow, friend, and now lover? She found she liked the thought of his kisses, although anything more filled her with dread. Yet they need not rush, despite Tybalt's eagerness. Rosaline was aware of her own uncertainty, that she changed her mind from one moment to the next. She knew Tybalt's deep affection would help him be patient. Soon she would have all the time she wanted.

She glanced up at the sky. "Daylight's eye is high and hot. We must go quickly to St. Peter's and find Juliet and Romeo."

Tybalt took her hand and, side by side, they raced along the street to the basilica.

When they reached the church, it shone in the afternoon light as if illuminated with gold leaf. A flock of doves alighted upon the steps, filling the square with their soft coos and spattering the front with shit.

Rosaline was ready to push her way inside past the stone lions guarding the great door, but Tybalt held her back. "A moment, Ros," he said, retrieving several pine needles from her hair with tender fingers.

Rosaline adjusted her skirts, and they took the steps two at a time. The nave was still and silent, restful as a forest. She scoured the aisles for her cousin, but there was only a monk kneeling in prayer.

"They're not here," hissed Tybalt.

"The chapel in the crypt," said Rosaline, running ahead, her footsteps clattering in the tranquility.

They descended into the dark, Rosaline becoming aware of her ragged breathing. When they reached the bottom of the steps, Tybalt and Rosaline hid among the slumbering stone effigies and jeweled reliquary skulls, the two of them the only living witnesses to this clandestine ceremony.

In the gloom of the tapering candles, a couple stood before

the altar, a friar joining their hands. Too intent upon the ritual, the little bridal party did not notice them. The girl was tall and slender, a nodding foxglove in her emerald gown; the bridegroom was steeped in love as he slid the ring upon her finger. The scent of incense mingled with mold and damp.

Tybalt nudged Rosaline aside and started forward, but she reached out and stayed him with her hand, hissing at him: "Tybalt, no. It is not them! See, the girl is not Juliet. Nor that groom Romeo."

For a moment Tybalt was too maddened to see the truth of it, and then as he calmed, he slunk back to Rosaline's side, complaining in a whisper, "How come they are not here? What trick is this?"

Rosaline seated herself on one of the low marble tombs and buried her head on her lap. She supposed it was possible that she had persuaded the friar to the stop the wedding, but when she thought of the Franciscan Bible in Cecilia's cell, she felt certain that he'd lied when he said he would try.

The wedding was happening in some other place.

She took a deep breath. "Romeo must have persuaded Nurse to give me or anyone who asked the wrong place. She never would have thought to deceive me on her own devices."

"Where else can they have gone?" whispered Tybalt, agitated. "Or are we already beaten?"

Rosaline licked cracked lips and tried to think. "There's only one place I believe possible. Friar Laurence's cell. Not far from St. Peter's."

Tybalt surveyed the dank chapel with distaste. "I do not like it here, where the departed bear sole witness. It is death in life. If you consent to be my wife, I should not wed you in a place like this, nor in some gloomy friar's cell."

"Where then?" asked Rosaline, curious, as they began to creep backwards into the shadow of the stairwell. They tried not to brush the dripping walls nor the tapers that were spitting wax. She too had always disliked it here, and Romeo's affinity for it had disturbed her.

"I should like us to be married on a riverbank among the kingfishers, or in a green wood with a choir of nightingales."

Rosaline was still not certain that she wanted to marry. She lingered for a moment, imagining the fresh leaves wet from recent rain, the whisper of the trees. If she could choose to remain by Tybalt's side forever without wedding him, then she would do so in an instant; perhaps she could be his not-wife always. They could live together in some other place as brother and sister—none who did not know them would question the arrangement, they looked so alike. Tybalt would love her and she would adore him, and they were already the very best of friends; what more was needed? But a voice nagged at her, whispering that to Tybalt the pleasure of friendship was not enough. She winced. She did not see how she could want him or any man after she'd been caught in Romeo's snare, been bloodied and tainted. Tybalt might not see it now, but the marks were there. One day he'd see them and despise her.

Romeo had spoken the truth—she was a spoiled and broken thing.

And yet, Rosaline understood that Tybalt loved her enough that he would wait. She had loved Tybalt before Romeo; perhaps she could love him after. She loved him already as her brother, nay as her twin self. All she was asking was for one affection to ripen into another, as a green apple swells rosy under the autumn sun. In time, it was possible her cuts would heal and fade from livid red to white. They were still only fifteen, and there was no hurry. She could run away with him, and perhaps in spring, next year or the one after, she would love him as he wanted. She'd ached for Romeo. One day, she might long for Tybalt. The seeds of desire were sown. Love would bring rain. She dared to hope.

Tybalt's foot was already upon the stair. "Rosaline, come!" He reached out for her and they ran up them together.

X

That villain Romeo

Rosaline led Tybalt through the archway into the series of physic gardens. The friars' dormitories were huddled around the edges of the lawn, the windows barred and black. She did not know which narrow cell belonged to Friar Laurence.

They paced the first cloister searching for some sign. It was peaceful there—a tepid breeze, warm as breath on her cheek, lifted the long skirts of a weeping willow, and the flower beds foamed with green fennel, its sharp aniseed scent carried in the air.

"How shall we tell which cell is his? Or have they gone to the chapel?" cried Tybalt, impatient.

Rosaline shook her head. She did not know. She feared their cause was desperate. The basilica bell tolled three. She scoured the garden again and with a start noticed the friar himself clipping daises in another bed.

She ran across the lawn to reach him, her stomach clenching with her dislike of him.

The friar noticed them approach and raised a hand in greeting. When he smiled, his teeth were as yellow as the hearts of the daisies at his feet.

"Well met, sweet Rosaline," he said.

"Are we too late?" asked Rosaline. "Did you marry them after all?"

She would not call him "holy father" now.

He laughed, a note of triumph in his voice as he turned back to tend his flowers. "Through the Holy Church, I have indeed incorporated two into one."

Rosaline felt sick. It burned in her throat. They were too late and Juliet was lost. For a moment there was no sound except the shrill of the blackbird as it hauled out a worm from the softly piled earth, its *pit-pit* loud, insistent.

Tybalt turned upon the friar, his face contorted with grief and anger. Rosaline could see that it took all his restraint to keep from shoving the old fellow into the dirt to grovel among his nodding violets and his sticks of nightshade.

"Please, Holy Confessor," he said, speaking between gritted teeth. "Which direction did they go?"

The friar smiled at him with false serenity. "Ah, the day is hot and all the Capulets are abroad."

"It's no good," said Rosaline, turning to Tybalt in exasperation. "He will not tell us. He's no friend of ours, only Romeo's."

The friar inclined his head. "Indeed, he is as a son to me. And now Juliet, my daughter." He simpered, pleased with himself.

Rosaline flinched. She had never loathed a priest or friar

before, but this man seemed to delight in her misery. There was a sourness to him. "How could you? You lied!"

"I tried, Rosaline; in faith I did. I promised you I'd do all in my power." He raised his hands in surrender. "But in all my time as priest, I've never seen a bride so fair, a maid so blazoned with joy and heaped with love. After we had done, she ran from here to await her groom's arrival, so eager was she to be enjoyed by him."

Rosaline felt the contents of her stomach clot and thicken. She was certain that the friar was envisioning Juliet, young and impatient, joggling on her truckle bed for her new husband. This holy man was in need of a confessor himself. She could see the rim of grime around his soul.

"Enough of this foul lechery," said Tybalt, reaching for his sword now and edging toward the friar.

The friar coughed, feigning frailty, and leaned on his walking stick. "Strike a holy friar, boy?"

Rosaline thrust herself between them and pushed Tybalt back. "Do not play the fool! There are friars and monks close by. All he needs to do is call for aid, and they will come. If arrested you cannot help us!"

Grudgingly accepting the truth of this, Tybalt sheathed his sword and stepped away.

Rosaline turned back to Friar Laurence. "From what you say, Romeo and Juliet are not together then, friar," she said sharply, the scent of roses thick in her throat. "Juliet is away to await Romeo. Alone."

The friar grunted, apparently annoyed that he had given away useful information. Tybalt became alert, ears pricked. Taking Rosaline's elbow he drew her away from the friar to the other side of the physic garden, murmuring, "You must go to Juliet then, and I shall to that fiend, Romeo. If I can find him before this marriage is consummated, then our cousin is free of him."

Fiercely Rosaline shook her head. She knew what he wanted to do, and she would not have it. Maybe it was the endless heat of these days that stirred mad blood and made them want to fight and brawl. She loathed Romeo, but she did not believe in a remedy at the tip of a sword. No angels or answers lay there— only death.

"Tybalt, no. I beg you. Come with me, and let us reason with her together. Only with the two of us united might we succeed. She will not listen to me alone."

Tybalt stared at her with eyes the rich brown of a hazel rod in May, but she no longer felt the same age as him. There had been a parting of the ways. She was ancient now, a crone on the inside, scooped out and shrunken. She wasn't Tybalt's girl anymore, full of light and mischief, but something darker, sadder.

As Tybalt continued to gaze at her, his eyes round, she balked, uneasy that she'd never be worthy of such regard. And yet, there again was that needling of hope. As long as they were together, they could save Juliet. She was convinced of it. Afterwards, there would be time to think of love and other things. She must prevent him from leaving, and there was only one way.

"Stay with me," she said, reaching out her hand. "We'll to Juliet together. And when this thing is done, afterwards we'll to the green wood and have no more of either Montague or Capulet, only Puck and Robin Goodfellow."

He paused—and came back to her, his face suddenly lit with unexpected joy. "Very well. Together then," he said. "Here's to love."

And he kissed her.

"Which way to go?" said Rosaline when they had finished. The scent of rosebay willow herb drifted in the air, and a shaft of light was caught in the blue leaves of a laburnum, stippling the ground. The sweet serenity belied her own turmoil, and she paused, unsure, her heart pounding. For a minute she could not decide.

Above the garden loomed the white finger bone of St. Peter's tower, pointing to heaven and fate above. How could she know which choice was right?

"This way," she said.

They quit the garden and took the road leading back toward the Capulet house. Rosaline did not know how far behind Juliet they were—whether minutes or an hour. The girl might yet be at the house. Romeo could already be with her, the marriage sealed. And yet, Rosaline took comfort in her guess that, like an imp, Romeo would not come to Juliet until dark. He would not risk entry to the Capulet place until he was safely hidden by night's face.

They walked for some time, until the afternoon heat had

lost its savagery, and seeing that Rosaline was tired from her exertions, Tybalt offered her his arm, and grateful, she took it. The sole of her shoe had worn loose and flapped, and there was a blister seeping on her heel; she rubbed at it tenderly. She limped in the trail of Juliet. Shops were starting to open again, but none of the traders paid the pair any heed. They were an unruly, wayward girl and boy roving the streets as dusk encroached. She beseeched the impervious saints above that she would not meet her father nor anyone who knew her.

After some little time, Rosaline noticed a slim figure ahead. She nudged Tybalt.

The light was gloaming, and it was becoming harder to see, but they quickened their pace, and Tybalt, unable to help himself, called out, "Juliet!"

The figure paused and slowed, tentative.

Rosaline, summoning all her vigor, scurried on. "Juliet! It is you!"

Juliet turned to look at them, her face wide with surprise on seeing them together. She started to run toward them, ready to hurl herself into the older girl's arms, before stopping just in front of her, suddenly hesitant.

"You told Tybalt, Ros," she said, full of reproach.

"I had no choice, Cousin. Believe me, I did not wish to."

"Please come with us now, little one," said Tybalt. "We will find some kindly priest, and he will annul this loathsome match."

"We love you, Juliet," said Rosaline. "More than that villain ever could. Please do as Tybalt asks."

Juliet edged away from them. "I do not want to quarrel, Ros," she said defensively. "Only kiss me and wish me well."

Rosaline stepped forward, reaching out and taking her hands, and kissed her with real affection. "I always wish you well. That's all I've ever done and wanted. But, coz"—she looked at her intently—"beggars are worth more than Romeo Montague."

Juliet stiffened with anger and hurt. "Do not speak of my husband so! It is not true. He's no beggar. He's rich in love for me. And he has coin. He showed me. Thirty gold ducats. We'll take all of it with us when we leave the city."

Rosaline gave a cry of exasperation. "Don't you see! The coin is my father's! It's the gold ducats Romeo bade me steal from my father's chest."

Juliet sucked the end of her plait and surveyed her cousin with steady hurt. "All will be well. Do not be bitter or shrewish. It does not suit you, Ros. Find it in your heart to be happy for me, even though fortune is cruel with you."

A pain ticked above Rosaline's eye from shame and from hurtling to and fro like a shuttlecock in the heat all day. Her heel was sore and oozed. She yearned to summon Juliet back to reason and to herself.

"The cause is not yet lost," said Tybalt with a frown. "She is but small. I can pick her up and find some place to hide her away until she comes to her senses."

Juliet darted away from him, afraid that Tybalt was serious.

"Hush," said Rosaline to him impatiently. "Don't speak at all if you will talk like this."

Rosaline thought of Cecilia and the young servant girl with the swollen belly. How many other girls had there been before her? She feared that soon fortune would be spiteful with Juliet, and Romeo would toss her aside, discard her as nothing.

But Rosaline wanted Juliet to understand that she was not nothing and that she was loved.

Juliet's cheek was tipped with carmine, rouged with the happiness that Rosaline longed to scrub from her. She wanted her to hurt too, to understand, but Juliet only surveyed her with unconcealed impatience, hopping from foot to foot, fervent to be gone and back to Romeo.

Rosaline sighed. She felt a nag of envy—she wanted to feel certain, happy, and beautiful again. And then she caught a flare of green, the flicker of a new leaf, wrapped around Juliet's slim finger. For a moment she forget to breathe.

"Let me see your ring," Rosaline asked, trying to keep her tone light.

Reluctant, Juliet presented her hand. Rosaline examined the ring, turning her palm over. The band was thin yellow gold, but the jewel was a fat emerald, brighter than the first buds of spring or grass after rain. At once, she knew it to be her mother's stone and the ring Romeo had reset for their wedding. She dropped Juliet's hand as though it had stung her.

Juliet stared at her, confused, but Rosaline offered not a word in explanation. There was no use. Juliet would not hear the truth of it. Her ears were stopped with poison.

Rosaline gulped and willed herself not to look at the ring

again. To Romeo, it seemed all girls and their rings were inter-changeable. It did not matter now, for Juliet would not see it; she was too imbued in love and had drunk too deep.

To Rosaline's anguish, the girl did not even ask what trou-bled her. Juliet merely hid her hands in her sleeves, saying, "I must hurry home," impatient to be gone.

"Let her go," said Tybalt, putting his arm around Rosaline's shoulders. "Her ears are blocked with his honeyed lies."

Rosaline nodded, dumb, and let her go. She stood in her broken shoe and watched Juliet rush away through the gathering dark. Let her look back, even for a moment, toss her a smile. *Turn around, Jule. I love you, while he only pretends.*

She did not.

Rosaline bit her lip to stop herself crying. Tybalt hugged her close, murmuring endearments, and covered the top of her head with kisses. It was warm and familiar in his arms. He smelled of willow herb and spring.

After a few moments, he gently pushed her away. "The hour has come, Ros. You must let me seek out the villain Romeo."

Fiercely, she shook her head. "No."

"Yes. We have talked enough, but words are only breath."

"While there are words and breath, there is life and hope." Rosaline took his arm and gripped it firmly, but he shook her off.

"Let me go, Ros."

"But I said yes to you and the green wood."

"And once this ugly thing is done, I shall find you." He smiled, and the light in his eyes was joy, but still he would not stay. He stroked her cheek with his fingertips and kissed her on the forehead. "O, heaven is here where Rosaline lives. Here is my heart."

Taking her hand in his, he pressed it against his chest so that she could feel the thrumming of his heart against the thin fabric of his shirt. Beneath it was tender flesh and the outline of fragile, boyish ribs.

Then, kissing her again, he was gone.

"No!" she cried. Tears pouring down her cheeks, Rosaline raced after Tybalt, but he was too fast. She ran at full tilt, her breath coming in gasps, but couldn't catch him. The street was empty. At the crossroad she looked down one narrow alley and then the next, but there was no sign of which way he had gone. She cursed into the darkness. She could only hope and pray that he wouldn't find Romeo Montague tonight.

The sonorous notes of the basilica bell sang out the evening. Monks and house martins gathered to chant vespers. Rosaline paced the city streets for so long that she heard the same voices sing out the hour of Compline. The moon was a high lantern, swinging in the sky round and bright, the sky pinned with too many stars.

Rosaline's eye was downcast—she did not care for the dazzle of the night as she scoured the city for Tybalt. Not one but two cousins in danger. Neither would listen to her. Even when she found Tybalt, she did not know how to persuade him home, and she did not know how else to help rash, lovely Juliet. All she knew was that she must. Rosaline wished there had been someone to save her from Romeo.

She glanced down at her soiled clothes and decided that they suited her. The dirt outside matched the filth within. Wretched and stupid, she deserved nothing better. She ought to have known Romeo was dishonest, to have seen it. She dug blackened nails into her palms until it hurt.

She started in surprise as a beggar woman emerged from a doorway and tugged on her skirt, pleading for a coin. Fumbling in her purse, she gave one to her, asking if a young man had passed along this road. The woman shook her head, retreating back into the shadows.

After weeks without rain, the river had shrunk and now slunk through a narrowed channel, smelling rank. The water was too low, and dead things floated, knocking against the rocks, or else had washed up, putrefying on the banks. The plague dead in their shallow pits festered too, but still Rosaline wondered if the stench was within her—that she was somehow rotten. Before Romeo, she'd feared she was invisible, and now it felt as if her body was not here at all or else not her own. Her blister seeped and bled, and yet even her heel did not seem part of her. Romeo had claimed her body as he fucked it, and she did not know how to make it hers again. He'd taken her virginity and her very self. Rosaline would not allow Romeo to repeat this story again and again with girl after girl. It must end with her.

She noticed another beggar crouched at the side of the river and called out to him, low.

"Did you see a man come this way? Not long ago." She paused. "A young man."

He shook his head and she walked on. Then, a voice called after her, hoarse and thin. "No boy alone, but I saw a mob of Montagues sometime past."

She turned on her heel, her heart stopping for a moment. "Which way did they go?"

He pointed. She ran. *Please don't let me be too late.* Perhaps Tybalt's path hadn't even crossed with theirs. *The city is large enough.*

Then, a sudden cry stilled her thoughts. Loud and harsh, a knife slicing open the smooth belly of evening. Rosaline halted, motionless. She held her breath, listening like a hare for the hunt. The screech of an owl, perhaps. *Let it just be an owl.* And then the cry came again, and it was no bird but a human shout, full of pain and anguish.

Worse than that, she knew that voice. *Tybalt.*

She ran, following the sound along the nearest lane. Sweat gathered between her shoulder blades and trickled down her back. Another voice answered. She could not hear what they said—only the notes of rage and hate. Her footsteps clattered, the loose sole of her shoe flapping as she ran along a deserted alley. The shouts and screams grew louder. She was close now. Nearly there.

Dread eased into her flesh like a summer chill. She paused

outside the entranceway to the graveyard containing the Capulet tomb. The fight was within the walls of the cemetery. From the din, it sounded like the dead themselves had risen.

Opening the gates, she eased inside and heard the yells coming directly from behind the tomb. Even though there had been no rain for weeks, the ground was wet and liquid mud oozed, staining her shoes. After the heat wave the stink was unspeakable. The mud reeked and was stained red in the moonlight. The dead were seeping upward, refusing to be forgotten.

She heard another holler, not from Tybalt but someone else she did not recognize.

"Now in these hot days, mad blood is stirring!"

"Thou art as hot a jack as any in Italy!" came another voice.

There were the sounds of a scuffle. Shoving and grunts. The clatter of metal on stone. *Please don't let him be hurt.*

"By my head here come the Capulets."

"By my heel I care not!"

Turning the corner, in the far end of the graveyard, she saw Tybalt and several Montague men—Romeo and two others, his friend Mercutio and another she did not know—circling each other among the graves, hurling insults like spears. Two young pages cowered at the far edge of the cemetery, clinging to one another in terror. She saw Tybalt poised aloft on a low granite tomb, wielding his sword, eyes lit with crazed anger. A wound on his cheek leaked blood, a dark slash that revealed a swinging flap of muscle. His jacket was badly torn and hung loose, but he seemed not to notice the injury either to his clothing or himself, as he balanced on the balls of his feet, ready to spring.

Below him, Romeo weaved among the graves, gripping his rapier in one hand, his dagger in the other, watching Tybalt with wolfish eyes. Unlike Tybalt, Romeo remained immaculately attired, as if ready for an audience with the prince. To Rosaline's dismay, she took in the two opponents' differences in proportions: Romeo was taller, broader, stronger in every way than Tybalt. Even now his beauty was unsettling, but as she observed the cruelty of his smile, she wondered that she had not always seen it.

"Get down from there!" she shouted. "The prince has expressly forbidden this bandying in Verona!"

Both men ignored her. It was as if they could not even hear or see her, so numb were they made by their own mad rage with one another.

Tybalt spat on the ground and, leaping down, lunged at Romeo, stumbling over a broken grave in his desperation to reach his enemy. "I know what you are!" he panted. "By morning, all Verona shall know too. Thou art a villain! I'll see thee hanged."

"Tybalt, peace!" cried Rosaline, scrambling to reach him, heedless of her own safety, but Tybalt, hot with fury, took no notice of her at all.

"Villain am I none," yelled Romeo, enraged. "Therefore farewell. I see thou knowest me not." He ran at Tybalt, slicing to and fro with his sword, and whether in the wildness of his anger or with indifference to her safety, in pushing roughly past Rosaline, he knocked her back against a tomb.

She landed heavily upon the stone, then retreated hastily to a corner of the cemetery, taking refuge from the slashing blades behind an arched mausoleum. Behind her, the cowering pages whimpered with fear, too frightened to flee in case they got caught in the brawl. Peering out, she saw that Romeo had clambered atop a high sarcophagus, well out of reach of Tybalt. He made a show of sheathing his rapier and dagger, and taking a long drink from his flask. He knelt in mock solemnity and pretended to pray, enraging Tybalt further.

"This shall not excuse the injuries that you have done me and my family. Turn and draw," said Tybalt, his voice already hoarse from shouting, the wound on his cheek smudged and shining with gore.

"I do protest I never injured thee," taunted Romeo. He held up his hands before taking another drink. Then, jumping down but careful to remain out of reach, he padded around Tybalt, nimbly dodging him, leaping from the stone lids of one grave to another.

Rosaline could see that Romeo took despicable pleasure in this, provoking Tybalt and then quickly withdrawing out of reach, toying with him as one would a feral pup.

Tybalt's wits and all his skill were lost in his fury. Enraged, he lunged again wildly.

"O! Dishonorable, vile talker!" he cried. "You did with violent lies and acts assail my cousin."

This verbal parry struck when all his other blows had fallen wide, and Romeo edged closer to Tybalt, where Mercutio and the other Montague could not hear. Only Rosaline was near enough to be privy to their exchange of words.

"We talk here in the public haunt of men," hissed Romeo. "Either withdraw into some private place and speak coldly of your grievances, or else depart." His manner to Tybalt was half aggressive posturing and half beseeching. He gestured to the others. "Here all eyes gaze on us."

"I will not budge for no man's pleasure, wretched man," spat Tybalt.

"Ignoble, vile boy," taunted Mercutio, now sauntering closer to stand at Romeo's side, sword ready in his friend's defense.

To Rosaline's dismay, she saw how Tybalt was outnumbered. She would not stay out of the fray and watch as he was hurt. Leaving the safety of the mausoleum, she clambered over a cracked tomb and, grabbing his sleeve with all her strength, hauled him to one side. He would heed her. "Tybalt! Come with me now," she pleaded, gripping his arm. "Leave this place to the dead and do not join them! Do not give Romeo reason to hurt you. Threaten him or his reputation and he will kill you."

Tybalt shook her off, unable to hear her warning. His skin was mottled all around his neck and chest, his temper was so inflamed. He dripped with sweat. A little way off she spied Romeo conspiring with Mercutio, a sly smile playing upon his lips. Whatever it was he plotted, it would not be good for Tybalt.

Desperate, she tried again. "Come, coz, you can't help Juliet if you're dead." Her voice snagged in her throat and she felt as if she could not breathe. "Please, return with me. Together we shall save Juliet, and then you and I'll to the green wood."

She kissed his lips and tasted blood. *He must heed me, he must.* "Or else if you prefer, we'll to Venice? Or even England. Truly, I do not care how wild the place, so long as I'm with you."

At this Tybalt hesitated, and he seemed to see her for the first time. Rosaline seized her advantage. "No grisly friar or moldering crypt for us. We can laze in the sun and read or quarrel as you wish. Only let's quit this horrid place and these wicked men."

She took his hand and to her relief he let her. She kissed his knuckles, felt the warmth of his skin, and began to lead him away across the churchyard. A bat fluttered above them, a tiny honor guard on black paper wings.

Then a voice called out, taunting him. *Mercutio.* "Tybalt, you ratcatcher, will you walk away?"

Tybalt stopped, stiffened. Rosaline tugged his arm but he was immovable. "What do you want with me?" he asked.

"Good King of Cats, nothing but one of your nine lives. That I mean to make bold with, and then hereafter, dry beat the rest of the eight. Will you pluck your sword out? Make haste, lest mine be about your ears before it be out."

And with that Tybalt was gone again.

"Tybalt!" yelled Rosaline in fury and fear.

He glanced back blankly but didn't even seem to see her, and then he was skipping across the smashed and broken tombs, drawing his sword and dagger as he was sliding in the muck, and rushing at Mercutio. Before Rosaline could prevent him, Tybalt had hurled himself at him, yelling, "I'm for you!"

Romeo called with gleeful delight, "Mercutio, put your rapier up!"

"Come sir, your passado!" shouted Mercutio, making an obscene gesture at Tybalt.

Rosaline was filled with horror and despair. Why wouldn't Tybalt stop? Why wouldn't any of them stop? She snapped around in anger, calling, "Won't you fight for yourself, Romeo? You use Mercutio as your pretty shield. Won't you duel with me? For I know how you like to fight in games with girls." She scrabbled across the graves and toppled stones toward him, pausing only to pick up a fallen branch, jabbing it toward him. "I've my fiddlestick here, if you want to go again?"

Romeo ignored her. His eyes were bright with savage pleasure as he directed the action from a careful distance, astride the top of a cracked sarcophagus, encouraging others to join the fray.

"Draw, Benvolio! Beat down their weapons! Hold Tybalt, good Mercutio!"

Benvolio and Mercutio drove Tybalt back against the boundary fence, where he stumbled and looked as if he were about to fall into the yawning mouth of an open grave. Then, to Rosaline's exultation, he jumped aside.

The air hummed with the mosquito buzz of their blades. The Montagues were a hunting pack and Tybalt their prey. But he was fast, and he had earned his name as the King of Cats: he skipped and parried. He drew the point of his rapier short and held his dagger aloft, grunting with each thrust.

Rosaline could not bear to look nor look away. She stood on tiptoe beside a small stone cross, straining to see.

Mercutio snuck closer and Tybalt feinted. His sword flashed, white beneath the moon.

Rosaline scrambled closer to Romeo, clambering across a smashed gravestone to his side.

"Make them stop," she pleaded.

He pretended not to hear. She was nothing to him now, one of the moths around the grave lamps.

Romeo's cheeks were rosy with pleasure. He relished this as sport. Her hatred for him thickened in her veins.

"I shall make you dance," cried Mercutio. They blocked and dodged. Tybalt jumped and ducked. His sword flickered and Mercutio jabbed. Too slow. Tybalt laughed. He was lighter and quicker, and Mercutio was tiring. Benvolio moved to help him, but Tybalt was too fast for them both, his blade a hornet sting.

Rosaline did not see the blow, only heard Mercutio cry out: "I'm hurt!"

Rosaline surged forward, then stopped. She stared at Mercutio, stricken, as blood rushed from his side and he fell to his knees into the muck. What had Tybalt done? She could not breathe. The air was too close and already smelled of death.

Tybalt gaped at the fallen man in disbelief and horror. It was Romeo he'd wanted, not this other man, this stranger. His face turned pale and bloodless except for the gouge upon his cheek. Below him Mercutio writhed and groveled in the dirt.

Romeo stepped forward with a frown, complaining, "What? Are you hurt?" He ambled over, reached down, offered Mercutio a hand, and tried to haul him to his feet, but Mercutio could not grasp it; his fingers were slippery with fluid. He slumped back. After a moment he laughed and blew a bubble of pinkish blood and spit, coating his teeth.

"Aye, aye, a scratch, a scratch. 'Tis enough," he said.

Rosaline swallowed. It was not safe here for Capulets. In desperation, she tried to draw Tybalt away. They must run, escape this place, run far from there, anywhere, but Tybalt could not, would not move. He stood rooted to the spot like the marble effigies surrounding them on every side, silent and immobile.

She turned to one of the pages hovering at the edge of the graveyard, his teeth chattering. "Fetch a surgeon," she urged. "Go!"

"Courage, man. The hurt cannot be much," said Romeo.

"No, 'tis not so deep as a well, nor so wide as a church door, but 'tis enough, 'twill serve," replied Mercutio. "Ask for me tomorrow and you shall find me a grave man." He snorted at his joke, but the laughter caused bubbles of blood to foam from his nose. He choked, beginning to drown in his own blood and water.

Tybalt gave a moan of horror. "I did not mean to kill him. Not Mercutio. Romeo, yes, but not this man. I hate all Montagues, but…"

Rosaline knelt at Mercutio's side, trying to repress her panic and revulsion, pulling out a stained and grimy handkerchief to stem the bleeding, but with surprising strength, he shoved her away, loathing in his eyes. "A plague on both your houses! Zounds!" He jabbed a finger at her. "A cat to scratch a man to death." He flopped back on the oozing ground, energy seeping from him.

Romeo crouched down and took his hand in his, but he too was shaken off. Mercutio stared at him, hatred and betrayal in his eyes. "A braggart, a rogue, a villain. The devil," he hissed.

"I thought it was for the best." Romeo's voice was the whine of a cart wheel.

"A plague on both your houses! They have made worms' meat of me. Your houses!" whispered Mercutio, eyelids fluttering.

Rosaline trembled with shock and guilt. She should have seen this affair would end only in death, but she'd been as blind as fate. She felt steeped with blame, as though she had inserted the blade into his soft flesh herself. Tybalt remained there stricken and unmoving, his sword limp at his side.

Mercutio thrashed a moment more and then was spent, gone. The silence throbbed.

Now, with a flick of his eyes, Romeo turned his attention back to Rosaline and Tybalt; his pupils burned with animosity. Rosaline's breath caught in her chest. It was clear that he longed to kill them both. His sword glinted. They backed away from him as he stalked them, stumbling over tombstones and the sludgy, uneven ground in their haste to get away.

Tybalt pulled Rosaline behind him. His hand shook, and his sword slid in his grip; he could not hold it steady, and it clanged against the tombstones as if knocking for entry.

"This day is black," said Romeo, his voice low, dangerous.

Rosaline stepped back again and nearly tripped. She crouched behind a grave, leaving Tybalt free to fight.

He stepped forward to face his enemy, his sword still juddering in his fist. He looked so lean and young, a stripling before a sturdy, full-grown oak. Benvolio came out from among the tombs to stand beside Romeo, while Tybalt stood alone.

"My very friend has suffered this mortal hurt on my behalf," said Romeo. "My reputation stained with Tybalt's slander. Tybalt that an hour has been my cousin."

Tybalt looked as though he might be sick.

"O, sweet Juliet, your beauty has made me effeminate and softened my temper," called Romeo, looking heavenward. Then, dropping his gaze again, Romeo moved toward Tybalt.

Tybalt raised his sword but once again could not stop it from shaking. He kept glancing at the figure of Mercutio huddled upon the ground, as though in a moment he might rise and all would be well.

"And the furious Tybalt, alive in triumph and Mercutio slain," continued Romeo, pressing forward relentlessly, his voice calm and steady, full of menace. He began to circle the younger man, slowly and deliberately, feinting here and there, toying with him.

Tybalt was numb and barely able to defend himself, all his

earlier skill and quickness forgotten. He clutched his weapon in both hands now, desperate to stop the trembling.

"Now, Tybalt, take the 'villain' back again. Otherwise, you or I must go with him," cried Romeo.

Rosaline rushed forward, desperate. "Plead for mercy, Tybalt, or he will kill you! You are outnumbered and he's mad with rage and cruel."

Bitterly, Tybalt shook his head. "No! He *is* a villain. I will not perjure myself nor grovel. And he deserves to die!"

"Perhaps, but even so I prefer that you should live!" Tears pooled in her eyes as she begged, but Rosaline could see from Tybalt's face that her words were futile. He was set upon his course, his hand steadier now.

He jumped up upon a mound, but Romeo was bigger and age had lent him experience and treachery. He feinted again and Tybalt followed him, then Romeo thrust out at him in earnest. Tybalt leaped away, but not quite quickly enough, and was caught by Romeo's blade. Merciless and cold, Romeo attacked again, pushing his blade between Tybalt's ribs. It scraped against bone; then there was a nasty, wet sound as it tore into softer tissue. Romeo withdrew and then inserted the razor edge again, slicing down Tybalt's belly and twisting.

Rosaline heard herself scream. Then the horrible clang as Tybalt's blade fell. And then, he slumped, dropping to the earth, silent, in a mess of blood and viscera.

"Murderer!" screamed Rosaline. "Murderer!"

Romeo stared at her. She raced to Tybalt's side. He lay

crumpled and unmoving, his clothes sodden with blood and sweat and shit.

"Speak, Tybalt!" she pleaded, seizing his hand, but it lay limp in hers.

He looked up at her. His first love and his last, his eyes large with surprise and pain. He opened his mouth to speak and she leaned forward, desperate to hear, but he said nothing at all. So she cradled him, drenched in his blood as his guts spooled out of him. In seconds she felt him slacken and die.

She shook her head. *It must not be.* Rosaline beseeched him, tears rushing down her cheeks: "Tybalt. No! Don't leave me now. Don't go!" But as she spoke, she knew it was hopeless; his spirit had fled. He stared with sightless and empty eyes, his face contorted in agony and shock. She gripped his hand in both of hers, slippery with blood.

To her revulsion, Romeo's friend Benvolio sprinted to his side, full of concern for him.

"Romeo away, be gone! The citizens are up and Tybalt lies here slain. Don't stand here amazed! Be gone, away!" he cried.

With a physical effort, Rosaline turned from Tybalt's corpse to Romeo. As if spellbound, Romeo surveyed the scene, taking in the slaughtered dead. "O, I am fortune's fool!"

She saw his features contort with self-pity, watched him shake his head in disbelief. Revolted by his display, she released Tybalt's hand, and rising to her feet, she ran at Romeo and shoved him hard, so that his sword tumbled to the ground. "This was not fortune's doing. This was yours! Thou art a fiend of hell!"

He stared at her, bewildered, as though all the evil he had brought about had happened in a dream, and he'd awoken to discover that it was real.

Benvolio pressed him again. "Why do you stay? Romeo, go!"

Through tearstained eyes, Rosaline watched, revolted, as Romeo tore through the gate of the cemetery. She lay down beside Tybalt's corpse and once again cradled him.

Romeo had stolen Tybalt from her, wrenched him from her, her oldest friend, the man who loved her best. Romeo was a villain, a murderer, and the thief of hope.

Tybalt had loved her, and now her heart was burred with hate. She kissed his forehead, his cheeks, his lips—and tasted metal. His eyes were open, unseeing. She tried to close them, but they would not stay shut, and her fingers were slick with his blood. The night smelled of meat, like a butcher's shop.

After a moment she realized the darkness had become full of voices. Capulet. Montague. They were coming. Torches flickered like an abundance of extra stars.

Benvolio crouched beside her, his arm soft upon her shoulder. She shook him off. "Rosaline? That is your name? They must not discover you here." He spoke gently.

She did not move; she did not care. Let them find her, but Benvolio persisted, entreating her again: "Come now, young Rosaline. They must not find you here among the slain. And when I tell them of this bloody fray, I shall not tell them you were here. This unlucky, fatal scene is no place for you. I swear this upon mine honor—I'll hide all sight and sound of you from this quarrel, or let Benvolio die. Go now too. Take my cloak to hide your bloodied cloths and hurry home, fair Rosaline. Tybalt would not wish you here. He would want you to turn and fly."

The truth of this made Rosaline falter. The voices were growing louder. They were nearly at the gates. She stood and, with one final look at the carnage in the graveyard, turned and fled.

XI

These griefs, these woes, these sorrows make me old. Shame come to Romeo!

The great deep basilica bell sung out midnight as Rosaline banged on the gate to her father's house. Every window was unlit—as if the place was already draped in a curtain of mourning black—except for the pinprick of light emanating from the lamp of the night watchman.

Opening the gate for her, he did not notice the stains on her dress hidden beneath Benvolio's cloak. "They were searching for you all day, signorina. I'm supposed to wake your father should you come home."

"I beg you, don't. Please, Samson, you've known me all my life."

He considered for a moment and then to Rosaline's relief shrugged and withdrew to his hut. She trailed into the house. It was deathly still. The only sound was her own breathing. At least her punishment for having disappeared for the day would be delayed until tomorrow. She could not face her father now.

Her legs were so tired that she hardly had the energy to climb the stairs to bed.

As she closed her bedroom door, she heard a furious knocking upon the front gate. She'd only just made it back in time; the watch was already here. Come to rouse her father and tell him the dreadful news. She felt sick. Footsteps banged upon the stair, then urgent, hushed voices. Someone ran past her door, but to her relief they did not come in. In this new disaster she had been forgotten.

She surveyed her small room with contempt. A fresh nosegay of pansies and larkspur was set upon the sill; apart from that, it looked the same as it had that morning. But the day's tragedy ought to be daubed across the walls. Instead, it was pristine white, unmarked.

Nothing in it was altered except for her.

Her fingers were numb with shock so that it took her several attempts to unfasten the buttons of her gown. The garment was black with muck and Tybalt's blood. It needed to be burned. Her slippers too were drenched with gore. Tears scorched her throat, but if she let them fall, she feared they'd never stop. She'd heard that the heart could swell with love, and a parent's grew with each new babe, but did the heart likewise bloat with grief and sorrow? *O rash, passionate, kind, stupid Tybalt.*

"O, give me back my Tybalt," she whispered to the empty room, her voice unsteady. "Now he is dead, take him and cut him out in little stars." She swallowed hard over the knot in her throat. "I will look up at the sky and see him there."

She gathered a few pieces of kindling along with the dress, shoving them all into the grate and, using the candle flame on her bedside, attempted to set fire to the blood-soaked gown. She was shivering despite the mildness of the night, and her fingers trembled so badly that it took her several attempts before the fabric caught. Naked now, and smeared in congealed and cracking mud and viscera, she hugged her arms around her bare legs, clenching her jaw to stop her teeth from chattering.

Curling up on the hearth, she watched the cloth scorch and tongues of flame flicker. The smoke was acrid and foul-smelling.

Tybalt had died to avenge her honor and no one knew. No one must ever know. Loneliness and bitter smoke choked her.

She awakened in the morning to find herself still lying on the rush matting before the hearth. Her hair reeked of cinders and her skin was freckled with soot. For a blissful moment, she thought it was all a despicable dream, and then she saw the twisted leather of her shoes wedged in the metal of the grate, the soles gnarled and smelling of singed meat. Through the brightness of the morning, the horror of it all swam back to her.

"Tybalt is dead. Tybalt is dead and Romeo murdered him." She murmured the words again and again as if by repeating them, they would make more sense to her, like a difficult catechism studied over. They did not. The world itself made no sense. Its order was misaligned and mutable, its spheres shattered and strange. That a creature like Romeo, foul and base, still walked and thrived while noble Tybalt lay cold and still, his flesh beginning to decay, showed how shattered it was. How could she pray to a heaven or a god that presided over an earth such as this? Her head hurt, her throat was parched, and it felt as if her very soul was raw and throbbing.

There was a rap on the door and then Caterina hurried inside. On seeing Rosaline lying prone on the floor, she ran to her and, kneeling, pulled her into an embrace. "You have heard the rumor then, but do not fear. It cannot be true! Our Tybalt is not dead. I will not have it."

"O, I wish it were not," Rosaline cried, inhaling the sweet familiar scent of Caterina's skin. Caterina hugged Rosaline so tightly that she struggled to breathe.

"We must tell ourselves that he's with Saint Peter now," said Caterina.

At this Rosaline began to sob on her shoulder and found she could not stop. She could only think that Tybalt would be bored in heaven and that he would miss her. Caterina wept too and held her tighter still.

After several minutes, when Rosaline's tears began to subside, the maid released her and, sitting back, finally took in that Rosaline was naked and smeared in filth.

"Where are your clothes?"

"I burned them," said Rosaline, not moving.

She waited for Caterina to ask her why, but unable to stomach any more horrors, Caterina only shook her head, her nose and eyes running. Smearing them on her apron, she rose to her feet. "Your father wants to see you," she said. Taking Rosaline's hand, Caterina drew her up from the floor. "He's mean with temper. We must clean you."

Rosaline allowed herself to be steered to a jug and pitcher of water. She stood as meekly as an infant while Caterina scrubbed at her, muttering at the unconscionable state of Rosaline's skin and hair and hands.

When she was finished, she found a clean gown in the chest and laced Rosaline into it. "You're to go to your father's room now. And he doesn't know that you've heard the awful news. I was under strict instruction not to tell you. He wants to break it to you himself."

Rosaline squeezed the maid's hand, grateful for the warning.

She trailed down the stairs, her feet heavy upon the treads. Nothing mattered now. First Emelia, now Tybalt. She was stalked by Death. He was on his black horse, watching her with cadaverous eyes.

The house was hushed, the mirrors turned to the walls and shrouded. She could not see her own grief reflected back at her, and for this at least she was grateful.

The study door was open and Rosaline entered without knocking. She stood in the doorway, observing her father bent over his ledger scribbling, for several moments before he became aware of her presence. The chamber smelled the same as always, dank as a tomb, the walls at ground level smeared with greenish mold. The miniature of Emelia eyed her with sympathy from Masetto's desk, the locked trunk sitting squat beneath the window the symbol of Rosaline's guilt.

As she looked at it, the box seemed to vibrate and rattle. Perhaps grief and unhappiness had broken her mind, and she was mad? She closed her eyes and then opened them again, and the box was still.

Masetto glanced up and saw her, his face contorted with displeasure. He set down his pen. "Daughter, I see I cannot trust you! How did you get out? This was a treason of the blood. I thought you'd run away. All day you were gone and most of the night! I thought you were abused. What if some harm had come to you?"

As he spoke, Rosaline experienced an unexpected pang of shame. She had not intended to worry her father. He did not usually notice her presence, so it had seemed likely that he would not be troubled by her absence. She bowed her head, contrite. Masetto pressed home his point, banging on the ledger with his fist, saying again, "Yes, indeed, what if some harm had come to you or your maidenhead?"

At this, Rosaline's eyes narrowed and the bubble of her contrition burst. It was her precious virginity that concerned him, not her personhood. It was her reputation—and therefore his—that was of value to him, and not her.

She offered neither explanation nor apology, merely defiant silence.

He grunted in annoyance and gave a dismissive wave. "You are untamable. You and your cousin Tybalt both. And now, alas, I must tell you, Daughter, he is dead!"

Even though she knew the ghastly news, Rosaline heard herself give a small cry. Tears began to run down her cheeks.

Her father sighed and observed her with discomfort and pity, then busied himself rearranging papers on his desk that did not need tidying.

Rosaline found her breath was uneven and that she was beginning to sweat. There was a humming in her ears. She roused herself sufficiently to ask, "How did it happen?" as if she did not know.

Her father glanced at her. "Tybalt disobeyed the prince and sought to quarrel with the Montagues. He slayed Mercutio and was in turn killed by Romeo."

She made no remark, as Rosaline feared that if she tried to speak, she would be sick. There was an acrid taste in her mouth, and all at once she was in the churchyard again, her feet sodden with sludge, Tybalt crumpled at her feet, his eyes open and sightless as a dead bird strewn upon the ground.

Masetto clicked his fingers in her face. "Is your tongue plucked from your head?"

Rosaline swallowed, tasted vomit. "I would that with these little hands I could avenge my cousin's death. I'd slaughter Romeo Montague myself."

"Indeed," said Masetto, pleased. "He shall soon keep Tybalt company. Then I hope you will be satisfied."

"I shall never be satisfied until I behold Tybalt again!" she cried. "My heart is dead."

"Enough," said Masetto, flustered that he had provoked

her too far. "God knows I tried to be a careful father. But as children neither you nor Tybalt would learn by rule of law or by the rod. And now grown, each of you so ungovernable, so unruly, subject only to your own whim and fancy. And alas poor Tybalt has paid the mortal price. I fear that you shall be next." He turned from her in anguish and regret. "Well, I wash my hands of you. By the time this day is out, you shall to the nunnery."

She stared at him whey-faced but offered no objection.

"What? No sullen rebuke?" he said, eyebrows raised.

"Your mind is made up. If I object, I shall only confirm your opinion that I am troublesome and petulant. My misery is absolute. I do not care where I am."

Her father sighed and rubbed his temples. "I see these griefs weigh heavily upon you," he declared more gently. "In acknowledgment for the love your bore your cousin, I'll allow you to attend the funeral. Afterwards, you leave at once," he said. "Now, get you to Juliet's. You and she can console each other for this unkind and untimely loss."

Rosaline withdrew without another word but, as she wandered out into the courtyard, concealed in her sleeve was the portrait of Emelia swinging upon its golden chain. Rosaline was already a thief. The first time she'd been reluctant and had to be cajoled into the crime. This offense she committed for herself and without hesitation. Her days at the convent might be spent in absolution, but this sin was worth the penance.

Juliet was waiting for her in the orchard, cradled among the plum trees. A blackbird perched atop a high branch, his beak a streak of yellow as he cast his joy upon the morning. Already the sun was a furnace from the smithy's yard, stoked till it could smelt and reshape the world.

Juliet opened her arms and Rosaline ran to her, and the two girls sat huddled together sobbing in the shade as the birds sang and the sun shone.

"That fiend killed our cousin," spat Rosaline when at last she could speak.

Juliet looked at her for a moment before scrutinizing her bare and grubby knees. "I cannot speak ill of my husband," she said. "And Tybalt would have murdered him."

At this Rosaline recoiled from Juliet. Her cheeks were stippled and red. "Your *husband*! You choose him still? Your twelve-hour lord? Romeo, who slaughtered our kinsman? Our playmate? Our Tybalt?" She spoke through a mess of tears. "Romeo played with him and killed him as if it was nothing. His life was nothing. Romeo sheathed his blade between Tybalt's ribs. I heard it go in. Wet and slick. I was there when Tybalt fell and when he died."

Juliet eyed her cousin in dismay.

"And when poor Tybalt's life had ebbed away," Rosaline continued, "Romeo had no regret except for himself and his own predicament. His only thought was for himself."

Folding her arms, Juliet turned away from her. "It isn't true.

Romeo is an honest man. They fought and he had no choice but to defend himself from furious Tybalt's blade."

"I tell you it is true, for I was there and bore reluctant witness to the whole cold and brutal dispute." Rosaline's voice cracked and she glanced away, wiping her eyes. She could smell the mud of the graveyard again. The blood and rot and cries of pain.

Juliet stared at her agape and then, reaching for her, declared softly, "I did not know you were there."

Rosaline shook her off. "No one does. Benvolio Montague swore he would not tell and it seems he kept his word. But for what purpose? For what purpose any of it if you stay with Romeo? Tybalt fought and died for us."

"He killed Mercutio, Ros! He would have slain Romeo!"

"Yes, to avenge my honor and yours. It was rash and typical of him. He was full of youthful impetuousness. And yet to ignore it utterly renders his death void of meaning. Don't do that, Juliet. Give him meaning and valor. I beg you."

"How?"

"Tell me you are not with Romeo. That you do not love Romeo."

"I cannot, coz. I shall not be forsworn."

Rosaline shook her head. "Then you kill Tybalt twice. You kill his memory too."

"Stop! Cousin! That's too cruel. I suffer too."

"How so? You seem well, for all that you weep."

"Romeo is banished for his part in this. I'm sentenced to a living death without him."

"Ha. This garden, these fruits, these friends," said Rosaline, plucking a budding apple and a green plum and hurling them upon the ground. "This is no living death. One day, if you so choose, you can fly to him." She paused, distress making her breathless and her head swim. "Yet I fear that before long, you will discover what Romeo truly is, and then you will find not merely a living death but death itself."

Juliet put her hands over her ears. "Fie! Hush. Do not speak like this. I shall not hear it."

Bubbles of rage crackled beneath Rosaline's skin, and yet she did not want to part from Juliet full of animosity. Rosaline at least understood who the real enemy was, even if Juliet did not yet. Taking a breath, she tried to sound temperate. "I do not speak to wound you, Juliet, but out of fear. From tomorrow I cannot help you. We must part today, and I hope as friends. I'm to the convent this very eve."

"O, Rosaline! We're both condemned. You to the wall and me to purgatory."

At this, Rosaline's temper snagged once more. "Waiting to join your lover in Mantua is not purgatory! Tybalt is done and gone," she said, nearly shouting now, her resolution for calm quite forgotten. She surveyed Juliet in fury, her pulse ticking in her temple. Juliet had adored Tybalt, and yet this diabolical love for Romeo appeared to insulate her against even the keenest knife of grief. Juliet might weep and insist her heart was broken, but her cheek was touched with roses as well as dew.

The two girls fell silent, both lost in unhappiness and

unable to comfort one another. They remained cradled in the lap of neighboring apple boughs, knees almost touching, and yet Rosaline had never felt so bereft, so alone, while in the presence of a friend. She knew of no words that could reach Juliet and persuade her of Romeo's wickedness. This monstrous love had armored Juliet against her.

There was a commotion from the house, and then Rosaline saw Lauretta stalk across the scorched grass toward them, shielding her eyes against the glare of the sun. She called to them across the garden. "Has she told you the news? There are joyful tidings in the midst of our sorrow. Won't she be the most beautiful bride?"

Rosaline was perplexed. Her aunt could not be satisfied with Juliet's marriage to Romeo. Surely Juliet had not informed her of it?

Lauretta reached them in the orchard. She wore a fine mourning veil stitched with exquisite embroidery pinned in her hair and had tossed a black velvet cloak over her shoulders. This, Rosaline supposed, signaled her melancholy at the loss of her nephew, for her expression displayed none. Her eye was bright and not dejected, and she smiled with good cheer. *A spoke of fortune's wheel must indeed be snagged and broken.* Lauretta displayed happiness on the day after her nephew's murder. Even Juliet flitted from joy to sorrow like a magpie; her thoughts moved from love and marriage to Tybalt's untimely death and back again. Rosaline's own were fixed only upon Tybalt, and she resented the intrusion of Juliet's bliss.

Juliet shriveled beneath her mother's gaze. Lauretta clapped her hands in anticipation. "Next Thursday morn, the gallant and noble gentleman Paris, at St. Peter's church, shall make her a joyful bride."

Juliet did not say a word. Rosaline surveyed her with pity, now understanding why Juliet too considered herself condemned. This was bitter news indeed.

Lauretta preened, reveling in the prospect of the upcoming wedding and prattling on about the expected *contra-donora* such a wealthy gentleman must bring. A magnificent selection of clothes and precious jewels to present to his bride, and O, the honor of being joined with such an intimate friend of the prince and, indeed, the gold and cash. Lauretta rattled on quickly and without pause as Juliet grew paler and paler, waning like the moon.

Rosaline detested Lauretta for her happiness at such a moment. How could she think on anything other than Tybalt? Her love ran shallow as a summer stream, while Rosaline's own was a river, deep and wide.

At last, when Lauretta's chatter and excited self-regard had dried up, she left them alone beneath the apple trees once more.

Juliet turned to Rosaline, her visage gray and stricken. "Now do you see? How can this match be prevented? Do you have a word of comfort?"

For once, Rosaline did not.

Juliet plucked a leaf and shredded it between her fingers.

"Nurse urges me to forget my Romeo and to marry Paris. 'For he's a lovely gentleman.' But my husband is on earth and my faith is in heaven! Comfort me, counsel me, Cousin!"

Rosaline slid her arm around Juliet's thin shoulders. "All is not lost," she said, knowing it was but meager consolation. At that moment she could think of little else to say. Juliet was being bartered to a rich man and she to God. Neither of them had any choice in their destiny.

"Paris is old and fat and I do not love him," Juliet said with disgust. "He looks at me as if I am a griddle cake he wants to stuff into his mouth."

Rosaline held her.

"If all else fails, I myself have the power to die," continued Juliet, smearing her hand across her cheek to wipe away tears before they fell to the ground.

Rosaline shuddered despite the heat of the day. "No! Is this you, or is it Romeo who talks thus? We have had enough of death. I beg you, no."

Romeo was an infestation. He twined around girls and blighted them with thoughts of death and self-injury. Before she'd met him, loved him, Juliet had never once spoken thus.

"I would rather leap from the battlements of any tower than marry Paris," insisted Juliet. "Or instead chain me with roaring bears. Or hide me in a charnel house with dead men's rattling bones. And I will do it without fear or doubt."

Rosaline hugged her tightly. "I do not question it, but let us hope it will not come to that."

Juliet reached into her sleeve and pulled out a short dagger with a rusted blade. She flicked it toward Rosaline, saying, "Or else I have this knife."

Rosaline tried to snatch it from her. "Juliet, no!"

Juliet concealed it again in her dress before Rosaline could take it from her.

"You are too young and quick to speak of death," said Rosaline pleadingly. "Have you so little regard for life?"

"For such a life as this is, Cousin, yes."

"You are the sweetest flower, and I shall see to it that Paris does not pluck you," insisted Rosaline. "I beg you, trust me and not Romeo."

Juliet did not reply, but Rosaline saw some color return to the white lead of her cheek.

Rosaline hoped that Romeo had been gentle with her on their wedding night, that for those hours at least he had been kind and pretended love as best he was able. He was well practiced, after all. But as the dagger slipped, protruding from Juliet's cuff, causing her to tuck it back into its hidey-hole once more, Rosaline noticed ugly crimson scratches scoring the inside of Juliet's wrists.

Furtive, Juliet caught her gaze and hurriedly pulled her sleeves lower. Rosaline said nothing but her stomach twisted and twisted. It did not matter whether Romeo had wielded the blade or Juliet herself, these wounds were caused by him.

Every part of her that had once been full of love for him was now steeped in hate.

Just before midday, as Rosaline walked homeward along the empty streets, her heart skittered, her thoughts tumbling over each other. Juliet was Romeo's prey, and only Rosaline knew. The loneliness of this awful knowledge frightened her. But she could not tell, for if discovered, Juliet too would be walled up in the nunnery, despoiled and spurned.

Rosaline was certain that Romeo understood how parlous was Juliet's predicament. As with Rosaline herself, Juliet's vulnerability was part of her appeal to Romeo. He was a vigilant hunter. He selected girls with diligence, ensuring that while Cupid shot his arrows blind, he never missed. Romeo did not fall in love but stepped with care. He preferred girls young and friendless and easily swayed by his quick tongue and remarkable looks. Grown women were not so readily convinced by either wit or a fine eye. Rosaline considered him the worst kind of predator, beautiful with clean white teeth and a perfect smile that promised life and delivered death. Love with him was carnal and delicious and all consuming; he wasn't just a hunter but a thief, stealing from girls their very selves. She thought of the marks on Juliet's wrists. Juliet might not know it yet, but her destruction had already begun. Rosaline felt that inside her own self; she was now completely empty, void as a ransacked tomb.

It was this rotten city that allowed Romeo to rise and move unseen. The worthy citizens, mothers and fathers, had allowed him to slink through unstopped, like the rats and feral dogs. These good people refused to see him for what he truly was, and it was because of their blindness that Rosaline and Juliet and the other girls had fled into his arms. He appeared to offer an escape from invisibility and indifference, or a marriage ordered by a father that felt like the bars of a prison cell. At present, Juliet was glutting herself upon Romeo. It was only when she'd finished gorging that she'd realize—too late—the feast was rotten.

Rosaline's bitterness with Juliet's parents simmered into rage. What was wrong with Lauretta and Old Capulet—even Nurse? They had been birthed under some misshapen star. How could they urge Juliet to marry Paris? Juliet was still only thirteen. What Juliet said was true—Paris's mouth did water when he looked at her; he was greedy for her. Yet if Paris was too old for Juliet, so was Romeo. It saddened Rosaline too that Juliet had lain with Romeo, married Romeo. Why had Nurse encouraged her in this, enabled that wayward romance and not warned her against it? If Juliet's parents knew of that clandestine love, they would be dismayed and shun her, and yet with this political, expedient match to Paris, they were content. Nothing would distract them from it, not even Tybalt's corpse, still warm, his quick brown eyes clouded over.

It was because of Lauretta and Nurse and Old Capulet and the good honest *hypocrites* of Verona that Juliet believed it was well and good for her to wed a man when she was still a child. While trying to break her in for Paris or his like, her family had seen to it that she was nicely softened for Romeo. Her arms had already been open and ready for him.

Still lost in her furious reverie as she entered the courtyard of her father's house, Rosaline was knocked sideways by Caterina, who flew at her, pulling her into an embrace, as she cried, "What a day is this! Tybalt was such a good boy. Nay, I must not lie, he was the naughtiest, but I loved him."

Rosaline nodded. "As did I. He was my best friend. And now I'm all for vengeance."

Caterina paused and stared at her through puffed and swollen eyelids. "Nay. Leave it be. Vengeance is not for you."

Rosaline balled her hands into fists. She was tired of being told what was for her and what was not, even by those who loved her. If she could fight Romeo herself, she would do it. She gave a tiny laugh—she was becoming as hot as Tybalt. Perhaps it was this infernal weather heating her blood.

She trailed Caterina into the kitchen. Unthinking, Caterina began to reach for ingredients and started to cook. Stricken with anguish, her mind did not know what to do, but her hands did.

Rosaline settled on a bench beside the open range and watched as she had a thousand times before as Caterina squeezed transparent lumps of lard between her fingers before rubbing it into snowy peaks of flour. Tears sprang to her eyes once more. As children, she and Tybalt had sat there, squatting beneath the pine table, stroking the ears of the kitchen spaniels and watching Caterina cook, vying with the dogs for stray scraps. Now, she felt her friend's absence as a dark void beside her. She wanted the comfort of his ghostly presence, some childish phantom of a boyish Tybalt licking the spoon or sucking a sugared cinnamon stick, but there was nothing. Just the tick of the cicadas and the spinning dust from the flour as it snowed to the floor.

Unhooking the great rolling pin from above the scrubbed table, Caterina began once more the spooling out of pastry upon the table and pressing it into a dish. Again, a brown and coiled heap of eels lay in a knot on the wooden butcher's block. They smelled of fresh rivers and mud and fish and childhood summers. Caterina picked up each one between her fingers, skinning them with her knife, picking out the bones and discarding them, the blade click-clacking at speed but never nicking her thumb, the pile of black and mirrored skin and naked, gored river slugs growing as she laid the sliced eels onto the base of the pie. Last, she grated nutmeg in before sealing shut the lid.

Rosaline gave a sad laugh. This was her last eel pie in this house. Her days there had indeed been measured out in eels, laid end to end.

"I leave tomorrow, Cat," she said softly. "The time has come. When I go, will you come?"

Caterina slid the pie in the oven and straightened. "Never fancied myself as a nun, for all that I love you."

Rosaline smiled. "No, in the abbey kitchens. They must want a cook like you. Will you?"

Caterina looked at her. "I'll think on it. Even as a nun, I fear you'll need some watching over."

"I will," agreed Rosaline. She studied Caterina and then said, "And maybe, one day, not at once, but in month or even a year, we could find a way to escape the convent together and come to a new life. After all, I don't know what you did or were before you came to us, but I think perhaps we could change ourselves?"

Caterina looked sad and did not answer.

"Come, it's possible," insisted Rosaline. "We'll sail to Illyria, or even England."

She'd once hoped to make this journey with Tybalt but that was not to be. It was a bitter thought to offer up their adventure to Caterina. The maid said nothing, lacking all Tybalt's quick excitement.

At last she said, "Speak to your abbess and see if I may enter your kitchen, then. So long as servants can come and go freely there, I'll think on it." The scent of pastry began to fill the room, curling up toward the ceiling. Caterina came to sit beside Rosaline and stretched out her legs. "At least you are free of Romeo," she said carefully. "He can seek some other girl to play the part of his lady."

Rosaline bit her lip in shame, reminded again that it was her fault that he had found Juliet. If it was not for Rosaline, he would not have been at the Capulet ball. She longed to peel away her guilt like the eels in Caterina's pie had lost their skins, but it clung to her.

"He has discovered the actor already for the part," said Rosaline quietly. "And married her."

"Poor girl! We must pity her."

"It is Juliet. Romeo has married Juliet."

Caterina gave a cry of dismay.

"No one knows the truth of it but us and Tybalt. And he took it with him to his grave. Nurse shares the secret but will not tell."

Caterina shook her head in disgust. "She's but a capon. She never cared for my pie." She continued fretting. "Our poor, dear Juliet. And isn't she to marry Paris?"

"That is her parents' wish. But she says she will die instead. I don't know what to do, Caterina."

Caterina sat back and studied the wooden cross pinned to the wall. "We'll pray on it. The Virgin save me, I should have stopped you from going to that masquerade. And now Juliet, the little wretch. If you tell, it will not go well for her." She sighed. "Indeed, we'll pray on it."

Rosaline wished that prayer would suffice against Romeo, but she took what solace she could in the familiar comfort of Caterina's kitchen. The smell of the pie. The dusting of the goose wing brush as Caterina stood up to sweep. The whirr and tick of the cicadas beyond the open window.

A few minutes later there was a rap at the door and a ragged boy peered around the kitchen door.

"I don't have anything for you," Caterina snapped. "There's nothing but fish skins today, and you'll have to fight the dogs for them."

"I don't want your scraps. I want Madonna Rosaline Capulet—?"

"Whatever for?" Caterina asked.

"She's to follow me, good lady. A maid is asking for her. A sick one. Mistress Rosaline must come and quickly."

Rosaline studied him for a moment in puzzlement and then slid to her feet and made as if to go with the boy, but Caterina put out a strong hand and stopped her. "No. Not again. You're not striking out alone to goodness knows where with some vagrant boy."

Rosaline gave a grunt of frustration. "Then come with me."

The boy was fidgeting, impatient. His feet were bare and made dirty prints on the brick tile floor. "Come alone or both of you, but quickly now."

They followed him.

Outside the day felt hotter than the kitchen oven. Rosaline's skin prickled. Following the boy, they turned away from the wealthy and familiar parts of the city and down toward the area beyond the fish market to the tanneries, where all effluence and filth flowed.

They walked in silence and after some little time, Rosaline observed that many doors were marked with red plague crosses. Here the pestilence still reigned.

"Who is it that asks for me?" she demanded of the boy, trotting to keep pace with him.

"You will soon see."

The houses were half tumbled down and ramshackle. Most of the shutters on the windows were broken. There were no geraniums in tubs nor frescoed Madonnas on the walls, only dried fish strung up on string like shriveled and stinking streamers.

Several of the buildings lacked doors, and half their roofs had fallen in and they appeared abandoned, until Rosaline saw that ragged washing was threaded in loops between the balconies. The streets here were quiet, and the few people who sat on the steps sieving stones from lentils were too busy with their own concerns to take notice of Rosaline, Caterina, or their skinny snaggletoothed guide.

The air caught in Rosaline's throat. The stink from the tannery spread over the streets in a haze, while the smell from the old fish market had seeped into the cobbles for a hundred years, the excrement and piss flowing downhill through the streets to the river and becoming lodged there. There were no mule carts or elegant horses, only the occasional screams of thin babies waiting to be fed. The spire of St. Peter's basilica was far off, its tolls supercilious and distant. These poor souls were beyond its purview.

"In here," said the boy, pointing to a door.

Rosaline thanked him and paid him. The house was even worse than those that surrounded it, if what remained of the dilapidated shell could still be called a house.

"I work hard so I wouldn't have to come to places like this," snapped Caterina. "Why can't you let it alone? Why must you go with every boy who knocks on the door?"

"I do not know. And I'm sorry, good Caterina, but you didn't have to come."

Rosaline pushed open the door with her shoulder.

The smell hit her first. It was even worse than the stench

in the street outside. Death. She could barely see for the reek of death. Something had lain here dead and decomposing for days. She glanced around for the corpse and saw a small, cramped, and gloomy room, with an open hole instead of a fireplace. There was a heap of blankets on the ground, and beside this makeshift bed, a tiny box crib draped in black. Tucked inside the blankets was a dead girl.

As she stared at the scene in horror, the corpse blinked, then with great effort lifted an arm. Rosaline watched in revulsion. Then another woman emerged from the shadows at the corner of the room and wiped the brow of the figure in the bed with a rag.

Rosaline edged closer. Caterina clung to the doorway, as if afraid to leave the daylight.

"You came," said the girl, looking at Rosaline.

Rosaline tiptoed closer, hands tight and moist at her sides. "You," she said. "Of course it's you."

The thin, childish figure was the maidservant Romeo had seduced and abandoned. As Rosaline peered closer, she saw that the blankets were stiff and black with dried blood. She tried not to look at the silent crib draped with black. Something scuttled across the floor.

"Don't stay long, mistress, or you'll tire her," said the woman gripping the rag.

"What does it matter?" said the girl. "I'll die anyway."

"Have it your way, then. Don't listen. I'm only staying out of charity and pity." As the woman marched out of the cheerless room, slamming the door, Rosaline watched in dismay.

"Go after her, give her this," said Rosaline, pressing a coin into Caterina's hand. Relieved to be released from the chamber, Caterina hurried away.

Rosaline turned back to the small form huddled in the nest of stained blankets. "Tell me your name," she said, crouching beside her. "I did not ask it before."

"Laura. I was his Laura. For a while at least."

Rosaline took the girl's thin hand. The bones were as thin and fragile as that of a bird's. If she pressed them too hard, they would snap.

Laura lay back on the filthy blankets, her stomach still swollen beneath them. She looked both childlike and gaunt and old.

The smell of rot and death, Rosaline realized with horror, was emanating from Laura. She must be decaying from the inside. Even the abbess with all her wisdom could not save this wretched, suffering girl. She would not rise from the birthing bed.

"I'm happy you are come. He would not," said Laura.

"Did you send for him?"

"Yes. The child pains came too early. And I sent word to him. I think perhaps he cared for me a little, as he sent Friar Laurence. He sat with me and prayed and read to me."

Glancing to the side of the bed, Rosaline saw another neat, leather-bound Bible bearing the same heraldic stamp as the friar's own and the one in Cecilia's cell.

"The friar gave me a vial of liquor to drink when the agony became too much to bear," continued Laura. She gestured to the corner of the room near the empty grate, where a bottle stood.

Rosaline fetched it and turned it over in her hands. It was of brilliant blue Murano glass, the color of a June sky. The only bright note in the colorless room. A drop of distilled liquid glowed in the bottom of the vial.

"Did it help?" asked Rosaline.

"My child was born dead. What medicine is there that can aid with that? And now I'm dying too. Some part is lodged inside me, putrefying. They cannot drag it out, though my god, they've tried."

Rosaline once more squeezed the girl's hand and closed her eyes. She felt death all around her in this small and fetid room. Yet Death himself was pitiless. He sat watching, waiting, and did not collect. Beads of fever anointed Laura's brow. Rosaline reached for her handkerchief to dab them away and Laura closed her eyes, exhausted.

Rosaline reexamined the bottle in her palm. "Can I keep this?"

"Take it."

She secreted the vial inside the small embroidered pouch hanging at her waist.

"I heard you are free from him now?" asked Laura, opening her eyes to look at her. "Is it true?"

"It is true that there is no truth in him," said Rosaline, unable to keep the bitterness from her voice.

"Ah, he's true when he's in love, but he falls in and out of love with the tides."

Rosaline nodded. "His kisses are Judas's own children."

"But taste sweeter," said Laura, rueful even now. She closed her eyes again and seemed to drift off to sleep, but then said softly, "Without a candle I must go dark to bed. Pray for me. And weep when I'm no more."

"I swear by my troth I will," said Rosaline, stroking the matted hair away from the girl's face.

Soon after, Rosaline left the dank and dark room with sadness and relief, holding open the door so the goodwife could slink back inside, bribed to return with Rosaline's gleaming silver coin. Out in the daylight, Rosaline looked again at the blue glass vial in her hand. Were the contents made to ease pain or to hurry death? The abbess would surely know.

Rosaline and Caterina began to meander back through the sun-hardened streets to Masetto's house, weariness weighing down Rosaline's limbs. She confessed to Caterina how Laura had come to the house, and whose child the girl had been carrying.

Caterina listened in silence, revolted by Romeo's further crimes. "It could have been you or Juliet in that foul room," she said at last.

They walked on without speaking again, each busy with her own unhappy thoughts. Laura was dying before she'd had a chance to really live. The babe had never lived at all. Rosaline hoped that Laura wouldn't suffer much longer. As she'd promised, she'd see to it that Laura was buried properly with her child, and not in a pauper's grave.

The women continued on, their backs warm from the fierce afternoon sun. Caterina was wrong. Prayer alone was not sufficient to keep the living safe from Romeo.

XII

Romeo...madman, passion, lover

As they neared Rosaline's father's house, they saw that the gates stood wide, several sweating, stamping horses and grooms lingering in the street. With dread, Rosaline entered the courtyard, Caterina close at her side. Her Uncle Capulet's horse was being brushed down and watered at the trough. What had happened here and why was her uncle come? When she'd left Juliet earlier, her aunt and uncle had been busy with preparations for Juliet's wedding to Paris. Had some accident or sudden sickness befallen Rosaline's father? It was not the plague, for then both fear and the watch would have kept them all away. There was no red cross daubed upon the door.

"Where is my father? My uncle?" she asked the groom urgently.

He pointed to the house and she ran inside, leaving Caterina in the courtyard. What new catastrophe had befallen the family? Servants scuttled through the hall but all looked away from her and would not meet her eye. The doors to her father's room were thrown open, and she found him sitting in his study, pale and disheveled, surrounded by papers and books tossed all about him. He looked up at her, his expression bewildered and lost.

"Are you ill?" she asked, taking in his disordered state and pale cheek.

"Ill luck. They have taken my ducats and my wife. Emelia has been taken from me again."

Glancing beside him, she saw that the sturdy money chest was unlocked, the lid yawning, and all at once Rosaline understood that her crime had been discovered. Was her guilt uncovered too? Her heart beat frantically in her chest.

Masetto ran his hands through his hair, making the few strands stand on end. "I've been robbed. All the money that was to go with you to the convent is stolen, Rosaline," he said. "It was a tidy sum and it has gone. I am robbed of coin and dignity—and my wife."

It was clear from his tone that he did not know it was her who had taken them. She breathed again. He pawed his face with his hands. "I was a fool for not being more fastidious. And I must plead your forgiveness, for when you go to the convent, it shall not be in such comfort as I'd intended. I shall send you with the coin I can spare. Can you forgive a silly old man?"

"For this, yes," said Rosaline slowly. "Though verily perhaps it is a sign that I should stay at home."

At this Masetto almost smiled. "Hush, or I'll start to believe that you stole it to stop me from sending you away."

Rosaline thought it wise to say nothing further. She felt almost guilty for stealing the miniature of Emelia. It burned next to her skin beneath her dress.

Masetto rose and surveyed his room once more with distress. "O, loss upon loss. The thief took so much. My gold and your mother. The criminal could not have wanted the portrait—her beloved face was not the jewel he wanted, but the emeralds and rubies and gold adorning the frame."

Rosaline experienced another tickle of shame, like sweat easing down her spine.

"Your cousins come here to offer consolation," he said, "but really they are here to mock me in my dotage. They insult and exult at once. I do not want their feigned pity. There is no satisfaction and no revenge to be had. I shall not find this thief."

Seeing his real consternation at the loss, Rosaline felt some remorse, but not enough to confess to either of the thefts—if she did, her punishment would be absolute. Instead, she took his hand. "You are not in your dotage. And my uncle's hair is hoarier still. Pay them no heed if their pity is not real, but I believe it is. Do not worry for me. I do not need comfort in the convent. I shall I have what I deserve."

Her father was both surprised and pleased by her affectionate concern and patted her hand before pressing into it a single shining ducat. "I had unlocked the chest to take out money for Tybalt's gravecloth. There was not time to find purple or gold to wrap your mother's corpse. Honor Tybalt—do not send him to his tomb ill-favored."

Rosaline surveyed her father in surprise, struck by this last consideration toward Tybalt. It was more than Capulet pride or fear of God; it was something close to a tenderness of which she had not believed him capable.

As she thanked him, her Uncle Capulet pushed past her into the room, eager to speak with his brother. "None of the servants know anything, or claim as much," he declared. He began firing a quiver of questions at her father, who sat meekly, head bowed in humiliation, absorbing the assault. "Is the window always left open so? And why do you do not hang the key about your neck, Brother? Are you so careless of your wealth?"

Her uncle shooed Rosaline out, closing the door behind her. As she walked toward the hall, their muffled voices pursuing her, she hoped fervently that none of the servants would fall under suspicion for her own sins.

The circle of the coin her father had given her was heavy and warm in her palm. It was a melancholy task she must perform. She'd once hoped to be given gold ducats from her father to choose wedding clothes for her trousseau, but instead she was to buy a gravecloth. The last act of compassion for the man she'd loved most perfectly.

She emerged from the womb-dark of the hall into the hot light of the afternoon. The air was sweetened with honeysuckle and jasmine, and thick with the purr of bees. She thought of Laura in her foul and darkened chamber. There was no one to purchase a golden gravecloth for her when the time came. Glancing to the east of the house, she saw lobes of grapes on the loggia swelling in the heat, their leaves shading the terrace beneath, where, to her surprise, Juliet lingered, staring out at the garden beyond.

Rosaline wandered over and perched beside her.

Her cousin did not appear to notice her and continued to gaze out, unseeing.

"Where are you, my lady? Not here, I think," said Rosaline.

Juliet started and looked around.

"My father has been robbed," said Rosaline.

"Indeed, I heard the news."

"You heard it before today for I told you it myself. I am the thief. I took from my father's chest thirty golden ducats. I'll wager the very same sum that Romeo Montague showed you and proclaimed, triumphant, was for your new life in Mantua."

Juliet grew quiet and still. "Perhaps he showed me some ducats. If it was the same sum, I do not remember."

"Liar."

Juliet flushed. "You would not do it, Ros. I know you would not steal from your father."

"Ah, but I did. Would you not do anything Romeo asked of you? Would you not die for him if he asked?"

"I would," replied Juliet, her voice solemn.

"Then, sweet girl, what he asked of me was not as dear. He did not want my death, only a few shining coins. He persuaded me that they were mine already and that I stole only from myself." She stood and plucked a grape. It was small and hard and covered in a chalky layer of dust. "What are thirty ducats beside a life? My price was cheap compared to what I fear he shall ask of you."

"I do not mind. I love him. I'd die for him willingly."

"Then I cannot change your mind. But know that the man for whom you'd die is a vagabond and a thief."

At this Juliet grew angry. "*You* were the thief. The sin is yours."

"That I cannot dispute and I shall do my penance. But I was Romeo's instrument. I no longer have the gold. He keeps the spoils of my crime."

Juliet was still annoyed, her cheeks hot. "Was Tybalt perfect?" she demanded. "Or was he rash, intemperate, and quick to hate? And yet you loved him."

"I did, for he was my friend and other self. And he was all those things you say, yet his faults were mended by my love, or else seemed so. But he was also kind and loyal, and he loved me as fixedly as the sun and stars. Your Romeo is the moon. Changeable and cold."

"Fie! Not with me." Juliet took a breath to steady herself. "I can't marry Paris, don't you see?"

The thin shadows of the vines played on the skin of Juliet's cheeks and hands like veins, aging her. Rosaline recognized her cousin's desolation and that her fear made her reckless. The tip of the dagger protruded again from Juliet's sleeve and, for a second, Rosaline could picture her bloodless in her grave.

Juliet met her eye. "For all your words, Ros, you cannot help me. I went to speak with the friar today. He is Romeo's friend and mine. He has a scheme and hopes to unite me with my Romeo." In petty triumph she held up a small blue Murano glass vial, as bright as a cloudless June sky. It caught in the light, brilliant as lapis lazuli, and shone as she shook the contents, tiny bubbles rising upward.

"Tonight, when I'm abed, I am to drink this distilling liquor, and then, presently, through my veins shall run a cold and drowsy humor, and no pulse, no warmth, no breath shall testify I live—"

"Juliet, no—!"

"The rose in my lips and cheeks shall fade to ashes and my eyes' windows fall like death. Each part shall stiffen, stark and cold, and appear like death."

"Like death or as death? O, Juliet, I beseech you, no." Rosaline placed her hands upon the younger girl's shoulders as she implored her, but resolute, Juliet shook her head. She would not even look at her.

"He promised me, Rosaline, that after two and forty hours I shall awake as if from a pleasant sleep. And in the morning, my bridegroom will come to rouse me from my bier and take me from my tomb and bear me to Mantua and a new life, free from all this present shame. The friar is sending one of his Franciscan brothers with speed to Mantua, to Romeo, bearing a letter of our plan."

Rosaline shook her head slowly.

"I don't believe he will send Romeo such a letter. He wants him safe in Mantua after the prince's decree. If Romeo returns to Verona, his life is forfeit and his death will be grisly. The friar would not risk him coming here. Not for you. He is not your friend, only Romeo's." Juliet refused to look at her, but Rosaline would not stop. "This friar is false and feeds you honeyed lies. He is cunning and cruel."

She reached into the pouch about her waist and held up Laura's bottle. The two were sisters.

"The selfsame friar mixed herbs for another of Romeo's girls—his once beloved Laura. It's from her side I come this afternoon. The birthing bed will be her deathbed too. Perhaps she would have died without his help, but I do not believe your holy friar, your misnamed friend, mixed herbs to aid her pain but to hasten her dying."

Juliet stared at her in disbelief.

"Do not drink this liquor," said Rosaline. "What if it is a poison that the friar has subtly administered to have you dead?"

Juliet studied the bottle in her hands, uncertain. "If I drink and die, at least I won't have to marry Paris. I'll be with my Romeo," she said at last.

"Ah, but Romeo will not die with you. He does not even visit Laura as she lies dying, and he'll certainly not die with her. She will die unhappy and alone, save for a woman paid to tend her. And he lives on." Rosaline took a deep breath. "Please, my love. Don't drink this." She tried to pry it from Juliet's fingers, but the girl tightened her grip around it.

Rosaline trembled in fury and frustration. "There are others who love you beside Romeo. Or am I nothing?"

"No, of course not. I love you, Ros." Juliet looked stricken, but still she wouldn't surrender the vial. She rose. "I hear my father call from the house."

No one was calling. There was only the song of the blackbird and the stirring of the vine leaves overhead.

Juliet began to hurry away. "Tonight we must part, Ros. There is no choice for us. I must trust to fate."

"Trust to fate then, but not to Romeo!" she called.

Juliet hesitated and then walked on.

There was the faintest gleam of doubt in her cousin's mind. Rosaline could sense it. Her love for Romeo was fraying, and that must suffice for now. Rosaline would work to tug upon the thread until it unraveled. But there was so little time. Rosaline watched her make her way through the garden and back into the house and disappear.

That blue vial did not hold sleep but death. Rosaline had lost too much already. She would not lose Juliet. She would not.

Rosaline stood in the cloth merchant with Livia, bolts of silk spread before them. Her father would not allow her out alone. He said he worried that she was not safe with the uncaught thief still abroad. Rosaline felt certain this was a lie and really he feared she would run away before he dispatched her to the nunnery.

The merchant spread another dingy rainbow of gray silks before them. Livia squeezed her arm. "I'm so sorry, Rosaline. Tybalt was like a brother to you."

Rosaline found she could not answer. Her voice was knotted in her throat.

More and more cloths were heaped upon the counter. Layer upon suffocating layer.

"Is there one you like, Ros?" asked Livia tentatively.

Rosaline shook her head. Tybalt needed something glorious. And then, she noticed one at the back of the shop. A cloth for a prince. It was the most lavish and gorgeous shroud she had ever seen, made of crimson velvet, backed by the finest linen. Emblazoned on the front in the best silk was a vast white skull and crossbones, the femurs snapped and jagged. Life is transient and brief, stalked always by death.

She pointed.

Livia took Rosaline back to her uncle's house to prepare for the funeral. Tybalt's body had been washed and laid out in the small hall. He looked younger and thinner in death. His wounds had been cleaned, but the congealed gashes were stark against the smoothness of his skin. Jars of rosemary, fennel, and roses rested on the mantelpiece to mask the scent of death. The burial garment was large enough, thought Rosaline, that it could enfold them both. She could slip into the peaceable dark with him. Yet, she realized, much as she wasn't ready for the convent, she wasn't ready for death.

Cradling him with the utmost tenderness, Rosaline, Juliet, and Livia wrapped Tybalt's stiffening corpse, tucking him into his shroud for his eternal sleep. This was her last time with him before the men would come and carry him to the Capulet tomb, and intuitively Juliet and Livia withdrew to a corner of the room to pray quietly, leaving Rosaline with him.

As she looked down at the swaddled form, Rosaline found she did not know what to say to Tybalt's body. Already he did not look like himself: paler and more yellow than he had been in life. She felt uneasy, as though he were some stranger. She didn't like to touch him. "Where are you?" she whispered. "Give me back my loving, black-browed knight. I don't know you."

His silence taunted her.

She unpeeled the shroud a little and placed a book in his dead hands, not a Bible or prayer book, but the volume of Ovid's tales that Tybalt had stolen for her from Valentio so many years ago.

"To read upon your journey," she whispered. "I do not want to read it without you. What are these stories without you to share them?"

The other two prayed louder to give her privacy, and yet she became aware of some other, more ribald sounds coming from another room.

"What noise is it that disturbs us?" she asked.

Juliet and Livia exchanged glances. "It is players preparing for a play," said Livia reluctantly. "After Juliet and Paris's wedding feast, there is to be a performance. Your uncle wishes it as part of the celebration."

Rosaline's mouth fell open. "He could not wait until Tybalt's buried?" she said, outraged. "They are intruders here, their very presence an affront!"

"I do not want any part of it," said Juliet. "It is not my fault."

Livia moved toward the door. "I'll tell them to speak more quietly."

"No, I shall do it," said Rosaline. She left the chamber, brimful of bitter anger. How dare her uncle allow the players to rehearse here tonight when Tybalt's corpse lay stretched out upon the table? It was a cruel insult. The laughter grew louder. The players were in their cups on her uncle's good wine.

Then came another voice. She stopped, listened. *It could not be.*

"Ros!" it called. She knew that voice. It was as familiar to her as her own.

It was not possible. And yet she heard him.

"Tybalt!" she called back, uncertain. "Where are you?" He was not buried yet, so perhaps his ghost still walked the shade? She followed the voice. It led her into the great hall, where several actors stood drinking, surrounded by half-unpacked painted backdrops, wooden props, and boxes of costumes. One juggled as another played the fool; they did not even notice her come in.

She looked about, confused. Perhaps she had been mistaken. An actor began to recite a speech, and it must have been that she heard. She drew breath, ready to scold the players, and then she heard him call her again.

"Ros. Here."

She searched the room again. At first she did not see him, and then there he was, standing on the stair leading up to the galleried landing. Grinning at her, wet with gore and blood

leaking from his side, his white teeth speckled with red. He
lingered on the stairs.

She ran to him. His cheek was colorless; he was not of this
world, and yet he did not frighten her.

Three actors shambled along into the long hall, one wearing
a curled wig, and all grasping mugs of beer and mumbling lines.

"Good evening, mistress," said one, raising his hat and
bowing to her.

She ignored him as, to her frustration, Tybalt turned and ran
up the steps and disappeared from view. Why did he not unsettle
these others? But no one among this crew of players seemed interested in a dead man. Either they could not see him, or else they were
only concerned with their mugs of drink and pacing out their lines.

Tybalt waved from the gallery above and beckoned to her.
She raced up the stairs. She wondered if she was indeed mad and
dazed from grief, or else parched from too much sun, and yet she
found her hand was steady.

He was sitting on the floor, waiting. She settled beside him.

"Tybalt?" she whispered.

"How fare you, Rosaline?" he asked, smiling mournfully at
her through his red-stained teeth.

"I do not know. Happy for you are here. But unhappy for you
are dead and part of my own self lives with you."

"You cannot live in death, Ros. It is not possible."

She tried to swallow and found she could no longer speak at
all. Eager, she reached out for his hand, but it was not there. He
looked at her sadly but did not speak.

Below the actors began to rehearse. Snatches of lines drifted up.

Two households both alike in dignity
In Babylonia where we set our scene

Rosaline remembered that she had been furious at the players' callous lack of feeling. Now as she looked upon Tybalt's
much-loved face, paler now in death, she realized her rage had
fallen away. She gazed at him in bewilderment. "I am mad," she
said.

"Why?"

"To see your ghost. I am mad with grief and love."

"Then I'm mad too," replied Tybalt, smiling gently. "We are
made mad together."

They sat quietly together for a moment, and Rosaline longed
for the cool of the woods, the sylvan green and scent of damp
earth. Perhaps Tybalt's footprints could still be traced through
the layers of pine needles, and she could follow him down, down
into the underworld. The smell of his blood was still in her nose,
the feel of it on her hands, warm and sticky, clinging to her fingers. She wanted instead to remember him as he'd been during
their days at the river, his hair slicked back like an otter's, with
water and not with blood, printing the hot stones with the pads
of his feet, blinking water, looking only for her.

There was a noise from the hall beneath, and Rosaline turned
to Tybalt, asking, "Pray, what piece is it being performed?"

"Ovid's tragedy of the lovers, 'Pyramus and Thisbe.'"

Rosaline thought of the precious book tucked beneath Tybalt's dead hands in the other room. The stories they would not read again. She sighed. Below, a swinging moon was hoisted above the makeshift stage, glinting sharply in the light. A fiddler began to bow and the sound was reedy and mellifluous, like the wind through the marsh bed at dusk.

"Are you really here, Tybalt?"

"Yes and no," he answered.

He is not here, she thought. *He is some part of me, the part that died. Somehow I have summoned him back.*

They turned their attention back to the action below. The play was crude and performed by green actors, yet it was uncannily familiar to Rosaline.

From ancient grudge to new mutiny...

I have read this story a hundred times, but more than that—I know this story for I have lived it. And now so does Juliet, decided Rosaline. The story playing out below had a ghastly familiarity: Pyramus and Thisbe. Romeo and Juliet. Rosaline and Romeo. Two households and a cankered hate. Two lovers, confessing their secret desire for one another. *I am watching a play, but I am also watching myself.*

She surveyed the actors with a frown, kneeling up for a better view.

A pair of star-crossed lovers take their lives—

"It ends in death." She sighed. "It only ever ends in death. Pyramus and Thisbe. Laura. Cecilia. You."

Tybalt looked at her sadly and said, "I died. But, Ros, your end is not yet done. There is more to come. There is still hope."

She shook her head and turned back to the players.

"How is this Pyramus? A lover or a tyrant?" she asked. "And what is this version of the play?" she added, puzzled. "It does not sound quite like Ovid."

"It changes each time it's told. It lives in the telling. The story is written in choice Italian. Listen now," said Tybalt, gesturing for her to hush.

They watched in silence for several minutes, but Rosaline really only observed Tybalt, taking in his beloved face, the curve of his cheek, his high forehead. The perfect arch of his lip, O, why had she not noticed it before when it was not too late to kiss?

"The best in this kind are but shadows," whispered Tybalt with a smile.

"It must be in your imagination then, and not theirs," she said. Yet as she spoke, she wondered how it could be in his imagination. Could dead men dream? Rosaline studied Tybalt. Her lovely ghost. Her love. Her dreams were his. If, as she believed, part of her had died with him, so it was her own self and soul that she now saw conjured there.

He surveyed her sadly but said nothing.

Rosaline understood that the answer to it all lay upon the stage before her; the part of Tybalt that resided in her heart had led her to the gallery to watch this rehearsal. What did he want

her to see and understand? Her eyes were raw with grit and tired-
ness. Why couldn't she see? She must, for her own sake and for
that of Tybalt's ghost.

The story on the stage below reached the end, and Pyramus
and Thisbe died.

"You see," said Rosaline in frustration. "It always ends in death."

"No," said Tybalt. "See now?"

The rehearsal being concluded, the actors stood, stretched,
and yawned, resurrected.

Rosaline's own ending, and that of Juliet and her Romeo, similarly remained unfinished. There were numbered pages yet to go.

Ovid had conjured the story of Pyramus and Thisbe, or
else had captured it in ink. Who had been the playwright of
Rosaline's love, and who had turned it into hate? Rosaline considered how something insignificant, even a mote of dust, could
turn the balance. Romeo had tried to mold her and create her as
the artist ordered his material, but she did not fit into the shape
he wanted for her. One day soon neither would Juliet. Then,
disaster would come. He fell in love with an idea of a woman and
then, realizing his mistake, discarded her. She could sense the
gruesome inevitability of it all. Their lives were following Ovid's
art like the wagon ruts worn into the stone of the Verona streets
and hewn into the sunken pathways that threaded through the
wooded hills; this way they must pass, and no other.

Rosaline would not have it. She'd force the great wheel of
fortune out of its smoothed rut and onto another track. If Ovid
conjured his story through the power of his imagination, then she

must amend theirs through hers. If only she could simply wield her pen and conjure a different ending for them all. That was the playwright's art, and she, Rosaline Capulet, was no playwright. She must find another way.

Yet what if Tybalt was right, and some of what had happened so far was a rehearsal too? Might Rosaline's own ending not be changed for the performance itself?

It was time for Juliet and Rosaline to break free from the story. She must peel life away from art, separate the rind from the flesh of the orange, and cast one into the flames. She did not want to end as a shadow or a ghost. She was flesh and she would live. So must Juliet.

It was for Rosaline to create a new path and a new ending.

She glanced around for Tybalt, saying, "Tybalt! A jot, a word will turn the balance! I understand what I must do."

He did not answer. Perhaps she had freed his shade when she'd discovered the truth of what he'd wanted to show her? She felt a physical jolt in her breast, longing for one final good-bye before he vanished into the underworld. She stood up and searched all around for him, leaning over and peering out as far over the edge of the gallery as she dared.

He was not there.

The bell tolled a quarter past five. There was only an hour until Tybalt's funeral. The actors had recommenced dragging the painted scenes into place, unpacking props, and pouring more drink.

Rosaline descended the stairs and watched them for a moment. "I enjoyed your rehearsal. I wish you well with the performance of 'Pyramus and Thisbe.' Sadly, I shan't see it."

If all went to according to her scheme, the wedding would not take place and the play must be canceled, but Rosaline did not say that. Still, the actor gave her an odd look.

"Thank you, good lady. But it is not 'Pyramus and Thisbe' that we perform but a midsummer comedy. 'Pyramus and Thisbe' would be a melancholy choice for a wedding." He paused and then added, "Mistress, we have not yet begun our rehearsal. We've done nothing but unpack our boxes and set out our scenes." He shook his head. "I fear we intrude too much upon your recent loss and for that I am sorry."

With a bow, he turned away from her. Rosaline stared after him. Had she dreamed or conjured the play from the darkness of her own imagination, along with Tybalt? Were they dragged from the blackness of her unquiet mind? And yet the dream, if that's what it was, for all its darkness, had helped guide her to a new possibility.

While the players were busy at the other end of the hall, Rosaline slipped past, helping herself to a plain cloak and hat. Thus disguised, she slid unnoticed out of the back gate of the house. There was something she needed to do before she kissed Tybalt's green lips and bid him a last farewell.

Juliet had said that the friar was sending a letter with one of his brethren friars to Romeo in Mantua. She loathed the friar almost as much as she did Romeo. The very thought of him was vinegar. When she'd talked with Friar Laurence, his gaze and lascivious grin had not been that of a holy man, and when he spoke of Juliet, his leery eye was lit. Rosaline suspected the two men were in this foul scheme together, although did not know how. Did Romeo's discarded girls end up in the friar's bed, or was that only a lecherous dream?

She swiped at the blackflies that thrummed all around her, nipping at her face and arms, multiplying in the heat and dirt. She drew her borrowed hat low over her brow and turned toward St. Peter's and the chapter house.

When she reached the chapter house, Rosaline glanced about the physic gardens with trepidation. The beds and lawns of the first garden square were full of barefoot Franciscan friars tending to it, tiptoeing across planked walkways. To her relief, she did not spy Friar Laurence among them, neither in the first garden nor in the next.

Tugging her hat down to shade her face, she approached a huddle of Franciscans in the second garden, plucking slugs from plump cabbage leaves. "Please, holy fathers. Which of you is going to Mantua for Friar Laurence? For I have a letter to send with that good man. I only hope I am not too late."

One of the friars, a large man with a nose that looked like one of the papery, purpling bulbs that he clutched in a wicker basket, scrutinized Rosaline. "Who are you, daughter?"

"Madonna Laura Montague, worthy Romeo's cousin. Friar Laurence said I could send a letter for my cousin."

"The letter is being sent with Friar John, but he's gone."

"No, no," said another. "He's out visiting the sick. He departs on his return."

"Then you can leave the letter for your cousin with me," said the bulbous-nosed friar. "I shall put it in Friar Laurence's cell. Friar John will take both letters with him when he returns."

Rosaline forced a smile and shook her head. Her scheme would not work if this kind friar took her letter—which she had not even written. She must go to the friar's cell herself and search for his missive to Romeo.

"I thank you, holy father, no. I do not want to trouble you in this. Let me go myself."

The friar looked unconvinced, but to her profound relief, the bell for afternoon prayers began to sing out. He reluctantly agreed. "Friar Laurence's cell is the one with the white roses blooming beneath the window," he said, gesturing toward one of the dormitories.

Rosaline thanked him and hurried at a pace around to the side of the abbey house before he could change his mind again. The dormitory was a redbrick building, single story, with a low tiled roof. There were rows of plain wooden doors and small barred windows, but beneath the sill of one flowered a wilting rose bush. The curled, brown-edged petals had snowed to the ground in the heat, and the scent of the residue was sickly sweet. Only one rose still bloomed, its petals not pure white but with a bloody tint like a spattered handkerchief. Its macabre beauty disturbed Rosaline.

This marked the cell of Friar Laurence. The door opened at her touch and she slid inside. So this was the lair of a monster. It did not seem sinister. There was no pile of bones or glistening dagger. It smelled of ash and the scent of roses from the open window. The room within was bare. A thin mattress. A wooden cross nailed to the wall. A water jug and wooden cup. A set of rosary beads. No blanket or chair—such items were unnecessary worldly comforts. It reminded her with a pang of Cecilia's room at the convent, resolving Rosaline to what she must do. She must find the letter to Romeo.

She noticed that beside the jug sat a blue Bible, the crest the perfect match of the ones in Laura's room and in Cecilia's Rosaline picked it up. It was well-thumbed, the letters faded, as if the prayers were worn out from frequent use. She was about to set it down again and continue her search when she saw, concealed in the edge of the leather cover, a tiny snag of paper. At first she thought it was a rip in the fabric, but when she tugged it out, came a piece of paper, folded very small and covered in tiny, spidery writing. For a moment she thought she'd discovered the letter to Romeo. But why would that be hidden in a Bible? Unfolding it carefully, she saw two columns. It took her a second to understand that she was looking at two lists of names: girls' names on one side and men's on the other. She recognized several of each. The men were among the wealthiest and most illustrious citizens of Verona. There were men from each of the Capulet and Montague households inscribed there. Signior Martino. Balthasar Montague. Gregory Capulet. And here was County Paris. To her relief, she did not find her brother's name, although she checked for it twice. She was glad of this.

Then she saw dotted lines linking the women's names with the men. Romeo's name was written beside every single girl's, his name the first to appear beside each one. Sometimes a woman was linked with two, three, or even four or five men. With a grim realization, Rosaline understood that this must be a list the friar kept of fallen girls and the men who used them for loathsome purposes. With a sickening pang, it struck her that she had heard of some of these women. She'd believed they had died. And either that was what the families had been told, or it was what the families had allowed to be known when their daughters ran away or disappeared.

Rosaline felt herself become covered in a cold sweat, and her head began to spin. Some of the names upon the list were scored out with black. These girls, Rosaline concluded, were those who had subsequently died—whether from natural or unnatural causes she could not know. It struck her that half of the names were obliterated with black ink, and a low cry escaped her lips. She murmured a prayer for them and swore vengeance for them all.

Wiping slick palms on her dress, she studied the paper again. Here were two more names she knew: *Cecilia*. And *Laura*. Both were scored out. Laura was dead, now then. *May her rest be sweeter than her ending.*

And then a noise suddenly hummed in Rosaline's ears, and her legs felt soft and strange.

She must not give in to fear, even though the foulness of it all was too much to bear. Was Romeo the honey to lure in all these girls—that must be the reason his name appeared first and beside each one? Rosaline felt sure this was how it was done—after all, it had worked so easily with her. Whether he loved them or not, Romeo must know he left a trail of ruined and broken girls behind him. And when the thrill of love waned and he tired of each young girl, the unholy friar would discreetly appear to rid him of the nuisance so he could love again without encumbrance. The girl would then disappear—to be passed around the wealthy men of Verona, presumably for a price. And when they tired of her or it became too dangerous? What then became of her? Rosaline again pictured the vials of blue Murano glass and the treacherous black lines scoring out the girls' names. She shuddered. This could have been her fate. And it might yet be Juliet's.

The friar was no man of god, but a man without conscience or regard for the human soul. A scorpion in holy rags.

The bell of St. Peter's tolled. She must hurry and be gone before the monks and friars finished their prayers. She slid the list into the pouch at her waist, snapping the Bible shut and replacing it beside the jug, hoping the friar would not notice it had been disturbed and his despicable scheme uncovered.

Her heart raced. She still must find the letter. Surely it was not hidden—she must simply have not looked carefully enough before. She glanced around the room again and saw a corner of paper half-hidden beneath an ewer for water on the floor, where she'd missed it earlier, only a corner peeking out. Removing it, she read the direction inscribed, *Romeo Montague*. It was sealed shut with wax. She hesitated for a moment and then broke the seal, unfolding the letter and reading quickly.

Benedicite, my good son Romeo,

On Thursday morn, Juliet is set to marry County Paris. I swear to you I'll do all I can to prevent the match, but you must not come back to Verona. Your presence here is death. The prince runs hot with fury at this feud, and you must not return to the city. Rosaline the shrew is vengeful and thick with hate for you. Do not come here to die for Juliet. You are a waverer in love. Remember, Romeo, once you and all your woes were for Rosaline. Then, in a day you were changed. Pray stay safe in Mantua. Love will come again.

Your friend,
Friar Laurence

Rosaline leaned back against the wall. The limewash plaster was cool and flaked under her fingertips. Of course Friar Laurence had lied to Juliet. This letter was not the one he'd promised her he'd write. He did not urge Romeo to make haste to Verona to awaken Juliet from her tomb and take her back with him to Mantua. And while he assured Romeo that he would prevent the match to County Paris, he did not say how. Rosaline feared that she knew, even if Romeo did not. She was almost certain now that the tiny blue vial contained death and not sleep.

Why did he not confide his scheme to Romeo? Was it out of fear that his missive might be read by the wrong eyes, or because he knew that for now at least Romeo still loved Juliet? But his passion would not last; it never did. It would dissolve like soap in tepid water. Friar Laurence understood that—his missive brimmed with accusation. Romeo the waverer, the falsehearted, and the fickle. When he grew bored of his girls, the friar would take them from him and use them for himself. That was how the diabolical arrangement worked.

For her ruse to succeed, Rosaline needed Romeo to come back to Verona. This letter must not be sent. If she stole it, Friar John would simply ask Friar Laurence to write another. She thought for a moment, the letter dangling between her fingers. Where had his brothers said Friar John was at present? Visiting the sick. That would serve her purpose most conveniently. Rosaline replaced the letter beneath the ewer, pinching the seal closed as best she could.

Rosaline took the alley leading to her brother Valentio's house, shaded by the long thin shadow cast by St. Peter's tower. There was so little time left. She began to run, her breath becoming ragged and short. When she reached the gate, she banged upon it with her fist and the watchman opened it with a scowl.

"I beg you bring me the children's wet nurse," she said between gasps. "But please," she pleaded, "do not tell my sister or my brother I am here. Just bring me the nurse."

The watchman stared at her in confusion. "Why not come in yourself, Madonna Capulet?"

Rosaline shook her head. "Please, I beg you make haste." She pressed a coin into his hand to pay off his curiosity, and the watchman lumbered off.

Bending double, Rosaline rubbed at a stitch that was poking her ribs. After several minutes, he returned to the gate, the nurse at his side. She appeared annoyed to have been pulled away from her charges.

"Rosaline?" said the nurse, bewildered.

"Madam, before you were a midwife and a wet nurse, you were a searcher?" asked Rosaline eagerly.

The nurse shuddered at the memory. "As I told you before I believe, I prefer life to death."

The nurse turned as if to go back into the house, impatient, and Rosaline grabbed her sleeve. "I lost my mother to the pestilence."

"I know it. And I'm sorry for it too."

"You know where to find the watch, I think. And they listen to you."

The nurse frowned. "I hope so. I was a searcher a full twelve months and saw to it most carefully that no more were infected after I carried out my visits. I did my duty."

"I do not doubt it, good nurse. Verily, I do not." Rosaline bowed her head. "In truth, it's why I came here. For I heard, at the chapter house, Friar John telling his brother friars how he was in a house of pestilence and plague visiting the sick. I heard him describe in horrid detail the oozing buboes about their armpits, but he came away quickly so as to avoid quarantine and being shut inside the pesthouse. He said he's traveling now to Mantua. I fear he will carry the sickness there."

The nurse stiffened with anger. "These people who think the duties in this regard don't apply to them! We'll never stamp this pestilence out so long as they evade the law! The clergy are among the worst." She clucked her tongue in annoyance and looked at Rosaline. "I may no longer be a searcher, but I can still summon an officer of the watch. Can you show me to him?"

"I can if I must," said Rosaline, glancing downward, as if full of trepidation.

The nurse nodded in approval, saying, "Let us go at once, and we'll seek out the watch upon our way. We'll make sure this miscreant priest is nailed inside his cell upon his return, a crimson cross painted on his door."

Rosaline hid her smile. She would wait until Friar John was searching Friar Laurence's cell to find the letter and point him out then. The unfortunate friar would be sealed up with the letter to Romeo. Neither would travel to Mantua tonight.

XIII

These violent delights
have violent ends

The horses jerked the wagon, their breath huffing and mouths frothing with spittle. Even at this late hour, the air was stiff with heat. Rosaline unpicked gnats from her hair. The river spooled out, smooth and limpid black, like molten metal in the evening light. A lemon wedge of moon dangled high above the city, its reflection shining in the water.

Rosaline was relieved to be taking the journey to the convent alone. Her father had offered to accompany her, but she'd refused. The funeral had been Tybalt's, and yet it had also felt like hers. After this night, she was no longer truly a Capulet. She must shed that name like a lizard loses its tail and grow another. Rosaline Capulet would be laid to rest and Sister Rosaline reborn. Tybalt now slumbered in his tomb, Rosaline Capulet beside him. She was a bride of Christ, and yet to her it felt only like death.

Perhaps she *could* find a way to escape her fate. With Caterina working in the convent kitchen, there was still the possibility of fleeing the nunnery. Smuggled out with the flagons of wine or sacks of grain. She wouldn't be the first novice to try to seek another life on the other side of the wall. Verona was impossible but there were other cities. She could shed her skin again.

The sorrowful goodbyes to the dead and living had already been made. Livia weeping, kissing her, and holding her so tight her fingers printed her skin. Those red marks were more precious to Rosaline than real rubies, and she wished they would not fade. Livia and Juliet swore that they'd visit her at the convent, Livia to bring the children. Yet to Rosaline it hardly mattered, for she would not touch any of them again. She could not hold them to her and kiss them, nor wipe away their tears, nor nudge them on hearing a joke. Sadness seeped into her, cold and deep. Even if they came to see her, she'd be sealed behind a wall, not only physical but metaphysical. She would no longer be their Rosaline, but God's. Every part of her would belong to him, that little word *sister* now a line between them. She was not theirs but his, not of this world but of the next. And she did not want to be. Heavenly joys were not for her. It was earthly pleasures, however messy, that she yearned for. She crackled with resentment.

The rhythm of the horses rocked her to sleep. As she slumbered, she dreamed of green gods dancing with Tybalt, leading him down into the underworld where Hades waited for him with Emelia on one arm and Laura upon the other. Rosaline called out to her cousin, but he did not hear her, for he belonged to her no longer, and as she watched, they all disappeared into the blackness.

When she woke it was in the borderland of dusk. The horses puffed and sighed and began to slow, straining with the effort of pulling the wagon up a steep hill. The wagoner crooned, encouraging them on in clicks and grunts. Rosaline stood up in her seat, straining to see. A precipitous crag leaned over them, crowned by the hulking shape of the abbey itself, which seemed to arise from the rock as if it had been carved from the granite by some divine hand and not been built brick by brick. Then, high above, a bead of light appeared, orange as polished amber. As the wagon drew nearer, the light came closer, brighter, and sharper. The horses foamed and sweated. The driver's soft words were replaced by his whip. Then, at last, they reached the open gates of the abbey, and the horses slackened their pace and stopped, the wagon rattling to a halt in the cobbled yard.

The driver held out his hand and helped Rosaline down. She laughed. Unless she escaped her prison, this man with his fingertips veined with grime would be the last she'd ever touch.

A torch flame flickered. A pale nun of middling years scampered out to greet her, lamp clenched in her hand. "Who comes here?" she demanded.

"It's me, Rosaline."

"Come, come."

The nun dismissed the driver, bidding him refresh his horses in the abbey stables, and guided Rosaline inside the belly of the convent. This time, as soon they were through the vast wooden doors, they did not proceed to the *parlatorio*—Rosaline was no longer a visitor—but straight on into the cloisters.

Once again, the moment Rosaline was inside, she was struck how the grim and austere exterior belied the charm within. Jasmine and honeysuckle clambered about the arches of the porticos, perfuming the air with their heavy scent. They wove through one another in an unruly tangle, reminding Rosaline of Juliet's uncombed hair. The lawns were rolled and starred with pinpricks of daisies, their petals clamped shut like eyelashes. Low triangular hedges of trimmed box separated the lawns of the cloisters, the leaves appearing black in the dark. The sky was filled with a hurry of wings, flying low enough that she felt the rush of air. The shrill of bats mingled with women's voices singing Compline.

"This way, please," said the nun, toying with the rosary around her neck.

Rosaline hurried after her. The evening smelled of sweet peas and lavender, the women's voices rising on the air. Rosaline looked around impatiently for the abbess. The women's voices were clear and strong as they sang the evening prayers, but she did not recognize the melody. The prayers of Compline swelled—a river becoming a torrent. The melody was strange—it was at the edge of her memory—perhaps something her mother had sung to her in her cradle.

"Please, I must find the abbess," said Rosaline with a frown, tugging on the nun's sleeve.

With a grunt, the nun led her out through a low door in the cloister, both of them forced to stoop, leading straight into the refectory. The room was empty; all the other nuns were in the chapel.

A single place with a pewter plate and cup had been set at one of the long, scrubbed tables.

"Here, sit," said the nun. "You must be hungry."

Rosaline dutifully sat down on the bench, but despite the ripeness of the cheese and peaches, she could not eat. "Pardon me," she said. "Truly I must speak with the Mother Abbess."

The nun laughed and then, realizing Rosaline was not in jest, answered, "She's still at Compline. She does not greet novices herself."

"I must have an audience with her," said Rosaline, taking the other woman's hand and squeezing it so tightly that she flinched.

"Hark at that! Tomorrow. Eat, and then we'll find you a habit to wear."

Rosaline began to panic. She must speak with her tonight or all would be lost. Reaching into her dress, she drew out a small bottle the brilliant jeweled blue of a June sky and pressed it into the nun's palm, closing her fingers around it.

"Take this to her and tell her I would speak instantly with her. I beg this of you."

The nun studied her for a second and then, muttering, did as she was bid.

Rosaline sat alone in the silence of the refectory. The room was lit by a single candle, cheap tallow and not wax. It smoked and spat, reeking of pig fat. She could not eat or drink. Bundles of rosemary, sage, marjoram, and lavender were laid out upon the far end of the table, drying. On another, rows and rows of snail shells were being soaked in vinegar, like tiny, coiled turds, a heavy pestle and mortar lying poised beside them. Whatever paste or unction they were destined for, Rosaline did not fancy it.

After some delay, the abbess herself entered the refectory. Rosaline scrambled to her feet, nearly knocking over the bench in her haste.

"Why did you send me a bottle tainted with cursed hebenon?" demanded the abbess.

"Cursed hebenon?" asked Rosaline.

"Put this in any liquid you will, and drink it, and if you had the strength of twenty men, it would dispatch you," replied the abbess, holding up the vial. She stepped closer to Rosaline and examined her for a moment. "What grief has set these jaundices on your cheek?"

"A villain named Romeo. Murderer. Seducer. Tyrant. And now husband to my cousin. It was his friend, a friar, who mixed that vial."

"That's grief enough. A friar?" The abbess's voiced was heavy with disdain.

Rosaline pulled from her small pouch the friar's list and slid it across the table. The abbess took it and read it in silence. If the contents surprised her, she did not show it.

"Where did you find this?"

"I stole it from Friar Laurence's own cell. It is written in his hand. Here is proof enough of Friar Laurence's villainy and Romeo Montague and half of the men in Verona. They are depraved, and their souls tarnished with the very worst of sins."

The abbess's expression was somber as she took in Rosaline's words. She looked again at the list. "The girls scored out in black are dead. I have buried some of them myself. May the Lord bless them and keep them."

Rosaline took a breath and proceeded to tell her about Laura and her dead child. The abbess listened gravely, turning the glass bottle in her fingers.

"This extraction would mean the babe was stillborn and there was no disgrace to Romeo and the Montague family," said the abbess. "The girl would expire after some little time, depending when and how she drank. If she'd been given a potion to counteract the poison, she might have been saved."

Rosaline felt sweaty and sick. She had guessed as much but now she knew. She thought of Laura dying in that filthy room, unloved and alone, the cradle draped in black.

"The friar has given another tincture to my cousin Juliet. He claims it is a philter to make her sleep, but I fear that sleep will be forever."

The abbess glanced again at the pretty bottle in her palm. "And you want my help in this?"

"I do. Juliet is not the first to be seduced by this Romeo, and neither was I. He loves us and discards us as dandelion seeds on the wind." Rosaline tried not to squirm but to meet the abbess's steady eye, although in truth her blood felt hot and treacly with shame. She was supposed to enter the convent and was here confessing a mortal sin.

The abbess watched her with brown eyes, which Rosaline for once wished did not look so much like her mother's. She forced herself to meet them, and to her surprise saw there was no judgment there. She supposed the abbess had heard more tawdry confessions.

"I shall help you unarm the friar and Romeo Montague," said the abbess. "I'll provide you the philter to make your cousin sleep."

"And the potion to stop the poison?"

"If you think you need it, I could," said the abbess.

Rosaline wished she could embrace her. "In you lies the proof of the goodness and virtue of men," she said, her voice warm with effusion.

"Of women. And my help comes at a cost," warned the abbess.

"I'll pay it."

The abbess stood and walked to a cabinet. She took out a bottle of wine and poured two glasses.

She drank, watching Rosaline steadily. "You have not yet said your vows, so tonight you may leave the convent. I will send you with a driver and our own cart back to Verona. You can give the vial of philter to your cousin and make her sleep. But tomorrow, when the business is concluded, you must return here."

Rosaline nodded. That much she could do.

The abbess gestured to her to drink and continued: "If once you'd thought to escape and flee this place, you must swear an oath to me here and now that you will not. That you will return and say your vows and live out your mortal life in this convent."

"Why?" cried Rosaline. "What use can you have with me?"

"I want you. I see you and your mind, quick and clever. You discovered not only the friar's wickedness but the proof of it. We have long suspected evildoing among some of the brother friars but have not found out how the web was woven, for all our listening."

Rosaline absorbed her praise but remained uneasy.

The abbess continued: "In time I know you will be happy here, or at least not unhappy."

Rosaline was silent.

The abbess considered for a moment. "I think perhaps I will teach you how to write our chronicles. That will be good for you and us. Herbs and gardens do not hold special interest for you, I can see. And you will play music for us too. We'll give you knowledge and understanding. It's not an incarceration. Your soul will be free."

"And my body?" asked Rosaline quietly.

The abbess smiled. "Well, the convent has porous walls. Rome is far away. They cannot see everywhere all at once. Sometimes visitors may enter. It has been known."

Rosaline inhaled sharply. "But can I leave? Even for a day?"

"Once you've said your vows? There is always a sacrifice, Rosaline. Once you return here tomorrow night, you shall not depart this place until death."

Rosaline could not breathe. A prison was still a cage, however perfumed the night jasmine and neatly mown the lawns. She would never belong to the world below again, only gaze down upon it like the kites and gulls surfing on air. She'd become an echo, a song in the wind.

But if she refused, Juliet would die tonight.

"Will you pay my price?" asked the abbess softly.

Rosaline nodded. "I will." She was silent for a long moment and then spoke, her words full of anguish. "What will happen to the friar and to the men on his list? Is there to be no vengeance for the girls they harmed in this life? Must we leave it all to God?"

A strange expression came over the abbess's face. She glanced behind her at the rows of tinctures in their bottles and then looked steadily at Rosaline. "I sense another plague coming to the wicked men of Verona."

The city was smeared with darkness. All was quiet.

At the Ponte Pietra bridge, Rosaline called out for the driver to stop and jumped down from the cart. "Go to the stables here in the city. And you know what you must do next?"

The driver nodded.

"I'll send a messenger when I need you to come," she said.

The driver whistled to the horses, and they disappeared over the bridge. Rosaline stood alone in the stillness and drew her cloak about her. She brushed the tiny glass vial in the pouch hanging about her neck to be certain it was still there, feeling its shape, solid and thinly curved, like a finger bone. She then checked the golden ring upon her forefinger, which the abbess had lent her. It was too big and she was scared of losing it.

The basilica bell tolled the quarter hour. Nearly midnight. She murmured a prayer. Juliet would be in her bedchamber. *Please don't let her have drunk from the friar's bottle, not yet.* Ignoring the scratch and scuttle of the rats in the gutters, she walked quickly along the empty streets toward her uncle's house. She was glad of the darkness; it was a better disguise than the simple traveling costume that the abbess had lent her.

On reaching the house, she hesitated. She could knock and announce herself, and the watchman would allow her entry, but there would be uproar that she'd fled from the convent. It was better that they all believed she was still safely sealed away.

She looked up at the solid wall. It appeared smooth and impenetrable, and yet Romeo had succeeded in finding his way from the street onto Juliet's balcony. If he'd managed to do it, then it must be possible.

Rosaline paced the walkway outside the house to and fro, trying to picture in her mind which rooms lay behind the outer façade. Behind was the great hall where the Capulet ball had been. The windows were positioned on the other side, facing out onto the gardens and loggia beyond. Beyond the hall was the minstrels' gallery, and above it lay Juliet's bedchamber, its balcony poised vertiginously over the orchard below.

Rosaline needed to find a way to clamber up to that balcony. When she and Tybalt had been children, she'd been a habitual tree climber. But there were no trees against the house. Not a plane tree nor an ash or a scrawny cherry. With a skittering heart, Rosaline realized she had no choice but to scramble up the wall itself.

She walked along far from the watchman and found a

spot where ivy grew thick as a man's wrist. This was the place. Glancing up at the basilica, she saw that she needed to make haste; the moon shone on the clockface on St. Peter's tower, the hour sliding toward midnight. Reaching up, she sought out a handhold and, hoisting herself up, began to climb.

The stone crumbled beneath her fingers, but she refused to let go and hauled herself farther up, searching with her feet to find a toehold in the ivy. Scrabbling and heaving, she pulled herself higher a few inches at a time, sometimes clinging to the ivy and other times searching the rough surface of the wall for a crevice for her fingertips.

In a few minutes, however, her fingers were seeping blood, her nails snagged and torn. Her breath came in rasps, and sweat trickled down her back. She cursed her traveling cloak and skirts. Romeo would have done this in britches and a shirt, with a dagger to help him pry loose the mortar to find handholds.

Her skirts tangled in the stems of ivy, catching fast so that she had to hold on with one hand and lean out to release them, slipping and nearly falling to the ground below.

Panting, she eased around the edge of the building, higher now, and scrabbled along the stonework until she reached the thick arm of a wisteria. She wriggled onto it, scraping off a layer of skin on the flesh of her thighs. She bit her lip to stop herself from crying out in pain. At least she was above the gardens now, hidden from the watchman and the street. She must hope that no one was taking a late walk through the villa courtyard or garden.

The leaves shook and blew, tapping against the lead of a

window. All the windows were illuminated, most thrown open in the hope of catching a breeze, a tower of glowing yellow squares stacked upon one another, and Rosaline couldn't help but notice how charming the lit scene was within.

She heard voices drift out through the wisteria toward her. "We shall be short in our provision. 'Tis now night."

Her aunt Lauretta.

Stiffening with terror, Rosaline slunk lower beneath a branch, banging her head.

"All things shall be well, I warrant you, Wife," came her uncle's voice. "I'll not to bed tonight. Let me alone and I'll play the housewife for this once. Go to Juliet."

There was the sound of a door closing, and she guessed that her aunt had gone. Stretching so that she could peer around the edge of the sill, Rosaline spied her uncle Capulet, standing alone in his bedchamber. He could not see her out here in the darkness. Then, her foot slid from its hold and she slipped, grasping the branch to steady herself, causing a flutter of leaves and snapping twigs.

Her uncle moved to the window. "What ho!"

Rosaline froze, certain he must either see her or else hear the frenzied beating of her heart. He stood there for a minute, looking out, then muttered, "Cats, pigeons, they are all forth," and walked away.

As soon as he had gone, Rosaline began to climb again. She must reach Juliet's chamber. Climbing up and up, she stretched out to reach the overhang of the stonework that marked Juliet's balcony. Here and there, the mortar had been pried away, and there were scuffs and scrabble marks upon the wall, and balding patches of leaves upon the climbing honeysuckle and magnolia where other fingers had grasped and slid. She felt uneasy that she was threading her way through Romeo's path to Juliet.

Pulling up her skirts, she hauled herself onto Juliet's balcony, landing with a soft thud as if onto damp earth. She crouched, holding her breath, heart pounding, terrified that she had been seen.

The balcony doors were ajar, a candle burned within, and she could see silhouetted the plump figure of Nurse and, to her profound relief, Juliet herself sitting on her bed. Juliet's bridal array was spread out on the chest beside it: a green velvet gown embroidered with silken pomegranates, and on a tray, Rosaline caught the glint of jewels dispatched from the groom.

Nurse fussed with the dress, picking it up to smooth it and setting it down again. She plucked up a pair of earrings, rubies like pricks of blood, and held them against Juliet's cheek, but Juliet swatted her away like a mosquito.

"Gentle Nurse, leave me to myself tonight, for I have need of many prayers to move the heavens to smile upon me. As you well know, I'm cross and full of sin."

At this, Nurse chuckled and rumpled Juliet's hair, murmuring objections.

The door opened and Rosaline saw Lauretta ease inside. Nurse and Juliet fell silent.

"What? Are you busy? Need you my help?" asked Lauretta, almost smiling.

"No, madam," replied Juliet. "So please allow me now be left alone and let the nurse sit up with you, for I am sure you have your hands full in this so sudden business."

Lauretta nodded. "Good night." She leaned over and laid a kiss on Juliet's forehead, so quick her lips must have barely touched her daughter skin's at all.

"Farewell," replied Juliet.

Rosaline did not like that Juliet replied thus. It was as if she knew that the contents of the vial contained a death that she was eager and willing to embrace.

As Rosaline watched from the balcony, Nurse helped Juliet into bed, tucking the sheet in around her before closing the door, leaving Juliet alone.

"God knows when we shall meet again," called Juliet after her before throwing off the sheet and rising. "I'll call her back again to comfort me. Nurse!" She slumped down again, hugging her knees, crying, "What should she do here? I must act alone. Come, vial."

Rosaline stood and moved to go into the room, only to find that her skirt was caught fast on part of the balcony rail. She tried to wrench it free with both hands, but the fabric was absolutely stuck, and she was wedged fast. She tugged and heaved, but it was hopeless. Tears of hapless rage prickled her eyes—it was absurd: she'd climbed a building endangering her life if she fell, only now to be defeated by a skirt.

"Juliet!" she hissed.

Juliet did not hear.

She must call out louder, but if she did, she risked alerting the entire household to her presence. She yanked at the stupid dress. The fabric ripped a little but did not free her. She had no choice.

"Juliet! Juliet!"

Still the girl did not hear.

Juliet raised the vial to her lips and then lowered it again. "What if this mixture does not work at all? Shall I be married then tomorrow morning? No, no! This shall forbid it."

"Juliet! Stop! No!"

Then, to Rosaline's horror, she saw that Juliet had put down the vial and had withdrawn the small dagger. She laid it across her throat, pressing it into her skin, but before Rosaline could cry out again, Juliet dropped it and it skittered across the floor. Her cousin was in a state of extreme distress, ghastly, eyes wide and unseeing, so that for a moment Rosaline thought she was too late and she'd already drunk from the vial.

"Or if I wake," Juliet continued, "before the time that Romeo comes? Shall I not be then stifled in the vault where bloody Tybalt lies festering in his shroud? Where, as they say at some hours in the night, spirits resort—?"

At last Rosaline wrenched her dress free and pushed her way through the doors and into the room.

Juliet stared at her, bewildered, her face eerie pale, eyes black. "O, look, methinks I see my cousin's ghost seeking out Romeo that did spit his body upon a rapier's point."

Rosaline put out her hands and tried to take Juliet's, but she snatched them back. "Stay, Tybalt, stay!"

"Juliet! Coz. 'Tis I, your Rosaline."

Juliet stared at her with unfocused, wild eyes. Rosaline was terrified for a moment her mind was overthrown. She stepped toward her once again, and this time Juliet did not recoil.

"It's really you, dearest Ros. Will you stay with me while I drink?" asked Juliet. "Even though you do not believe Romeo will come and redeem me."

"I will make sure that he comes, but it will not be to redeem you. But do not be afraid, for I have found a way to keep you safe."

Juliet stared at her. "Is it possible?"

"'Tis true. Do you trust me?"

"I do."

"Then when you wake, you'll be free. Of Paris and of Romeo."

She studied Juliet, uncertain how satisfied she'd be by this last part, but the worm of doubt had furrowed deep into her brain, and she looked relieved. Then, she frowned again and said, "And what of my parents and their next decree? Will I be free of them?"

"Of all earthly chains."

Juliet looked frightened. "That sounds like death."

"A sleep like death, and then you shall rise again to enjoy this new life, I swear. And I'll stay with you in the tomb while you rest. I'll not abandon you among the ancient and newly dead, or the night spirits."

Rosaline helped her back to the bed and patted down the sheets around her, kissing her tenderly and stroking her hair behind her ears. "I'll not leave you, little one. Not now or later."

She looked at Juliet anxiously, but Juliet's face had softened and relaxed.

"Where's the vial?" Juliet asked.

Rosaline held up a small blue bottle from the chain around her neck, the size of a dead man's finger. "Here. But drink first this glass of wine."

Rosaline fiddled with the gold ring around her finger. Inside the tiny compartment lay several grains of powder, which she poured into the wine before passing it to Juliet, who took it and drank. Now, Rosaline unstoppered the vial and gave it to her cousin. "Come, close your eyes," she said. "I'll sing you to sleep,"

"Here, I drink to thee," said Juliet and swallowed the contents of the vial.

Rosaline settled beside her and thought of her song. It was an old one she'd learned from her mother. She began to sing. "*Ye spotted snakes with double tongue…*" As she sang, she envisioned Romeo and his honeyed words.

Ye spotted snakes with double tongue
Thorny hedgehogs, be not seen;
Newts and blindworms, do no wrong,
Come not near our fairy Queen.
Weaving spiders, come not here;
Hence, you long-legged spinners, hence!
Beetles black, approach not near;
Worm nor snail, do no offense.

By the time she'd finished her song, Juliet's eyes were closed as if asleep. But this slumber was indeed like death; her cheek was white, all color fled. Juliet was a stranger in another country now.

Even though she knew that it must happen, Rosaline felt her guts cramp and tug. Leaning over, she placed her ear beside Juliet's nose and could not feel a tickle of breath. Had she fed her milk from the wrong vial? But she saw it was the abbess's bottle that lay empty and discarded on the pillow, and she tucked it into her pouch. All was well. She reached up and this time fastened the friar's bottle around her neck.

Could she be certain that Juliet would wake? She trusted the abbess meant well, but herbs and brewing was an art, and if she had rendered it too potent, it could be poison. *No, that is the friar's vice.*

The fierce little dagger lay half-concealed beneath the pillow, and Rosaline took it. Juliet had no need of it.

She stepped out onto the balcony and hesitated, reluctant to leave Juliet, who lay still and silent, a sleeping effigy.

Steeling herself, Rosaline climbed back over the railing and edged her way along the stone balustrade, trying not to look down to the swirling dark below. The leaves tickled her arms and the branches scratched her skin. Most of the windows were still lit; all remained open, like panting mouths gasping for air. As she scrabbled lower, she peered in through the windows of the great hall, where the servants were preparing the chamber for tomorrow's wedding feast.

Her uncle was there, directing them all with good cheer. "My heart is wondrous light!" he declared.

Rosaline was filled with bitter hurt and fury. How could he speak thus? Tybalt was hardly green, and already they'd forgotten him, their thoughts quickly turning from death to love. She spat a curse between her teeth. She and Tybalt were cheap Capulets, family but in name, easily discarded and disregarded. Were they less worthy or loveable; was their blood less red?

Her uncle called out again, "Hold, take these keys and fetch more spices, Nurse!"

Nurse's arms were already full, and she bustled past him, complaining, "They call for dates and quinces in the pastry."

Rosaline left them to their preparations in disgust, sliding out into the garden wreathed in darkness. She wanted to keep watch on Juliet. When they discovered her living corpse, she must be close by.

She was so tired from all her traveling and exertions that she longed to find a place to crawl into and sleep. Tomorrow she'd seek out Caterina. She crept across the grass to the orchard and found her way into the cradle of apple trees, and there among them where she'd lingered many times before with Tybalt and Juliet, she hid herself and slept.

The sun wheeled around the earth, driving out the dark and rising again, newly polished, but Rosaline slept on. The cockerel crowed and crowed again, but still Rosaline did not wake. She finally roused as shouts of alarm and grief penetrated her dreams. For a moment she did not know where she was, and she

sat up sharply, hitting her head against the bough of an apple
tree. The cries were frenetic and fierce. Through the web of
leaves, she saw Nurse run out onto the balcony.

"Lady, lady, lady! Help, help! My lady's dead!" she called,
running back inside and then out again. "Some aqua vitae, O!
My lord, my lady!"

It took all Rosaline's resolve not to leave her hiding place
but to remain as audience to this awful scene and merely watch
all the other actors unwittingly play out their parts. She had an
excellent view of the house, and it was displayed before her like
the set of a theater. She watched as her aunt Lauretta hurtled
up the stairs, her face appearing briefly in each open window of
the stairwell. Lauretta was about to enter as the mother robbed
of a child.

"What noise is here?" came Lauretta's voice from Juliet's
room, loud, annoyed.

Rosaline could not distinguish Nurse's reply, but a few minutes later Lauretta ran onto Juliet's balcony, breathless and shaking, leaning out over the balustrade so far that for a moment
Rosaline thought she might fall. She rocked to and fro, calling,
"O me, O me. My child, my only life."

Lauretta turned and fled back inside.

Rosaline wrapped her arms around her legs and flicked a
wood louse from her knee, trying not to picture the scene within.
Juliet's death may be borrowed, but their grief and loss was true.
For the first time ever, she pitied her aunt. In her mind she saw
Lauretta kneel beside the bed, lift up her daughter's limp arm,

and feel the icy cheek. There was cruelty in this plan and Rosaline felt it keenly. These people had made her and Juliet suffer, and yet revenge was joyless. And she could not step forth and stop it.

For Juliet to live, first she must die.

Now from her hiding place, with a coil of dread, Rosaline spied her uncle walking up the path to the house with Paris, a violet pinned to his jacket, clutching a nosegay of more violets in his hand. The bridegroom grinned at the morning, full of happy cheer. In her mind, Rosaline saw Paris's name upon the friar's sordid list. For him she had no pity for what was to come. But Rosaline's heart ached for the others, and she wished she could look away.

As he reached the loggia, her uncle glanced up to Juliet's balcony and saw Nurse standing there. He called up, annoyed: "For shame, bring Juliet forth. Paris is here."

"She's dead, deceased, she's dead," cried Nurse, her voice cracking, and she began to weep once more.

Lauretta wandered into the doorway of the balcony and stood silhouetted there, trembling and repeating, "She's dead, she's dead, she's dead."

Capulet stared at his wife. He did not speak but seemed to shrivel, turning inward upon himself, face growing claggy and gray. Rosaline feared that he might fall; he suddenly appeared frail and aged in a single moment. Without a word to Paris, he tottered unsteadily into the house.

Rosaline could see his progress as he made his way slowly up the stairs. She wished that she could comfort him and tell him that it wasn't true, but for him it was. From this day forward, Juliet must be dead to him. They had all killed her. They'd dressed her up and sweetened her and served her with spice to Paris. Paris, who now stood on the loggia squeezing to death his bouquet of violets so that their little heads crumbled and fluttered to the ground.

Rosaline was filled with loathing toward him. This suffering was due, in part, to him. If he had not wanted Juliet, paid for her with a good, ripe bride price, then she might not have run to Romeo. And if, in their greed, Lauretta and Capulet had not groomed her for Paris or another like him, then she could have stayed a child longer, her ear not so willing and eager to listen to Romeo's lies.

Paris slumped down onto the stone steps of the loggia, his head in his hands. He was close enough that Rosaline could see the flecks of gray around his temples and the ooze of flesh around his waistband as he slouched. Handsome but overripe. And not the man of Juliet's own choosing. She desired death over him.

From the open balcony doors came the noise of fresh weeping. A father's howl tore open the air, joining the women's wails in a broken song. It raked Rosaline's ears. *It is not my fault. You have your own selves to blame for this.* Juliet lay as dead—it might only be a little death, but it was real enough for them. Still her uncle howled.

Rosaline put her hands over her ears, desperate to stop the noise. It was too pitiful and she could not bear it; however much they all deserved it, she could not stand to witness this torment. She envied Juliet, lying snuggled in pretend death, cold and indifferent as the stone monuments in the Capulet tomb. Revenge was not sweet but rotten.

From her hidey-hole among the apple trees, Rosaline spied Friar Laurence make his way through the garden toward the house. He dawdled along, looking up merrily at the cloudless sky. Rosaline's hatred for him bloomed like the plants he nurtured in his physic garden. His smiling demeanor, his jaunty air—it was all a prettily tended lie. He already knew that the household lay gutted, its heart plucked out, and that it was all because of him.

"Come, is the bride ready to go to church?" he called out pleasantly.

"*Liar,*" muttered Rosaline to herself.

Her uncle wandered out onto the loggia. He'd aged in half an hour. His mouth sagged open, clacked. He shuffled, lost. "Ready to go but never to return," said Capulet.

The friar started, but his surprise was studied, as though he'd been practicing his reaction in the reflecting glass. Rosaline detected no real pity in his eye.

Her uncle shambled forward and clasped Paris's wrist. "O, son, the night before your wedding day death has lain with your wife." He jabbed up toward her chamber with a stubby finger. "There she lies, flower as she was, deflowered by him."

Paris tried to lead him to a seat, but the old man shook him away, angry.

"O, life, O, love—" started Paris but the old man cut him off.

"Death is my son-in-law. Death is my heir." He shuffled farther away under the loggia, trampling fallen figs. "My daughter he has wedded. I will die and leave him all—life, living, all is death's." Slumping into a seat, he stared out over the garden. "With my child, my joys are buried."

The friar crouched beside him and spoke in a firm but tender voice, as though he addressed a wayward child. Rosaline shuddered to hear him. "Peace, for shame. Heaven has her now. You could not keep her from death. She's married best, that dies married young. Dry up your tears and stick rosemary on her fair corpse and, in her best array, bear her to church."

As Juliet's father blinked and nodded, allowing the friar to bless him and offer him false consolation, Rosaline longed to hurl herself forth from her concealment and tell them all that Juliet's would-be murderer was this unholy friar. But to give him up was to spoil her careful scheme and cunning. She must be silent, still—and hold in her hate.

XIV

Romeo is coming

It was still early, and mist bandaged the church spires, if not the wounded hearts of the Capulets. Rosaline knew it would take some time for the women to prepare Juliet's body for the tomb. While the mourners streamed through the gates, come to deposit their sympathy and posies upon the unfortunate household, Rosaline slid out unnoticed.

Outside the entrance she concealed herself in the shade of the stone pine and watched the mourners come and go. Caterina arrived, but she came with Rosaline's father and Rosaline could not call out to her. An hour later, Rosaline spied her emerging alone, and she sprang from her hiding place and caught hold of her arm, drawing her aside into the shadow of the tree, hissing at her to be quiet.

"Please, it's only me. Be still."

"Why are you here? You are not supposed to escape the abbey yet! O, if they find you here, I cannot bear to think on it! Alack, this unhappy day!" Caterina wept in confusion and distress, rubbing already reddened eyes.

"The abbess let me out to save Juliet," said Rosaline.

Caterina sighed. "Then, alas, poor girl, you are too late."

Rosaline smiled, relieved that she could at last offer consolation and hope. "Juliet is not dead but sleeping."

Caterina gave a moan of despair. "O, Rosaline, after all that you've suffered and all your griefs coming so quick upon each other, I fear you've lost your mind in this last tragedy."

Rosaline was both touched by Caterina's concern and frustrated. It took some time in explaining how she'd swapped the bottles to convince Caterina, and even then she appeared reluctant to believe her.

With a sigh, Rosaline tried to tell her what she must do to free Juliet from her fate. "This evening I shall go to the Capulet tomb. I must be waiting for her before they seal her inside the vault with the other dead."

Caterina shook her head. "Rosaline, no. I do not like this scheme of yours at all. What if the noxious vapors of the corpse should prove fatal to you too? I am not so very sure that Juliet is not dead. I saw her body. There was no breath. And you cannot really think to remain in the darkness with Tybalt's corpse, for all that you loved him. He's starting to...rot."

Rosaline tried to appear brave, though indeed the thought frightened and repulsed her. "There is no choice. It must be done. But I must ask two favors of you, Caterina."

"Anything," she answered, looking nervous.

"First, bring me an iron crow and candles, lamps—as many as you can find."

"And the other—?"

"Is more difficult. Can you follow Friar Laurence from my uncle's house? See where he goes and what he does? He wrote a letter to Romeo; I tried to frustrate its delivery and must know if I was successful in the attempt."

Caterina mumbled a prayer. "I shall do my best in this and meet you at the tomb at nightfall."

The women embraced and parted.

With trepidation, Rosaline walked down to the river, the boats bobbing and dipping upon the tide as the fishermen gathered in the catch. All at once the air was livid with the squall and shriek of gulls, the sky brushed white with wings.

As Rosaline crossed the water, her mouth dried up like salted fish. This was Montague territory. Where was it that the Montague men loitered? Romeo had told her once, and she tried to pull it from her memory. It was a place she'd only heard about—the sycamore grove that grew to the west of the city. Rosaline increased her pace, avoiding taking the path directly before the Montague villa where there were too many greedy eyes even at this hour.

After a quarter of an hour, she passed beneath the western city gates—ones she'd hardly used before—and found herself on the empty road outside Verona. Exhausted from lack of sleep, and only the urgency of her task keeping her going, she walked some distance along the road as it curved through the hills, the route shaded with cypress trees. Soon, she spied the covert of sycamores at the edge of a cornfield, golden in the early light of the sun. She hesitated. The reputable citizens were all within the city walls. No one with good intentions was without. It was not safe for her here, not for any woman—let alone a Capulet.

"Juliet," muttered Rosaline. "What little honor I have left belongs to you."

Hearing men's voices, she moved through the field, the corn scratching her legs, and approached the trees. In a clearing beside the remnants of a fire, she saw two men, disheveled and filthy, wrestling among the ashes. At first glance neither of them appeared to be gentlemen, and yet one of them sported elegant clothes, velvet hose, and fine leather boots, if dust-covered and filthy. They fought and grappled in the grime, punching each other, half-drunk.

"Pustulant knave," said one, aiming a hard kick.

"A bubo in your groin, sinner," replied the other, kneeing him.

The one in the velvet hose winced in pain and writhed on the ground.

Rosaline approached and stood over him. He flopped onto his back, and she recognized him, despite his wild appearance.

"Benvolio? This is an unfortunate position in which to find a gentleman," said Rosaline. She hoped that by naming him so, she would remind him of his obligations.

Benvolio peered up at her from his vantage point on the ground. He was sweating profusely, there was a cut upon his forehead, and he stank of ale. "I know your face," he slurred, staring up at her.

"But not my name," said Rosaline, relieved that he was too drunk to remember her.

"It will come," he replied. Then with a groan, he sat up. "You are Rosaline! Juliet's fair cousin."

"I am her cousin. But I am not fair."

"No, it's true they all praise her complexion above gentle Rosaline's. They say she is fair and you have too much color. But I say, for all that you are brown, you are fair."

Rosaline felt heat come to her cheek. She had come here with a purpose, not to be teased by a drunk man. She had thought well of Benvolio, for a Montague, but why must he speak to her like this? Anger and resentment pricked her. Sensing he had offended her, Benvolio changed topic.

"How is Juliet? I am supposed to write to Romeo to let him know that she is well."

Rosaline glanced at her feet, as though trying to find her words. "I saw her laid low this morning. Her body is to sleep in the Capulet tomb and her immortal part is with the angels."

Benvolio stared at her in horror.

"Pardon me for bringing this ill news," said Rosaline.

Benvolio staggered to his feet and nudged his companion with his foot. "Get me ink and paper, Balthasar. I will write and send word to Romeo." He sat down on a log, poised as if ready to scribe a letter in the middle of the grove, a twig for a pen and a tree stump for a desk.

Balthasar stared at him, slack-jawed and swaying.

Rosaline knew him to be another of the names on the friar's list and surveyed him with disgust. She also understood at once that Benvolio, still mostly drunk, needed to be persuaded to play his part. She perched on a log opposite him and asked, "Will you not go to Romeo yourself? Hire post-horses. Tell him this awful news in person. A letter is not enough."

He stared at her with round watery eyes. After a moment he nodded. "Yes, you speak the truth. I must." Benvolio rose and, with a bow to her, began to weave his way out through the trees and the cornfield, to the road that led to the city.

"And make sure you tell him where Juliet lies—in Capulet's tomb," called Rosaline.

He raised a hand. "I go at once. Balthasar, you stay and tell them I have gone."

Rosaline had one last melancholy task to fulfill before nightfall.

She'd promised Laura a proper burial with her baby. Before she returned to the Capulet tomb, she would see to Laura's body. With a sigh, she began to walk back to the city, coins jangling in her fist.

The cicadas were beginning their frenetic evening chorus; Rosaline heard them as finger taps hastening the flow of sand through the hourglass.

She lingered outside the tomb among a circle of yew trees.

The dipping sun bathed the Carrera marble in rosy light, turning the stone of the tombs pink and orange. Gulls and crows circled above, the air pulsing with their cries. How she loathed this place with its stink of death. When she closed her eyes, she saw Tybalt's last fight with Romeo played out again, the macabre dance of death among the graves. All paths she took somehow led her back to this grisly place.

She heard the sound of footsteps and panting breath, and hid.

"Rosaline?"

She eased out from behind a sarcophagus. "Caterina. You came."

The servant thrust a basket into her hands. "Here are candles and a tinderbox to light them. And the iron crow. I do not ask for what gruesome purpose you want it."

"No, do not ask. And what of the friar?"

Caterina lowered herself onto a gravestone to catch her breath, wiping her forehead with her sleeve.

"I heard from a maid who works at the abbey house for the Franciscans there, that Friar John could not take the letter to Mantua nor get a messenger to take it. The searchers of the town, suspecting he had been in a house of pestilence, sealed up the doors of his cell and would not let him forth."

"Good," said Rosaline, clapping her hands together with relief. "Something has gone right in this. What is he doing now?"

"As I was leaving the abbey house, Friar Laurence was calling for a wrenching iron to open up his cell. Friar John was sealed up inside with the letter before he could depart."

"It does not matter. It will be too late. But Friar Laurence is likely on his way here with Juliet's funeral procession. I must hurry and get inside the tomb. Pass me the basket and the torch. Kiss me, and then stand back."

"I'm afraid to stand alone here in the churchyard. I pity you, Ros, in that tomb. But I shall stay here and wait."

"Thank you. I shall feel less alone in this, knowing you are here."

Among the graves rose the voices of pallbearers. With a last, longing glance toward the sinking sun, Rosaline slid inside the Capulet tomb.

Rosaline waited until the last mourner had gone before she crept out of her concealment. Nurse and Lauretta were the last to leave, clutching each other and weeping. Even after the door to the tomb was shut, she could hear their cries as they walked away along the path.

The darkness was thick, but from the glass cupola above, she could see the heavens as perfectly as if in an astrolabe. With trembling hands she lit a candle, needing several attempts with the tinderbox. The shadows leered and the marble effigies seemed too lifelike in the gloom. Taking the iron crow from the basket, she set about opening the vault laid into the wall. She must free Juliet from her prison.

The air was stale and warm, and in a moment she was panting as she worked, taking fetid gulps. The iron tool slipped from her moist hands and clanged on the stone, the noise echoing too loud in the blackness. At last, heaving and hauling at the stone on the vault door, she pried it open.

For a moment she stared at it, unnerved and unwilling to venture inside. The candle in her hand puffed out. Trembling, she lit it again.

There was no choice. She could not leave Juliet alone in this vault beneath the earth. The pounding of her heart in her ears reminded Rosaline she was alive, seemingly the only living thing in this place. Even the mice and rats had deserted the tomb. Candle grasped tightly in her fist, she descended the stairs into the womb of the dead.

The smell of death was putrid and waves of sickness burned in her throat. Still she did not stop, stepping down and down. The taper guttered, illuminating walls of black and green. She felt as if she were plunging into hell itself. Finally, she reached the vault, a cave hollowed out from the bedrock, housing generations of Capulets. There were bunks of the dead laid out upon their wooden racks, bundled in their shrouds. Skeletons in rags observed her from empty eyeholes. With a cry she recognized her mother by her black hair, but her face was shriveled and gone, worm eaten, collapsed in upon itself, her eyes fallen back into her head.

The worst stench came from Tybalt. She recognized the flash of white on his crimson shroud. She must not look more closely. She must not. She willed herself to turn her head away.

And there was Juliet, sleeping peaceably among them,

untroubled and perfect. Rosaline hesitated, stricken. She could hardly bear to remain here with Juliet amid this horror, but when she ran to her and tried to lift the girl, the burden was too much. There was no possibility that she could heave her up the narrow stairs without injuring them both. She would have to wait for her cousin to wake.

She sat in the gloom and closed her eyes, gripping the candle tight in her fist. A scalding dab of wax dripped onto her skin and she hissed in pain. The minutes slid by. Straining, she could not hear any sounds other than her breath and the terrified patter of her heart. Juliet was as silent as the true dead. Rosaline hoped that when this thing was done, the abbess might have some remedy to make her forget this night, this tomb; else every dream would bring her back to this hour and place.

There was a sudden noise above: the echo of the outer tomb door slamming and then footsteps upon the stone floor. Rosaline's eyes flicked wide. She was alert, wary as a fox cub. Seizing the candle, she ran up the stairs to close the vault door. No one could know that she had opened it or suspect that someone was already there.

As she reached the top, she did not absolutely seal it shut, leaving a narrow chink, or else she and Juliet would both be locked inside. The very thought made her light-headed with fear. She crouched beside the tiny gap, listening. Her hands were beginning to shake. *Please let no one notice that the vault isn't sealed shut.*

On the ground just beyond the doorway, she could see that

a tiny spill of light from her candle was seeping out through the opening and casting a light upon the floor. With dismay she blew out the candle and was drowned in darkness.

"I am almost afraid to stand alone here," said a man, his voice low.

Paris. Through the gap, she could see that he'd brought flowers, the very same violets and pansies that were to be in Juliet's bridal bouquet, their sweet herbal scent mingling with that of decay and purification but not strong enough to overcome it altogether.

"Sweet flower, with flowers your bridal bed I strew," he murmured, wiping his eyes. He knelt, leaving the posy at the entrance to the vault—just beside where Rosaline crouched, holding her breath—and mumbled a prayer.

She wished he'd hurry up and leave. It was not safe for any of them to be there. His presence could be ruinous to them all. Why did he have to come tonight? He was neither loved nor wanted.

Almost at once, there came a loud clatter and the sound of the outer tomb door opening again. Torch light spooled inside, illuminating the stone effigies, toying with the marble of their skin, so that for a moment they appeared to wake again. Then, the light moved off and they were stone once more. There was the soft pad of feet as someone else entered the tomb. The footsteps joined with the rapid thud of Rosaline's heart.

"What cursed man wanders this way?" called Paris, rising. "You disturb true love's rite."

Rosaline smothered a murmur of alarm and shrank against

the wall on the other side of the vault. She had not planned for this. Why had Paris not returned with the others after the funeral?

"Live and be prosperous and leave, good fellow. Farewell," said another voice. One she knew well.

Romeo.

As soon as she heard Romeo speak, Rosaline found she could not breathe. She strained to see them. She willed Paris to run. Romeo was offering him the chance to live.

"You are that banished Montague!" Paris cried. "The murderer of Tybalt. It is out of grief for her cousin it is supposed my Juliet died."

"*Your* Juliet? You dare name her so? You urge me to fury with this affront! She is mine in life and in death," said Romeo.

There was a grunt and sigh as Romeo hit Paris hard, and he fell back into an altar. The candlesticks there clattered to the ground, rolling across the floor. There was the sound of a scuffle, and then she heard Paris cry out again, "Vile man! Stop!"

As the men edged back into view, through the narrow chink in the vault door, she watched Romeo try to shove Paris aside, but Paris pushed back at him hard, reaching for his weapon.

Romeo laughed. "Do not tempt a desperate man. Fly away and leave me. I beg you, you oversized boy. Do not put another sin upon my head."

"Go with me now. You are a condemned felon."

Romeo shook his head. "Do not stay here. Be gone and live. Hereafter, say a madman's mercy bid you run away."

"I will apprehend you."

"You will provoke me. Have at me then, man!" Romeo wielded his torch in one hand and his blade in the other, waiting almost languorously for Paris to lunge. When he did, Romeo parried easily and fast—neither man was young, but Paris was plump, and already he was perspiring, his sword sliding in his grip. It was a wolf toying with a spaniel for sport. There was only one way this would end.

Rosaline was paralyzed with fear. She did not like Paris, but she did not want him to die here like this, as she watched.

Romeo distracted Paris with the flare of his torch, shaking it and drawing his eye. He nicked Paris's forehead, so that it gushed and he could not see through the film of red, the man lunging wild and wide. Romeo laughed, calling out—teasing him. Paris lumbered on, moving slower and slower, Romeo stalking him around the tomb, until at last he stumbled and fell beside the entrance to the vault.

Romeo knelt above him, his sword pricking his throat.

"I beg you be merciful," pleaded Paris. "Let me leave this place and live."

"No. I offered you mercy before and you did not want it. It was cheap then. Now it is too dear for you."

As Rosaline looked on aghast, Romeo sliced Paris's throat. Blood spilled out in black ribbons, seeping through the crack beneath the stone door where she crouched, drenching the floor and pouring down the staircase leading into the vault. She stared down at her feet, now bathed in gore.

It was her fault that Paris was dead. She had lured Romeo back to Verona. It was she who had summoned the devil out of hell, and now Paris had paid the price. How many more souls must perish at Romeo's hand or that of his cursed accomplice, the unholy friar? Girls, families, men laid to ruin. She would see it stopped tonight.

Then came a horrified shout from another man. Rosaline saw that Benvolio had entered the tomb and seen Paris's mutilated corpse. Now he stopped dead in fear. As she watched, he backed away from Romeo. "I will be gone and not trouble you," he said.

"Yes, fly!" said Romeo, then paused, reaching out for the tools that his friend had brought. "Hold! Give me that mattock and the wrenching iron."

Benvolio did not move for a moment, apparently rooted to the spot in fear and revulsion at the sight laid out before him.

Romeo took the iron crow and began to work away at the vault door, prying it open. There was the ringing sound of metal on stone, each blow bringing him closer to Rosaline and Juliet. He glanced back toward Benvolio. "Upon my life, I charge you, whatever you hear or see, do not interrupt me in my course. Why I descend into this bed of death is partly to behold my lady's face, but chiefly to take thence from her dead finger a precious ring."

With dismay, Rosaline understood the ring he spoke of was the one now set with her own mother's emerald. Silently she descended the staircase to Juliet, the stones now slippery with Paris's blood. Hands shaking, she lit another candle.

"Be gone!" she heard Romeo call again to Benvolio.

She wondered if Benvolio would summon the watch, or whether in honor of his old friendship to Romeo he would hold off.

In her wooden bunk, Juliet slept on, surrounded by the silent dead. Glancing about her, Rosaline snatched a gravecloth from a long dead Capulet and draped it about her shoulders. To her relief, it smelled only musty, but she tried not to look too closely at its brown and rusty stains.

"Ha, open, you rotten jaws," shouted Romeo, and there came the crash of the door that sealed the entrance. He was inside.

Rosaline shrank back against the wall. She blew out her candle and was swallowed in absolute darkness. He was coming.

And then, in her sleeve, she felt the prick of the dagger she'd taken from Juliet.

She saw the yellow light of his lantern upon the wall first, and then Romeo himself. He entered the vault, taking in the bunks of stacked dead, his enemies' bones fastened into their shrouds like kindling.

"Ah, Tybalt, do you lie there in your bloody sheet?" he asked, prodding the gravecloth, and then recoiled, choking at the stench as the corpse released foul vapors.

He glanced around the dismal tomb and then stopped suddenly, startled on seeing Juliet, perfect, untouched by death or decay, her cheek almost rosy. Rosaline feared that any moment she would wake. With his fingers he reached out and brushed her lips, her hair. He set down his lamp and knelt beside her, his eye gentle with love.

"Ah, dear Juliet, why are you still so fair? I should believe that some abhorred monster keeps you herein to be his paramour. Yet worms are your chambermaids."

He leaned over and kissed her lips, slowly and fully, and then started to stand, but changed his mind and stooped to kiss her again. When finally he stopped, he took her hand.

"You have no need of this, my love," he said and began to pry the ring from her finger.

Yet whether it was the effect of the drug or the heat of the underground tomb, the ring could not be forced from Juliet's finger. Romeo cursed and, after a moment, began to rub tallow from the lamp upon it, but still it would not come.

"It is no matter. The doors of breath are sealed, this will not hurt," he said. To Rosaline's horror, he withdrew a knife from his belt and, seizing Juliet's hand, made to cut off her finger.

Rosaline screamed out. Romeo dropped the knife in shock, and it clattered to the ground. Rosaline stepped out of the shadow, the shroud draped around her head and shoulders like a ghastly bridal veil. "You would violate the dead body of your wife? This is villainous shame even for you," she hissed.

Juliet slept on, not stirring. He only stared at Rosaline. "Rosaline? Is it you or some phantasm conjured from my guilt?"

Rosaline did not answer, saying quietly, "I believed you'd come here out of jealousy and misshapen love. But you only came to steal."

Romeo shook his head. "The dead have no use of gold or jewels. I did return for love, for one last kiss."

"What love is yours? Your love lasts less time than a drag-onfly wing. The tombs of Verona are fed with your discarded lovers."

Romeo stood back and stared at Rosaline.

"Why did Juliet kill herself?"

"She did not. Your friar did this to her. He mixed her liquor and bid her drink it. He knew you'd tire of her. She drank, and you can see here the consequence."

"No. The friar is no murderer."

"O, you wanton self-deluder! He is the accomplice in your crimes! You enjoy the swell of love, but when it withers and falls, the friar sweeps up the dust. Look here now, upon the destruc-tion you have wrought."

Romeo covered his face with his hands.

"Don't weep with false sorrow. Your love will soon run dry, so dry your tears too."

Romeo looked at Rosaline again and saw that she had drawn Juliet's dagger. He threw his head back and laughed. "O, Ros. For pity's sake, do not make me fight you. For we have done it before and it did not fare well for you."

Rosaline slid toward him across the vault. "Cur. Villain. Murderer."

Romeo stepped back but did not draw his sword. "What do you want with this? Aren't enough slain tonight? Do you want to further stuff this grave? You cannot kill me, Ros."

"No. For I cannot kill what is already dead."

He stared at her for a moment, puzzled.

A smile played upon Rosaline's lips. "Do you feel quite well, sweet Romeo? I see a dew seep across your brow. And your hand begins to quiver."

For the first time Romeo looked frightened. "What have you done, witch?"

"I? Nothing. Your death was sealed when you kissed Juliet. Her lips were brushed with Friar Laurence's own poison."

Romeo stared at her for a moment, his face stricken with disbelief. Rosaline met his eye, resolute. Neither moved. From far above them, the deep basilica bell rang out, a hammer strike upon an anvil.

It summoned Romeo back to himself, and he moved forward and snatched at Rosaline, but she stepped easily aside. He lunged toward her clumsily and then began to choke, his expression pale and filled with dread. Rosaline edged farther back. Trying to draw his sword, he discovered he could not grasp it. He fell to his knees and reached for her again.

She moved away but this time was not quite swift enough, and he grabbed hold of her ankle, yanking her toward him. She fell and, with a smile, he tugged her face down toward his.

"Come, I will kiss your lips in case some poison hangs on mine," he said, but she wrenched her head away. Again he tried, but his strength was fading quickly now, like the moon at the coming of daybreak, and she wriggled out of his grasp.

"Here's to my love. O, Rosaline, you are a true apothecary; your drugs are quick," he said, turning paler still.

As she slid through his hands, he seized her fingers and brushed her knuckles with his lips one final time.

"With a kiss I die."

He crumpled at her feet and lay there unmoving.

Rosaline stared at him for a moment and then ran to Juliet. Looking down at her, Rosaline saw that her cousin's eyelids were beginning to flutter, her hands to curl and flex.

Stroking Juliet's cheek, she observed that her skin was now warm to touch, while a tiny smile played upon her mouth. She no longer appeared dead but asleep. Rosaline drew her fingers through the tangle of her hair.

"Where is Rosaline?" said Juliet, opening her eyes.

Rosaline took Juliet's hand and kissed her palm. "I am here."

Dawn was just breaking among the trees as they rode out of the city for the final time, the yellow light puddling around the trunks of the cypresses. Caterina rode at the front of the wagon with the driver, while Rosaline and Juliet sat behind, Juliet's head resting on her cousin's shoulder, bobbing as the horses drew the wagon through each dip and furrow of the road.

Together, they'd carefully set the scene before the watch arrived, summoned by Benvolio. It was a scene written in blood and bodies upon the ground. A duel fought between two suitors, both wild with love and grief. Paris dead, in a pool of blood at the end of Romeo's sword. Then, Romeo killed by his own hand with poison, at the side of his young bride, unable to bear life without his love, a vial of June-blue glass shattered at his feet.

Rosaline had seen to it that the poison that slayed Romeo so fast did not harm Juliet, for the previous evening she'd taken the remedy given to her by the abbess and laced Juliet's cup of wine. When she'd brushed Juliet's lips with the friar's own poison in readiness for Romeo, it was with the knowledge Juliet would not be hurt.

No one noticed that, wrapped up in the Capulet shroud was not the body of Juliet but another young girl, one Laura and her infant, brought there to lie eternally in her place. The driver from the convent had carried the two small corpses down into the tomb according to Rosaline's instruction, making certain that Laura's body was lying carefully in Juliet's place before the watch arrived. The smell was such that none examined her too closely and noticed the deception. Rosaline had promised Laura that she wouldn't be buried in a pauper's grave. Instead, she was wrapped in a silken shroud with her babe concealed in her arms. One of Romeo's loves swapped with another. A secret family united in death.

Yet the citizens of Verona knew none of this. They only saw the scene that had been set for them. Rosaline hoped that the people of Verona would spread the story that they'd discovered in the tomb, of Romeo and his Juliet, and she supposed that in time, as the years passed, the account would grow and change with the weft and warp of history.

As they traveled higher, she smelled pine and larch and the coming of rain. Dust motes swarmed in the light all about them, but to her surprise Rosaline did not feel the heat of the day. Instead, she noticed that bulbous clouds were rising upward, dark and black, ready to disgorge. At last, the heat split apart. The women stood up in the wagon as the rain poured down, lashing them, the droplets tilling the soil in the fields on either side of them and turning the road to mud. Verona shrank and vanished in the cloud, not to be seen again.

Rosaline and Juliet laughed and held up their hands, drenched in a moment, their hair soaked into snakes. *I have saved you*, she thought as she looked at Juliet. *One day, if you wish it, you can go out into the world again and live. You shall live for us both. I have given you this.* There was no one to save Rosaline, and yet with this act, she had salvaged some part of herself. There was pain in the sacrifice—she gazed upon eddies of pine needles spinning in the wind with greedy eyes—but there was also joy.

When they finally reached the convent, the air was cool and clean. The horses stopped outside upon the cobbles, huffing, steam rising from their backs. The abbess herself was waiting for them.

Author's Note

Before Romeo loved Juliet, he loved Rosaline, but in the play she never gets to speak. We only hear about her through the filter of the men: Romeo, his friends, and the nefarious friar. The closest we get to a description of her is the invitation to the ball where she's referred to as Capulet's "fair niece." It's in order to see her there that a lovestruck Romeo sneaks into the masquerade. Romeo's buddies—notably Mercutio—discuss her in lewd terms but we never actually get to see her directly or hear her voice. She's hidden among the crowd, or concealed among either Romeo's generic courtly extravagances or his friends' brash obscenities. So in order to build my Rosaline, I decided to turn to Shakespeare's other Rosalines.

There is a Rosaline(d) in *As You Like It* (the name is essentially the same, spellings varied during this period) and also Rosaline in *Love's Labours Lost*, and I use both characters to create my version of Rosaline, to both give her a voice and imagine what she looks like. Rosaline(d) in *As You Like It* is strong-willed, witty, and is defined by her fierce love of her cousin, Celia. Rosaline is banished and the two girls retreat into the forest of Arden, a liminal wood at the edge of the city, which I've borrowed and placed at the edge of Verona. Like many Shakespearean women, Rosaline(d) dons breeches as a disguise.

The Rosaline from *Love's Labours Lost* is one of Shakespeare's most brilliant, powerful, and clever women. It's an odd, sad play where life and art get muddled. Also, this Rosaline is definitely a woman of color. She is as "beauteous as ink" and a "beauty dark" who is "born to make black fair / her favour [beauty] turns the fashion of the days." Shakespeare wrote several iconic characters of color as well as Jewish characters. My Rosaline is inspired by the remarkable Rosaline in *Love's Labours Lost* in both temperament—her delight in words—and in her physical appearance.

Romeo and Juliet has a sister play, the comedy *A Midsummer's Night's Dream*. The setup is almost identical: a young woman refuses to marry the man her father chooses for her, and the punishment if she persists is either the nunnery or death. The shadow of each play is felt upon the other—the darkness in "Midsummer" and the echo Romeo and Juliet contained in the play-within-a-play of Ovid's "Pyramus and Thisbe." The lovers run mad within the wood. In *Romeo and Juliet* in the intense July heat—the play takes place over four days at the end of the month—the wild heat stirs the blood, provoking "mad" temper, fighting, and passion.

Shakespeare loved the idea of Italy, setting thirteen plays there, but almost certainly never visited the country. Italy seemed exotic and enticingly other, as did the Catholic Church with its monks, friars, and references to saints and holy ghosts to a now Protestant

England. Yet although the play is set in "Verona," it is still recognizable as Elizabethan England. Shakespeare wanted his audience to recognize themselves and their concerns in the characters—he was not trying to create an accurate historic vision of fourteenth-century Italy but an enticing suggestion of Verona. The place names like "St. Peters" are anglicized as are the names: Romeus and Giulietta become Romeo and Juliet, and the Montecchi and Cappelletti families in turn the Montagues and Capulets. Women are "Lady" or "Madam" while men are "Signior."

My novel is similarly set in "Verona-Upon-Avon." It's an imagined landscape or a landscape of the mind, as if created by someone who is enchanted by the idea of Italy but has never actually traveled there. The monster garden that I've given to the Montagues in their country villa, for instance, was created in the Renaissance but is in Virtubo in Lazio.

Even in the world of the play, the characters are uneasy about Juliet's extreme youth; it's the only Shakespeare play where a woman's precise age is given, and we're told not just once but five times that she's a child of only not yet fourteen. It's important and we're not supposed to be okay with it. In the sources that inspired Shakespeare, Juliet is older (she's barely sixteen in Arthur Brook's poem) but Shakespeare made her even younger. Nurse and Juliet's mother worry about her being married so young—she might die during childbirth as her body is only pubescent. Shakespeare wants us to be uneasy about this relationship. It's not the romance that it appears to be. Romeo's actions have always been transgressive, even in the Elizabethan era.

Yet for generations, we've used the story of Romeo and Juliet to define the idea of love for young people. It was the first Shakespeare play I read, and as a teenager it defined my idea of romantic love. I thought this was how relationships were supposed to be—furtive, doomed, and that it was okay if boys were pushy with an edge of violence, where they pressured you into sex.

Only, Romeo is no teenager; it's just how he's usually cast in modern versions. There is no evidence in Shakespeare that he is actually a boy. Shakespeare does not specify his age. Romeo could be in his twenties or even thirties (men courted and married much later than women)—he just likes young girls. The word "boy" in the play is frequently used as an insult. The men hurl "boy" at one another as they fight to belittle each other. It doesn't mean they necessarily *are* boys.

As a teenager, I believed it was the doomed love between Juliet and Romeo that made the story a tragedy. Rereading the play as an adult—alongside my sister who works in child protection—I understand it very differently. The real tragedy is that none of the adults protect the children. The Capulets are all culpable. Like all groomers, Romeo has a pattern, a predilection for young girls, and Juliet is the youngest of them all. He chooses girls who are vulnerable and desperate for an escape and then fills their need with sex, empty promises, and ultimately violence.

Rosaline is the girl I wished I'd been when I was a teenager. The girl who's ready to fight back against Romeo, the only one ready to defend Juliet.

Reading Group Guide

1. What are Rosaline's objections to entering the convent? Would any of her other options allow her to have all the things that she wants?

2. What initially attracts Rosaline to Romeo? How does he initially compare to her idea of "a Montague"?

3. Describe Rosaline and Tybalt's relationship. How does their time apart change their childhood closeness?

4. How does the feud between the Montagues and Capulets color Rosaline and Romeo's early interactions? How does she feel about keeping their identities secret while out together and the truth of their relationship to herself?

5. What does Romeo want from the girls he seduces? How does Rosaline disappoint those expectations?

6. How does Tybalt react when Rosaline finally tells him the truth of her situation? What did she hope to gain by telling him?

7. Rosaline struggles to get Juliet to see the danger that she is in and knows that she was just as stubborn in Juliet's position. Can you think of a character that Rosaline might have respected as she eventually breaks through to Juliet?

8. What role does pride play in the book? In what scene does a character's pride cause the most harm?

9. How do Paris and Romeo compare in their pursuit of Juliet? Are their goals the same or different? Do you agree with Rosaline that Juliet's parents are to blame for the way the two men made a victim of Juliet?

10. At the beginning of the book, Rosaline's freedom is the virtue she holds most dear. By the end, she sacrifices it to earn the abbess's help. What changed for her?

A Conversation
with the Author

Was it daunting offering a new take on a story as well-known as Romeo and Juliet? What was most exciting about developing an alternate interpretation?

I was so daunted! It's one of Shakespeare's best-loved plays, and everyone knows the story even if they've never read it or seen it performed. Also, I took a firm, unequivocal stance on the play and the character of Romeo, and I knew from the beginning that some people would really resist my interpretation. The more books I've written, however, the braver I've become. I'd prefer to write a novel that some people absolutely adore and feel really passionate about than a safer story everyone likes. I've learned to be bold. There was only one moment when the thought of readers' reactions did wobble me, so I spoke to a good friend who's a well-known Shakespeare director. He told me to think like a director of a radical production, not like an author, and to imagine my book with its two covers like the wings of the stage: whatever happens on my page, as on the stage, belongs to me. This novel is my vision, my production. That's not to say that others can't exist too. That's the joy of Shakespeare—there are so many interpretations. We reinvent him for every age.

How did you first become interested in Shakespeare's work? What has been the most surprising thing you've learned from your studies of his plays and historical context?

I read Shakespeare at school, but I don't think I really connected with his work properly until I played Hermione in *A Winter's Tale*. I was seventeen, and it's a story of marital jealousy, loss, and the hope of redemption. An unlikely choice for a school play but I loved it. I also had to wear a massive pregnancy belly, and when my granny saw me in it (she hadn't been warned), I heard her scream across the theatre.

I find it useful to think of Shakespeare as a jobbing writer and actor as well as a genius. His plays are marvels of the English language. We talk and think in his words and see the world the way we do in part because of him. Yet while his genius is unquestionable, he was also under pressure to produce content quickly for a demanding and varied audience. He reuses turns of phrase and ideas. Partly because, as like all writers, the same themes fascinate him again and again but also because he was often short on time and under pressure.

Rosaline first balks against the loss of her freedom but then chooses it in service of the greater cause. What do you think her definition of "freedom" looks like now?

The "freedom" she has in the convent is the freedom not to have her life dictated and controlled by a man. She's free from the dangers of childbirth. Raising children and running a household took almost all of a women's time, and so she had very little left for intellectual pursuits. Rosaline will have a creative and intellectual freedom. But there is also the sense that she has made a sacrifice for Juliet. She loves her so much that she was willing to make that choice, but there is a cost. Rosaline is still forced to relinquish much of the world.

Speaking of freedom, the conversation with the abbess hints that there was much more than met the eye going on in the cloisters of nunneries. How did nunneries serve as an alternative society for women?

In Italy, families would deposit their unwanted daughters in convents. Marriage required a significant dowry, and to marry off multiple daughters was incredibly expensive. While poor women were needed as labor, unmarried wealthy women proved troubling for their families. They wanted them safely and cheaply kept away from mischief and the tempting lure of men. The convents required a dowry but a much smaller one than a groom would expect. If a father or a brother paid enough to the convent, a nun could experience a relatively easy life in a furnished, comfortable cell, and she was released from the most exacting parts of convent life—like the very early or late prayers—or more strenuous work. But even if she was lucky

enough to afford the material ease, she still remained sequestered from the world.

**You chose to have Rosaline save Juliet, sparing her from the
tragedy. What do you imagine might be next for Juliet? How
will she need to change to escape the romantic notions that
led her into the Capulet tomb?**

I imagine Juliet spending some time in the convent with her
cousin Rosaline and growing up in peace, unharassed by any
more Romeos. I don't think she needs to change. We all make
mistakes while growing up—it's how we learn and develop as
people. Juliet made a mistake with Romeo, but she was not even
fourteen. I'm not sure it was so much romantic notions that led
her to fall for Romeo's nefarious charms. He seemed to offer
an escape from her forced marriage to Paris. She felt trapped,
and he apparently showed her a way out. Only it was really the
same option: marriage and sex with another (older) man. In the
convent, she can have time to decide who and what she wants to
be—if she wants to remain in the convent or be with a man one
day. But she can make that decision as a grown woman and not
as a child. It will be her choice to make.

**What is the most satisfying part of a story for you to develop,
and why?**

The most satisfying part of writing *Fair Rosaline* was

ensuring that my story wraps around the original play. I loved Tom Stoppard's *Rosencrantz and Guildenstern,* and I wanted my novel to work in a similar way where we feel the edges of Romeo and Juliet just off the page. I include some of the same scenes, but the angle is different. When you go to the theatres and see *Romeo and Juliet,* I want you to imagine the events of *Fair Rosaline* happening off in the wings, only just out of sight.

Acknowledgments

I started *Fair Rosaline* during the final lockdown. While most of the UK was trapped in drizzle, I roamed Verona. Yet I didn't write the book alone in my studio. Usually writing is a very private thing for me. I listen to music, watch the wind comb through the tops of the willows through the glass, and I work. I do my best to ignore everyone. This stage of the book, however, was different. I had a small, loud office buddy in the form of my then five-year old daughter, Lara. She was supposed to be doing lessons on Zoom with the rest of her class but the headphones "made her ears hot"(and her temper hotter), so she sat at her little table beside me, yelling phonics at the screen. A good deal of this book was written not to the soundtrack of Eric Satie or Brahms but twenty-five children shouting over different Zoom connections while the teacher tried to signal them to mute.

I'm not going to pretend it was easy. It wasn't. Lara and I were loud and cross. I wanted to work, and she didn't want either of us to do that—the world is big, and there's not enough time to play. And yet, it is something to write with love in the room. My daughter is fierce and brave and tender. Rosaline became suffused with her and my love for her. It's not surprising that the book is a celebration and exploration of the power of young women.

My sister, Jo, helped me so much with this book and was willing to think about the play again from her perspective of working in child protection. She answered endless questions about groomers and told me what to read. I'm full of gratitude and admiration for her. Thanks as always to my parents, Carol and Clive, for their patience and baby-sitting. Thanks to my Rosaline(d), Ros Chapman for being the best possible friend. My book agent, Sue Armstrong—you're a marvel: calm, patient, and sensible. All things I am not. I'm so lucky to have you on my side. A big thank-you to my amazing screen agents, Elinor and Anthony at Casarotto.

This isn't my first book, and like most authors, I've weathered a few squalls. And I've also learned to take nothing for granted—and oh, my goodness—the team at Bonnier, you are the absolute best. Your passion and excitement and your brilliant ideas! I feel lucky every day that I get to work with you all. Thank you to my amazing editor, Sophie Orme. You are the best champion, and I love getting to spin ideas with you—I'm so happy we're working together. Thank you to Shana Drehs and the remarkable team at Sourcebooks in the U.S. Justine, thanks for being so patient and reading the book again and again with such care. Thanks to Mirielle, whose sympathetic sensitivity read was very useful. Thanks to the fabulous publicity and marketing teams—Ellie, Eleanor, Vicky, and Clare—it's such a joy working with you. And thanks to the indefatigable sales team—Stuart, Mark, Stacey, Vincent, Jeff, and all the wonderful sales reps across the country. Thank you Ruth, Stella, Ilaria, and Nick for championing Rosaline around the world. Thank you to Emily Rough and Holly Ovenden for the most beautiful cover I've ever had.

And I'm extremely grateful to my brilliant friend Edward Hall who read early drafts of this book, patiently listened to all my panics, and diffused them with great kindness and wisdom. Also, a massive thank-you to all the booksellers who I met on tour with my last book. I started the tour in a maudlin place—and your kindness, enthusiasm, and warmth helped me reconnect.

And lastly, thank you and a big hug to my family, David, Luke, and Lara. Thanks for putting up with me. I'm sorry I sometimes forget to make dinner. I love you.

About the Author

Natasha Solomons is the author of six internationally bestselling novels, including *The House at Tyneford*; *I, Mona Lisa*; *The Song of Hartgrove Hall*; and *House of Gold*. Natasha lives in Dorset with her son, daughter, and her husband, the children's author David Solomons, with whom she also writes screenplays. Her novels have been translated into seventeen languages. When not writing in the studio, Natasha can usually be found in her garden.

INSTAGRAM:
@NatashaSolomonsAuthor